BIRDS ON A WIRE

WILL WYCKOFF 10-12-16

DANIKA~

IF WEALTH IS EVER MEASURED BY PATIENCE & ACTS OF KINDNESS, YOU WILL HAVE MADE ME A WEALTHY MAN.

Will Wyckoff

This is a work of fiction. Names, characters, places, and incidents either are the product of the author's imagination or are used fictitiously. Any resemblance to actual persons, living or dead, events, or locales is entirely coincidental.

3rd Edition

ISBN-10: 1467957674
EAN-13: 9781467957670

For Zach,
contest winner extraordinaire,
who helped me with my cover

ACKNOWLEDGEMENTS

My sincere thanks to family and friends who were supportive of me as I wrote *Birds on a Wire,* my first book. Each of you, in your own way, formed my safety net. Special thanks to my family who tolerated my absences whenever I escaped to the "Recluse Room". To those of you who played the role of editor/confidante (Lori McCurdy, Chuck Wyckoff, Sheila Becker, Ellen Smith, Glenn Kimble, Teofilo Newsuan, Stephanie Dein, and Florence Singley Simmons), thanks for being candid and observant. To those of you who helped me with my research (Bill Bea, Maurice Meagher, Jr., Dave Smith, Seth Hubbard, David Yadlosky, Carl Beilman, Dan Drake, and every member of the English Clan out west), thanks for helping me with facts regarding your respective fields and your patience when I took the liberty to be *creative* with that information. Thanks to Dylan Hubbard, Tami Haas, and Dawn Carter for their help in winding up the process. Last, but not least, my thanks to my Wayne Highlands Middle School students and their pen pals in Lori McCurdy's Polson Middle School class who, after reading excerpts along the way said to me, "May we please have your first book some day?" You sounded so certain that I could write a book, and I did not want to let you down.

Hi, Mac! Hi, Rupe!

PROLOGUE

Mitchell Dirlam knew espionage was dangerous. He could only imagine what his capture would entail. All operatives might deny it, but before each assignment they mulled over the personal and national ramifications of being captured. Would public humiliation be the end product for Dirlam and the United States, or would it be his demise, occurring with lightning bolt quickness followed by an equally fast denial on the part of his government? Of course, there was always the threat of torture that preceded a slow, agonizing death. Without exception, he and his colleagues believed that torture would be the worst, and now, knowing she was coming for him, brought back memories from years ago.

Training at Fort Cary was intense. Mentors, nicknamed Spy Vees, were espionage survivors. These men and women were walking/talking resources whose personal experiences were never discussed, yet somehow they became the stuff of legends. Occasionally students noticed not-so-subtle scars, a missing finger, and even some pronounced limping, but not one teacher ever disclosed specifics about his or her assignments. Such discussion was deemed counter productive. Each former agent was secure in the knowledge that what he had achieved was necessary, believed what he did was right, and was worth any risk. Enemies had been thwarted.

Near career's end, the Spy Vees at Cary felt their most daunting task was preparing their protégés to enhance and maintain national security. Spies had long been an invisible-yet-necessary extension of government, and their sort would always be required to maintain a strategic edge in the future. Mitchell Dirlam took their teachings to heart.

Lessons based on years of experience were shared during training. From the outset, veteran agents emphasized that learning to blend and not arousing suspicion were of paramount importance. Without the ability to move about unnoticed, success was quickly compromised.

"Become a local, and think like one," advised Alexander Nix, a Mid Eastern Spy Vee. He emphasized that location dictates the role of anyone under cover since different cultures spawn varying political philosophies and agendas. Nix felt that once agents grasped the very root of a culture's core beliefs, they could best understand their enemies.

Dirlam learned physical presence was an integral part in the merging process, too. Many times missions were re-assigned at a last moment when an agent with a more appropriate appearance became available. Nix explained, "There is always a solid reason when agents are finally chosen and, quite simply, there are times when appearance comes into play. For this reason, skilled operatives vary in race, age, and physical attributes."

Observation skills were honed as well. Successful spies, those with the longest careers and life spans, were those who were comfortable no matter where D.C. sent them. "Be flexible and be observant," veteran agent Hanners reminded her students. "For security reasons, you might not be the only covert plant on location acting as a native. Never judge a person by what comes out of his mouth. Note his actions. Learn who you can trust."

Above all else, Spy Vees stressed that appropriate behavior was crucial. If a mission sent an agent down Fifth Avenue along the Metropolitan Museum of Art, it was important to assume the pace and prevailing attitude of the thousand pedestrians that day. Nix told them, "If New York City is tired and moving slowly, if it's terribly hot and it's late in the day, you must appear to be equally lethargic. And if an assignment lands you in the world of high finance, you had better be wearing a power tie and speaking intelligently. When in Rome..."

Years later, after many foreign missions, Mitchell Dirlam received an assignment in New York. He knew the political climate, for he had been working for the President of the United States as part of an inner-circle detail. And on this occasion, ethnicity and age were not a factor since he was meeting his contacts at the United Nations Headquarters, located in the Turtle Bay area of Manhattan. Diplomatic status and its immunity were guaranteed for this sensitive issue. It seemed Dirlam had finally caught a break: an easy case.

His behavior? *That* had to be spot on. Dirlam was being asked to apply all he knew regarding the cultures of North and South Korea as well as the slippery slope they both walked.

On this occasion, he was not the middle man. This time Qi Se-Hoon, a familiar contact from South Korea played that part. Se-Hoon, an elderly gent, stood to gain the most since his reputation and safety were at the greatest risk. Having been covertly approached about defection by a North Korean scientist, Yi Po, who was also a prominent human rights activist, Se-hoon quickly contacted Dirlam in the hopes of gaining some favors.

Yi Po was unaware of America's interest in his work or that an American operative would ever become privy to North Korean nuclear secrets. He thought his information stopped in South Korea. Unaware that his trail might eventually lead to Dirlam and stir up an enormous amount of national resentment, the physicist was careless and left several loose ends behind. Scraps of paper upon which the names of contacts and directions were scrawled, as well as any conversations with unsuspecting acquaintances, became indicators of American involvement.

As a result, security began to unravel. Qi Se-hoon was out of his league. The silver-haired South Korean had been equally sloppy. As a poultice, he had provided Dirlam's name to Yi Po in order to quell the defector's fears and thereby secure any nuclear secrets coveted by the United States. The defecting scientist found his freedom, and valuable Intel was gained, but left behind was enough information to dissolve

Dirlam's anonymity. Carelessness and poor judgment on the part of Qi Se-Hoon caused Dirlam and his co-workers to become targets of The Democratic People's Republic of North Korea, including its most relentless assassin.

PART ONE

From: Eli Parks <eliparks@usg
To: Rita <sparky7@usg
Sent: 9:00 p.m. est
Subject: Like you...

A lit single candle, the tiniest of flames, has the power to hold off the dark.
The song of a scarlet cardinal, across distances, keeps loneliness at arm's length.
A cool, gentle breeze over our skin can bring wonderful relief on a hot summer day.
Each of these is like you in that they bring comfort.
Thank you for that. I love you so much.

....

From: Rita <sparky7@usg
To: Eli Parks <eliparks7@usg
Sent: 7:35 p.m. mst
Subject: re: Like you...

Like everyday, from afar you have shown me that you're in love with me.
I love you right back and anxiously await our wedding day.

CHAPTER 1

Rita kissed Eli at the doorway as she headed off to play poker with friends. The game was not for high stakes, but it had become an anticipated monthly ritual, much like when they were school girls awaiting weekends and the Saturday Matinee.

Rita still struggled with the nuances of the game. "Have fun tonight, Sparky," he whispered as he slid his arm around her waist. She was taller than many women, with a shapely yet sturdy figure, but Eli was a bit taller at six feet. "Don't take all their money."

She playfully slapped at him, and ran her hands over his shoulders. "Look at you," she teased. "All that training is turning you into an Olympic athlete." They were like kids in love. His brown hair was of modest length; only the touch of gray splashed upon his temples hinted that he was fifty three, a few months older than his wife. She kissed him one last time and grabbed their truck keys.

Technology made it possible to be home more often for moments like this, and for that he was grateful. In fact, computers helped them bridge distances before they married. Eli was a romantic, so e-mails and texts suited him, and his love of writing offered escape from his analytical mind. His written words played an immense role in winning her heart, and after they married, they still enjoyed leaving emails for each other.

He watched Rita head down the gravel driveway and then returned to their cabin's loft where he picked up the novel he had been reading, *First Family* by David Baldacci. His plan for the evening was to enjoy a chapter or two, do a little fishing, and wait for his bride of four years. As a respite from the chaos of D.C., they would star gaze Montana's big sky, provided there were no clouds to mar the occasion. Happily they anticipated a bright moon to enhance the romantic atmosphere. Theirs was a second chance at first love. They knew it, and they were determined to make the most of it.

Through one of the cabin's large, front windows, Eli enjoyed the lake's mirror-like effect. Saving his book until later, he grasped his light pole by its cork-covered handle and stepped out into the evening just as the local bullfrogs began croaking their nightly chorus. First he heard a few, and then a few more. By the time he reached the shore and was ready for casting, he was surrounded by their deep, throaty calls. A bass named Pete was overdue.

Each night before sunset, as red-winged blackbirds sat queued upon a power line over their lake, soaking in the final golden pieces of daylight, the large bass splashed loudly. The sound it made, a *ka-thunk*, sent smaller birds skittering from nearby branches bordering the shoreline. Its weighty girth smacked the lake water forcefully one time, and Eli considered the large fish's conspicuous display an invitation to a healthy competition.

On those nights, as concentric rings expanded, Eli would cast line from his open-faced reel to the center of the wavelets. Since his stepson, Edward, was into scuba diving, he was able to advise Eli about hiding spots an old, wily bass might choose. Having seen the monster bass among some large, slime-covered branches that fell victim to a windstorm years ago, Edward excitedly told Eli his lightweight pole would be tested if he ever hooked the lunker they had mutually named Pete.

The bond between stepfather and stepson took shape by degrees, and their relationship took on a natural progression; however, it was still a work in progress. As he threw in his line, Eli recalled how, at first, Ed had been skeptical of his stepfather's motives. Their relationship had improved noticeably after Edward overheard Eli explaining to Rita how he felt that leaving college and pursuing other interests might be a good thing for her son. No other adult had ever given Edward the benefit of the doubt. Days later when he learned Eli's own son, Jake, had not been ridiculed when he never entered college, Edward understood that Eli had spoken from his heart.

At another point, when the scuba gear proved to be costly, Ed felt Eli had treated him like a man when they came to terms concerning a loan. Respect between the two had begun to form. Rita noted her husband's efforts, and she believed that Edward was as important to him as his own twenty year old son.

Now, on Poker Night, while he stood along the shoreline in the dusk under a few tamarack trees sixty feet in height, Eli enjoyed the quiet which was punctuated by the sound of his amphibious neighbors. He recalled how twenty years earlier he had enrolled in a pair of post graduate Environmental Ed classes. During one of these, he had experienced a night pond search. On that night his suburban eyes and ears were introduced to the world of nocturnal animals. Once, over dinner with Edward and Rita, he had recalled this experience. "I'd never paid attention to ponds, at least not at night," he said over a dessert of homemade German chocolate cake. "The crickets and cicadas were louder than you can imagine, yet when one of us snapped a branch underfoot everything became silent temporarily."

Sincerely curious, Edward asked, "What did you see?" He was a young man in his early twenties. He was nearly as tall as Eli, his hair was dark and thick, and his body was a burly, perfect match for it, giving him a rugged appearance.

Eli shared how he saw all sorts of critters headed for the water. "I'd never thought about how important a pond or lake is to the food chain. Our class saw several raccoons, a few deer, a possum and its brood, and we enjoyed the songs of the peepers and bullfrogs which were incredibly loud." Because they both enjoyed the outdoors, that night's anecdote and others like it also managed to gradually tie Edward and Eli even more close together.

A loud splash of ol' Pete's tail snapped Eli back from his reverie. Smoothly retrieving his line, it was just seconds before Eli had his old-fashioned Jitterbug flying its silent rainbow arch in Pete's direction. A weighty lure, the Jitterbug caused Eli's pole to jiggle as he reeled in a little line. He paused and reeled some more. Above the gurgle of the lure, katydids sang their staccato, nighttime song. Brilliant stars sparkled in a night sky colored the indigo blue of an artist's ink.

As he fished, far off in the distance Eli heard the unmistakable sound of Edward's high-pitched cycle climbing the back roads to their cabin. The previous fall Ed had purchased a yellow and black Kawasaki Ninja 650, and he rode it whenever he could. After Edward's arrival, Eli was splashed by a pleasant quiet as the machine was rendered silent. It was not long until his stepson's careful footsteps, and the crunch of gravel beneath knobby tires became audible as he approached.

"Catch him yet?" Edward asked quietly. Then he laughed softly as he imagined Eli trying to act calm if he ever caught the overgrown lunker. "Sorry, dumb question."

Eli turned smiling. "If I'd caught that fish, I'd have met you at the bottom of the hill. I'd have to tell someone!" They laughed together comfortably, and Eli offered the reel to Edward. "Want to cast a few times? Try your luck?"

Both men enjoyed the serenity of the cabin, the lake, and even the paths their lives had taken. The cabin offered an escape from life's day-to-day grind. It was largely a field stone structure accented with wood planking on each end and conveniently located a few miles northwest of Falls Port, just a half a mile off 93 N towards Kalispell.

Theirs was not a difficult existence by any means although both their jobs were demanding. In scientific circles, Eli was world-renowned as an acoustical engineer. In local circles, since leaving school, Edward was gaining respect among construction workers as an artisan. At the cabin they found solitude and peace in the simplest of homes. It was an old cabin with a beautiful fireplace, two large bay windows and a deck overlooking a small, picturesque lake. Most of all, this is where they shared and loved the same woman...mother and wife.

Neither of them had made life easy for her. Eli's career and previous marriage contributed its share of strife, while Edward's teenage years provided her with rollercoaster moments, too. He had enjoyed more than a few beers, had foolishly submitted to peer pressure on occasion, and had ignored his mother's curfews from time to time. Through it all, however, she loved them both unconditionally, and now the trio was together more often than not.

Edward cast a final time, but their trophy was not taking the bait. The unlucky anglers called it a night, and side by side they trudged back to the cabin while exchanging what their day had been like, not realizing that a challenge far greater than catching ol' Pete was ahead of them.

CHAPTER 2

"Rita! You had no business betting fifteen cents with nothing but a pair of sevens," lectured Kathy. The others laughed. Few of them really knew the ins and outs of poker, but Rita admittedly knew the least.

Music played softly in the background as the group continued their game of chance. Cary's house was perfect for entertaining, and she enjoyed sharing her good fortune with Rita, Kathy, and the rest of their mutual friends. Her house overlooked Flathead Lake, a much larger man-made body of water which attracted thousands of tourists during summer months unlike the smaller lake where Rita lived not too far away. The home's interior was tastefully decorated in a rustic theme, but never once could Rita recall Cary putting on airs about her success. She was always a genuine friend. Money, no matter how much she had acquired, had not gone to her head. Her personality had not changed since high school where Rita befriended Cary during her gangly, awkward stage.

Little by little, time had washed over their hostess, slowly reshaping her boney appearance like a shallow stream smoothes its pebbles with a gentle and steady cascade. She grew to be a tall, slender woman. Her smile was attractive, and it was accented by fuller lips. However, she never forgot her roots and what these friends had done for her when she went unnoticed by boys during her awkward teenage years.

On the other hand, during high school days in Falls Port, it was Rita who caught the eye of many a male classmate. She was taller than most girls and had long, chestnut hair that waved gently upon her neck and shoulders. Yet what endeared her to many was that even as a teen her friends meant more to her than appearance. Early in life Rita's parents taught her that friendships were something to value.

Falls Port High was small, so small that their senior class trip required only one bus. Cary was in many of Rita's classes, and they spent time in the halls together when their schedules permitted, as well as during their free time away from school. Both liked to write, and they joined a literary club and journalism class together as well.

Looking back, Rita admired Cary's work ethic. Sure they had partied together in college, but Cary always excelled in the classroom. Professors liked her and believed she would do well in the future. As an adult, money that Cary spent was money she earned and deserved. The good fortune she shared with her friends was the residue of her hard work.

Alan Wing, Cary's ex-husband, was a blip on the screen, a mistake from which she learned a valuable lesson. Early in their marriage he was exposed as abusive and lazy. To use a local phrase, "throwing him back," was not a tough decision. Fortunately no children were involved, and the last anyone knew Alan had disappeared into the Canadian provinces. He was no longer a topic of discussion around the girls' poker table, a beautiful oak table covered for poker games with a red and white checkered tablecloth, the kind one might expect to see in an Italian restaurant. Tonight the nickels and dimes seemed to find a home in front of Rita.

As trusted playing friends do, they discussed things openly. They laughed about the new checkout guy at the local Super One grocery store as well as rumors regarding co-workers at school. "They're fools," Pat commented. Pat was shorter than most of her friends, and she was of a more solid build. A wonderful friend to everyone, there were still moments when her edgy comments seemed to reflect her powerful figure. "Rita, I know you like Marie, but she has two kids. Why the heck didn't she wait for her husband's return from Afghanistan?" There was a brief silence as the cards were shuffled.

It seemed everyone in town knew about Marie's new love interest, but the girls wanted to know exactly what Rita knew. Too, they knew Rita had been through a divorce. Having successfully survived bad experiences made both their hostess and Rita doubly interesting. Both had been down that uneven road and might provide some insight on the subjects of separation and a new life. "Who are we to say what's right?" Rita finally responded. "Is staying where you are for the sake of the kids always better? I do know this: Marie tried and tried with Kevin before he was deployed, and now she's moving on. What's wrong with that?"

Her comment left the floor open to others with an opinion. It seemed Edward and Eli were not the only ones fishing that night. And Rita, like the clever bass named Pete, had just wiggled herself off the hook. She swallowed the last gulp of her beverage, set her mug firmly on the table and smiled as she threw in her ante for the next round. "Let's play cards."

As a rule, poker came to a halt around ten o'clock. The girls did not depart at game's end, however. The view from Cary's porch was phenomenal most nights, a vacation for the eyes. Its layout was well planned. Facing the northwest sky, the vista offered its share of beautiful sunsets and even the Northern Lights on occasion. Cary's home was set in a private location at the end of a wooded cul-de-sac with her closest neighbors a half mile down the road, so on a monthly basis these ladies could have their fun, and no one would complain.

On this night the conversation was light, the sky beautiful and drinks went down easily. From the beginning, they agreed to take turns being the designated driver, and it was Rita's turn to drive. She had enjoyed a lite beer or two as they played, but backed off by night's end.

Elyse, who was comfortable with her weighty image, snacked as she reclined on Cary's stuffed lounge chair and addressed no one in particular as they sat upon the deck relaxing. "Cary's traveled a lot, but do any of you wish you had traveled more?" The question arose as a conversation starter.

There was a brief quiet following Elyse's seemingly innocent question. Ice clinked in glasses. For the most part, they seemed like a happy lot, and not any of them secretly envied Cary. To her credit, Cary did not flaunt her travels as if they were to be envied like so many gold medals in a trophy case. Yet the question was thought provoking. Other than Cary and Rita, the others had not traveled much at all.

Kathy spoke first. As a rule, she was not the most assertive member of their group, so it was surprising that their diminutive red-headed friend spoke before anyone else. It was as though the topic of travel had unleashed something normally restrained within her. "I'd like to ride a train across the states. I'd like not to have to answer to any deadlines, not do any driving; just take in the sights." She paused as the others looked in her direction. The mental image of Kathy aboard a train caught them off guard. "I'd want the kind of arrangement where I could get on and off the train whenever I wanted," she continued.

"My God, Kathy, why don't you just take a stagecoach!" interrupted Pat. The others laughed lightly upon hearing the effects of the chilled wine passing Pat's lips.

"Sorry, Patricia, but I think a lengthy train trip would be fun and romantic," Kathy countered. Everyone laughed again, all in good fun.

"Kathy! You horny thing, you!" teased Rita. "I never knew that side of you."

Kathy then turned to Rita and spoke softly, but loud enough for all to hear. "Really! I'd *like* to ride a train across the states. What a trip! I have to tell you. If I could, this is exactly what I'd love to do!"

As if the lock to her secret thoughts had been unfastened, she continued. "Another fantasy of mine is renting a cottage on a tropical beach and just living life day to day... maybe writing a book or making jewelry from seashells! I don't think I've ever told any of you before. I sometimes feel so confined in my marriage. I feel as though there are so many things I'd like to do, but I lack the liberty to pursue them."

Kathy paused here, and her friends were silent. They were flabbergasted actually. This was not the Kathy they knew. "That really sounds selfish, doesn't it? Even with the wine talking I *know* that it is selfish of me. I am so fortunate to do the little traveling that I get to do, and I can tell that none of you ever knew I am not completely satisfied. But who is?"

Again she paused and seemed to revel in the thick, almost palpable silence around her. "I am blessed with wonderful daughters and really good friends and parents that are still alive and a sister and nieces, but in my marriage I feel I lack control of my life. It makes me feel ashamed that I tolerate this, but leaving is complicated, and I would sacrifice so much if I did. So, I carry on. Do you think less of me because of this?"

Rita started to speak, "Kathy..."

"This is *not* the wine talking. The only thing that the wine allows is to loosen my thoughts and permit me to say what I normally wouldn't say. I think all or many of us have a wish bottled inside of us, but it is not easy to pursue our wishes. That takes courage, and sometimes taking action is not worth the necessary sacrifices."

Elyse stood up quietly and simply stated, "*This girl*'s living proof that boys must be careful with the quiet ones." Kathy's face turned red, but she actually enjoyed the teasing. And she knew she could trust each of these friends with her feelings she had long kept inside of her personal vault.

Above the deck, the stars shone brilliantly and the milky blue-white moon rose higher. The night sky created a milieu that relaxed everyone captured under its spell. Little did Rita realize that the relaxed atmosphere and camaraderie of this evening were pleasures to be denied in the weeks to come. She would not play cards again with anyone for quite some time.

CHAPTER 3

A person never knows how a divorce will affect people, whether it be the couple involved or those whose lives they touched. It is easily as tricky as marriage and certainly more harsh. And in the case of Alan Wing, a Native American briefly married to Cary, it did not go so well. Cary's friends had noticed Alan going into local taverns more often than they would see him going to work. "To research the word *loser* in a dictionary might well result in finding his caricature next to the definition," was a favorite Patty-ism.

When Cary first dated him, Alan was working as a manual laborer on weekends and during the summer after graduation. His parents advised him to consider a trade school if not college, but he resisted. Alan was likable, but he just was not driven. Since he was a handsome young man, only a handful of her younger friends questioned Cary's choice at the time of their engagement. Right up to the day of their wedding, more than one young lady was willing to flirt with Cary's husband to be. His six foot two inch frame was tan nearly year 'round, and his job kept him in pretty good shape after he left high school where he had done well in several sports. He excelled in track events, once setting a school record for the 400m run at 44.7 seconds. He was not the only rooster in the Falls Port High School hen house, yet he drew the attention of many hens. Always running with his dark black hair tied behind his head, he was easy to pick out in a race.

Truth be told, a few of the local adults in her life had questioned Cary's decision to marry him, including her own grandmother. However she was a high school girl when she first saw Alan, and from afar she was enamored by his charm. She never gave a future with him much serious thought at the time. Not long before high school, Cary's gangly ways gained her little notice by any of the boys, so she enjoyed Alan's attention immensely.

High school days passed, and they were followed by years in college where Cary earned both a bachelor's and Master's degree. Alan chose to stay in Falls Port. Their separation during her college career kept the romance fresh. Whenever she returned to Falls Port, they were seen together and seemed comfortable in each other's company. They would party with lifelong friends, boat on Flathead Lake through the summers, and promise to be faithful when summer's end rolled around, sending Cary back to school. She grew more and more beautiful, slender, and at the same time athletic. Alan hated to see her go.

Both were twenty-four when they married, and it was then that their time together as husband and wife caused irritating philosophical differences to surface. Cary, who was always active and an advocate of hard work, was at times confused by her husband's complacency, but not enough to give up on him.

They settled up East Shore Drive in Big Fork, a sparsely populated area surrounded by rolling hills on one side and their beloved lake on the other. Cary would commute nearly thirty minutes to her job in Kalispell daily. She was assisting as a grief counselor there, and her clients loved her. Her compassion and her abilities became well known in the area, and her connections grew as more and more professionals learned to appreciate her abilities. The quantity of references she received grew quickly. Word of mouth was a powerful ad agency for Cary. With her success came a greater demand for her service, so she deemed late night appointments were necessary, and that meant she often came home later in the evening.

"I'm sorry, Alan," she said to her young husband over the phone or over a meal together. "These people are in dire need of counseling. They are going through some terrible issues. I hope you understand." Through the early days, he claimed that he was not inconvenienced or bothered by all the time she spent in Kalispell, but over many months her absence eventually began to bother him. She occasionally asked for help cleaning and cooking. However, from his buddies he became brainwashed into believing such work was meant for women, and he began to grumble about it often. When she heard him, she confronted him about his attitude but not in a demeaning manner. In each instance, she thought they had resolved the issue.

Despite his occasional squawking, the time soon came when Alan's attitude toward her was altered, and Cary's late appointments quickly began to suit him. The time alone he had on his hands ended up being more time in a local tavern or time in front of their television. He did not work a forty-hour week since the season for farming or caring for the area's cherry tree crop was not that demanding. As it turned out, Cary's involvement with her job and her dedication to her clients enabled Alan to work less and experience no guilty feelings. Finally he just did not seek any temporary or permanent employment. Staying at home suited him just fine.

One Thursday night in summer she came home earlier than usual. Her mood was upbeat, and she had called Alan to let him know she was on her way. He agreed to throw some steaks on their grill. Steaks were not what she found when she arrived at their small home they were renting just off the highway. She discovered he had done nothing at all.

"Alan, I thought you were going to help me out tonight?" She caught him in one of his insecure moods when he was feeling sorry for himself. She suspected he had been drinking. At times like this he justified his actions, no matter what they were, by claiming she did little to help him.

"Hey! You're never here to help me!" They had been down this conversational avenue before, and Cary was tired of it.

"Alan, I'm not having that discussion with you again." She set her briefcase by her desk off the kitchen.

"Shut up!" he yelled from their overstuffed chair in the corner of their tiny living room. "You think you're so special. Let's all bow to the great professional!" His voice quickly became malevolent. Never had she seen him like this before. "You think that because you're the big bread winner that I'm supposed to be a housewife?" He stood from the chair where he had been slouching, stumbled a bit, and began to yell and then scream. "I'm not somebody's housewife!"

Cary was taken back. This side of her husband was new to her, but she kept her composure as long as she could, largely due to her experiences at her office. Then a few moments into his tirade she countered whimsically, "Honey, you couldn't cut it as a housewife to be honest." She wished she had not said it. It was out of character for her to make such a comment. She knew it. He knew it.

When it really hit home with Alan, he quickly flipped the small, oak table where they sometimes ate together. Alan's eyes were bulging. His neck was tightly muscled. When he grabbed her arm, Cary felt physically threatened for the first time in her life. His breath disgusted her, and his powerful grip caused her not a little pain.

She twisted and tried to escape his commanding hold. "Alan! Let go of me!" To her, it was like a movie scene developing right there in their kitchen; a malicious and despicable moment. She wanted out, and she wanted out right away. When the phone rang and he stepped to answer, she took advantage of the welcome distraction. That was the last moment she was ever alone with him. She heard him speaking into the phone angrily as she made her escape out the front door. She locked her car doors immediately and pulled up to the highway, briefly debating her options.

When their marriage came to an abrupt end, Cary felt no remorse about it. She never looked back as she continued to pursue her goals of happiness and financial security. For a while, she ran her day-to-day affairs from the safety of her grandmother's home and eventually she found her own place to live totally alone for the first time.

As for Alan, legal matters and all contact with his ex-wife had drawn to a close, and life became lonelier for him. The courts were not unkind, but he had made some serious errors. His chauvinistic attitude came back to haunt him. Word of his behavior and poor work ethic spread quickly around Falls Port, having the effect of a toxin that flows into fresh water. It minimized his chances of survival in the region.

However their divorce did not rake him over the coals. In fact, considering what he brought to the marriage, things might have gone a lot worse for him. Cary was too fair in the eyes of some who were privy to the divorce details. Pat said aloud what more than a few of her friends believed and privately thought to themselves when she chided Cary with, "I'd have squeezed his balls really tight." Cary was just eager to move on while Alan just drifted and landed in many uncomfortable situations over the next two decades or more.

CHAPTER 4

A seat at a roulette table is a bit more subdued than the S.R.O. circus around a craps table. Nevertheless, roulette is no less exciting. It just appeals to the more quiet nature of its clientele. It actually might be more dangerous when a player feels settled.

Unless provoked, Alan was not vociferous by nature. That was why Cary, who had never seen him so upset, was so surprised at his threats that awful night ten years earlier. His seat at the roulette table was perfect for him. Much of the room was in front of him; no one was at his back. Large, beautifully framed pictures depicting the Mission Mountains were in view of his velvety, high-backed chair. After a single wager, a fortuitous one, he was seventy-two dollars in the black. He pondered a larger bet. Then Alan made a mental error commonly made by many a novice: he believed he was now playing with someone else's money. Players who realize money they have won is their own money always play much more intelligently, becoming more guarded about that which is their own. Poor Alan had not yet learned that important lesson and lost his seventy-two dollars as quickly as it had been won. Greed is a terrible thing.

If indeed there was a bright spot, Alan met all sorts of characters at the roulette table. One older gent in particular seemed to pride himself in knowing the game's history. The man was well-dressed, but what made him stand out was his shock of thick, white hair atop his head that was accented by an equally white goatee. As he shared his pearls of wisdom, he never took his eyes off the little ball circling the wheel. "As legend tells it, François Blanc supposedly bargained with the devil to obtain the secrets of roulette. The legend is based on the fact that the sum of all the numbers on the roulette wheel (from double zero and zero to thirty-six) is 666." For some odd reason, that was a lesson Alan never forgot. He enjoyed sharing it over the years when he played at other casinos, enjoyed how it felt to sound like he knew what he was doing.

Late one night he finally tired and was about to leave his table. With but four twenty-dollar chips in front of him, all that was left of his winnings, he shrugged his shoulders and carelessly put them all about the felt-lined table. Reds, blacks, and rows of numbers mesmerized him as he cast the chips aside. In a blink he had lost eighty dollars that he could surely have used to improve his financial situation for the next day. Eventually Alan's life came to that: living day to day. For more than two decades, the casino life was a temptress too difficult for Alan to resist. He needed cash, and the gaming arena lured him in with its get-rich-quick siren song.

Unfortunately or fortunately, that was almost what happened. Alan had enjoyed some good evenings at the tables. In fact, there was a stretch of successes that not only enabled him to afford his meals, but also to take up residence in the casino's hotel. His attire improved as well. He never forgot the classy, old, white-haired story teller, and he fancied himself to be his equal, at least in the wardrobe department. Alan was not a high roller by any means, but time and again he was lucky enough to live comfortably for quite some time.

That is not to say he did not find some work. He liked the gaming tables, but he was smart enough to know he had to get away from time to time. He took on some odd jobs which he discovered were available one day when he stepped out of the casino and visited a local diner. Chatter was everywhere, and the locals greeted him kindly. Construction workers he met were unaware of his lifestyle, and they thought nothing of offering him a job at a decent wage. During some stretches of part-time employment, it felt to Alan as if he was laying pipe along various highways for weeks on end.

Like the game of roulette and the sounds and smells of the casino, manual labor grew tiresome. Alan was ready to explore new frontiers. Why not Vegas? Atlantic City? Why not the relatively new yet famous Mohegan Sun in Connecticut? He had become restless.

However, just before leaving Montana to enjoy new adventures, Alan sat at one more roulette table. "I'll give it another chance," he said to himself that night while celebrating his forty-fifth birthday.

The stakes, as stakes go, were moderate. What attracted him at first was a table permitting a five dollar minimum wager. No matter where he played, Alan felt the five-dollar table was well within his means. He had to wait his turn, so he made the most of it by being observant. As always, he was fascinated by the game's croupier. Those who ran the games of roulette were quiet people with the ability to enforce House Rules. He could tell by their demeanor that they tolerated no nonsense, yet somehow they always were able to remain courteous. He found himself wishing to be like them. When a seat finally opened, he felt he was ready, and that this night was going to be special.

There is something about a casino that is hard to describe. As a rule, the atmosphere is exciting and upbeat. It has been said that casinos pump in pure oxygen to keep their guests alert and feeling good about their luck, not to mention the rush they are experiencing when they occasionally win. Combine that with the lights, a few bells, and the excited reactions of the various audiences, such an establishment becomes an oasis from one's mundane life, especially when life is centered around hard work. Or so it seemed to Alan. Then there is the constant sound of money. Slot machines create a din that would be tolerated no place else. Theirs is the song of fortune, however. It becomes part of the allure. Trained professionals are not loud enough to be heard above the slots, but anyone walking the floor has no problem keying in on what each table has to offer. By combining this huckster-like mentality and an almost carnival-like atmosphere with the laughter of a few lucky winners, visitors can get caught up in hope quickly and easily. It is absolutely infectious.

It was not long after Alan was seated that he had become even more of a roulette addict. His initial five dollar wager on what he called "lucky red seven" quickly paid him a cool $330 return on his minimal investment. That was about all it took. He felt twenty-five again and invincible.

A focused player can sit for long periods of time and never note those who come and go on his left or his right. Combine the thrill of winning money with the hypnotic tympani of that little ivory ball as it defies gravity on each spin by the croupier, and faces become insignificant quickly. Yet oddly enough every player can recall the clacking of that same ball as it finally drops, bounces, and lands in any one of thirty-eight cups on the seemingly frictionless wheel of red, black, and two green wedges. Similarly, there is no forgetting the sound of chips being raked or distributed across each table's green felt. For Alan, long ago that clicking and stacking of his chips had been seared in his memory forever. "Finally! It's about time," he thought happily.

Casinos do not install windows. They are a timeless place in which players can escape the real world and its deadlines or schedules at least for a while. That was fine for Alan. He had no pressing engagement. Cary no longer cared where he was, and sadly he was for the most part friendless. When this first roulette game began to exhaust him, he was surprised to see it was nearly two a.m. He played for eight hours and had somehow managed to win more than $750. Cary would have been surprised to learn he actually tipped the croupier. That was not the old Alan's style. He picked up this behavior from other winners. "I'll be back someday," he uttered quietly, and he was wished a pleasant evening by the cute table master on that shift. She smiled a million dollar smile with her dark-brown eyes, and he liked that, too. Still twenty years after their divorce, he could not stop himself from thinking of Cary as he left the gaming table, wondering what she would have thought of him on this night.

CHAPTER 5

Poker night was over, and Rita happily saw to it that everyone arrived home safely. Pat was the last friend to get out of the truck. She was one of Rita's closest neighbors. Their conversation was light, and they relived the highlights of their evening with abundant laughter.

"I thought I'd bust a stitch listening to you teasing poor Kathy!" chuckled Rita as she carefully negotiated a curve in the highway.

Pat laughed aloud. "She might be a wild one! But to be honest, I'm glad she has such dreams. It's good to have dreams."

"Life's more fun that way I think," replied Rita as she smiled privately on the inside. She had dreams of her own.

Finally alone after saying good night to Pat, Rita popped in one of her favorite homemade CD's. Her selection of songs meant something special to Eli and to her, and she was in the mood to hear some of them.

Years ago, when they were dating, they both were keenly aware of different levels or stages of involvement through which romance took them. In D.C., it was flirtatious and fun. The next few times they were in contact from afar and later on when they were together, it was incredibly exciting for both of them. They had not expected to ever love again. Secretly they both began to examine whether or not they had found someone who meant so much. Was a second chance at first love possible?

Then one night as they kissed goodnight, Rita spontaneously whispered, "Meet me at the sandbox tomorrow." She was hooked. She was feeling so lighthearted, so like a little girl again, and she loved him for bringing that feeling back into her life. On this particular night upon this particular CD, the recording she made featured a song that referenced a sandbox where a little girl liked to meet her beau, the boy of her dreams. For Rita, Eli had become that boy.

They married on May 23rd. The ceremony was kept austere yet tasteful. As she drove, Rita recalled exchanging their vows. Recalling the occasion made her smile.

The breeze was deliciously refreshing after rain fell earlier in the week. It had the slightest hint of coolness to it, felt as if it had a texture all its own. Morning light bathed the yard which was lush and green. During recent days, buds exploded into emerald green leaves against a deep blue sky, the perfect spring background for their wedding. Captured on canvas any artist would have been proud to call the setting her own. As she dressed that grand morning in May, the future Mrs. Eli Parks noted all of this and stood recalling what brought her to this point.

Then as car doors closed outside, Rita was awakened from her reverie. Her nerves were measurable but not unbearable. To Rita, butterflies were part of the fun. She had patiently waited for the day, so jitters were not going to spoil any of it.

"Mom! It's time!" Edward called from the bottom of the stairwell. He was thrilled at the double honor bestowed upon him. Not only did he get to give his mom away, Eli had asked him to be his best man. They truly enjoyed each other. Careful not to engage one another too quickly, their relationship had blossomed. Rita was proud of Edward for being so open-minded.

After all their guests were comfortably settled, their minister began. "Friends, we're gathered here today in the presence of God to witness the union of Eli and Rita. They have composed their own vows and will exchange them with each other this morning, asking that you be their witnesses. They are honored that each of you has come here to their home today for this blessed occasion."

With a nod from the officiary, a taller and thinner man adorned in traditional gray and black, Eli took his cue and turned toward Rita. With the exception of an occasional trill from a meadowlark, the atmosphere was blissfully silent. Hearing their vows was no problem. Eli first reached for Rita's wedding ring, and he took it from Edward's hand. He placed the band of gold upon her finger, and when he was about to speak he realized she had never looked more beautiful. He whispered to her this private thought, and then Eli began his vow comfortably and loud enough to be easily heard.

"Friends, family...Rita, I stand here in front of all of you today, the happiest day of my life, to promise to you that I will cherish your love and friendship for the rest of my days. When I need support and care, it is you who I wish to be at my side. At sunrise, I want to watch you stir and awaken. When I see a sunset, I want to witness it with you. And when I put out the final lamp at night, I want to look and see you there by my side. In return, I only ask that you feel the same way."

Then it was Rita's turn to speak. A light breeze blew, and it tickled the leaves on the branches while far above wisps of white clouds floated across the bluest of skies. She gently brushed a few strands of hair back from her eyes and took Eli's hand. She placed a simple gold ring upon his finger, thus completing their union. Her hands trembled slightly, but her voice was confident as she spoke.

"Eli," she began, gazing into his eyes, "I've waited for you all my life. Today we celebrate the official beginning of a love story started long ago, and I can't wait to act out the chapters within. Wherever our travels take us, whatever events shape our lives, I'll have everything I need in this world because I have you. You are my endless love, and my happily ever after." As she drove home that night after a game of cards, as her favorite songs played softly, Rita remembered that their wedding was truly a simple and lovely ceremony.

She pumped up the volume. The louder she played her music, the more free she felt she was becoming. Rita enjoyed her private time riding alone with her windows down, the wind blowing through her hair, and listening to songs that reminded her of time she spent with Eli. More than once he told Rita how he loved her willingness to let her hair down, how she let it blow freely in the wind. It was almost symbolic of how they had hoped they would live their lives together: carefree.

As she drove home, more memories flooded her consciousness. "Wake up," Rita whispered to her husband one morning as he lay sleeping next to her. He did not stir. Eli had been up late working on one of his stories. She was one of only a few people who knew that Eli Parks enjoyed writing. With music playing and the wind rushing inside the cab, Rita was reminded of how that morning's cool breeze lifted the curtains of their bedroom window. It was from their room they enjoyed witnessing morning's first light as the sun rose over the Missions. Eli had found the cabin for them, and the eastern windows had been one of the selling points for them: a beautiful start to their day. Every day. To find such a place was one of their dreams, the sort of dreams tucked away by Kathy and myriad others.

Driving home that night she recalled how that day she snuggled closer to Eli, touched his arm, and then kissed his shoulder softly. Coffee was brewing in the kitchen, but Rita chose to stay where she was, close to the man she loved. Meadowlarks sang her back to sleep.

They were not overly spontaneous, but they enjoyed suggesting ideas to one another and being able to occasionally act on some. She recalled night time walks, swimming in the lake during a downpour, and the crunch of snow as they sometimes left the comfort of their cabin's fire to go snowshoeing. Her absolute favorite was when they would surprise each other with little gifts. That happened each month, and those surprises ranged far and wide.

On this night, as she stole a look at the stars through the windshield, she remembered how Eli had mailed her a letter to her school from overseas. When she opened it she was dumfounded to find he had filled the envelope with golden glitter that scattered all over her carpet in her classroom! Her custodian friend was not very happy with her fiancée that day. When asked later about what he was thinking, he just quipped, "At the moment it seemed like a fun thing to do. I didn't over think it."

For the most part, they enjoyed the privacy of their home. Just driving home to Eli stirred up yet another beautiful moment she had shared with him. It was winter. Bits of ice could be heard tick tacking on the window. Occasionally a gust of wind sent creaking sounds dancing around the quiet cabin. Things were quiet, but in the dark there were always noises. This night was no different. Even an occasional pop of an ember seemed louder in the dark.

They had spent the day together reading, snacking, talking and watching the weather worsen around them. Because she kept the fire going, Eli's job was to make sure plenty of wood was in store. By evening the two of them began to enjoy sipping on a bottle of a favorite Pinot Noir. Later they had a light dinner by lantern light just for fun. Married in the spring of 2015, the Parks were still like kids together. After dinner they changed pace and enjoyed some Bailey's over ice as well. As she thought about it, Rita could still imagine the sound of the cubes clinking in their empty glasses.

Together they had tidied up. While he showered Rita tended to the fire one more time. When Eli came out of the bathroom, the flames painted an orange and yellow glow about the room. Shadows danced upon the walls, and it would not have taken much to convince a time traveler that what they had created was a Currier and Ives setting in which they were riding out a storm during the 1800's. Twenty-first century technology seemed far off in the future because of the mood that was set. Eli found his bride reclining on the couch.

"C'mere," she whispered as she extended her arms and looked up at him with those beautiful, dark brown eyes. "I want you to just hold me," so that's exactly what he did. As she snuggled into his side and took hold of his hand in hers, Rita realized she had found Heaven on Earth.

With many fond memories of her recent past going through her mind, she became even more anxious to get home. The old, red Dakota smoothly passed among the pines and tamaracks while creamy white moonlight splashed over open stretches of the road ahead of her headlights. Many visitors who did not grow up in Montana considered this sort of road to be desolate. To others, Rita among them, such scenes were beautiful and peaceful. From a country song they both enjoyed, the lyrics "...I get to come home to you..." added to the moment. The music, like the night's incredible moonlight, seemed to safely blanket her.

Each curve of the road was entertaining, like a kaleidoscope, as shadows danced all about. She was never a city girl, so Rita could not imagine what life among the taller buildings would be like. Could the thousands of lights from skyscrapers ever take the place of a starlit night? She did not think they could.

Gravel rolled, and its unique sound under her tires announced her arrival as she advanced up their driveway to the cabin. She smiled as she prepared her mock confession. "Honey, it's so beautiful tonight, I nearly kept going." Rita knew her husband would react good-naturedly. She was anxious for his witty reply. Rita smiled again, for she had never felt so much in love.

Upon their deck outside the kitchen, Eli was enjoying the stars and the moon against the indigo night sky. Only a few peach scented candles illuminated the cabin's interior. Rita spotted Eli waiting for her in their favorite lounge chair atop the steps. It was soft, comfortable, and spacious enough for two. She knew he was waiting, but it was a good kind of "Welcome home, I missed you" type waiting.

He had some ice and a bottle of Irish cream liquor on the picnic table next to their seat. It was the same old picnic table under which they had first privately rubbed knees years ago. In fact, she learned that Eli was quite a romantic when he surprised her with a rather unusual gift. At the time that very same picnic table was deemed no longer useful by Rita's brother, Eli claimed it. He then refurbished it, and thereby rescued their private memory forever.

"Hi, Baby," she whispered as she kissed Eli softly. She felt him tremor slightly. Rita still had that effect on her husband after all this time, and it made her feel good. "Honey, it's so beautiful tonight, I nearly kept going."

He held her there for the kiss, and then returned softly,

"You couldn't. I've installed explosive devices on the back tires. I have ways of stopping you. You cannot escape."

"Uh huh," she answered, sliding next to him on the lounge chair. He slipped his arms around her and the two cuddled. "Where's our boy?"

Eli pulled her closer and told Rita he had slipped Edward some cash and sent him off in search of the perfect girlfriend. Rita laughed at that. They were alone together on a beautiful night. They had been married four years, but the day-to-day excitement was still there between them; a kind of newlywed jitters that never went away. As they kissed, Rita draped her leg over his as a silent suggestion. The romantic moon was their backdrop when they made love on that silent starry night.

CHAPTER 6

As a youth, Graham Witworth was the high school standout moms and dads hoped their daughters would meet and bring home. Standing six feet tall and in great physical condition, his blonde hair, green eyes, and square jaw made several girls consider him an Adonis. A look at his Maple City yearbook portrayed a young man who was going places. Class president, co-captain for a wrestling team that won a district title, and co-captain for track and field's league champions were achievements just oozing leadership qualities. A member of his high school's National Honor Society, he finished at the top of his class. The yearbook dubbed him "Most Likely to Succeed" as well. No one balked when his quote beneath his yearbook photo read, "I've always wanted to be rich!" Like him or not, his classmates thought Graham would be the class's first to make a million.

All of that aside, his graduation speech as valedictorian never hinted at materialistic traits, nor was it self-serving. Upon Graduation Night, his words were impressive enough that most folks in attendance that sticky, hot Friday night in the gym offered him their full attention. Temporarily at least, Graham Witworth helped everyone forget their discomfort.

"How many of us have stood at the edge of the diving board twelve feet above our local pool? How many of us hesitated that first time or two before we jumped? How many of us looked back and wished we were back by the ladder?" He paused and let his questions land in everyone's lap. "Well that's where we are tonight," he continued dramatically. "We're upon a precipice, but we're not about to dive into our pool, but leap feet first into the rest of our lives. I can't speak for all of us, but I know I have looked back these past few days. Each memory is a rung upon the ladder that helped us arrive here tonight."

Graham Witworth looked at his robed classmates over his shoulder as he took the microphone comfortably into his hand. He turned and looked to them. "Tim, you were the first eighth grader we knew to earn a driver's license. Most of us still remember the day we followed you to the middle school office amazed that you had the courage to ask Mr. Clift, our principal, for a place to park your truck! We thought it was the bravest thing we had ever witnessed." Then Graham again paused for effect for he was speaking directly to a student who many thought would never finish high school. He continued by saying, "Yet through you, Tim, we learned valuable lessons. We learned about courage from you and fairness when Mr. Clift assigned you a parking spot right next to his own car."

Next he nodded at his high school principal as he spoke. "And who will forget the day we stole Mr. Rodda's desk for Mr. W- ? We gave up our lunch period for that little caper. It taught us the fun in a harmless prank, the value of good planning, and how to share a good laugh like Mr. Rodda did that day."

Now the audience was chuckling, for until that very moment, it only knew the sterner side of the man who ran their high school. At this point, Graham Witworth had the audience's full attention, more so than the adults who spoke after him that night. He went on to share a few more steps down Memory Lane, and then he closed.

"Sure it's great to look back, but now it's time to move forward. It is finally time to dive into the pool we call Life. For those of us who might be a bit more uncertain, you should find comfort in the shallow water. Me? I'm going to stay out on the deep end. But that's just me. Just remember there's a spot somewhere in the pool for every one of us."

With that he returned to his chair on the stage and the audience rose to its feet. He had reached the kids like Tim who did not like school all that much, but who had the tenacity or good sense to finish. His words reached the kids who liked to goof around while simultaneously his metaphorical approach even reached the scholars in the class, challenging them to do more with their lives in the deep end of the pool. He even remembered to honor classmates who unfortunately died at some point during the class's school career.

In the fall, R.O.T.C. called to him at the University of Scranton, and Witworth continued to do well. He was near the top of his class all four years while setting a few track and field records as well. No one could touch him in the field events when he was there, and to this day his distance of 59' 2" in the shot put is still a record. Having chosen the Navy for a career, Graham Witworth proved to be prophetic for he eventually became a submariner, indeed headed for the deep end of the water.

Successful leadership came at a price. An officer right out of college, Witworth's youthful appearance made it difficult for some enlisted men to accept orders without question. Such a phenomenon is not at all unusual. Resentment based upon the belief that college grads were automatically arrogant and unsympathetic toward enlisted men and women demanded that young, inexperienced officers earn any crew's respect.

Clinging to time-honored rules and traditions, he proved to be fair, consistent, and willing to listen. More experienced officers found him to be likeable, and that helped. Officers are not a "we vs. them" brotherhood, but to some degree successful officers find it necessary to care about their crewmembers from a distance. As Graham Witworth went from first being an Ensign, and then a Lieutenant (J.G.) twenty-two months later, and Lieutenant after four years, he chose to occasionally stick his neck out for the crew when he felt it was the right thing to do.

While deployed to Bahrain as an Ensign Witworth's captain was contacted by the local police officials concerning crewmember violations of a local custom: wearing short pants and short sleeves while on shore. It was not a violation of U.S. Naval regulations, but the affair needed to be addressed diplomatically. Witworth was assigned the task, performed it with courtesy, and he had the men returned to their boat without further ado. When the time to record annual evaluations came around, no mention of the incident was noted. In fact, the crew found his reports to be complimentary when they were passed along for the Captain's signature.

Having his backside ripped by a superior officer for the sake of a sailor, in this case for not informing his crewmembers of the local custom, carried a lot of weight with all the crews on various boats. In the cramped quarters of a sub, word of such loyalty traveled quickly.

While assigned to Connecticut's Naval Submarine Base New London, he met Louise at a fund raiser for local charities. Since her dad was retired Navy, it was not surprising that she understood the reality of lengthy missions which translated into lengthy absences. Lieutenant (J.G.) Graham Witworth felt he was fortunate to find a woman who might be willing to live the life of a naval officer's wife. They were married long before troubles intensified in the Middle East, and upon learning of his deployment she told him she felt it was odd that a campaign entitled Desert Storm required submarines. For years, they enjoyed a good laugh over that.

Over the next eight to ten years he earned the ranks of Lt. Commander and Commander. By continually making decisions that were effective and honorable, eventually Witworth moved on up to Captain.

All of this upward mobility did not come easily. Stress upon married officers was often an underlying issue since naval requirements move officers from one boat or ship to another every two or three years. This practice was deemed necessary in order for officers to gain the experience needed to assume command. Change often required movement to different ports and naval activities creating a hardship on spouses and children as well. For Graham Witworth, having to periodically purchase a new home for his family became a financial burden since the home being left behind did not always sell quickly. It was not unusual for officers, Witworth included, to find themselves holding more than one mortgage for an extended period of time.

Together he and his wife began a family with the arrival of a son. Often forced to play the role of a single parent, Louise occasionally expressed that should the opportunity ever arise she would like Graham to take a stateside position where he could continue his career in relative safety and closer to home. It was not an uncommon conversation between military spouses. From time to time, he passed over such opportunities, and tensions at home began to arise. Before long, deployments became welcome respites. He tried to deny it, but it was true.

Subsequently a divorce ensued. Despite an amicable parting, expenses caused by bad investments and college tuition began to mount. This part of his life was out of his control and made him vulnerable. Over the next decade, crew members began to notice their captain displaying irritation on occasion, although his ability to command was never in question. And it was doubtful that a single man under his command ever gave Graham's most animated argument with a Mr. Eli Parks and some "boat doctors" a second thought. That situation obviously had been resolved, or so they thought.

In the autumn of 2016, Witworth was in Sasebo, Japan at one of the United States' most important naval bases when he was first approached about his finances. He never knew just how Koreans learned of his money woes or why they were in Japan. Perhaps they just felt all Americans were greedy or that American naval officers were underpaid. He was sure he had been private enough to never let such information slip out.

The first time he was approached was like a blip on one of his sonar screens; there one minute and gone the next. Over a few drinks, he had casually conversed with a Korean couple who were smartly dressed in American clothing. They were in a quiet out-of-the- way bar that many Navy officers frequented. It was not a dark and mysterious setting by any means. In fact, it was quite a pretty place which was nicely lighted. They had been talking about career choices. An engineer by trade, she was an attractive Asian woman who merely offered an observation. "I don't know many military people who couldn't use a little extra money." Her cohort agreed. Five minutes later they thanked him for his part in polite conversation, and they were gone. He never saw either of them again. However they did leave with two things: his name and the fact that he was interested in making "...a few extra bucks."

CHAPTER 7

Eli had worked at the United States Naval Warfare Center fifteen years before he met Rita, fell in love, and married her. Their courtship evolved naturally. They felt a keen attraction to one another while in Washington, D.C., and they enjoyed staying in touch even after she was back in Montana. Rita and Eli became the envy of closet romantics everywhere once they married and their story was known.

While she was in our nation's capital, Rita befriended several Japanese citizens, but it was her friend Megumi she cherished most.

Eli found Rita at the kitchen table wrapping a baby gift for Yusuke who was Megumi Naka's new son. She arranged the blue and white hand-knit sweater suit, complete with bear ears on the hood, in a Baby Gap box and then covered it with tissue. "When Megumi and I reunited in Washington, she claimed she was *never* going to marry Takashi," Rita mused. "Now here they are-the happy couple with a new baby!"

"That makes two happy couples," Eli commented, brushing her hair aside to kiss her neck. "But *our* baby is over twenty years old!" He watched her cover the gift-wrapped package with brown shipping paper, then copy an Osaka address from her book near the phone. "I thought you'd have Megumi's address memorized by now," he teased. "You send each other packages all the time." He grabbed a pitcher of iced tea from the fridge and poured a glass for each of them.

"Well she is the one to thank for introducing us!" countered his wife. In 2013, Rita had spent three weeks in Washington as a recipient of the Congressional Merit Award for Teaching Exellence. Along with forty-nine other educators from the U.S., she had been wined and dined by Japanese educators and U.S. Department of Education officials, as the two nations compared cultural beliefs and educational systems.

In 2011, prior to her journey to D.C., Megumi had worked in Rita's middle school classroom as an exchange teacher. They remained great friends as they corresponded after Megumi's return to Japan. When Rita learned her dear friend was being honored in Washington as well, she composed a private itinerary of attractions to visit. The two friends spent a memorable weekend touring the sights of the city, from the Washington Mall to the White House. For a brief time, Rita's father lived on the east coast, but Rita was there for the first time. "I'm not much of a tour guide," Rita apologized when they walked up a wrong street for a second time. "At least I can still read the signs," she said teasing her friend.

Once the packing project was complete, Rita put scissors and tape back in the drawer. She returned to the table and slid onto Eli's lap, resting her hand on his back. "Remember that banquet at the Hamilton Crowne Plaza?" she teased. "Millions of people in Washington, and Megumi had to turn and spill sake on you! She about died as she stood there looking up at you!"

"That made two of us," Eli smiled. "So much for first impressions."

"Oh, you made an impression, Mr. Engineer. You know I have a thing for guys in ties. Even ties soaked in sake." Her hair brushed against his face.

"Apparently." He smiled at the thought, remembering how flustered Megumi was after the incident, as she tried to wipe off the spilled wine. Too, he recalled Rita's first comment, "He looks like a big boy, Megumi. He can take care of himself." Eli assured the women he had survived worse. Eli accepted their invitation to sit together for dinner that evening along with a few teachers Rita met from North Carolina and D.C. From across their table, they exchanged glances and sly smiles all night long. He was taken by her intense brown eyes, and she enjoyed his humor.

"I kept trying to find out where you taught," Rita reminded him as she snuggled comfortably. "I assumed you were a teacher. You were awfully vague about what you were doing in D.C." Then she added, "Just how did you end up in that particular event for dinner?"

"Classified information," Eli answered. "Your tax dollar was at work. But you didn't stop asking questions even when we strolled around those store fronts after dinner. If you'd been quiet for two seconds, I'd have kissed you."

"You can kiss me now," she said, and he was about to oblige when Edward stormed through the door.

"I'm starving!" he announced, opening the door of the fridge to check on whatever he could find. "Are either of you love birds going to feed a hungry son?"

Eli stood up, nearly dumping Rita on the floor. He grabbed her playfully before she landed. "We've got hungry men to feed around here!" He headed out to the deck to light the BBQ grill and to begin cooking some burgers, while Rita collected baby spinach, carrots, and other salad fixings.

"You can grate zucchini," she told Edward. "That'll take your mind off how hungry you are."

The three of them sat at the table just visiting long after their barbecue was finished. Rita watched Eli and Edward's easy relationship continue to grow. Eli worked at it and hoped to fill a gap in Edward's life. Her first husband left when Edward was ten. To her, it seemed Edward was grateful for Eli's genuine interest in him as well as any common interests they shared such as fishing. Above all, she knew, Edward appreciated how Eli treated his mother.

"Tell me again why you found Mom so attractive," Ed requested.

"I wanted to marry her as soon as I learned she was a baseball fan," Eli told his stepson. "You should have heard that woman cheer for the Nationals at the ballpark!" He winked at her across the table.

After their conversation over lunch, they spent much of the afternoon boating and fishing on the lake. In the evening they met on the deck again to talk some more, this time over steaks. They relaxed together until the sun slipped behind the Mission Mountains closing another perfect day. They were evolving into a tightly knit family.

Early the next morning Eli was thinking how Northern Montana was perfect for him. The hectic pace of his work in D.C. combined with its occupational dangers was the polar opposite of life in Falls Port. That is not to say its inhabitants were hicks or hillbillies. Montanans were wise in their ways. He admired their understanding of what was really important. They seemed to get caught up in superficial things less than others he had ever met. For example, he witnessed more old pickups in the Northwest simply because a vehicle's appearance was less important than its dependability.

Edward joined Eli as the two enjoyed some homemade waffles. He was so naturally curious. Edward knew that prior to meeting his mom and falling in love, Eli had been married before. Edward had learned that with their son, Eli and his first wife lived in the suburbs of Allentown in Lehigh County. Edward had heard how the couple was originally from New Jersey, but when a promotion made it possible to move across the Delaware River into a quieter area, they made the leap. Eventually what was once largely a farming area in rural Pennsylvania became the suburbs of Allentown. It was not as crowded as where they had lived in New Jersey, so they were seemingly happy with their choice. This much Edward knew, but was curious to know more.

He sat down as Eli leaned against the railing. "Why did it take you and Mom so long to marry? She met you in Washington when I was seventeen or eighteen, but you didn't marry until I was twenty."

"There are friends who'd tell you that our wedding would have taken place sooner; that your grandpa had a hunting buddy, who was an attorney, intentionally drag out your parents' divorce proceedings to irritate your mom. The truth be told, it was my work that was responsible for the delay."

There were details which Rita had not explained to her son. She had not told him some specifics; how Eli was married to Erin at twenty-six, and their son Jake was born nearly six years later. As he grew, Eli and Erin followed their son around to the various activities little kids choose to pursue: soccer, scouts, and youth baseball. She had not yet explained how Eli did the best he could while secretly traveling and working for the U.S. government at nearby Willow Grove Naval Air Station. And she did not tell Edward that it was unfortunate how Eli was absent when many of Jake's activities took place, events other fathers were able to attend. It was not always easy to make young Jake understand why his dad could not be at various functions. Rita and Eli felt that Edward would learn enough about this part of his past when the time was right, and Eli did not want Edward to worry that his step dad's job would make him neglectful.

When it came to Edward, Eli purposefully was careful discussing details regarding his work. For example, Ed did not know his step dad was recognized early on to be an extraordinarily talented acoustical engineer and technician; that he and his partners were engineers and inventors with few peers. Too, Edward did not realize that Eli's job was sometimes awkward and dangerous.

It had never been explained to Edward that since Eli was not a military man by profession, there were Navy lifers who resented Eli's arrival upon their respective ships, boats, or bases. The nature of the work that Eli's team was sent to do was demanding and exact. Upon boarding a sub, for example, Eli automatically was granted full charge of the boat's itinerary. This did not sit well with some captains, but with Eli in charge, that which needed to be done could be done more quickly.

In 2016, a year after Eli married Rita, Eli and his partners were assigned a mission that required boarding the U.S.S. Helena, a Los Angeles Class nuclear submarine first launched on June 28, 1986. At a cost of approximately $900 million, it was built in Groton, Connecticut. The boat measured 361 feet in length. When submerged it displaced 6,200 tons. Armed with Tomahawk missiles, Harpoon missiles, and Mk-48 torpedoes, the U.S.S. Helena presented a formidable adversary. But technology must be kept current, and that was where Eli fit in. The

Helena had the ability to lay mines, but if it did not run as quietly as technologically possible, enemy mines scanning for sounds would find the Helena and destroy it. Eli's job was to update vessels of the U.S. fleet and keep them running as quietly as possible.

The Helena was home for fourteen officers and ninety-eight enlisted men and women. Its captain, Captain Graham Witworth, was not totally cooperative during one particular overhaul. Most visits by the *boat doctors,* as Eli and his team had become labeled, meant interrupting what Captain Witworth thought were items of vastly greater importance. In reality, it was Witworth's ego that was of greater importance to himself. He argued with Eli in front of Eli's partners and crewmembers of the sub over ordinary maneuvers. Finally Eli requested a private meeting with the captain in the Captain's quarters, and it was granted.

"Parks, I've little time for your interruptions, but I'll give you the few minutes I have," barked Witworth. "What is it you want to say?"

"Captain, I find it hard to believe," replied Eli in a quiet voice edged with frustration, "that you do not realize that what we are doing might keep you and your crew alive." Eyeball to eyeball, he went on to say, "You'll never know whether or not The Helena slips by mines trying to detect your presence, but I assure you the programming we're installing will do just that. I need you to make the maneuvers I request, in order to test the sub once the technology is installed."

Witworth just stared at Parks. He had been a captain for twelve years and captain of the Helena for half of them. His crews toed the line. It irked him that a civilian seemingly wanted to take over, albeit temporarily. "Well, Mr. College Boy, it is I who captains this boat."

At that Eli had heard enough. He now knew it was personal. He had been warned that such a day would come. Wisely he was given a trump card he had hoped he never would have to play. Eli feared it was tantamount to calling his big brother to fight his fight for him. But the Helena's crewmembers' lives were at stake. After a pause, trying to remain visibly calm, Eli reached into his wallet, pulled out a card, and said, "Captain, I believe you need to contact this number today. Failure to do so might result in your suspension of duties." As the captain read the card, Eli waited. "I will be with you when you make the call," was the last thing he said in that meeting.

After that, Captain Witworth could not have been more cooperative. Everyone aboard the Helena noticed the change. The President of the United States himself told Captain Witworth right where he stood in relationship to Eli Parks, and Eli's old college roommate did not pull any punches.

In Eli's mind, this was the sort of experience Edward need not know. He wanted to impress his stepson on his own merit, not by the fact that the President was his close friend.

To Rita, Eli was an open book. He once told her how long ago at night he had lain in bed and explained to his wife that he learned not to take any captain's coolness toward him personally. "I can't blame them. It's as if I'm walking into their business office, in this case a mega-million-dollar vessel, and I'm given carte blanche to fix things they don't even know might be in disrepair." And Eli meant it. After all, when he was done nothing seemed different. Many crewmembers' lives were saved as a result of the boat doctors' alterations, but crewmembers never knew it. "It's like a tune-up or oil change," he explained to her. "They're necessary, but we would never realize their importance until it's too late."

He told her how at first Erin seemed to understand and respect his passion for his work as well as the rush he experienced after enabling an atomic submarine to avoid sound-activated devices. She had even been introduced to several people who most civilians never meet, and he was certain she enjoyed that part of their life. People in their circle organized galas or parties so that job-related tensions could be abated, if only for a short time. In Eli's case, some were formal affairs in the White House. Others were more like barbecues at a friend's home. Erin Parks was well received and acted as if meeting the spouses of Eli's co-workers was a joy.

However the excitement evidently wore off over the years, and Erin Parks became immune to the fact that her husband and his team worked for the President and the fact that his work saved hundreds of lives time and again. She began to envy neighbors whose husbands worked regular hours and might be home on weekends. Maybe if Erin knew what he and his crew sometimes went through to get to their workplace she would have been a bit more patient. After all, theirs was not always an ordinary commute.

Night does not get much darker than it does when the sky is overcast over the middle of the Mediterranean. Aboard a ship like the U.S.S. Chanticleer (ASR7), a surface support ship officially decommissioned in 1974, but secretly used by the Navy for covert government missions, a great deal ran through Eli's mind. No matter how many times he had taken part, Eli was always amazed what took place when he boarded a sub at night while out at sea. Weather was a non-factor. Neither secrecy nor war would wait for better weather.

He marveled at the efficiency of the crewmembers to whom he and his team entrusted their lives each time such a transfer was deemed necessary. No one was more professional than those who worked upon those tremendous ships and boats.

Then, of course, there was the stealth of the sub. Standing with a few seamen one minute on the deck of a ship like the Chanticleer, hooked to a greased steel cable not much thicker than a golf ball, and glowing like Christmas trees due to the dozen or more Glow Stix they had attached to them in the event they fell into the sea at night, it was always an amazing surprise that an atomic submarine could silently surface, run adjacent to a ship, and never be heard approaching. Not there one moment but there the very next, only the machinery noise from the ship and the commands to the crew were ever heard. None of the gushing of ocean water pouring off the side of a sub was heard. Perhaps he was too excited to notice. And as quickly as it arrived, the boat covertly disappeared back into the dark sea with a slightly wet Eli inside along with his team. Having delivered its passengers, the seemingly insignificant Chanticleer headed back to port.

Eli felt all of this was too much to share with Edward over waffles that morning on the deck. He felt it was inappropriate since it seemed like creative story telling. A better, more appropriate time would someday come. Much to his credit Edward did not pry; however, he did appreciate Eli clearing up the part about Edward's paternal grandfather and his tactics.

Casually they moved to other topics. "Did you know your mom was a jock?" he would tease. Then Eli would quickly list fictitious awards his wife had won as a teen.

"Don't tell him that," she would counter as she smacked her husband's arm. "Edward, it was all I could do to tie my shoes. I was not an athlete. Do not believe everything this man tells you."

CHAPTER 8

Despite the hour, more than 2,000 miles away nine men, most of them military, huddled around an oak conference table, surrounded by windowless walls and an array of American flags from earlier periods in history. To heighten the significance of any conferences held in this room, it was tastefully decorated in American lore. Important documents and antique guns, for example, were on display inside gilded frames and under glass in ornately carved wooden cases.

Each individual had his own comfortable chair, legal tablet, Cross pen, and an assortment of non-alcoholic beverages. Papers were shuffled as each man silently read reports. The President, dressed casually in jeans and a soft, red flannel shirt, pushed up his sleeves as if he meant to get to the task before them. After clearing his throat, he asked the others for their reactions to the documents at hand.

Andrew O'Neill spoke first. His handsome, physically fit, six-foot-one-inch body frame made him a White House poster child for the press, but to some in the room he was considered too young and inexperienced to be the "Gatekeeper", the person deciding who speaks with the President. As Chief of Staff, one of his many jobs was that of White House liaison between the President and any operatives of Homeland Security. It was their job to track individuals deemed especially dangerous or posing threats to the United States. "Mr. President, despite the never ending efforts to track suspected mercenaries and terrorists, one in particular has slipped through our security network. The NSA/CSS has deciphered foreign communiqués that lead us to suspect this individual is an agent of North Korea, and as a result, our sources believe one of our staff, Mr. Parks, is in Harm's way." He cringed when he was forced to admit that last bit to his Commander-in-Chief.

"Parks? Eli Parks? There was noticeable consternation in his voice. Any workers in trouble concerned this President, but being a personal friend of Eli Parks made his fear more discernable. Not a man in the room could ignore it.

"Yes sir. Eli Parks. But the threat could also spill over upon members of his unit as well."

"Who are the other members in Parks's unit?" the President inquired. By his tone he left no doubt that he was equally concerned for the others.

"Sir, their names are Jeff Ripkin and Gabe Winters. The three of them and any researchers supporting them have frustrated hostile governments more than once."

President Rittenhouse shifted in his chair. Rittenhouse was as physically solid as the sound of his surname. Like the previous President, he was an African-American. Unlike his predecessor, who reveled in letting voters see him play basketball or football in an attempt to send the message their President was both in shape and in touch with the common man, and unbeknownst to the public, this President worked out privately in the bowels of the White House gym when time permitted. He looked directly at O'Neill. "Is it that they've done anything immoral? Have they done anything wrong?"

At that a few chuckles were heard around the table. General Stephen Conte spoke up before O'Neill had the opportunity. "Mr. President, they are a pain in the ass to people who like to brag about killing Americans." The balding, bespectacled General folded his hands tightly and leaned forward. "Men like Winters, Parks, and Ripkin keep people like us alive."

"Navy folks in particular, Mr. President," interjected Admiral Bea. Admiral William Bea had met the Parks unit on a few assignments and was duly impressed and grateful. "As you well know, more than once they have made it possible for us to move inside hostile waters undetected."

The President turned to Bea. "Admiral, tell me why North Korea in particular would single out these three men. Surely there are several, even thousands, of acoustical engineers on this planet. Why have the names of these three men come to the surface? No pun intended."

The Admiral was a Presidential favorite. He was sixty-seven years old, blessed with a full head of white hair, and had not one iota of fat upon his body anywhere. He took a moment to think, took a deep breath and delivered. "Mr. President, I'm sorry, but I have no idea unless it's because North Korea believes Parks and his teammates are solely responsible for having invented technology that frustrates them. Various scientific periodicals have recently put Winters, Ripkin, and Parks upon a pedestal, and terminating a personal friend of the President would be the proverbial icing on the cake. Again, I have to admit that this kind of reasoning is purely speculative."

Not pleased with that answer, Rittenhouse barked, "Then we better quickly find out."

At this point in the conversation, Andy O'Neill felt compelled to lay some cards on the table. Over the years, he had earned some respect from all those attending this meeting, so he had no qualms about being blunt. "Mr. President," he began slowly, "it's entirely possible that North Korea won the favor of one of our sailors; perhaps one of our officers." The silence in the room was palpable. He struck a nerve when he said "officers". The men around him were patriots. Of that there was no doubt. He had to have his facts straight if he was going to suggest treason was the act of one of their own.

"Go on, Andy," replied the Commander in Chief. He understood the difficult position Andy O'Neill, a civilian, was in at the moment, and Rittenhouse was holding wolves at bay intellectually with his position as President.

"Well, Sir, it's a combination of things, a combination of possibilities." O'Neill looked at the others, too, as he spoke. "First there's the politics of it. Trying to figure out North Korean politics is like figuring out a Rubix Cube. It's not impossible, but it's difficult. There's no set line of succession when it comes to authority." O'Neill was feeling more comfortable with himself and his audience, so he continued uninterrupted. "Years ago the Supreme People's Assembly confirmed Kim Jung-il's power over North Koreas 23.5 million people, including Kim Yong-nam who is the President of the Presidium there. Since the SPA is the most powerful organ in their government, for now Kim Jung-il is considered their leader. The country has even nicknamed him "Dear Leader".

General Conte snapped at O'Neill, "We don't need a civics lesson, son. Get to the point." His face was bright red, and his countenance indicated he had little patience for O'Neill. Nevertheless he was a brilliant military mind.

President Rittenhouse told Conte to hold his tongue and then told O'Neill to cut to the chase. In so doing, both men were not embarrassed in front of their peers. Rittenhouse knew what to say and when to say it. Conte was put back in line, but O'Neill had been told to move his presentation along.

"Mr. President, it's impossible to get solid, confirmed reports about Jung's health. Did he have a stroke? Who is in charge? Despite the naming of his third son, Jong Un, as his choice as his successor, North Korea is not a very stable place right now. And the lack of a clear successor in North Korea opens the door for anyone in any office of any kind to be assertive. It's possible that one of our men was approached...bribed by an individual working for his own benefit. Information from a United States military officer would be a huge feather in his cap. The rest of the North Korean government factions might not know it is being attempted."

The President nodded for Andy to continue. Everyone was glued to what it was he was saying. "Now combine that possibility with a reality we all know exists, that some naval officers resent turning over control of their boats to Parks when he and his crew come aboard, one of those officers might just give in to temptation." At that O'Neill paused for rebuttal.

Rittenhouse didn't leave time for any rebuttal. "What you're suggesting is that North Korea has possibly been provided the names of Ripkin, Winters, and Parks by a disgruntled naval officer. Am I understanding you correctly, Andy?"

"It's a distinct possibility, Mr. President."

"Certainly we have the resources to do background checks and recent financial activities concerning any officers with whom this unit has worked." He looked at O'Neill and spoke sternly. "Get on that, Andy, now. I want that to be a top priority. I want the names of each officer who has worked with Parks, Ripkin, and Winters. As soon as you have that information, we will reconvene. Questions, Gentlemen?"

The room was silent. As the President of the United States of America rose to depart, everyone stood out of respect for the man and his position. Only the sound of his muffled footsteps upon the plush, dark blue carpet could be heard as he exited.

CHAPTER 9

Hyun Lee, professional assassin for the country of North Korea, was not permitted to carry a portfolio or any notes concerning her assignments. To do so would be a security breach of enormous magnitude. She had researched the life, times, and achievements of Mr. Gabe Winters, Mr. Eli Parks and Mr. Jeff Ripkin with intense scrutiny. Above all else, she was particularly careful to note patterns her subjects might display.

Three years earlier, she had been assigned the task of terminating a European whose talent enabled her to intercept transmissions out of North Korea to its field agents. Her name was Andrea Cutter, and the headaches she caused for Hyun's nationals were manifold. Cutter was, however, as fond of mountain biking as she was technology. She regularly biked the parks or forests of Inverness in northern Scotland. She found the panoramic views there to be spectacular, and the trails were dangerous enough to earn a four-diamond rating. Only bikers and ski enthusiasts of the highest talents dared attempt such trails. Andrea Cutter was one such soul.

During Cutter's biking, Hyun Lee observed one instance when the agent would let her guard down repeatedly. There was one time...every time...when she was most vulnerable: she always stopped by the lakeshore to photograph and capture various daytime scenes. Cutter's home was like a gallery seemingly constructed to share the results of her hobby. Once she was assured of Ms. Cutter's constant habit, Hyun simply waited for her to stop at an opportune moment. The North Korean sharpshooter dropped Andrea Cutter from 200 yards, and the lake became her grave.

The biker's body, camera, and Diamondback bike were never discovered. One bullet was all it took. Andrea Cutter had been too predictable.

From her observations and studies, it was apparent that Eli Parks and his teammates were not much different than most of her targets. Except for those driven to paranoia, everyone had an element of predictability about them. Their work, by nature, kept them on the move, and sometimes they were employed or assigned to foreign locations for long periods of time. That unto itself made them more difficult to approach since their work put them under water in yet another nuclear submarine. Hyun noted that despite D.C. being the headquarters for their work, they constantly traveled all over the globe.

Unlike most D.C. commuters, however, Eli Parks retreated to the Northwest rather than the D.C. suburbs near his workplace. To Hyun Lee, his most glaring tendency was in the realm of family. Yet it was more complex since Eli Parks, one of the subjects of her next assignment, had two families. To make him even less predictable, each family was separated by 2,000 miles. A son by his first marriage lived with his mother and, by and large, they could be found in Pennsylvania. Eli loved his twenty year old son, Jake, so he visited him in Pennsylvania whenever he could. His current wife and his stepson called Montana and the Northwest home.

Winters and Ripkin, too, departed the D.C. area when they chose to go home. Both lived in Northeastern New York state and not too far apart. Like Parks, Winters enjoyed returning home to his bride. They had no children, but both were family-oriented. Ripkin, on the other hand, was a bit more of a free spirit once he was home. He lived with his parents when he returned to New York, but their house was more of a base from where he operated, for he was often on the move while enjoying his youthful social life.

Hyun felt she had done her homework. "I'll figure all of you out, gentlemen," she would murmur to herself as she gathered information. "You're a challenge, but I'll figure you out." Her last contact indicated they were busy at work in D.C.

Parks was a wild card in a much different way. It was not difficult to believe Eli Parks would visit the President since they were long-time friends. His D.C. visits were common knowledge once they took place; therefore, he possessed too great of a profile when he was there. She had to be patient, yet stay within the liberal time parameters assigned to her. She would only approach Eli Parks in D.C. if time forced her to do so.

At the present, she had no time constraints upon her whatsoever. For Hyun, that was rare. Yesterday she had been in Florida, and today she awakened in the Hyatt of Baltimore's Inner Harbor. Under the guise of a vacationer, no one would ever question why she landed at Reagan National Airport and then traveled to Baltimore. It is true that the Reagan airport was used largely for corporate entities, but there were some commercial flights as well. Blending as a tourist was easy.

Her flight enabled her to check in before 6 p.m. Having visited the harbor previously on a recon-type mission, she had heard of Little Italy's D'Napolis, an often-crowded, tiny restaurant known for its tremendous veal chops. Rather than just sitting around, she let the Hyatt arrange for a town car to pick her up at the hotel's entrance. The service was classy, and her countrymen would appreciate the fact that it was free. The chops were not a disappointment, and she was back in the Hyatt's Pegasus, a top-floor lounge, by 11:30 p.m.

Hyun enjoyed her privacy both at dinner time and as a traveler. She liked to observe people. Her observation skills were important to her trade. During her second day in Baltimore, she found an index card on the lobby's guest bulletin board. Upon it was a general invitation to "... anyone interested in a game of tennis". She called the room number, and a young man's voice greeted her. In very little time, they agreed to meet that evening to play.

The gentleman she met, a Mr. Barry Elkins, was tall and as athletically built as she was. He was friendly, but had the air of a man who was going to take it easy on her once they hit the court. Little did he know Hyun was a superior player, and he was somewhat embarrassed to have lost to her in straight sets, not having won a single game. His ego took a hit, for there was little conversation when the match was over. She laughed to herself, because she was sure Barry thought tonight might have gone differently once he impressed her with his own tennis ability.

That evening she returned to the Pegasus Lounge atop the Hyatt. Its night time view of the harbor appealed to her. After a glass of wine and some decent, softly-played background music, she decided a good night's sleep was just what she desired. It was after ten o'clock.

She tossed her key card upon the cherry dresser and stopped before the vanity's mirror. "No wrinkles yet," she whispered to no one but herself, and then she let down her hair as she removed the amber combs at the back of her head. At 5' 6", she was beautiful, and she knew it. Athletic since childhood, Hyun continued to take care of herself.

From her fifth floor suite she could see many of the harbor lights whose glow created a relaxed atmosphere in the otherwise darkened room. Only a plate glass window separated her from the cool evening air. Tired, she climbed into bed and fell into a comfortable sleep.

In her dreams, she visited North Korea and her friends. As a child she was always happy to see Mia who lived down the street and Ayuku who she saw at school every day. The three of them were inseparable when their school schedule permitted. When Hyun's latent physical talents were discovered, she saw less and less of Mia, but Ayuku often remained at her side, for she excelled in the gym as well. Sadly, Hyun was forced to begin specializing in the field of tennis, costing her valued time that she and Ayuku enjoyed so much. Eventually Ayuku found her niche as a swimmer and excelled at the World Games of 2000. Hyun was happy for her, but still felt a pang when she realized how little they were permitted to live their lives as children. As an adult, Hyun looked back on those days with mixed emotions.

Occasionally Hyun dreamed of time spent with her father. For decades he was a North Korean police officer. His counterparts knew of his daughter's successes on the court, and they envied how the Lee family's image had improved in proportion to her accomplishments. Her exploits made members of Hyun's family more well known. At one point, her father began parading her around Police Headquarters enjoying the attention she brought upon both of them.

During one such visit, she was introduced to the headquarters' firing range. A huge, well-lighted facility, it was there that she initially discovered her interest in target shooting. Hyun's father could not have been more pleased when his superior officer offered lessons which resulted in the discovery of yet another latent talent: marksmanship. Competitions ensued and quickly word spread that Mi Hen Lee's daughter was more talented than most men and women on the police force. Arrangements were made for her to meet coaches with the North Korean National Team which was, of course, affiliated with the North Korean Army. The combination of her talent with weapons and her new associates eventually led to a career that North Korean officials euphemistically called a government position.

If she was awake and happened to recall her dreams, she sometimes resented how her family's station in life was directly correlated with her own successes. The more Hyun and Ayuko succeeded, the better their families fared as well. Remembering how the effects of her athletic achievements altered her youth was often unsettling. She had distasteful memories of her father and brother berating her when she occasionally stagnated talent-wise, or her progress appeared to level off.

On the other hand, her mother was gentle and appreciative of her efforts. Her reveries concerning her mother and North Korea were riddled with anxiety caused by the men in her life. As an adult, she vowed no man would own her or dictate her life. She actually preferred the company of women. Perhaps that was why she enjoyed embarrassing the "Barrys" of this world.

Hyun slept deeply. Her breathing was rhythmical and relaxed. When she awakened to her phone's computer-generated chime, it was late in the morning. From the Hyatt in Baltimore she logged onto the Internet and began researching Montana, New York state, Pennsylvania, and Maryland. She finally decided a visit to first New York state and then Montana was in order. There was reconnoitering that needed to be done.

CHAPTER 10

Cary had neighbors not too far down her road in either direction. She knew them all and knew them well. In fact, all of them were proud of the fact that Falls Port had been their home for generations, and over the years her parents had introduced her to each and every one of them at some point while she was growing up. Everyone around her had done well for themselves, and most of her neighbors were retired. It was a neighborhood consisting of homes equal in beauty to her own. None were too close by, nor were they too far away.

Feeling introspective, Cary went out alone for a walk one Saturday night. Despite having neighbors in all directions, it still seemed as if she was alone, as if the road, all the trees, and all the night sounds were her own. To her, the solitude was not unsettling. It was more like a protective barrier or even a blanket into which she could bundle herself and escape with her private thoughts. The night air was cooler; a pleasant change from the warmer temperatures earlier in the day. It was a pleasant change, too, from what had just occurred.

It had been a busy day, so her mind was full of thoughts that ran the gamut from silly things to absolutely serious. Early that morning, she spoke with Rita on the phone as the two of them exchanged bits of gossip and sipped their beloved morning coffee.

Rita rambled on about how her next door neighbor had for some reason created an unusually deep-sounding wind chime that he had hung from a thick rope in a large, old tree. "I would compare its sound to that of an anchored marker buoy's gong as it was swaying up gentle waves in a harbor someplace."

"Does it keep you awake?"

"Cary, the funny thing is that I found it relaxing!" At that they both laughed and moved on to another frivolous topic.

By late morning the sun was high in the clear sky over Montana, and she had grass to mow. Her yard was miniscule, for she preferred the trees and wild growth on her property to that of a finely groomed lawn. She did choose to have a small lawn to let in more light through the day, thereby keeping unwanted moisture and mildew off her home. The yard was tiny by comparison to the yards of her closest neighbors, and she mowed it by hand with a push mower. When Cary had finished cutting the grass it was nearly noon. Her white tank top clung to her skin, bits of grass stuck to her sweaty arms and legs, and she was ready for her shower.

Her afternoon was spent calling clients to see how they were faring. It was a personal touch she provided some weekends. As she spoke with them about some of their decisions and the ramifications, Cary carefully took notes that would be of use to her when they met in her office a day or two later. Saddened by some of those conversations, from time to time she still thought of how Alan would never have understood why she chose to bring work home, at least that's how he would have perceived it. To her, it was not work but a passion she enjoyed: helping people.

When evening tiptoed into darkness, she felt she had a good day. A call from Patty brought some more laughter, and a glass of red wine helped her to mellow as she listened to some of her favorite music. Upon her couch, she was covered with a soft, chenille throw and in for the night. Then there was one more telephone call.

Not long after that final call of the evening Cary chose to go for her walk. Like all nights when she walked alone, she was armed. She carried the Smith & Wesson M+P 45 semi automatic her father had given her only because she felt it was prudent to have for protection against a bear or mountain lion that she might accidentally encounter. To her knowledge, attacks had never happened in the Flathead Lake area, but she felt better protected anyway.

As she walked slowly in and out of moonlit surroundings and the shadows that painted her lengthy, blacktop driveway, she recalled her youth. Cary was fond of recalling her parents. Both were deceased, having died of similar bouts with cancer not long ago. They were instrumental in shaping her values, her confidence, and her willingness to work.

She loved recalling, too, how her dad taught her to handle and respect guns. When Cary was a young teen, and because she did not possess terrific social skills, she had few people she trusted as friends. Perhaps her dad pictured her being alone more often than not. Perhaps he felt she would be vulnerable. For whatever reason, he felt it incumbent upon himself to pass along what he knew about gun safety to his only child. All of this made her chuckle to herself and think how the boys in her school had no idea she was better at marksmanship than they were.

"I won't always be around to protect you, Cary," her dad told her as they walked the length of the outdoor range to retrieve their respective targets. "And you might not ever have to use one of these, but it's good to know you can if you must." She found it comforting to think that her dad was still with her when she was armed. It was a lesson well-learned and appreciated. Cary did not feel as if having a gun empowered her or made her a threat. She did not feel she was someone to be reckoned with, but being competent did make her less fearful.

Occasionally a creature scurried through the darkness. A grazing deer picking up apples cracked some branches as well. But as a rule, the night sounds soothed Cary. Night sounds also ranged from crickets to breezes stirring gently as if whispering to her through tamarack branches. And it was not at all startling when she heard coyotes yipping up in the hills. Those were her favorites.

Off in the distance, the occasional 18 wheeler growled its way along Route 93's West Shore Road. And like that driver off in the distance who shifted gears of a fully loaded rig, Cary shifted gears mentally and tried to digest why Alan, her ex-husband, might have called her and why he began speaking to her the way he did.

"Well hello, Cary. It's been quite some time. Hasn't it?" Alan spoke to her quietly. It sounded as if he was trying to appear mysterious. "You *do* know who this is. Right? I was once the man of your dreams." Briefly she acknowledged him and let him go on a bit more. His voice deepened and he spoke more slowly and more distinctly. "I'll never forget you, Cary, and I doubt you have heard the last of me." It was not so much what he said, but the manner in which he spoke to her. He was creepy.

His former wife gathered her wits and told him to never call again. Then she hung up the phone gently. At that very second she feared hanging up the phone with any force would signal the degree to which he had upset her. She worried he might actually arrive at her door. Deep inside, Cary knew that all he heard was a click, but at that very moment she could not risk being wrong.

Never had Cary said much of anything to anyone about him; certainly nothing derogatory. She had been careful not to do that. She wondered what instigated his desire to call. He was not enraged. Alan did not necessarily speak dramatically to unsettle her or make her feel threatened, yet that was how she felt. Perhaps he was just drunk and feeling sorry for himself. She was glad she had dismissed him, but at the same time, wished she had listened to his ramblings more carefully. Next time...maybe.

CHAPTER 11

Eli was awake just enough to hear Rita's Montana twang. "Cary?" Caller ID told Rita the origin of the early morning call. She was surprised that Cary would call before 6:30.

"Morning, Rita. Sorry to be calling you so early," Cary began. Rita sensed an edge in Cary's voice, so she was not caught off guard when she heard Cary ask to meet her at the Driftwood for coffee or breakfast.

"Are you okay?" Rita asked. By now she had tossed off her side of their powder blue duvet and was sitting on the edge of their bed. There was a brief silence. After she hung up the phone, Rita turned back onto the bed to face her husband, and ran her fingers through his hair. Eli slid an arm around her.

"Everything okay?" he asked sleepily. His hair was a mess and his face unshaven.

"I'm not sure," she said. Then Rita kissed his mouth gently, glad to have him there to help in unsettling times. She knew Cary had no one in her life at the moment, so Rita felt fortunate in that regard. She stood up from the edge of their bed and peered out the window. "Cary wants me to meet her at the Driftwood."

"Want me to come with you?"

"Later, Baby," she smiled and headed toward the shower. "I want you to be there, but give us thirty minutes to sort things out. Besides, I might be back sooner than you think, and I could make you breakfast." Eli dropped back into the pillows. In no time he was snoring.

If Rita had been taken into the Driftwood Café blindfolded, she would still have known where she was immediately. Like most cafes and diners in Small Town America, the Driftwood had its regulars with their ongoing conversations plus sounds and smells all its own. Chris and Dave Sampson, brothers who the townies described as joined at the hip, always sat with Jim Kaufman each morning on the three stools adjacent to the cash register.

By contrast, the loudest patron in the café, old Gene Hopkins, usually sat by himself behind the morning paper in the most remote booth the place had to offer near the café's large front window. Hoppy, as his friends called him, lived in Falls Port most of his life. He knew everyone, or so it seemed. Despite his rough social graces, to the locals he was considered part of the Driftwood's charm.

The aroma of freshly brewed coffee permeated the café, and Rita loved her coffee first thing in the morning. One of the many things Eli appreciated about his bride was that, like him, she thoroughly enjoyed the first meal of the day. Eli and Rita were Driftwood regulars, so it surprised no one that she was there. The Sampson brothers nodded and smiled as Rita and Cary settled into a booth of their own. Jimmy tipped his cap. Abigail sauntered over with two coffees and then left them to chat. She was in no hurry to take their breakfast order.

Rita smiled at Abigail and then caught the eye of a high school friend, Brenda Miller, the cook. "Hey, Brenda! How are you?"

"Hey, Mrs. Parks!" old Hoppy bellowed from the back of the café. "You tell that husband of yours I'll be glad to go fishin' with him when he's ready!" Actually most people believed Gene Hopkins knew more about fishing Flathead Lake than anyone else in town and perhaps Lake County.

Rita smiled back at Gene. "I'll tell him, Gene. He and Eddie didn't catch a thing last night."

"Still trying to catch that bass in front of your cabin?" Like diners everywhere, the sounds of a dishwasher and thick white plates being stacked blended in with the conversation of customers.

"Still trying, Gene. That fish is Eli's dream catch." Only then was Rita able to refocus on Brenda. She smiled. She understood that tolerating Hoppy's interruptions was part of her job.

"Hi, Rita!" Brenda replied finally given the chance. "Where's Eli this morning?"

"Truth be known, Brenda, he was snoring when I left."

She turned back to Cary. "I wonder how old Gene Hopkins is now."

Cary sipped her coffee and held the mug in both her hands as if it were a source of warmth to her. "He's older than my dad so he's at least seventy-five. He's still a big man." They didn't know it, but Gene had indeed tipped the scales at more than 250 pounds earlier that week in Vogler's Feed Store.

Rita took a glimpse at the sun through morning mist over the lake and marveled at how serene life appeared. In the meantime, Abigail had taken Rita's order and was serving it. She could only stir her coffee so many times before she finally asked the obligatory question, "Are you going to tell me why on earth you called so early?" Abigail placed scrambled eggs, wheat toast, and sausage patties in front of Rita as she sat back, ready to listen.

Cary looked at her friend. "Alan called. He didn't have time to say much because I told him not to call again, and I hung up on him."

"Alan?" Rita sounded surprised. "Has he called before?"

"Hardly ever," Cary answered. "But this time his tone was malevolent. And it was creepy. It bothered me even more because it was his birthday." Cary had not ordered breakfast, but nibbled on a triangle of buttered toast from Rita's plate. "And get this. It motivated me to go for a walk most of the night—well, 'til 3 a.m. I even drove by your house early this morning after my walk."

"Cary!" Rita chided her in a heavy whisper. "You don't have any business roaming the area in the middle of the night!"

"I had my pistol," Cary blurted out.

"What!" The café briefly became silent as customers stared momentarily, then the noise level in the Driftwood returned to normal.

More than a little self-conscious, Cary looked over her shoulder and spoke softly. "What's the big deal, Rita? You know I have a gun. You've seen me target shoot."

"Yeah, but you went out at night feeling unsettled and took it with you. You might have shot someone! What were you thinking?"

"My dad taught me how to handle guns." She bit some more toast from Rita's plate. Then she wiped a few crumbs from her lips. "I know more about gun safety than most men know."

Rita's brown eyes were intense, and they showed frustration. "That was to defend yourself from animals, not humans," she persisted.

Cary said nothing. She just stared at the lake. Finally she turned back to her best friend. "You're right. That's why I called. I want advice from you." A few customers passed by slowly, so the girls did not talk for a moment.

Rita calmed down a bit as she cut her sausage patties in to bite-sized pieces. "Why was this phone call so disturbing to you?"

"It was his tone," she answered. "During other calls, he never once gave me the impression he'd ever wanted to hurt me. He never sounded threatening before. But last night he said something like, 'I'm sure you'll be seeing me again' or something to that effect. Last night he sounded so mysterious and so weird. Plus I had no idea where he was. Not knowing only served to double my anxiety."

"So he had you at a disadvantage. He knew you were home, so you felt safer getting out. Right?"

Cary sighed, tired after a long night. "I guess so. I can't honestly say. I have no one like you do. Usually the quiet and darkness are soothing to me, but he made it quite unsettling."

More locals entered the café and were greeted loudly by Gene Hopkins. He created a "You're always welcome here" atmosphere without even knowing he was doing it.

"Do you always take your gun when you walk?"

"Usually I do. I take it in case I walk into the path of a bear or something like that." Cary was staring out the window with her chin on the palm of her right hand. Upon the table she quietly drummed the fingers on her left. Her long nails clicked gently as she did so.

Rita shook her head. "Okay, so what are you considering? A security system? A dog? Floodlights? Moving altogether?"

Cary admitted that those options all sounded good, and told Rita she had already had the security system installed months before. "I'm afraid. Alan never sounded like he might want to hurt me until last night." She paused. "Are you going to eat that toast?"

Rita pushed her plate toward her. "Do you want to stay with us?

"For a couple of nights?" Cary asked.

"Stay as long as you want. Now eat the toast before I change my mind."

"About staying with you?

"No," Rita laughed, "about the toast."

No sooner had she spoken when Gene Hopkins bellowed, "Hello, Mr. Parks! Here to check up on the little woman?"

Eli waved toward Gene and slid into the seat next to his wife. Abigail brought him decaf coffee.

"Good morning, Brenda!" Eli called out.

"Hey, Sleepy! How are the other dwarves this morning?"

"Very funny, Brenda. Very funny." He laughed. "Try not to burn the scrapple this time!"

Breakfast played itself out casually. Rita and Cary apprised him of Cary's situation. When they were done he explained he had been called back to D.C. "I just received a call from work. I have to fly out sometime today. It depends on how fast I can get a flight." Then he became amusingly sarcastic and said, "As you can see, I'm rushing to get out of here." Eli liked his work, but he loved his home. Little did the girls know that somewhere in Missoula the U.S. government had already made sure he had a flight out of Montana that very morning.

Eli had biked to the café. He enjoyed a morning ride. As routes go, the ride to the café was an easy one—mostly flat and partly downhill. When they left the café, Rita saw his bike had been tossed in the back of their Dakota, so she knew he planned to catch a ride back home.

"Honey, you don't mind if Cary stays with us. Right?"

He put his arm around his bride who, as always, sat next to him in the middle of the truck's bench seat. They took a lot of teasing over this, but secretly, those who teased them admired the fact that they still acted so in love. It was no act.

"Sparky, that's what friends are for. Besides, since I have to go to D.C., I'm glad Cary will be there to keep you company. Maybe the two of you can finish staining the deck." At that, Rita slapped him playfully.

Eli's phone call had been that of a serious nature, of course. However, he explained it away as everyday business. Until he knew the reason for the meeting's urgency, he was not about to create a worry for his wife. He called his son, Jake, in Pennsylvania, and later spoke to Ed as well. Ed promised to keep an eye on his mom, and later that day the two shook hands as Eli hopped in the old red and gray truck.

"I'll be back as soon as I can," he said to the two of them. "And I'll call tonight." Then he leaned out the window and kissed Rita one more time.

Ed was not at all put off by this. He was happy to see his mom receiving some long overdue affection. She stepped back and put her arm around her son. Ed was pretty sure he heard his mom say softly, "God, please watch over him," and it made him wonder what exactly his stepfather did for the government. Until now he really did not know too much about Eli's work. Next time they went out together, he would broach the subject with him.

As he drove toward Missoula, Eli assured himself that turning down a helicopter ride from Falls Port was the right thing to do. Such an event would have brought too much attention. By driving himself to the airport he maintained an air of normalcy.

CHAPTER 12

After his birthday, Alan decided to visit Kamiah, Idaho not only for its casino attraction, but also for its Native American history. He hoped to feel as if he fit in better socially since he, too, was a Native American as were many of the locals. The Kamiah area, inhabited by the Nez Perce people for hundreds of years, received its name from their tribe. Alan learned that it meant "many rope litters," as Nez Perce manufactured "Kamia" ropes in the area to fish steelhead. Alan also learned that according to Nez Perce tradition, the Appaloosa horse was first bred in the area. After a brief tour of the area, he was ready to settle in and play.

Upon arrival at the River Casino, he had not only checked in but made the decision to pay his bill ahead of time. The decision proved to be a prudent one. In the wee hours of the morning, he fell asleep after a frustrating outing. Early on, Alan had hit upon a streak of good fortune; again it was at the roulette table. However luck had turned its other cheek shortly after midnight. Not able to walk away while still a little ahead of the game, he lost a lot of money by the time he quit playing, and a new day's sun had begun to rise.

At first he slept uneasily, lying on the queen-sized bed in his jeans. He had barely enough energy to pull off his sweatshirt, and that was all he managed to do. He had not even removed his shoes before he fell asleep. Irritated by his losses combined with Cary's unwillingness to listen to him over the phone, Alan's anger seemed to fight the sleep he needed. After much tossing and turning, his body gave in to exhaustion, and he began to rest more easily. His tan, physically fit torso, inhaled and exhaled rhythmically. Always a good looking man, Alan somehow managed to continue taking care of himself physically. That was an enigma to those who knew him, especially Cary, because by nature he was lazy. Staying in shape was his saving grace; it was the one area in which he applied himself.

As he slept, he drifted in and out of a graphic, recurring dream about his family history. The Wing family name was proudly adopted several generations before Alan was born, and he began dreaming of his ancient Wing ancestors more and more often. As long as he could remember, his family's stories had been passed along as part of a wonderful oral tradition. As if in a vision meant for him alone, the stories of his male ancestors of long ago and their respective vision quests, a tradition practiced by several Native American tribes, he often had the same detailed dream.

Settling into a deeper sleep that morning upon his bed in the casino's posh hotel room, his dream permitted him to watch, as if unseen and omniscient, an older man sit atop a Montana butte at dusk. A fire crackled and the old man chanted as he reached occasionally to the stars. Beside him was a young man, a boy by comparison, who eventually the old man would abandon. It was the boy's turn to seek a vision, fulfill his quest, and determine the path his life might provide. Before his departure that night, the grandfather passed along a pouch made of leather with little or no ornamentation upon it.

A fire between them crackled occasionally, and from the distance could be heard the yipping of coyotes. Outside the ring of firelight, darkness was draped like a thick curtain. As the tribal elder spoke, the young man listened. Alan, too, listened as if he were experiencing an out-of-body observation. "Your elders have permitted you this opportunity, young one. It's time for you to choose your path." The old man's hair was long and had the appearance of spun silver. It was tousled by the evening breeze. He paused and then continued. "The Great One will provide you with one sign or perhaps a few. Be alert. Don't overlook the significance of anything—great or small."

At this point in the dream, each and every time in his sleep he softly uttered the same words, as did the young man in his dream: "I'll be alert, Grandfather. I will be on my guard. I'll make you proud. I will not be lazy like the cattle in our herd that need to be driven." At that moment, the pouch was passed and the old man appeared to evaporate into a night spangled in countless stars.

In his dream, Alan revisited the Wing family's story to conclusion. As one might hope, the boy returned to his people days later, starving but unharmed, with a tale that included an amazing chapter about the stars. And whenever Alan dreamed this particular dream, the young man always awoke upon the butte to find not one but seven feathers of an eagle placed about the blanket under which he finally slept. As the boy slept alone atop the butte under the dark night sky, the Great one spoke to him and told him to follow the flight of stars, and the eagle's courage would be his. To Alan, for some reason, none of this made sense. It did not seem to apply to him. Other than the possible connection between the discovered feathers and the Wing family name, he wondered on many occasions what this dream had to do with him. When Alan awoke in the casino's room on the third floor it was early afternoon.

That same afternoon, the government jet that awaited Eli lifted off smoothly. Earlier as he walked through the airport, Eli fondly recalled previous trips when Rita would meet him there. Eli loved to mentally escape to the day when on an the airport elevator he had first been brave enough to kiss Rita. What always brought a smile to his face was the fact that she actually initiated the kiss. He had not stopped enjoying the taste and texture of her kisses ever since. Eli told Rita on more than one occasion that when life got a bit rough, he escaped mentally to his happy place—their elevator. He found it comforting and inspirational to mentally transport himself there.

On this flight he sat alone, but when flying commercially Eli enjoyed observing others. He especially enjoyed watching those who he felt might be flying for the first time. To him a dead giveaway was how they enjoyed looking out the portholes as they cruised thousands of feet above the earth below. It seemed to him that children especially loved the clouds, even that child inside each adult with whom he sat on various flights. But this day was different. He was the sole passenger upon the flight, and he would cross the United States more quickly than usual.

Not long after departure, Eli fell into a deep sleep. He did not know it at the time, but somewhere between Missoula and D.C., he dreamed of days long ago when he lived in the suburbs of Allentown. His childhood memories were often sports-oriented while many adult memories involved his family, including his previous marriage to Erin.

Family meant a great deal to him. It always had. He had older brothers who were his heroes. When Eli was a little boy, Jamie often pedaled his newspaper route with Eli on the handlebars. Local boys working for the Philadelphia Evening Bulletin met in someone's garage to wrap and bind the evening papers for delivery. Eli always felt special when he realized his brother was the only paperboy who brought along his kid brother from time to time.

When sports came into Eli's world, brother Bernie seemed to be the one who was around to help Eli get his fix. How many times and how many hours did Bernie play football and baseball around the house with Eli during his teen years?

And when he thought of his brothers, he could not forget his brother Wally. Wally was the one who helped him the most when dating became part of Eli's world. Eli could not think of a time when Wally would not let him borrow his car. A favorite memory recalled how Wally insisted on a game of straight pool to decide whether or not Wally's new car would be available on Prom Night. Somehow Eli overcame an incredible deficit to win that game; surely Wally had let him win. But that was the beauty of his third brother: with him you just never knew.

It was his loyalty to family that made his divorce most strenuous. His wife was a good person. Many of her values were his. Nevertheless, the things they did not share or agree upon ate away at their happiness. Sometimes when he would dream of unhappy times he would awaken with a feeling of guilt that he could no longer make things work. He wondered if others ever experienced the same emotion.

During this particular flight he dreamed of the night he had been sitting on the team bench during a high school basketball game. He was not a regular, but he enjoyed the team nevertheless. He was sixteen; a sophomore. Eli clearly recalled details of that specific night. In the dream, from the bench he saw his dad enter the gym, a dad who did not enjoy basketball, and therefore never attended his games.

His father felt that basketball game officials had too much control over the physical nature of the game. "When I was a kid, the game was actually played in a cage. We were called 'cagers'. The game was more physical. Now you can't touch an opponent. At least in baseball a pitcher can purposely plunk a batter or tag an opponent hard. And, in football, players can tackle or block a man roughly. Basketball is too soft."

So on this night when he saw his father enter the gym, immediately Eli suspected the worst. Sure enough his dad had arrived to tell him that his sister-in-law, Martha, who earlier in the day had given birth to her third child, a baby girl, had died suddenly for reasons unknown to the family. Eli's dream recalled his departure from the gym to the background roar of an unknowing audience.

Why Eli even dreamed of this particular event is anybody's guess. He dreamed about it from time to time and never knew why. He once shared it with Rita, and she suggested that perhaps since it was unexpected he recalled that night subconsciously whenever he was facing the unexpected. In this case, he had been summoned to a meeting by his college roommate, now President Rittenhouse, and he did not know why. When Eli was awakened by the announcement that they soon would be landing, he felt unsettled. The dream of Martha's death evaporated quickly, and his flight landed during the middle of the Capitol's rush hour.

As he walked the tarmac to an awaiting ride, he used his personal cell phone to contact his wife. "Sparky, I'm not sure how long this conference will last. I'll call when we're through if it's not too late."

Rita loved his pet name for her. Even after a few years of marriage, she thought it was sweet of him. As for herself, he had always been Eli. Rarely did she deviate from this for she felt his name was solid, and it suited him well. "Nooooo you don't, Eli," she quickly interjected. "I don't care how late it is. Call me."

"Yes, Dear," he countered and waited playfully for her wrath.

"Don't you dare, 'Yes, Dear' me! she retorted.

"Yes, Dear." He barely could contain his laughter.

There was silence for a moment, for she missed him already. "I love you, Eli."

"I love you more," Eli whispered back. A rear, passenger-side door into a shiny, black SUV was opened, and he was rushed to the White House to meet his old friend, the President of the United States of America. That concept still amazed him. "If they only knew what we were like as kids," he whispered to himself.

CHAPTER 13

Clearance for admittance to the White House had been arranged, so by all appearances Eli's arrival was ordinary. Nonetheless, Eli made a point to refresh his memory regarding names of several staff members in several departments.

No matter how many times Eli met with President Elijah Rittenhouse, he marveled at the grandeur of The White House, felt respect for its history, and was in awe of his college roommate's zest for his position. He had not, at least in front of Eli, let any of his political power change him as a person. When he was cordially ushered into the famous Oval Office again, the President crossed the room to greet him. The President, still in fine shape physically, was equal in height to Eli. When the two shook hands, everyone in the room saw that the bond between them was heartfelt. Then Eli was reintroduced to those in attendance around the room: Chief of Staff Andy O'Neill as well as the heads of the FBI, the Secret Service, and the National Security Agency.

Eli quickly learned that this night's meeting was largely about him. Without pretense, the President relaxed in the presence of his friend. Leaning casually against his desk in the Oval Office, he dispersed with idle chit chat and quickly got to the heart of the matter. Besides Eli's issues, the President did have other domestic and global matters his staff insisted he must address. Eli knew this, so he was not at all put off when there was no college roommate banter on this occasion.

"Eli, there's no way to sugarcoat this, so I'll be straight forward." He finally sat next to his old friend upon the golden, suede-textured couch that paralleled his own desk in front of the large windows overlooking the White House lawn. Upon the carpet was a Presidential Seal that was ten feet in diameter. White book shelves, that he was sure were filled with historically significant texts, lined the walls to their right and left. Rittenhouse continued as he looked out that famous office window. "More than ever, I fear for your safety and the safety of your family. I fear for the members of your team as well."

The word "family" immediately struck a chord with Eli. "What is it, Mr. President?" he asked tensely.

"As you know, most of what you have been asked to do for our country has been classified Top Secret, yet we would all be fools to think secrets do not get loose and travel about." Now the President looked Eli squarely in the eye. "My people cannot assure me any longer that you have not been compromised. You are believed to be an assassin's target."

"God Almighty!" Eli whispered to nobody in particular. Such language was uncommon from Eli Parks. The President knew that about Eli as did the other staff members scattered throughout the Oval Office. The quiet was palpable. They gave Eli time to react, and he did so admirably. "Mr. President, what do you need me to do?"

The glances that passed from face to face around the room traveled at lightning speed. The President's people immediately understood why Eli Parks was so special to the President. This man had just been told he, his family, and his co-workers were the target of an assassin's bullet, or soon might be, yet he immediately and unselfishly offered his services to the nation first. Even the President was caught a bit off guard.

"What? Why are you looking at me like that?" Eli pondered aloud. He looked around. "Certainly you've called me here with some sort of plan in mind. Right?" His eyes darted hopefully from place to place.

"You never cease to amaze me," replied the President. "Yes, we have a plan, and it does involve you. Speaking for everyone in the room, I just didn't think you would make it so easy to present. As I've learned a hundred times, you are an incredibly unselfish friend."

Eli was a bit embarrassed by the praise he had just received. In his way of thinking, he had just reacted in a manner that appealed to him. In his mind, he was being assertive. He wanted to be a part of whatever it might take to make his family and friends safe again. "Thank you, Mr. President, but I'm only interested in how I can expedite my family's and friends' well being. I must at least admit that. I'm not a saint."

Rittenhouse turned to his Chief of Staff and spoke. "He's all yours." Then turning to Eli, he added, "I hope you know I have my best people on this. Please trust them completely. I'll be back with you as soon as I can. Right now, Roomy, I have to go avert a war."

Both men stood and shook hands, and then hugged briefly. With that, Rittenhouse was gone, leaving his famous Oval Office to his friend, and it did not go unnoticed.

CHAPTER 14

Time has a way of passing, and reality began closing in on Alan Wing at long last. As if on a pendulum, his luck at the tables had begun to swing in the opposite direction. He had not even enjoyed an occasional lucky streak in days.

Some folks would argue that it is not true, but roulette is a simple game, and the chances of winning consistently are not in a player's favor. Alan employed all sorts of systems to beat the house, finding it hard to believe that luck was on his side for a while and that his earlier good fortune had nothing to do with his skill. His ego would not accept that his talents were insignificant. This is a difficult lesson to learn, and until it is understood, success is fleeting more often than not.

Permitted to watch from behind the chairs where serious players sit on the roulette table's boundary, Alan would stand quietly and observe patterns or occasions where he saw Red or Black be announced the winning color several times in a row. On one particular night, he waited patiently to bet on Red while the game's mesmerizing, tiny little ball found its home in the arms of Black on nine consecutive spins of the wheel.

"Surely Red is due," he thought to himself, "and if it doesn't come up I will just double up on the eleventh spin and recoup my loss." Selecting the correct color pays two-to-one, so Alan was certain he was about collect double his twenty dollar bet on the tenth spin of the wheel or break even after his bet of forty bucks on the eleventh. The verisimilitude of Red bringing Black's reign to a halt was too much to resist, and Alan was compelled to bet. The desired result never took place. The run on Black continued right through the fourteenth spin by which time Alan realized he was dangerously close to losing everything he had. There was no more house money to wager; everything he had won on previous outings was lost. He had pitted himself and all of his skills against the mathematical odds of the game, and he had been defeated.

To compound his troubles, his jeep was in need of maintenance—tires, a tune-up, not to mention car insurance. His was not an uncommon story. A legion of gamblers before and after Alan Wing lost touch with reality and never recovered. At least Alan still feared finding himself destitute. His gaming had limits, because someplace in the recesses of his mind, Alan's means of transportation was a high enough priority that signaled he had to walk away.

A gambler close to addiction, Alan still managed to find work doing odd jobs between his visits to a casino. Many were the moments when he thought about never entering a casino again. The extra cash in his pocket came slowly, and he knew he worked hard to earn it, but eventually the lure of easy money was just too great.

When he won, he slept in the accommodations offered by various night clubs. On those occasions he again suffered from illusions of grandeur, for such nights reinforced that he had finally figured out the system, a way to beat the house. He became almost gladiatorial in attitude. Many a player has made that mistake. Undeterred he returned to the arena to do battle. As had happened before, when his fortune at the tables worsened and his opponent had revealed to him any flaw in his protective armor, he found shelter in deplorable motels, tried camping on different occasions, and even slept in his Jeep.

One of his last nights in a casino was spent at the Cal Neva Resort, located on the California/Nevada border and along the northern shore of Lake Tahoe. His losses had been staggering. As Alan entered an elevator he overheard a well-dressed woman comment to her husband about an inappropriate guest she had watched blow hundreds of dollars over the course of the evening. "He just didn't seem to get it. He was such a loser. He even lost his temper." It was obvious that what she had witnessed through the evening was distasteful to her, and it had made her quite uncomfortable.

Curiosity prompted Alan to turn and see who was speaking. Then he realized that not only did she have a familiar face, for she had been seated near him at a roulette table most of the evening, but he also quickly understood that she had been describing him. From the rear of the elevator, she recognized him when he turned, and it was an equally embarrassing moment for both.

A new direction in his search for success slowly manifested itself. As a result of his misfortune, Alan eventually resorted to visiting various acquaintances he had discovered during the course of his travels. They tolerated him for as long as they could at each stop along the way. In each instance, he burned bridges behind him. What had begun with "Alan, how are you? Sure! Stay with us," always ended with "...and don't come back!"

In northern Idaho, Fate once landed a high school classmate in his lap, someone with whom he was once close friends. On a Friday afternoon while putting gas in his Jeep Alan heard a voice quietly ask, "Alan? Are you Alan Wing?"

He turned, and in front of him stood Charlie Littlehorse. Alan had not seen or spoken to Charlie since he went off to college. He recognized Charlie's smile immediately.

"Charlie! Imagine seeing you here at the top of Idaho!"

Alan's first impression was that his high school friend had done well for himself. His clothing was impeccable and stylish, but it was the immaculate 1969 Chrysler Newport that sold him on the idea. It had a charcoal gray body with a creamy-white roof. Like many Chryslers of its era, it was huge. It was a four-door sedan, and Alan was certain it guzzled up gasoline like a thirsty dog slurps water from its bowl.

"I live here, Alan. How about you? What brings you to Bonner's Ferry?"

Alan put on the charm and began spinning his tale. He told Charlie that the urge to travel while he was still single had finally won out. He was honest about Cary, and he even took the blame for the failure of their marriage. He was impressive in a humble way.

"How about you, Charlie? What do you do for a living way up here near Canada?"

Charlie laughed. "I'm sure you're familiar with all the old Native American stereotypes regarding the Redman, whiskey, and gambling. Well I'm an assistant manager here in Bonner's Ferry at the Kootenai River Inn and Casino." Charlie put his arm around Alan's shoulder as if he was sharing a secret. He told Alan he was fighting the good fight, defeating White Man by taking his money away from him slowly. At that, they shared a good laugh.

"Alan," Charlie continued, "have you seen many casinos? Ours is state of the art."

Alan lied. He spoke of seeing a few in his travels, and he told how the concept of a casino, despite its spectacular appeal, scared him a bit. "I'm not sure it's a good place for this warrior, Charlie."

"Look...where are you staying tonight? I can put you up at the Inn free for a night." Never suspecting what kind of door he might be opening, Alan's old friend continued. "We'll have dinner and catch up a bit more. Right now I have to get going."

Alan was gracious in his acceptance of Charlie Littlehorse's invitation. "Before you go, I have to ask one question: How can you afford to drive that tank around?"

"Thank the White Man!" Charlie called back to Alan, laughing as he accelerated back onto the local main route.

Later that night, after a fine charcoaled steak dinner and a few beers, Charlie turned over one hundred dollars to Alan in casino chips. "Play for a while, Alan. Don't be scared. If you lose it, and you probably will, you lose it. Just have fun." They shook hands as Charlie excused himself to make his rounds. "I'll stop by if I see you on the floor. If not, sleep well, and we'll meet in the restaurant across the street for breakfast about ten. Okay?"

Alan continued his portrayal of a humbled friend. "I wish I could be a success like you, Charlie. I can't thank you enough." With that Charlie waved off Alan's compliments and left.

Suspecting that Charlie Littlehorse had cleared the arrangements with his boss, and realizing that his own behavior would reflect upon his old friend, Alan was careful about his conduct that night. He did not take a single free beverage, and he tipped the croupier generously when he called it an early night. After winning nearly two hundred dollars, Alan was feeling as if Fortune was smiling down upon him.

The accommodation was small, a single bed in a clean, nicely-decorated section of the Inn. His room offered a shower, a flat screen television, and a view facing the Canadian mountains off in the distance which he spotted in the morning.

As agreed he met Charlie Littlehorse in the restaurant directly across the street from the casino and inn. "This time I'm buying, Charlie, and I want to return the $100 you spotted me last night." Then Alan stepped out of himself for a moment. "In fact, I won $100 or more last night playing roulette. I'd feel better if you took it back."

"That's not necessary, Alan. Thanks." He paused and added, "We let you win. It's something we do for beginners. We like to give you a false sense of security in the hopes that you and your friends will return someday soon." Charlie looked at his breakfast and could barely contain himself. He looked up. "Relax, Alan. I was kidding."

The look on Alan's face signaled that Charlie had sold him the idea. Quickly his visage flooded with relief. "Wow...imagine if you *could* do such a thing!" Then there was quiet. "Charlie, you really can't do that. Can you?"

Charlie Littlehorse wiped off his mouth and smiled. "No, Alan. We're good, but we're not *that* good."

When they had finished their breakfast, they walked outside and shared plans with one another. Charlie's day was not a busy one until near dinner time, but he had casino-related chores requiring his personal attention. Alan announced he thought he would be leaving Bonner's Ferry. "Probably this afternoon."

"Why don't you stay one more night? You're not on a schedule. Are you?"

Alan watched a few cars go by the restaurant lot. He really did have a good feeling about the casino. He turned gently to his friend. "Only if I pay my own way, Charlie. It would be awkward to take..."

"Nonsense! You'll be my guest or you won't stay here at all." He was adamant. He sounded sincerely offended by Alan's conditions.

As if he was warding off an adversary, Alan put his hands up and conceded. "Okay! Okay! I'll take a spin around town for a bit. Then I'll catch up with you again tonight. Is that agreeable?"

The two shook hands, and Alan watched as Charlie started up his Chrysler, backed out of his parking spot, and pulled off into light traffic. "God, that's a big car!" Alan uttered to himself aloud.

After another fine dinner, Saturday night did not go as well as the first. In fact, Alan became frustrated when he lost all his house money early. He seemed to forget just how much he was ahead of the game since his lodging and dinners for two nights had been gratis. However, he wanted to play more.

After suppressing a pang of guilt, he strolled to the Front Desk and asked to speak to Charlie Littlehorse. When he was told Mr. Littlehorse had gone home for the evening, Alan enacted his scheme. "Did Mr. Littlehorse leave any messages for me? I'm Alan Wing, a long-time friend of his. He has me staying here in the Inn."

The staff member asked others working with her about Alan's inquiry. "No, sir. It appears there's nothing here for you."

Quickly Alan assumed the role of an indignant guest. "How can that be? We had dinner together again tonight. I was told by Mr. Littlehorse that an envelope awaited me here at the desk. Like last night, he was going to leave me $500 in order for me to play roulette in your casino." He stood taller, attempting to intimidate the clerk. It appeared for a moment that it might work.

Then the castle made of cards collapsed. He heard and then watched the Front Desk Manager who was at the switchboard toward the back of the Front Desk. "Mr. Littlehorse?" A pause ensued. "Yes, Sir, I'm sorry to interrupt your evening. There's a Mr. Wing here at the desk, Sir." There was another silence. Both Alan and the young woman across the desk from him were facing the Evening Manager and listening. "Well, Mr. Littlehorse, he's demanding that you agreed to leave him a $500 cash credit in an envelope. He said you did it last night for him as well." Again she listened.

Alan Wing knew right then that he had gone too far. Silently he backed away from the desk, for he had no idea where Charlie Littlehorse lived. He began hoping it was not nearby. Alan had to return to his room, gather what few things were his, and he had to get out of Bonner's Ferry immediately.

Alan's legs became 500 pound weights. His heart was pounding out explosive beats like an oversized drum. He had begun to perspire, so his shirt was sticking to his chest and back. His hands were shaking nervously.

Finally able to reach the parking lot and open his Jeep's driver side door, he threw in his things and got the vehicle started. Seconds later he heard Charlie's horn blaring as he raced into the Inn's lot. The Chrysler's brakes squealed loudly. Alan was physically fit, but he was no match for Charlie Littlehorse. One of life's many ironies was Charlie's last name.

However, it was another event years later that turned his head back in the direction of home, back in the direction of Falls Port, and it took place later after a week-long stay with a distant cousin, Henry. Henry was one of Alan's relatives on his mother's side. Henry and his wife Carla lived alone 200 miles east of Reno. They took Alan in and made him feel as welcome as extended family members might possibly do. Over a home cooked roast of beef, Alan brought them up to speed concerning his life, but he did not share with them any knowledge about his gambling. "After our divorce, I decided to travel occasionally and catch up with family." He had a way of spinning his well-rehearsed tales in such a way that they were almost romantic. By the end of that first sumptuous meal together, he had Henry and Carla feeling flattered that he cared enough to stop by.

While he visited, Alan was clever enough to come and go while they were at their respective jobs on work days. Henry and Carla were under the impression that Alan was looking for work as well as enjoying the local tourist traps. He did not eat much, and Alan was careful to be neat during his visit. But the reality of it was that Alan finally resorted to stealing from Carla's grocery stash. After witnessing how she kept some extra cash in a fake vegetable can deep in their pantry, temptation overpowered their guest. However, he was careless, and she caught him taking most of it. Before Carla could finish her phone call to her husband, Alan once again grabbed all his belongings and took off. He left most of the money behind in the hopes Henry would not chase him.

Two hundred miles from home, fifty-two years old, embarrassed that he had been seen for what he really was, and recalling the "loser" label a perfect stranger had hung upon him much earlier, he finally believed it was time to regroup. That which began to consume him was a subconscious realization that he had hit rock bottom, and Alan decided to head back to Falls Port. It was bad enough to be down and out, but to be in such a way so far from home was too disconcerting for even the likes of Alan Wing. "If only I can get back home," he thought to himself remorsefully, "I think I can start all over."

Desperate for money, he felt that the only way he could get back to Falls Port was to head thirty miles south to Troy where he could sell his vehicle and use some of the cash to buy a bus ticket to Kalispell. He did not feel up to a long drive. Not anymore. Alan was worn out.

PART TWO

Following the Equator
by Mark Twain
"Man is the only animal that blushes. Or needs to."

CHAPTER 15

Upon landing, Hyun sought the rental service desks. To her surprise there was but one. "Welcome to the Northwest," she whispered to herself. The desk clerks at the rental center were more than surprised when she requested a 4 x 4 pickup truck. As an attractive young lady, they had quickly stereotyped her as someone who would rent a BMW or Volvo. To further surprise the clerks at Hertz, upon being presented the keys, Hyun produced a Grizzly baseball cap and put it on her head. The burgundy cap, the tight gray tank top, and tight jeans left them with a mental image they did not soon forget.

She relaxed just outside Kalispell, Montana for only two days, in a rental cabin near Foys Lake, and to her surprise the surroundings had begun to appeal to her. Her appreciation of privacy and solitude made it easy for her to understand why Eli Parks sought this environment as his home.

Eventually Hyun headed toward Falls Port in a relatively new burgundy F 150. She did not know when or where Parks would show up, but she needed time to research his family. Once that was done, she was certain she could smoke him out. She had taken another day to relieve some job-related stress when she hiked to the top of Mt. Aenas in the Jewel Basin. She had seen it promoted on the internet back in Baltimore. The trail had been wide and easy in the beginning, but became more difficult as she climbed the ridge. Along the way, she had visited a stretch where last year's forest fires had charred the mountainside. Not thirty yards away, on the opposite side of a ridge, was pristine scenery.

At the top, she and other hikers she had met along the way waved at a pilot who flew a few hundred feet above them as they stood at the pinnacle. His red plane with wings trimmed in bright yellow shone brilliantly in the sun, and the pilot tipped his wings to salute them. From on high, the view out over Hungry Horse Lake and its surrounding thousand square miles of wilderness was spectacular. She envied the pilot for all that he could see from the plane. Hyun stood there feeling a quiet breeze and was at peace. She was ready to move on.

Later that evening and miles down the road, she spied an individual along the highway looking dejected. Initially she had passed him by but was able to slow down soon enough to attract his attention. Upon further inspection, despite a sullen appearance he was actually handsome. It was evident he needed assistance. Seemingly middle-aged, the man was sitting next to a badly worn pickup truck whose tire had blown out along a desolate stretch of highway. Being afraid of a stranger was a concept foreign to Hyun Lee, and that which made her offer help was the fact that the roles were reversed: she, a woman, could rescue a man. That appealed to her nature.

Alan stood up as she pulled in behind the truck. He brushed off his jeans. An hour earlier Alan had chosen to sit. He was not necessarily waiting for help to arrive. It was not his plan to be rescued. Alan Wing, reservation evacuee, ex-husband, and drifter did not have a plan. He had just decided to sit alone on a Montana roadside. Voices in his head confirmed what others had said: he was a loser. He had arrived in Kalispell and rented a motel room for a night. He ended up staying for three. At some point, after meandering around the city, he found a car lot and purchased a rust bucket of an old, white Chevy Luv with more than 200,000 miles on it for $100. "This will get me where I need to go," he thought, and did no negotiating about the price. Like the truck, he was just worn out.

A new pickup motored by him as others had done, but it did not mean anything to him. However when the driver slowed and began to back up in his direction he found within himself a spark of interest, more than he previously thought he could summon. He watched as Hyun climbed out of her pickup and heard her ask, "Is there anything I can do to help?"

Down on his luck until that moment, Alan did not know if he should be more surprised by her beauty or the fact that someone had bothered to stop. He turned on what was left of the old Alan Wing charm. Little did he know it was falling on deaf ears. He felt self-conscious though as he admitted sheepishly, "I'm without a spare. I'm grateful you would stop. Would you be headed toward—"

"Falls Port?" she interrupted with a smile. "That's along my way." Then she pointed to his vehicle. "Do you want to lock it up? Leave a note?"

"Good idea," he said once again in a why-didn't-I-think-of-that tone. "Give me a minute." He grabbed his travel bag and locked up the truck. Only a brief note was left. He figured that in addition to the note, his license plate would provide more than enough information. Even though 93 was traveled regularly, odds were he would be back before anyone would even bother to investigate his truck's appearance along the roadside. Campers, hikers, photographers, and fishermen often left cars parked along the highway.

Alan Wing dropped his bag in the back of the 4x4's bed and climbed in the pickup. He looked into Hyun's eyes, wondering what she was doing in Montana. He thanked her again.

She did not offer her name, but replied, "We all have our bad days. Let's go."

Alan wondered if his fortune had not just turned for the better. He was quiet for a few miles before he reiterated his gratitude. "I want you to know how much I appreciate the help. Not everyone would take a look at me, stop, and offer assistance especially with me all dirty like I am."

"Think nothing of it,' replied Hyun. "So are you a local?"

Not used to being a passenger, he was actually enjoying the ride. "Yes, I am. I've been away for a time and, believe it or not, you're giving me a chance to look around and recall how pretty home is."

"It's a scenic place," she agreed. She asked about the area and whether locals experienced much of a growth here.

"Nope, Montana doesn't attract many people other than tourists," Alan answered. "Few would want to move here and call it home." He pointed to the Mission Mountains and actually sounded nostalgic. "My people go way back in history when it comes to the settling of this land. I guess you could say I'm a Kootenai Indian who has been Americanized."

They continued the drive toward Falls Port, a small city at the southern end of expansive Flathead Lake. He told her about the dam and Flathead Lake, and how the area attracted thousands of tourists each year. "Is that why you're here?" he asked.

Without hesitation, Hyun explained that she had come to Montana for peace and quiet. She shared that she was a screenwriter and needed to escape the rat race life in any city she had called home over the years. She told of her plans to meet with a director, for her next story was about Montana and its people. She asked Alan if he was at all familiar with a film made in Ennis, a Steven Segal movie called "The Patriot."

Alan's eyes opened wide then and he spoke of how his ex-wife's sister rented her Ennis home to actors for that very film. Then he added how he had actually been an extra in the movie, but his part fell to the editing room floor. "That was the end of my acting career," he said, and they laughed.

Her passenger could not believe how well things were going. In the time he had ridden with Hyun Lee, he had seemingly struck a chord with her; for their conversation took on more substance the closer they got to Falls Port. She seemed to relax as the miles passed.

"You must think I'm terribly rude," she announced as she continued down the highway, window open, blowing her shoulder-length black hair in many directions at once. Alan found her conversation agreeable; without feeling awkward, he could gaze at her as she spoke. "My name is

Hoo Lin." It was an alias she had used before so it rolled off her tongue naturally. "And I never asked for your name either. Sorry."

He extended his hand, anticipating the touch of her long soft fingers. "I'm Alan Wing."

She seemed to balk at first, but after a noticeable hesitation, she exchanged the courtesy. He noted the strength of her handshake.

"So tell me about yourself, Alan. We have a ways to go. It will help pass the time."

Her request had been anticipated, and he was leery of the first impression he might make. As they rode and he thought of how to answer, night was taking hold in the Mission Mountain area, and Hoo Lin's headlights were having more of an effect. They witnessed what would be the first of several white tail deer, and Alan warned her of their abundance. It gave her cause to slow down.

Then Alan proceeded to share bits and pieces of his Native American heritage, including the retelling of the Wing family origin. Hyun seemed genuinely interested. With his ego inflated by this course of conversation, Alan Wing wished there were more miles to pass before they reached the city.

"Have you ever been married?" she finally asked. "Do you have what we call a *jagiya* or girlfriend?"

Ordinarily the thought of his failed marriage did not bother him, but on this occasion he nearly choked on the question. He thought it best to be direct and brief. He would not make excuses. "I was married briefly to a nice woman." Then he surprised himself when he added, "But I wasn't a very good husband." She looked at him and he continued, "I was a faithful husband, but I wasn't the most dependable man in the world. I screwed up."

His spirits rebounded when Hyun said she admired his ability to accept his share of the blame. "There are two sides to every story," she said. She let her right hand lightly touch his arm. "Mind if I ask more questions? Or am I prying?"

"I don't mind," Alan said, focusing on her touch.

"Family? Are they local?"

As he had mentioned, his sister had left the area a while back. His parents were still here. "I haven't talked to my parents for a while. My father and I didn't see eye-to-eye on things. He can be tough for me to take."

She asked about his work. Briefly he wondered if Cary had hired this woman to grill him. He summoned another stock answer. "Well, that was part of our marital troubles. I'm currently between jobs." He admitted he had been lazy since his ex-wife was successful enough for both of them. Alan expected rejection or a lecture then. What he heard caught him by surprise.

"I'm a pretty good judge of character as a rule," Hyun said. She ran her fingers through her hair. "I'm here to enjoy some privacy and hopefully wrap up a film deal here in the area. Are you familiar with the Winston property between here and Falls Port?"

"As a matter of fact, I am," he said. "My ex's friend lived there as a kid. I've been there a couple of times." He added, "It's a beautiful property, but the buildings have been neglected. Natives call that area just north of Falls Port 'Rollins'."

Hyun then asked Alan if he would like to work for her on the place. "I'm staying there tonight even if I have to set up a small camp. I expected repairs to be needed."

Alan was surprised. "You want me to become a caretaker?"

"I'll pay you well," she said. Her voice softened as did her eyes. She knew what she was doing. He did not know it, but Hyun already had plans for Alan. "If I had someone like you to help me, guide me, look after me, so to speak, "she said and touched his arm again, "you could make my job so much more simple."

Continuing their ride south on 93, Alan jumped at the opportunity for a week's paycheck. The amount she offered shocked him, but he had to agree upon protecting her privacy. "That might be your biggest challenge," she told him.

As the pickup cruised down the highway, dim views of the lake and gorgeous landscapes flew by on their left while mountain scenes dotted with groves of trees passed on their right. Their travels moved them closer to Falls Port and the Winston place. It was nearly twilight when they arrived.

CHAPTER 16

Late into the first day of planning, initial options were reviewed patiently a last time. Eli was then afforded an opportunity to present what he felt were flaws. Due to the gravity of the situation, no one was offended when he spoke his mind. After all, the President's men were trying to help.

Again it had been explained to him that government sources, specifically the National Security Agency with its intercepted communiqués, felt a North Korean agent had been assigned to kill him. He asked whether his coworkers or teammates were in similar danger. He was told that since the White House believed they were, Jeff Ripkin and Gabe Winters were being extended every caution he was receiving. When he asked whether they should be in on the planning sessions with him, he was assured it had been considered, but by separating everyone, their chances of survival were increased.

"Chances of survival," he muttered to no one in particular. "Then let me ask you this. When we come up with a plan, can we at least conference call and make sure we're all in agreement?"

"We don't have to wait that long," was the reply. Chief of Staff Andrew O'Neill was the President's lead man on this operation. He was not unknown to Parks, and that comforted both men. They had earned one another's respect over the years. Andrew turned to an aide who told him he already had Eli's two partners waiting for him on a conference call. Their images were brought up on the screens.

"Thanks, Andy, that means a lot." Eli knew and trusted his friends implicitly and was anxious to hear what they were bringing to the table. One plan discussed was to put his team on yet another submarine as if they were going about business as usual. The positive side was obvious—it protected Parks's team. It was also tempting in that the President might be able to identify any information leaks since he could announce one location, but actually send them elsewhere. The downside was that their enemy might be on a timetable and do something rash; he or she might try to bring all three to the surface by threatening the lives of their respective families. That plan was rejected quickly.

The most extreme plan was to publicly announce the three had died in a helicopter crash en route to a mission site. The proposed crash site was to be out over the Atlantic, and it was to be broadcasted that no survivors had been located. Only shards of wreckage were to be found as a result of this enactment. Again, it was rejected. Since family members were not to be informed of the truth until later, Eli vehemently insisted he would not put them through that. Besides, any agent worth his pay would suspect that ploy was a ruse.

Then Eli's partner, Gabe Winters, added, "And eventually we'd be back and our work results would surface anyway. Square one all over again." This plan, too, was scrapped.

Such were the extremes tossed about and considered. For a week, they tried to formulate a plan of action that would minimize the danger for everyone involved. Jeff Rifkin, the third member of the engineering team, said little most of the time, but Eli and Gabe attributed that to his young nerves.

During the evening of the final day, Eli asked Andrew O'Neill if he could speak privately with his engineering partners. Andy agreed.

About to leave the darkly paneled conference room they had been using since they left the Oval Office, Andy turned and politely added, "I'd be lying if I told you I wasn't curious about this dialogue, Eli."

Eli smiled slightly and replied, "Andy, I promise to fill you in. You'll understand my need for privacy when I explain it. Thanks."

~

As Rita towel dried her hair, she let Cary sleep later than usual. She had been a good listener again into the wee hours of the morning. Cary had been with her now for the better part of seven days. At that moment, Rita's thoughts were on her husband. Before they were married and even before they were engaged, Eli had a brief encounter with his health. Months later he finally decided to tell Rita about it. She was upset; not at Eli, but with the realization they were mortal. That day she asked that she always be kept informed—no secrets. To her knowledge, Eli had always kept his word.

He called a few times each day since departing for D.C. It bothered Eli that he had not yet been able to share his situation with his family. Back and forth, he argued with himself. To tell his family was to put all of them on edge, and for good reason. In an age when former President Bush assured the world that Americans would continue to live free as they always had, Eli was now beginning to see how that might be easier said than done. But he felt that telling them over the phone would be insensitive. He decided to tell them in person was best; most reassuring. However, he hoped he could inform them of the government's plan of action as well. Therein lay the problem. To date, they had no acceptable plan.

He picked up the phone and called. It rang twice and Ed picked up the other end. "How are you holding up as you try keeping Mom in line?" Eli asked him and Ed laughed. For a moment they exchanged small talk.

Edward caught Eli's attention with, "I nearly caught ol' Pete two nights ago!" He paused to let that sink in. He enjoyed Eli's reply.

"What? You hooked him? How?"

"It was easy! A buddy of mine lit a quarter stick, and I sent it into the lake with your old tennis racket!"

Eli laughed, picturing the site of the stunned fish atop the lake. "You had me going, Ed. Nice. I'll get even." Before Ed handed over the phone to Rita, he heard Eli say, "By the way, thanks for being there with your mom, Ed. It means a lot."

Ed smiled at the words. He and Eli were so much more comfortable with one another than they had been in the beginning. "No problem, Eli."

Rita sat on their forest green couch and visited easily with her husband. "I'll be home tonight," he said. "But it'll be late. Can you wait up for me?"

"I'll be up," she said. "I can't wait to see you."

"Gonna make me a German chocolate cake?" he inquired.

"Don't push your luck, Mister."

"Yes, Dear..."

As Eli flew to Montana on the government's private jet, he had time to reflect on the events of his past seven days in the nation's capitol. For the first time in days he felt as if he had some degree of control over his life; the butterflies that accompanied making big decisions were going away. He hoped his partners were enjoying the same sense of relief. When Eli called Andy back into the conference room, as promised he told Andy of their conference call. To say that some eyebrows were raised would be an understatement. Eli recalled the conversation as he took time to close his eyes during the smooth flight.

"Andy, I think you might want to sit down," was how it all had begun. "As you can see, everyone is still on line. I wanted you to hear our decision from all of us. I don't want to misrepresent the team."

"This doesn't sound good," was O'Neill's response. He made himself comfortable. The dark, cherry table seated a dozen men when it was full. At this meeting, only a few were in attendance. "Who's going to fill me in? Gabe? Jeff?"

From the split screen on the wall, Gabe and Jeff indicated they felt it best if Eli did their talking for them. Gabe was comfortably dressed in a blue pullover cotton sweater—no company tie today. Jeff followed suit. He was casually dressed as well. It was a meeting that would affect their lives forever, so they chose to be comfortable. Eli, of course, wore a tie. His wife liked it that way. Eli leaned forward.

"Andy, I'm not going to sugarcoat this." He looked at his team, nodded in their direction and told Andy they had decided to call it quits. "That's the way we've chosen to deal with this."

There was a tangible silence. Then Andy replied, "Certainly, men, that's an option, but I don't know that I can offer the protection you deserve."

"Andy, we appreciate that. We're not trying to be jerks or show some sort of solidarity. After all, there are only three of us. It's just that we feel we've endangered our families, and no plan we've come up with reduces the threat placed upon them. Please don't take any offense, but it's accurate."

"None taken," Andy replied. Eli knew his counterpart was wondering how he would break this news to the President.

From the screen Winters added, "We understood in the back of our minds that such a situation might someday arise, and now it's here. To us, our choice just empowers us to be with our families, or at least available to them."

"Anything you want to add, Jeff?" Andy addressed the screen.

Ripkin seemed less comfortable, but he nodded his assent. "Just that we're grateful for your support and your efforts. Please stress to the President that this is in no way some kind of power play. Okay?"

O'Neill assured Eli and the others that their sentiments would be passed along. "I won't insult you men by trying to talk you out of it," Andy said as they nearly ended the conversation. "However, I have to ask one more time whether or not any of you have an inkling why North Korea might be after any of you?"

Eli and Gabe simultaneously reiterated how they were stumped while Jeff Ripkin said nothing for a moment, as if to pause. Then he added almost cryptically, "If I was ever in North Korea, I think I'd remember it."

The jet touched down in Missoula, and Eli awoke to the toughest of all tasks. He now had to explain this most threatening and unsettling situation to all the members of his family. Seven grueling days of planning had come and gone, and he still had no plan for that.

CHAPTER 17

Not long after Eli's return in late August, Cary felt safe enough to begin spending nights alone in her home. Of course, there was good natured kidding about the noise made by Rita and her husband which kept her awake, but down inside where her feelings stirred, Cary was only a little apprehensive. For some reason, Eli's permanent presence added stability to her life as well. Ed offered to bunk at her place for the first night or two, but Cary knew she had to return to normal at some point. Ed's offer was greatly appreciated, but she felt it would only delay the inevitable.

In early September temperatures soared, and Rita's daily phone calls to her friend's house bemoaned the fact that the weather was more summer-like now that school had begun. Cary would invite her over to enjoy the late afternoon shade and breeze off the lake. Occasionally, Rita would accept and stop by after a day of classes. A Montana afternoon in late summer or early fall was always enhanced by the view from Cary's deck. The two women shared stories, gossip and an occasional beer.

During one such visit, Cary told Rita she had seen her ex-husband back in Falls Port. "I was coming back from Kalispell, down 93, and I passed him! I'm sure it was Alan, but he was driving a newer pickup."

"I suppose it's possible," Rita said. "Maybe he found work."

Cary's eyebrows arched at the thought of Alan Wing holding down a job. "That would be something," she said.

"Does it scare you that he might be back?" Rita asked Cary. "Do you want any of us to stay here for a while?"

Cary smiled at her friend's loyalty. "That's okay, Rita. I'm okay. Alan wouldn't hurt me. He's a lazy sort, but he's not an axe murderer." She leaned back in her chair and seemed at peace with the whole thing. Rita could not help but worry. Since the recent threat upon her husband and his co-workers, she was understandably more sensitive about safety issues.

Autumn had come to the great Northwest once again. Eli commented that it was easily comparable to New England's famous autumn splendor. Those who grew up or lived most of their lives in Montana were always glad to see summer and its warm temperatures arrive, but they were happy to see it pass as well, for it took so many tourists with it. Snow atop the Missions became more visible, and the beauty of the autumn's golds, reds, oranges, greens, and browns mixed as if from an artist's palette. Summer forest fires were a thing of the past, so nights were clear and Big Sky Country was even more beautiful.

Rita and Eli had grown comfortable with their new routine. They awoke at their leisure on weekends, shared coffee, and continued to discuss Eli's decision to retire. Rita was not at all surprised by her husband's choice. When he called her family together, she could see just how much he truly cared for the family he had inherited, so to speak. She also understood without his ever saying a word that he feared the danger he brought with him might cause them to resent him.

Never was she more proud of her siblings and her own son when they rallied around Eli, offering love and support. Both of Rita's brothers were quick to offer help.

"Eli, if we can help at all, let us know," Tyler quipped half-joking. "As Montana men we have a reputation to uphold. It wouldn't do at all for folks to learn we ran and hid at the first sign of trouble."

Ryan, the oldest, was more quiet. He just nodded his total agreement.

Eli had nearly cried while she held him close to her one night, running her fingers through his hair. It was such a relief to him to learn of their unconditional acceptance.

Breaking the news to Erin and his son was another story. Eli flew into Allentown and rented a car for the trip to see the two of them. At the most, it took him an hour to get from the airport to the front door of the house that once was his home. It was a modest two-story brick and stucco building; Tudor-like in appearance. Many of the homes on the block hinted at affluence, but they, too, were modest in size. He did not know what to expect once the door was opened.

For the most part, it went as well as could be expected. Erin asked questions about guaranteeing her safety as well as her son's, and rightfully so. "Are we safe here? And what if we need help?" They were not easy inquiries to answer yet he provided what he could.

"Erin, I won't mislead you. I'm only going to tell you what I do know, and what I think I know." He looked out the back window into the yard as he sipped his iced tea. Erin always made the best iced tea. "I do have names and phone numbers of government workers who are in the business of protection and rescue. Keep them handy. Make sure Jake knows their whereabouts as well."

" 'Protection and rescue...'," Erin said coldly. "*That* sounds disconcerting. What else do you have to share, Eli?"

He calmly sat down at the table and continued. "Along those lines, Erin, these folks understand your situation. If you note anything at all that you believe to be out of the ordinary, call them. False alarms are not a nuisance to them." As best he could, he hoped those words would comfort her to some degree.

He paused now and then to let her think. "And if you want my opinion? Don't consider relocating. Anyone who wants to find anybody can do so in this day and age." He reached across the table and took his ex-wife's hands in his. "Erin, I promise that I will be in touch as well. I hope that helps." She stared at him and held in some sharp words she promised she would not dump in his lap anymore.

They talked off and on for hours trying to cover as many bases as they could.

Strangely enough, the disturbing news of such a threat on Eli's life and new family might have brought Eli's son, Jacob, closer to Rita and Ed. He had flown back east to inform Jake and his ex-wife about what had transpired. He provided them with the available security names and phone numbers, which was a courtesy extended him by President Rittenhouse. The trip gave Eli the chance to spend a few days with his son.

As they had in the past, they fished, camped, talked about his mom and finally broached the subject of Eli's new life. "What's it like out there, Dad?" Jake asked him one night as they sat around a fire frying up their small catch.

Without missing a beat, for Eli had long waited for such an opening, he told his son softly, "Jake, you have to see it for yourself—the mountains, the lakes—"

"No, Dad, I meant what is your new family like?"

After a brief pause, he looked his son in the eye and said, "I'd like you to meet them." More quiet followed. "Jake, I'm never going to divide you and your mom. But for you and me...I'd like there to be some sort of middle ground. I'll bring them here, if you'd like, so you're not totally on the defensive. Meeting them on your own turf, so to speak, might be easier for you."

His son dragged a stick through the embers of the campfire. More than anything it was the result of nervous energy. "How's the fishing in Montana," was Jake's next question, but he already knew the answer. What fisherman didn't?

"Funny you should ask because there's a huge bass in the lake outside our back door. His name is Pete, and I can't catch him. I've tried." Eli wanted to handle this conversation carefully. "Son, if you want to visit, we'd love to have you. I want you to know Rita and Ed, but you have to decide that for yourself. They won't make you feel like an outsider. I can promise you that."

"We'll see, Dad," he shrugged noncommittally. "I won't lie to you. I hated you for a while for what you chose to do. Life goes on, I guess. I'm just trying to figure out what's real." He stirred the embers again.

As Eli unrolled his sleeping bag, he spoke one last time. "Take your time, Jake, but don't take forever. I enjoy your company."

It was a weeknight and Eli and Jake were the park's only campers. They had passed a few sites as they trudged up to the hilltop above the lake. They chose a campsite out of view of other camp sites, yet they had a great view of the lake below and the sky above.

The fire had reduced itself to a pile of orange-golden embers. As Jake threw another log onto the pile, Eli heard a crunching noise in the distance, and then they were startled by a beam of light. The pair looked at one another. It was after midnight and neither of them knew what to expect. No security agent or phone number could help with this.

To their relief, their visitor turned out to be an overzealous rookie campground ranger. He was a gangly sort of fellow whose clothes were loose fitting. Under his cap, his hair was cropped short. The ranger proudly told them he took it upon himself to check all the registered campsites to make sure no one was camping without paying. "And if I can be of any help, I'm in the cabin near the gate."

He must have been a lonely sort, for Jake and Eli also got a piece of his life history. Eli missed some of what the ranger had shared, for his inner thoughts were all about what if this had been the assassin? That night Eli vowed to protect his family a whole lot better when they camped out. The ranger finally made his way down the hillside, and Eli made a note to help Jake apply for a Pennsylvania gun permit by trip's end.

CHAPTER 18

It was not exactly what Alan expected, but the work around the Winston property proved to be less difficult after the first week or two, and the money Hyun paid him each week helped him go a long way toward paying off some local, long-overdue debts. He no longer felt he had to sneak back into Falls Port. If he was asked by anyone what he was doing for work, he simply shrugged and said he had been lucky enough to pick up some day labor outside of town. He liked the way that sounded. It was more impressive than admitting he was a *gofer* for a professional writer holed up at the old Winston place.

As summer slowly surrendered to early autumn, less and less he was asked to make structural changes inside and out. It appeared the old building was ample for his employer's needs, and that impressed him, for he knew several women who would never live in such rustic conditions. Furthermore she actually helped make the renovations Alan had suggested to her. She seemed to listen. Alan felt Hoo Lin was a special breed of woman, and he found himself becoming more and more loyal to her. He did not know if it was because she paid him well or because he admired her drive—her businesslike approach toward matters at hand.

One night in particular stood out. It was the night they had all but finished repairing the porch's leaky roof. He had gone to his apartment for the night and by morning, she had taken it upon herself to finish the repair because she needed him to tackle another job. She wanted him to familiarize her with the locale so she could better represent her story's setting in her writing. Alan never mentioned that he had seen her do little if any writing. That was her business.

On a regular basis Alan began driving Hyun all about Lake County. She seemed to enjoy photographing different locations; some were natural settings, some man-made, and others were shots of populated areas. "Taking pictures is much more fun than taking notes," she told him. "I can pick up so many more details in a picture. And how can I not take pictures of these beautiful autumn scenes?"

Alan was genuinely impressed. Strangely enough he saw in her qualities he had admired in his ex-wife. Temporarily at least he no longer felt he was a loser, and recognizing that he rebounded and was grateful for what he had to do each day—work. "Imagine that. I'm enjoying work," Alan would consciously think to himself. He was aware that the woman he knew as Hoo Lin had provided a wonderful chance for him to see life from another vantage point.

His beautiful boss seemed more interested in the area near the southern end of the lake, the area in and around Falls Port. As she snapped photos of Flathead Lake she commented how one day it seemed to be the lightest of blues, another day it might have an icy green tint, and then be cobalt blue on still another. She seemed to love its appearance more and more each time they took a boat ride upon it.

Hyun wanted to know all about the various coves and even any lore he could provide about the Mission Mountains to the east which towered above the lake, blanketed with spruce and aspens. She especially enjoyed the patches of golden trees mixed among the darker green.

More often they began chatting over lunches about people he had met, people she had met, technology that they both enjoyed, and life in general. On one such day, Alan found himself sharing information regarding his ex-wife and acquaintances he had made through her. He mentioned his ex's best friend Rita who had also divorced, and that she had married a second man named Eli Parks. It was impossible not to note the look of surprise on Hyun's face. "Do you know them, too?" Alan asked.

"I'm not sure. I did once meet a gentleman by that name."

During one such meal not too long after that, Alan proposed he take her to a landing across the lake from where he used to pick up Cary at her parents' home. It was a state landing set up for locals and tourists alike. Anyone could launch a boat, swim from a dock, or just picnic there at his or her leisure. "To see the house from the lake," he insisted, "is truly impressive. First we'll go to the landing, and then I'll take you to the see the house Cary inherited."

Off in the distance a fisherman worked, trying to catch some lake trout or not-so-tasty mackinaw that gave a good fight. From across the bay, Alan was describing life on the west shore to Hyun Lee. To his surprise, from her carry bag kept in the back of the truck she produced a powerful set of binoculars, an impressive digital camera and tripod. "Hoo, what else do you have in there?" Alan half joked. Seriously, he wondered.

"Just taking more notes, Alan," Hyun breathed quietly. "Looks like your ex is home and has company." Once on shore, she gestured an invitation to her naive guide so that he may look through her lens. Alan walked behind the tripod, nearly bumping into it, and whistled softly when he realized the magnification powers of her binoculars.

"Where the in the world did you get this equipment?" He looked across the lake briefly. With such binoculars, he could tell Hyun what the two women were wearing and drinking! "Cary's the gal leaning back in her chair, and the woman with chestnut hair is Rita Parks. I mentioned her to you a few days back." Trying to mask her feelings at such a discovery, Hyun resumed use of the binoculars and observed the women across the dark, choppy water. After a while, she put away her equipment and masked her excitement by chatting about the beautiful home Alan had shown her.

Then she casually added, "You know, since you brought up those names earlier, I have to wonder if she's the wife of the Eli Parks I once knew."

"If you'd like, I'll ask around town." Simultaneously and privately Alan thought about how he could not get over what it felt like to see Cary close again. Then quickly he continued making his point to Hyun. "I can do it so no one will know you're in Rollins."

"It's probably not him. I met him in D.C. years ago. What would he be doing way out here?" Hyun had just planted two assignments in the garden Alan called his mind. She knew he had become loyal to her, in a schoolboy-like manner. She merely needed to know if Eli was in town.

It was not too long after Alan showed Hyun his ex's home and her visitor, that he learned his employer was suddenly willing to visit Falls Port for the first time. At first he thought perhaps she needed a break from her retreat on the Winston place. Then he considered she might have writer's block. He also thought she might have just been doing more research to improve her material. It was when she began traveling into town on her own that he was really surprised. Up until then, he felt pretty important. He had been more like a professional guide than a custodian or handyman. Now he began to feel threatened; she might not need him much longer. Nonetheless he chose to keep his mouth closed about his concern. There was no point in making his usefulness a topic of conversation. He needed and enjoyed that generous paycheck.

As "Hoo Lin", she expected to open some eyes and turn some heads while walking the streets of Falls Port. There were not many folks of Asian ancestry in Montana, let alone Falls Port, but its Native American population helped her to blend despite the fact that she was very attractive. This city was not an ethnic melting pot like larger cities but their two cultures shared a similar appearance. She even found it gratuitous to label Falls Port a city. In her mind, at best it was a town. The city label seemed a misnomer. "I need to blend in," she whispered to herself as she threw on sunglasses and a baseball cap before each trip to Falls Port. She hoped she would draw less attention outfitted as such, but when push came to shove it really did not matter. "Hicks are hicks," she joked inwardly.

Pretty sure she could quickly learn of Eli's whereabouts from Alan, Hyun was more interested in any patterns he might be exhibiting on a daily basis. Did Parks drive down the same roads regularly? Did he go jogging? Did he do anything at all that could be considered a pattern? If so, when and where did he do it?

After a few visits in town, Hyun was frustrated by Eli's unpredictability. She had watched him bike once and maybe twice, but not only did he bike to different locations, he was not always alone. She had watched him work around the house and in the car, but never was he indicating a pattern of any sort.

Eventually she found herself picking Alan's brain for what he might know. One morning over coffee she questioned Alan about Eli under the pretense that she would like to be sure he was the same man she had met earlier in her career. "It would be embarrassing to approach him, a married man, only to learn he is not the same person I befriended years ago. I'd have to admit I couldn't be sure, and that would be embarrassing as well."

Alan thought her uneasiness about being mistaken was blown out of proportion, yet he had a concern of his own. "I have never met Eli Parks, but I don't want to risk appearing useless," he thought. As they finished their coffee that morning, he desired to sound useful. "I've heard it said that he traveled often. I know Rita told some people more than once that he flew back east quite a bit." Alan got up from the table to grab a second mug of coffee. As he looked out the window, he felt it would be wise to offer his own services. "I can ask around, follow him, or just plain visit him. Would you like me to do that?"

"Can you do that without him finding out that you're asking questions for my sake?"

"I'm not sure." He cringed when he admitted his uncertainty.

"Then don't. I just don't want to draw any more attention to myself than I already have." With that she changed the subject to photographing some of the city's streets and buildings. "I have nearly all the shots I need to block out a specific scene I have in mind, but a few more would help."

Later that morning, Alan found himself driving along with Hyun, for he felt he knew the best shots for what she needed. He had convinced her that from what she was describing, he could expedite matters. She wanted some shots from taller buildings, and Alan could quickly introduce her to the owners of the buildings that would meet her requirements. As they drove he asked, "What kind of scene are you working on?" Lately he had begun to hope that she might be able to use him as an extra at the very least. Somehow the idea appealed to him, so he began showing more of an interest in her film making.

"Oh...in every film it seems there's always a need for some shots of town whereby the camera pans over Main Avenue from above. It's a common ploy used by film makers to intro a new setting." Hoo Lin was wearing her cap backwards and her hair was tousled by the wind blowing through her truck's open windows. She pulled down her visor and looked into the little mirror affixed to its flip side. Having only been in the Northwest for a brief time, already the athletic, young Ms. Lin was losing her summer color.

Alan drove a bit further and repeated that he thought he knew enough store owners that he could help her fulfill her need. His new boss indicated that she was grateful for that, and Alan thought this might be a good time to ask, "Exactly how are extras picked for films?" He hoped he was not too obvious.

Alan's passenger leaned against her door and turned to her left to face him. She smiled a bit and replied, "You want to be in this film, Alan! Admit it!" She was teasing him, and he liked it.

"Was I that transparent? I just thought it would be fun."

"You just get me up on top of some of Falls Port's tallest structures so I can play sniper, and I'll see what I can do." They rode down the highway awhile when she added, "I never answered your question. Did I? I'm sorry. Generally speaking the business runs an ad in the local papers and runs a spot on local TV and radio. That usually does the trick."

By the time they had exhausted all of Alan's questions, they were pulling up along Kerr Dam just outside of town. He had crossed town to get her there. She had wondered what he was up to. "There's a nice shot for you," Alan suggested. "Do you see those wooden plank stairs and that wooden stair rail? My ex and Rita Parks used to hike the stairs to the bottom and back several times each day. From up here there's quite a view, but the view from down near the bottom is equally impressive, especially when they're letting water out of the lake.

"Maybe I'll try that," said Hyun as she looked to see just what bordered the steps to the bottom. "Is it safe?"

"No one's ever been attacked or eaten by a bear, if that's what you mean." Alan had no idea what she was getting at as he accelerated slowly and headed back into town.

CHAPTER 19

"Mr. President," Chief of Staff Andy O'Neill greeted Elijah Rittenhouse somewhat comfortably. Others stood respectfully as had O'Neill when the President entered the room. In attendance with the Chief of Staff were two Joint Chiefs of Staff, Air Force General Hummer and Marine General Forbes. General Hummer, a burly individual sporting a shaved head, served in both VietNam and Desert Storm. He was the sort who thought things through, but could do so in a timely fashion. Forbes was tall, thin, and wiry. His white hair thick and well-groomed. Few noticed it, but he was without two fingers upon his right hand, the result of a wound during hand-to-hand combat.

Rittenhouse, in jeans and a gray, chenille hooded sweatshirt, was again dressed more casually than O'Neill who some folks said wore a suit to bed at night. Initially the President seemed preoccupied with a portfolio as he strode into the Oval Office. Finally he spoke from the middle of the room as all in attendance stood around waiting for their leader to be seated. But on this day there was no need for the power he and past Presidents had exuded from behind their desks. President Rittenhouse consciously saved how many times he could play that card.

"Gentlemen, please give me a few moments alone with Mr. O'Neill." The office emptied quickly, and the two men sat comfortably on the couch that faced the President's desk from across the room. "Tell me about the North Korean assassin, Andy." Rittenhouse had nearly referred to it as the "Parks Situation", but caught himself in time. To be truthful, O'Neill would have understood, and he appreciated the fact that the President did not want to appear to minimize the importance of Winters or Ripkin.

"Yes, Sir. We have maintained periodic—"

"How often, Andy?"

"Weekly, Sir. That was their request. Respectfully speaking, Mr. President, to contact them more often would have been a nuisance to them. They felt it would have cramped their lifestyles." O'Neill went on to assure the President that his three former employees were entirely grateful for the White House's concern and the courtesy extended to them.

Rittenhouse stood and faced his Chief of Staff. "Secure channels are being employed each time?"

"Yes, Mr. President." O'Neill waited.

"Are we able to contact them...any of them, if there's a sudden, unexpected need?"

"Yes, Sir."

"Have you tested it?"

"Yes, Mr. President. We have experienced no problems either way." O'Neill had anticipated this question in advance, so he had instructed each of the three men to call occasionally as if on a whim. In each case, O'Neill was readily available which is what he knew his President would want.

"Can they contact each other?" It was becoming more evident that this issue of safety was weighing heavily upon Elijah Rittenhouse's mind.

"They have done so regularly, Sir. That is how they watch out for one another. If one neglects to check in with his team, we are contacted immediately. We have even tested such a scenario." By now, from the middle of the room, Rittenhouse was looking out the vast window behind his desk. O'Neill was still seated upon the couch. "But in reality has this occurred as of yet?"

"Yes Sir, Mr. President. Mr. Ripkin purposefully neglected to call his team in order to test the system himself, to gain some peace of mind if you will, Sir. The system worked. Then he went on to say, "Both Winters and Mr. Parks reported to check on Ripkin."

The President turned away from his view of D.C. Andy heard the silhouetted leader say, "My God, I hope they made the right choice." Rittenhouse did not say it, but deep inside he hoped that announcing the trio's retirement would satisfy Korea, and their assassination plans, if they existed, would be scrubbed.

"Mr. President?"

"Yes?" Rittenhouse was surprised how well his friend and confidante, Andy O'Neill, understood his President's needs.

"Would you like to contact Mr. Parks?"

The President replied with an affirmative nod, and in seconds he was able to hear Eli's voice.

"Parks here," were Eli's exact words. Ever the professional when he had to be, Eli impressed his old friend.

Able to shift into a casual tone quickly, the President greeted his old friend, "Eli, it's Elijah. How are you?"

Two thousand miles away a smile spread across his crony's face. "Mr. President! Are you worried about me?" Then he laughed his old, familiar drinking buddy laugh.

"Don't push your luck, Parks," was the President's retort. Then they both laughed. After a pause he asked, "Seriously, Eli, how is your family and how are you?"

For a moment, because he believed it was appropriate, Eli became serious. "Sir, everything seems quiet. I will admit that for the first few weeks the smallest of noises were unsettling. Now I'm less jumpy."

Looking at his watch, Rittenhouse knew he had to attend to his everyday duties. There are few spare minutes on the itinerary of a President. "Okay, Eli. As long as you are satisfied with this arrangement you've concocted."

"There is one item of business, Mr. President, if you don't mind."

'Yes?"

"You had better be sure to call Gabe and Jeff. When they find out I received a call from the President of the United States of America, they are going to expect one, too! To do otherwise might cost you a couple of votes." Parks began to chuckle.

However, once again the President proved to be his equal when he quickly replied, "Parks, I called them first."

Eli knew he had been outdone, so he surrendered. "Of course, you did, Mr. President. I should have known. Thanks for the call, Elijah." And then there was silence.

A few hours later the twenty-one year old red Dakota cruised up the gravel driveway off the county road and Rita could see Eli was attempting to surprise her with something on the grill. A thick blue-white smoke hung over their deck, a sure sign he had not yet mastered the art of cooking.

"The bugs won't be annoying anybody tonight!" she called out to her husband who she saw scurrying about on the far end of their deck by the kitchen's sliding door. She jogged up the steps and saw two well-charred burgers on the grill. A carafe of wine was on the picnic table, along with a plate of condiments and a bowl of chips.

Eli looked sheepish. "Someday I'll be more domestic," Eli promised. "I don't know why I still can't cook burgers."

Rita kissed her husband and thanked him for the gesture. "I love that you'd do this for me," she smiled. Sitting across from him at the picnic table, they ate off their burgers what they could and all of the chips. When the teasing and laughter between them subsided, Eli told Rita about the President giving him a call. "Elijah called tonight. He asked for you and sends his love."

Momentarily a chill grabbed Rita's spine. "Everything all right?" she asked with some trepidation.

"Yes. Actually it was a social call. I mean I know he was checking on us, all of us, but for the most part it was a social call." No matter how he shared it with his wife, Eli knew any reminder of their situation would make things at least slightly uncomfortable. Nevertheless he knew she would want to know of President Rittenhouse's call.

Suddenly Rita had an epiphany. "I can't believe I didn't tell you about Alan until this morning!" Eli asked whether or not he and Cary were back together. "No, silly," she said. "Cary would never do that!" As they sat there visiting over a glass of wine, Rita told Eli about her visit with Cary after school. She leaned over the table to kiss Eli, affording him a view down her red tank top. Eli reached under the table and ran his hand the length of her thigh. "You're distracting me," she said between kisses. "I'm trying to tell you about Alan."

"Screw Alan," Eli uttered playfully, reaching the edge of her light gray shorts.

"You won't be screwing anybody if you don't let me finish my news flash." From that point, Eli pretended to listen attentively about Alan's return to the area. "He was driving a new 4x4 pickup truck."

"A new truck? Ol' Alan's moving up in the world." With that, Eli ended the discussion by gathering up the dishes on the picnic table, and he put them into the kitchen sink. Back on the porch, he took Rita's hand and led her back into the house. "Now where were we?" he murmured, kissing her once they were inside.

Eli looked into his wife's eyes, and he knew all over again how much he wanted to be with Rita for the rest of his life. Standing with him was the woman he would love until the end of time. He once heard a song that expressed what he was feeling; each time they were together, it felt like the first time; he still trembled when they kissed and made love.

Rita slid her arms around Eli's neck, and with her long fingers, stroked the back of his neck. She leaned into him and kissed him softly. As if escaping into a world meant only for the two of them, they both closed their eyes and melted into one another.

Her husband slid his hands down her bare arms to her hips. He pulled her closer and his tongue danced with hers. Eventually, because there was no rush, he led her to their bedroom. Hungry for him, she slid off her own shorts, and then tugged impatiently at his jeans. Everyone else in the world was forgotten as Rita and Eli lowered to their bed together, her long legs straddling him as she whispered into his ear all the ways she was going to love him that night. And she did.

CHAPTER 20

Over breakfast on a Saturday in early October, Hyun told Alan she was flying back east that day. Her announcement took him completely by surprise. "Boy that sure came out of left field," he mumbled sarcastically. Quickly he realized how he must have sounded. He had to be careful. She was his boss and not a family member or friend who might be inclined to forgive sarcasm.

"Out of what?" Hyun asked. Evidently she was not one to follow baseball or its jargon. It gave Alan the necessary second or two he needed to regroup.

Pouring her coffee he continued. "Oh it's just an old Indian saying; out of Cleveland perhaps." He smiled at his own joke. "Forget I said anything." He sat down, and he sipped his own coffee briefly. "Your plan to fly back east today is a surprise to me. Is everything okay with your family?"

Hyun almost never mentioned her family ties, and little did he know he had touched a nerve. She looked up quickly then softened her gaze. "Oh it's just business. I need to personally assure my backers and publishers that my work is moving forward on time." She reached across the kitchen counter where they were seated opposite each other upon brown stools upholstered with leather. She touched Alan's forearm and stroked his ego. "Would you do me a few favors?"

Not yet having figured out she was manipulating him like a puppet, Alan nodded. Her most simple touch aroused him. With his mouth full of wheat toast, he was unable to speak.

"Please continue to be my eyes and ears. Notice things and events you think my readers might appreciate about your region." By now, she was up and standing over the kitchen sink. She placed her dishes in the dishwasher and continued. "Keep people away. I still want my privacy when I return, and keep this place looking lived-in. If you're not staying here while I'm gone, we might be asking for trouble."

"Sure," Alan replied having swallowed what he was eating and washing it down with some orange juice. He was greatly relieved she was not releasing him. Once he realized he was still on Hyun's payroll he relaxed. "Want me to drive you to Kalispell?"

"Thanks, but I'll be flying out of Missoula this time." Then she added, "I'd like to leave early enough to see the campus. That's possible. Isn't it?" In reality her concern was that she did not want to be recorded on security cameras in Kalispell any more than she had to be. In and out of Missoula would be a first for her.

Alan began to clean up. "Sure. How long will you be gone?"

Hyun had anticipated this question, so the delivery of her answer seemed to flow naturally. "I shouldn't be gone for more than two weeks. Meetings can be unpredictable with these people. They'll treat me like royalty, yet they will make it known that they are growing impatient." To further stroke Alan's ego, she added a trace of dependence. "Would you mind if I called you when I need you to meet me at the airport?"

"Not at all! I'll make it special. When you come back I'll hold up one of those large, white signs in case you forget what I look like." Alan was pleased he could bring a smile to her beautiful Asian countenance. Then he anxiously scribbled the phone number of his recently purchased cell phone. "Here...in case I'm not here."

Hyun looked at him quizzically.

"Oh, yeah. We don't have a phone here." He felt more than a little embarrassed. Hyun turned and pretended to be amused and giggle. Then she retreated to her room and began to pack for her journey back east.

As she readied herself to travel, Alan once again briefly wondered just exactly when she did her writing. He occasionally had this thought on and off since he had met her. He had not seen any evidence of it. Perhaps she wrote at night as he slept. To him, she seemed heavy on the research end of the spectrum when it came to the writing process.

She finally exited her room. She was not carrying much in the way of luggage, but he did recognize her high-tech equipment case he had seen her use at the lake. The quality of her equipment blew him away, and he wondered, too, what she would be observing back east. She noticed this and brushed it off with, "Alan, I've several stories going at once. I'm under contract for multiple books. How is it you cowboys put it?" This time, at the use of the term "cowboys" it was she who smiled at her own little joke. "I have several irons in the fire."

"Hoo, I'm the 'Indian', not the cowboy. Remember?" He feigned being insulted.

"Gotcha!" she replied quickly.

He laughed as he noted she briefly sounded very American. "By the way, what if I need to contact you?"

This question, too, she had anticipated. The assassin chose to regain the upper hand a bit with her carefully calculated reply. "Alan, don't be offended, but since I'll have my work with me, there will be no reason important enough for you to contact me. Understand?" She pulled her burgundy Griz cap firmly atop her head as if punctuating what she just said to him.

Any ideas Alan had of finding a chink in her social armor was vaporized by her answer. "Okay, Boss," was the best he could summon. In seconds they were headed out of the door and riding together in silence upon the old macadam road that paralleled the lake's edge, soon to be on 93 South around Falls Port, and headed toward Missoula International.

Hyun made it a personal rule to always work under the assumption that American agents knew she was out and about. She felt such thinking, even when inaccurate, helped her keep her competitive edge. For this reason, she made her destination a more inconspicuous landing site near Scranton, PA. The airport, roughly two hours west of NYC, proffered short trips to other possible job-related destinations as well. For example, Philadelphia was also only two to three hours from Scranton, just in a more southerly direction. She felt the TSA was not an issue for her, but first she had to get there.

Out of Missoula, Hyun flew into Salt Lake City, Utah. After all she had heard about it, she was disappointed by the appearance of the Great Salt Lake, yet she found the manner by which the city snuggled between the Rockies noteworthy. Salt Lake City and its urban sprawl seemed to have the organization and symmetry of a colossal geometric proof. From the air, streets, avenues and parkways were wonderfully aligned. Snow covered much of the mountains, but greens and browns were still largely evident in the heavily populated basin. Weather would not hamper her travel arrangements during this trip.

Once off Delta's 42-seat shuttle, she found traversing the terminal in Salt Lake City to be pleasant. All sorts of eateries and gift shops were brightly decorated and offered delayed passengers desirable places to keep occupied.

Hyun's connecting flight to Cincinnati Airport was posted as on-time as well. Once comfortably seated in the larger 747, she chose to catch up on briefs she had received back in Montana; information that set this new ball to rolling.

She perused what North Korea recently sent her via its night time contacts and felt disdain for what they described as an obvious attempt to divert North Korea's attention from Parks, Winters, and Ripkin. The United States government had publicly announced the retirement of three of its best, a crackerjack team of mechanical engineers, who were largely responsible for saving the lives of naval men and women around the world. Truth be told, they had indeed stymied several North Korean efforts at espionage, but there was more reasoning behind her assignment than engineering. The President hailed their efforts as no less than heroic. He went on to say it was a classic example of how private citizenry could merge talents with government and military for the good of all, making the world a safer place.

Hyun inwardly scoffed at the ostentatious ceremony associated with the retirement of these three white collar workers. She and her countrymen were sure Parks, Ripkin, and Winters would eventually be assigned new identities, and then they would get back to work on future acoustical advances and their other projects few folks knew about, just as they had before. To Hyun and North Korean operatives everywhere, the announcement failed to ring true. Never would the government let three men so well trained ride off into the sunset forever. Frustrated North Koreans felt these Americans were still a hurdle to be successfully cleared. That meant that retirement or not, Winters, Ripkin, and Eli Parks were still targets. Hyun still had gainful employment in the U.S.

This leg of the journey seemed the longest. Not traveling First Class created a degree of anonymity, but also made Hyun appreciate moments when she permitted herself to travel in style. Straight ahead and far behind her were rows and rows of travelers, nine across the fuselage, watching an overhead movie, sleeping, working on laptops, and having conversations. Flight attendants moved up and down the aisles distributing snacks and beverages. Graciously Hyun rejected the snacks but accepted a cold drink. She prided herself in her self-discipline, especially when she was amidst what she considered an obese American culture.

CHAPTER 21

An elderly neighbor found Erin upon her back on her kitchen floor in an massive pool of glossy, sticky, darkened, blood. Later the police would determine she had been shot one time; probably by a .22 caliber gun judging by the size of the wound. No bullet was ever located. Jake had not been home at the time of the shooting. He was working across town. Mrs. Eliot, a kindly soul who lived next door, decided she would visit for a spell before her retired husband of forty-four years returned from a round of golf with his cronies. It was not at all unusual for Janet Eliot to stop by for a chat. Having just returned from her hairdresser, she had slipped into an old fashioned house dress, and she walked in to show Erin her new hair style. As was her custom, as she entered, Mrs. Eliot knocked politely at the kitchen door she had opened so many times before, only this time she discovered a horrifying sight she would never forget.

The short, round woman screamed and momentarily experienced a nervous struggle with the decision of whether or not she should go near Erin's body. Finally she scrambled for the telephone to dial 911. As she spoke excitedly over the phone to the dispatcher, she began to panic and breathe irregularly. She could not stop crying, nor could she make herself stop studying the crumpled body positioned flaccidly at her feet. Erin's eyes were wide open as was her mouth. The look upon her face was expressionless; almost as if she was a wind-up toy whose key had become unwound, and she had fallen to the floor in a mechanical position waiting to be wound up again.

"Oh, Erin! Who would do this to you? Who would do this to you?" was all poor Mrs. Eliot could say over and over as she paced from Erin's side, across the Mediterranean tiled floor to the back door she had just politely opened moments ago. She saw no one coming to her aid, at least not quickly enough. She wrung her hands with worry as she wished she could undo what had been done. "Oh, Erin! Who would do such a thing!" The tears fell down her wrinkled, plump face as she sobbed, gasped for breaths, and cried out.

After what seemed to Mrs. Eliot to be an interminable amount of time, she began to hear cars pulling into Erin's driveway. Then she heard screeching brakes out front. Footsteps followed, rushed and hurried yet careful. From inside the kitchen she could hear the officers calling to her. They called for her to exit the house with her hands above her head. They were taking no chances. When she exited, she was finally taken aside gently, questioned very briefly about what they could expect to find in the house and whether or not she felt anyone else might still be inside. She advised them the best she could despite her sobbing and nervousness. It was not long after that she realized her husband was just returning from his round of golf, and that already curious neighbors were gathering as closely as they could. All of this became too much for her to process, so she began to babble loudly. The officers turned her over to paramedics who arrived not long after the police chief had pulled up to the house. George Eliot, a physically fit man for his age and nicely dressed in his golfing attire, wrung his hands, too, as he watched the paramedics attempt to comfort his wife.

Now Erin's home became a crime scene the likes of which most of the local police rarely had witnessed. It was not complicated in the sense that little seemed out of place. And, oddly enough, that was what made it difficult. It seemed nothing was broken, not even a windowpane on any of the doors. Apparently entry was not forced. There was no sign of a struggle. Could Erin Parks have known the shooter? Had she permitted her own killer to enter the house by the back door since her home's other doors were all locked? As best they could, considering how seldom they had been called to the scene of a murder, they canvassed the property for clues and began questioning the neighbors. There were no witnesses.

About thirty minutes into their investigation, a state police officer arrived escorting a pair of federal agents. The officer was a man of remarkable stature. It was obvious he was into physical fitness. Each of the agents, too, were taller gentlemen, but they were not as physically intimidating as their escort. However, their involvement truly opened the eyes of the local police. It was then that they were sure that something more than a murder had taken place. This was no domestic dispute and not a burglary, not if the Feds were involved.

From their opening dialogue, it was clear the state policeman knew the local Chief of Police. Walking carefully into the kitchen, they addressed one another civilly.

"Mike Monroe, this is Agent McGee and this is Agent Bystrom from the Secret Service and FBI respectively." The Chief shook their hands. He was on the tail end of a 35 year career, and the wrinkles in his leathered skin suggested he had put in a lot of hours during his tenure as the Chief. Short-cropped white hair on the sides of his head could be seen below his cap.

"Never nice to meet under these circumstances, but hello." The Chief got right to the point. "What brings you here? And how did you get here from D.C. so fast?"

Agent McGee smiled slightly and replied, "Don't get the wrong impression, Chief. We're not that efficient. We were assigned to the Lehigh Valley area on an advanced recon job for the Vice President's visit next month. We truly just happened to be in the area." Then with a more serious look upon his face he continued. "But that doesn't answer your biggest question. Does it? Why we're here."

The Chief nodded. "I'm not trying to be unfriendly. I'm sincerely curious."

"Well this lady we have here on the floor was under government protection, I guess you might say. She's the ex-wife of a gentleman, a government employee, who we still feel is the target of an assassin." He kneeled down as if to observe Erin's body more closely. "That's the long and the short of it."

"I appreciate your honesty, Mr. McGee. How can I best help you?"

It was then that Bystrom spoke for the first time since entering. "Did you know the late Mrs. Parks at all, Chief?"

All three men were walking about the kitchen slowly as they talked. The Chief leaned against the maze and black granite countertop which accented the room's creamy colored cabinets beautifully. "No, I've never met her. We like to think we live in a small town atmosphere, but we don't."

Partly to show they had no egos and partly to make the Chief feel good, Bystrom asked, "Any idea of how this might have happened?" All this time, Trooper Washburn stood and listened respectfully. Truth be told, he was interested in the kind of work Secret Service and FBI agents do. It would not hurt to listen and observe.

"Agent Bystrom..."

"Mike, please call me Ray."

"Okay, Ray..." and the Chief looked at Agent McGee as if to wonder what his name might be..."

"Chief, my name's Mike, too. Might get confusing." He smiled to show he was joking.

"Well, Ray...Mike, I guess it's pretty fair to say that the shooter had no trouble getting into the house. The security system in place has been compromised." He pointed to a cream colored keypad to the right of the door, and then he walked the agents outside to see a mounted camera as well, where wires had been neatly snipped. They had noted it and two others on their way inside, but they did not feel they had to tell Chief Monroe. They did not want to interrupt his presentation by appearing to pass judgment on what he might share. He might have lost his train of thought if they interrupted him, and interrupting him might have made them appear judgmental. McGee and Bystrom were actually gentlemen, something not all that prevalent in their line of work. "No damage is present. There's no scarring on the door jam, nor is there any broken glass or scratched paint. It's clean as entries go. Looks like the shooter just walked in or was invited inside."

Chief Monroe was suddenly summoned into the living room by one of his officers. She was an attractive woman who had been on the force for a few years. Her navy blue uniform fit her snugly, and her short sleeve shirt revealed the biceps of an officer who cared about her appearance. She was chiseled. When her boss entered the room, she stood looking down at a piece of shattered porcelain.

"What have you found, Ellen?" the Chief inquired. "Explain it to Agents McGee and Bystrom. I'm guessing they'll be taking over the crime scene. They're here from D.C."

The trio exchanged nods of acknowledgment, and she spoke. "Still no bullet, Chief, but how do you explain a shattered statue of China's Qilan left strewn all over the floor when it's obvious that Mrs. Parks kept an otherwise immaculate house?"

"Qilin, Ellen? What is a *qilin?*"

"Not so much what but *who,* Chief." As the four of them looked about the immaculately kept living room, she continued to explain. "I have a brother-in-law who travels. More than once he's brought me some items of interest from the Far East. Along with them come stories or explanations. Qilin, spelled with no "u" after the "q", is thought to be a sign of good fortune. I guess that's irony, but it goes back several dynasties in China, and there's even a huge metal statue of it in Beijing, also known as Peking. The city is a metropolis in northern China and the capital of the People's Republic of China."

All three of the men listened for a moment longer, and then Bystrom said, "Ellen, if you can somehow connect this shattered piece to the crime scene, I bet the Chief will make you a detective." She did not know if he was envious of what she knew or if the agent was having fun with her, but she smiled a nervous smile nevertheless. Then he continued. "No, I'm serious. Don't overlook any possibility. Okay?"

CHAPTER 22

At first there were the sirens. When the police cars went screaming down Main Street they caught Jake's attention since he was not working too far away from his home in the center of town. It was midafternoon. He was finished tamping down the new sod in back of Mr. and Mrs. Jackson's yard. They had installed an in-ground pool recently, and the sod was a finishing touch. Jake was part of Yardworks, a three-man crew that did landscaping all around Lehigh County. It was hard work, but it was work in which he took pride. When he was done he liked standing back, having a cold drink with his buddies and saying, "We did that." The sirens had interrupted that rewarding private moment.

The arrival of a lone police car came later. The Yardworks team was gathering equipment and calling it a day. The cruiser's siren was silent, but Jake thought it odd that its lights were brightly flashing red, white, and blue. Two officers stepped out of their car and left them on. He thought it was even more odd when he realized they left the engine running. Curious like anyone else, Jake stopped what he was doing and watched as his friend and co-worker, Alex, pointed in Jake's direction. Jake did not recognize either officer.

After pointing to Jake, Alex seemed be answering questions. Jake watched their conversation play out, and he wondered what the police wanted. Then they walked across the new sod toward him, and by their stride and serious demeanor he sensed he was about to learn something that would not be pleasant. An unsettling sensation crept over him quickly, and the closer they came toward him the more uneasy he became. Jake knew he had done nothing wrong, and he had time to wonder why he was feeling the way he was.

In a flash, his uneasiness brought back a memory of a high school incident. As incidents go, it was not particularly exciting, but since Jake was brought up to respect authorities who deserved his respect, he was uneasy that day in tenth grade when Mr. Boyce approached him with a look similar to those upon the faces of the officers who now approached him. Mr. Boyce was his favorite teacher that year, and Jake had heard earlier that someone had stolen Mr. B's briefcase. The look on his face made Jake wonder if Mr. B thought he was the one who had done it. As it turned out, Mr. Boyce only approached Jake to ask if he had seen anyone in his room that day who acted suspiciously. He had asked Jake because he trusted him.

The taller of the two officers spoke to him gently, snapping Jake from his reverie. The closer of the two first asked Jake if he was indeed Jacob Parks. The officer had a softened expression upon his youthful countenance, and he took his hat off before he spoke, revealing a full head of dark brown hair. He then introduced himself and his partner as patrolmen Skantz and McGrebe, but Jake never really heard their names. It struck Jake that the officer was behaving in a gentlemanly manner; not exactly what he was expecting. The second officer, also a younger man, stood respectfully silent at his partner's side.

"Yeah...yes, I'm Jake. Is there a problem, Officer?" He felt his heart rate increasing, and already he had become nearly dry-mouthed. Over their shoulders Jake could see his co-workers had stopped loading the company pickup, and that they were watching the scene unfold.

"Jake, is your mom Erin Parks, and do you live with her on Acorn Drive?"

"Yes. Is there something wrong with my mom?" Nervously he glanced at Skantz and then at McGrebe for some chink in their facial armor.

There is no tactful way to present the answer to such a question. Between the two of them, only Skantz had handled such a situation before, and that was the only time. McGrebe continued his respectful silence, listening to his partner and learning. Skantz hoped his courteous tone would offset his quick-to-the-point approach. He was once instructed that victims rarely remember what is said to them anyway, so getting to the point was probably the best route to take.

"Mr. Parks, there is no easy way to tell you this, but we think your mom has been murdered." That having been said, the officer tried to prepare for what might happen or be said next. The neighborhood was eerily quiet, or so it seemed. A mower could be heard further down the street.

Jacob "Jake" Parks just stared at Officer Skantz and then at McGrebe. He felt his knees weaken, and in his heart of hearts he was hoping this was some sort of horrible prank or error, but their countenances quickly assured him that it was not. He looked over the patrolmen's shoulders toward his co-workers. In micro seconds he wondered if the officers had spoken of the murder with them. Judging by their clueless facial expressions atop their muscular and tanned bodies, he did not think they had. Conversely, from their position near the property line fence, Alex and Bo could see Jake's face twist in horror. It was then that they suspected serious trouble.

Jake finally spoke quietly but rapidly and asked, "Can I see her? Where did this happen?" Looking at the new grass beneath his feet he added, "What makes anyone think it was murder?" He had dropped the tools he was carrying and nervously let himself be led to the car.

Skantz asked Jake's co-workers to help with his tools and requested Jake get into the patrol car. "Come with us, and we'll tell you what we know in the car."

Once they were inside the black and white, McGrebe finally spoke. "Jake we're going to take you to the station first. Once your house has been initially investigated, we'll take you home, investigate further with your input, and help you decide what to do next."

"What? Oh, thanks." He looked out the side window. "I'm sorry. My head is spinning." His anxiety was obvious as he struggled to settle upon the back seat. Then Jake wondered if his father had been contacted, so he asked. "Does my dad know about this yet?"

"Someone else is trying to get in touch with your dad. We might need your help with that." Little did all three of them know that not only had Eli Parks been informed, but the President of the United States knew about it as well. The "system" had failed, and the President was not happy.

As Elijah Rittenhouse saw things, his college roommate had been assured his ex-wife would be extended every courtesy to keep her safe. However she had been murdered in her own home, and it had happened on his watch. The President felt terrible about it, blamed no one in particular, but at the same time he felt he had disappointed his long-time friend in the most egregious manner possible. To Elijah Rittenhouse, the safety of Eli Parks and his family was not political anymore. It was personal.

CHAPTER 23

It was Ed who took the call. Eli was outside enjoying the sunshine on their cabin's deck and had asked him to answer the phone. It was around 2:30, Rita was off to school, and the men were enjoying some "man" time around the cabin. Ed had a day off from work while Eli was living the life of the retired government employee: he was ticking off chores left by Rita.

"It's a Mr. O'Neill from D.C.," Ed called aloud. "He says it's awfully important." As he walked through the sliding screen door that opened to the kitchen, Ed shrugged his shoulders as if to signal he knew nothing more.

Eli took the phone, lipped the words, "Thank you" to his stepson, and sought some privacy inside the cabin. The words "...awfully important..." made him immediately anxious. He thought maybe if he began in a friendly tone it would settle him. "Yes, Andy! How are you?"

Two thousand miles away Andy O'Neill handed the phone to Elijah Rittenhouse. Eli heard Andy quietly say, "He's on the line, Mr. President."

"Hello?"

"Eli? It's Elijah." His tone was subdued this time so Eli immediately suspected this call was not of a social nature. President Rittenhouse paused briefly trying to summon the appropriate words, words that he found difficult to use. How does one tell his friend that a member of his family has been murdered? "Eli, I have some terrible news, and I wanted you to learn about it from me."

"Elijah, what is it?" Eli sat down on the forest green couch that permitted him a view of the lake down in front of the cabin. The sky was a brilliant blue, and the lake was lightly rippled. He saw Edward had strolled down to the lake to offer him even more privacy. Such a mature kid!

"It's Erin, Eli. Somebody has taken her life." Then there was silence. The President of the United States waited respectfully for what would most assuredly be a series of questions from his long time friend.

Eli sat stunned. He could not fathom the truth of the matter even though they all knew it was a possibility. An assassin had begun his mission by taking the life of his ex-wife. "Elijah, how did this ever happen? Why her? She hasn't done anything to hurt anyone." And then he thought of his son. "Where's Jake? Is he all right?" All this time the President sat in silence until his college roommate from years gone by had finally run out of questions for the moment.

"Eli, first I have to apologize ..."

"Don't. It's not your fault," was Eli's quick reply.

"But..."

"Don't, Elijah. Just tell me what you know." He paused a second to prioritize. "Start with Jake."

"Jake is safe. He's been told, and the police have contacted your sister-in-law." The President excused himself momentarily. Over the phone, Eli could hear what he imagined were staff members briefing the President.

Eli sat on the edge of the couch waiting. "I've just been told by Andy that Jake is, in fact, now at Patty's home. You can reach him there. I cringe to say this to you, but it goes without saying she'll have protection."

He experienced at least a hint of relief and sighed. "How much time do you have to discuss this, Elijah? Or do you want someone else to fill me in?" As soon as his last inquiry crossed his lips Eli realized how ungrateful it might have sounded. "I'm sorry..."

"Eli, it's me. No offense taken." Elijah Rittenhouse began leaning forward as he sat at their dining room table in his private residence atop the White House. He felt closer and more sincere somehow, as if Eli could see him reaching out. "I'm upstairs, Eli. The world and its issues are on the back burner for now."

"Thanks." Again there was silence. Eli's years of training helped him focus. "Let's back up. Let me ask you about what you've been told."

"It seems the intruder had little or no trouble entering Erin's home, specifically her kitchen. I'm told there is no sign of forced entry. There was no sign of a struggle either."

"So she might well have known her killer." Eli took a moment to soak in that concept. He couldn't fathom being killed by someone he knew. "Elijah, how did she die?"

"You really want to know this, Eli?" The President was more than a little uneasy handling this question.

"Yes. I have to know."

"One gunshot, Eli, to the front of her head. There's a chance she never knew she was in any danger, never experienced fear."

"When? When did it happen?" By now Eli was on his feet moving about. He watched Edward down by the lake securing their rowboat to their dock. He was looking at a blissful, peaceful scene while at the same time discussing the worst thing that had ever happened to him.

President Rittenhouse briefly studied Andy's notes. "This particular report tells me it was late morning or early afternoon. An elderly woman, a neighbor..."

"Oh, God! Mrs. Eliot found her? She often stopped by unannounced to check on us. She adopted us in her own kind way. That poor woman." In micro seconds Eli pictured the discovery playing out in his head. It left a cold, cold feeling inside of him. He had lost his ex-wife, his son had been forced from his home, and he was feeling compassion for Mrs. Eliot. It was all so much.

"She stopped by around 4 p.m. She reported that it was not at all unusual for the kitchen door to be unlocked."

Eli knew that was true. Mrs. Eliot's visits were welcome escapes from Erin's day-to-day problems.

"Elijah, who is on this?"

"Local police, state police and for now there are at least two of our special agents at the scene."

Analyzing things was Eli's strength. He continued to think clearly despite the horror of the situation. "Did any of them note anything they felt was unusual? Anything out of place? Were there witnesses?"

Hand on his forehead, the President replied softly, "No, not yet. No witnesses. This shooter was thorough. Investigators haven't even located a bullet, a casing, or a weapon."

"Again, do you know from reports whether or not anything appeared out of place or were there things strewn about? Tell me that."

"Jake will be taken to the house after Erin's been removed. He might recognize anything amiss that investigators might overlook."

Eli was wondering if the murderer had been searching for any clues as to his own whereabouts. "Elijah, I'm guessing the shooter was looking for a way to find me."

"Couldn't he just ask? Why didn't he grill her first, if that's the case?"

"If this is a professional, he might be on a schedule. He might be hoping he'll flush me out."

"Eli, it could be a woman, too. Don't forget that." At that moment Eli overheard President Rittenhouse speak to Andy. His voice appeared to have increased in excitement for the moment. Eli pictured Elijah scanning the reports and having found something.

"Elijah! What is it?" he nearly shouted into the phone.

"Hang on, Eli." The conversation in the White House residence continued. "Just give me a minute." He knew Eli was listening.

Listening intently he overheard the President say, "Andy, is this what I think it is? Is this a reference to a porcelain statue with a Far Eastern or Asian background?"

"Oh my God, Mr. President." Right then Andy, the President, and even Eli spoke simultaneously to no one in particular. "It's her!"

CHAPTER 24

Never before in Falls Port had so many people taken the time to stop whatever they were doing to observe anything that was going on at tiny Falls Port Airport. Outside of town just west of the quarter-mile long bridge across Kerr River that led traffic up Route 93 north, the airport sat at the base of gradually sloped mountains that paralleled Irvine Flats Road. Few structures, private or otherwise, dotted the mountainside, so for observers it was a perfect backdrop to the airport. The runway and the gently sloped hills beyond could be spotted from most places in town since the airport was located at the base of the mountain about 100 to 300 feet above most buildings in Falls Port.

The three camouflaged military Bell UH-1N Iroquois choppers that landed there Thursday morning created a staccato approach that was heard throughout the river basin from a distance of four or five miles, far in advance of their arrival. Truly a surprise to locals, most had never witnessed first-hand such transportation ever before. There was an even larger surprise when later word somehow was spread that all three choppers were sent to pick up but one individual. Yet the greatest surprise was when the citizens of Falls Port learned the lone passenger was Eli Parks, husband of one of the teachers in their local middle school.

It did not take long for conjecture to circulate and tales to take flight, too. Stories about the event ranged from Eli's capture, since he obviously was a criminal wanted by the U.S. military, to a nomination into a national public office of such importance that it had to take place in this manner. One such story labeled him the next Secretary of State. For certain, all of Falls Port felt that to send that many aircraft and military personnel meant he must be pretty important one way or the other.

On Wednesday evening, Eli had received yet another call from President Rittenhouse. He explained to Eli that transporting him back east to reunite him with his son Jake was this President's new top priority. It was requested that their passenger be at the local airport the day of Erin's murder. The entire transportation process could have been carried out Wednesday night, but Eli requested time to get some personal things in order before leaving Montana for Pennsylvania and Washington, D.C. Eli had spoken to Jake, assured his safety and the safety of Erin's family as best he could, telling him that he would be with him at some point the following day.

As he settled in for his brief flight to Missoula International Airport where he would board his final transport, he had only a little time to collect his thoughts. He struck up a conversation, albeit brief, with one of the personnel aboard the Huey. Each soldier on board was truly professional in that they all had a function to perform that each was trained to do. A muscular lieutenant, whose age was much less than Eli's, was seemingly assigned to Eli to help meet his needs; therefore, he was willing to chat a bit.

"Mr. Parks," came out of his mouth rather matter-of-factly. His tone was business-like. "Are you all right? I mean are you comfortable, Sir?"

Eli was used to the military mindset, so he was not at all uncomfortable physically or socially. "Thanks, Lieutenant. I've been this route before." Eli and the lieutenant had to yell to each other over the mechanical noises, but their conversation continued. "Lieutenant, why were three Hueys sent to Falls Port?"

"It was the President's call, Sir. I work for him."

"But why three?"

The lieutenant remained business-like in his demeanor. He did not flinch when he explained. "Mr. Parks, if we are dealing with an advanced terrorist cell, chances of your survival are increased if the enemy doesn't know which chopper you have boarded, Sir."

It was then that Eli learned all three Iroquois choppers were following varied flight paths to Missoula. If they had clustered all the way, they would have been easier targets. Since Erin's life had been taken, perhaps it was a terrorist, or perhaps it was the very assassin about whom all of them had been warned. However what struck him most at the moment was that his very presence, his company, actually put everyone else around him in danger. The lieutenant and the crew, for example, were possibly in the line of fire thanks to him. No matter where he traveled, it seemed to him he had become a pariah. Eli's mood became sullen, and he chose to speak no more.

Finally back together and in formation, the three choppers banked to approach the airport. Out his small, oval-shaped portal Eli noted Missoula's famous, large, white, cement *M* on the mountainside overlooking the campus of the University of Montana and the entire city which was nestled in a valley under the Bitterroot Mountains. He recalled the first time Rita and Ed challenged him to walk to the *M* and its summit for a photo opp. Ed scooted up the serpentine trail with seemingly little effort. Huffing and puffing, Eli finally joined his stepson twenty minutes later as he sat upon the structure looking as casual as he could make himself look with a "what took you so long" grin spread across his face.

But any hint of humor that briefly crossed Eli's mind was suppressed when he thought of how he never had attempted the hike with his son Jake. "Poor Jake. What must he have been thinking about all through the night?"

Transferring Eli to a shiny Leer jet did not take long. It was one of several aircraft kept at Andrews A.F.B. designated for special Presidential assignments. The chopper had purposefully landed close to the aircraft. Rotors and blades stirred up the air violently, but they were not so loud that he could not hear the jet's whirring engines singing their high pitched song while prepping for takeoff. Also, he noticed several commercial jets lined up on the tarmac awaiting permission to take off. He knew that he had been given preferential treatment this day, and it bothered Eli that so many passengers aboard those waiting planes were held up because of him.

Once he was in the air again, Eli was surprised when he saw his flight had a military escort. "Oh, Mr. President, what have you done?" he muttered to himself.

"Mr. Parks?" A young steward seemed to have appeared out of thin air and was at his side. He, too, was younger than Eli expected, dressed in Air Force blues and wearing a name plate that told Eli the young man was probably Irish. He startled Eli, and he moved his gaze from the fighter jet just off to his right to the young man on his left. Eli felt sheepish about having been caught off guard and then managed a friendly glance upward.

"Sir, the Major requested that I inform you that we'll be landing at McGuire Air Force Base in two and a half hours, about fourteen hundred hours, Sir." He paused to let Eli do the math and realize just how fast they were flying. Then he added quietly, "Sir, at speeds like this you should leave your safety harness on."

Eli turned to his right once again and began to recall events of the hours that passed since Edward handed him the telephone yesterday. What he replayed in his mind was in no particular order but rather like a cluster of facts in a mental slide show.

He recalled his immediate reaction first. Yesterday he wanted to pull everyone closer to himself. Today he was not so sure that was smart. He was a target, and they could be caught in the line of fire. Yesterday he had hung up the phone and immediately called loudly to Edward. Right then and there he needed to know Edward was safe…alive.

Edward came inside, and Eli sat down next to the young man. He began telling him more than Edward ever expected could be true. After Eli finished explaining his former occupation, his reasons for his retirement, and the existence of his endangered co-workers, Eli finally summoned the courage to share what had just happened to his ex-wife.

There was silence between them briefly, long enough for Eli to note the quiet inside the cabin and out. It was a gorgeous day. "How could such a horrible thing happen on such a beautiful day?" ran through his mind. Then it dawned on him that the day was similar to September eleventh 2001. Eli recalled the unusually brilliant blue sky that showcased the horrible rubble during the Trade Centers' destruction.

Then Ed exhaled as if to signal he was mentally on board when he asked, "When do we tell Mom?"

"We're going to school and get her right now," Eli replied matter-of-factly.

"We?"

Stepfather stared at stepson. This was one of the moments that could solidify their bond or weaken it. Eli quickly understood how he might have sounded, as if Ed was a little boy. "I'm sorry. I didn't mean to imply you can't handle yourself."

"Don't apologize. You're afraid someone is coming after us." They both just stood side by side looking out at the lake. "This changes everything. Doesn't it?"

"Ed, right now to keep my mind straight, I'm thinking there is safety in numbers. I promise I won't make you live in a cage like this forever."

Leaning against the counter, legs crossed, and looking out the large window Edward said, "I can't imagine what you're feeling. If my company makes you feel safer, I'm cool with that. But Mom's gonna know something's up when she sees both of us."

Eli knew this was true, but there was no way to sugarcoat murder, and he had already left her out of the loop long enough. The two of them felt the same sense of urgency and jogged down the deck steps toward the old red pickup.

Once they had pulled into the school lot, Ed nearly suggested he would wait in the truck, but then he thought better of it. They trotted briskly down a cement ramp, passed a silver-colored, aluminum flagpole to their right and toward the modern, brick, one-story middle school entrance. The American flag snapped crisply in the breeze. After they buzzed the office and announced their identity and intentions, the door was electronically unlocked. The moment was not lost on them. More than ever they were sensitive to school doors everywhere being kept locked.

The jet hit some turbulence. For a moment, Eli snapped out of his reverie. The silver F-16 was right there on his wing. Right then he wished he could provide such protection for everyone. He looked about the cabin and then drifted back to thoughts of yesterday.

Ed was right. The look on his mom's face could be seen down the long, colorful school corridor. It was a look of concern. She was walking more and more quickly toward the office where her men stood waiting for her at the hub of the school. Eli took her arm and led her off to a private spot, out of earshot of the office workers. He had already arranged to use the counselor's tiny office. He had requested the favor of Benjamin, Rita's principal, as they awaited her arrival from her classroom. Upon seeing her, Ben had gone to Rita's room to cover her class, passing her in the hallway. She gave him a worried look as well.

"What's going on?" She was winded. Edward closed the door, and they sat down.

"Honey, I don't know how to say this without sounding dramatic, so I'm just going to be direct. I'll tell you what I know." Eli paused briefly and then told Rita of Erin's murder.

She was stunned. Physically she began to tremble and writhe. She knew all along that trouble was possible. They had been warned. Eli had retired. Arrangements for everyone's security had been arranged, yet this awful thing had still happened. She began to wring her hands upon her lap. "Eli, how did this happen? How could this happen?" she quietly moaned in fear.

As he flew across the United States, Eli could not help but think to himself, "She was terrified, and I was helpless to comfort her. We can't go on like this. Something has to be done."

CHAPTER 25

From the aircraft, Eli was able to contact Gabe Winters and Jeff Ripkin. He was relieved to learn they had not suffered similar fates. In Ripkin's words, it seemed their guardians were now on a higher alert. Via conference technology not offered on commercial airlines, Eli's friends extended their condolences. Neither Winters nor Ripkin had children, so they were spared that concern. Winters was married, but Ripkin, the youngest of their trio, was not as of yet. All were in agreement that they might never get used to living as if they were being stalked, and Erin's murder had only intensified their respective worries.

Before touching down at McGuire Air Force Base, Eli became uneasy about the upcoming reunion with his son, his sister-in-law, and her family. It was easy for him to imagine more than one scenario in his mind in which he might be verbally attacked for what had taken place. Years ago their divorce resulted in some wounds that seemed to heal slowly. Explaining to them how his occupation might have placed their lives in danger? That was yet another disconcerting thought.

There was no helicopter ride from McGuire Air Force Base to Lehigh County. A limo service transported Eli where he needed to go. During the ride, Eli recalled that outwardly, at least, Patty had never shown signs that she had taken sides against him throughout her sister's divorce proceedings. However, he felt it would be prudent to expect the worst.

His biggest concern, of course, was Jake. Had his son reverted to disliking him? Eli tried to anticipate any questions or arguments that

Jake might have saved for his dad. Over and over Eli rehearsed what he would tell Jake; tried to prepare mentally for his son's questions.

Since time was a valuable currency, none was wasted transporting Eli to Patty's house where he found Jake and others waiting inside her field-stone ranch style home. Patty's and Stan's front entrance of twin, golden oak doors, was accented by a pair of tall sycamore trees in the front yard. Hugs and softly spoken condolences were exchanged with family members.

At long last, Jake and Eli were reunited. Jake met his father in Patty's front hallway, and they embraced. Hurdle number one had been cleared. Eli suspected that eventually conversation regarding the entire family's safety would surface, but for now he was not concerned with that. On this subject of family safety, however, Eli continued painstakingly to organize in his head what it was he would carefully say later when he was certain the time was right.

Two of his three older brothers were in attendance as well. Jamie drove down from Northeastern Pennsylvania while Bernie arrived quickly from the New Jersey shore area. None of them knew the whereabouts of Wally. He disappeared years ago without leaving word, and he could not be contacted.

As it turned out, the neighbors were extremely generous in that they prepared and sent delicious foods to lighten Patty's load. Ordinarily Patty would have enjoyed preparing meals for everyone, for in accordance with neighborhood tradition, many times she had helped her neighbors by sharing her culinary skills. Now she was on the receiving end. Friends understood that this was a tragic event and that Patty had been drained of energy, so not having to cook was a tremendous help to her.

Thursday night Patty's dining room was set up smorgasbord style, and family members quietly and politely mingled around a large, oval table in the middle of the room. Neighbors sent breads, soups, cheeses, a baked ham, a pair of casseroles as well as various desserts. Under all of these delicacies flowed a navy blue table cloth that was accented by cut glass candle holders. The creamy white candles were never lit, for a soft light from an overhead, brushed nickel lamp bathed the setting. During happier times, neighbors passing by would have glanced through the bay window and surely assumed they were witnessing a celebration, but on this day they knew better.

The foods provided a topic of conversation for at least a little while. Jake seated himself next to Eli who had found a small couch not far from a brick fireplace. By meal's end, nearly everyone had left the dining room and meandered into Patty's living room along with Eli and Jake. All were silently hoping that comfort would be found in numbers.

Scanning the room, Eli felt that it was time to speak to everyone at once rather than to catch up with them individually. He feared he might innocently be inconsistent and forget some details if he shared his story with different family members at different times. He wanted to speak his piece, allow time for questions, and clear the air. Too, he felt it was better to speak of their mutual experience in house, thereby avoiding awkward discussions that might arise spontaneously in a less private setting. He knew that the information he was about to share might eventually be retold inaccurately outside of Patty's household, but at least her family would be informed firsthand.

Before he asked for everyone's attention, Eli briefly experienced a flashback to his college days. Specifically he recalled his public speaking professor. He recalled what was probably his professor's stock opening monologue shared at the beginning of each new semester.

"Not long ago," his professor began as he casually plopped himself atop the edge of his old, heavy, wooden desk, "I came across a book entitled *The Guinness Book of Lists*." He went on to explain how it might be confused with *The Guinness Book of Records* and how the two were different. He recalled how he was thumbing through the book of lists until he came across "Man's Greatest Fears" in the table of contents. "I fully expected this survey to reveal that death is man's number one fear. What I found atop the list," and here he would pause for dramatic effect, "was public speaking! It means that people would rather die than speak in public settings!" All of this ran through Eli's mind in micro seconds. At last he called for everyone's attention. In but a few seconds all were quiet.

"Folks, I'm not quite sure how you will process the information I'm about to share. As all of you know, I have remarried, I live in the Northwest, and I have a stepson, Ed. My wife's name, his mother's name, is Rita."

At this point, if the proverbial pin had fallen, even if it fell on Patty's soft, beige carpeting, it would probably have clanged. Eli did not know if the quiet was the result of curiosity, respect, or if the people in the room were stunned by what they felt was his audacity when he mentioned his new family.

"I only bring them up in this setting tonight because I want you to know that what I'm about to share with you I have already shared with them. You are no less important to me than they are." Eli could feel the intensity of their respective stares. "Erin knew this as well and, God bless her, she coped with it throughout my second marriage as best she could."

Just like his college professor, he paused for dramatic effect. What he was about to share had to be presented clearly. "My line of work has caused me to become the target of an assassin. It is suspected that Erin was easier to locate than my wife, Rita, so her life was taken in order to bring me back here."

Immediately the room began to fill with nervous murmurs. It did not take long for everyone to understand that their respective association with Eli might endanger them as well. Erin's and Patty's father spoke to him first. "Are you saying that any of us might be in danger now that you've returned and are among us?" There was more than a trace of irritation in his voice. Eli's former father-in-law was red-faced, he was physically shaking, his jaw prognathic.

Eli looked at all the concerned faces about the room. Then he focused on Erin's father, looking him straight in the eye. "That's exactly what I'm saying. You deserve to know."

"Then why in God's world did you return?" The older man's emotion was palpable.

Eli waited a moment as all in attendance quieted again. "Had I not returned to pay my respects, had I not returned to check on Jake, your grandson, and the rest of you here in this room tonight," again he paused as he prepared an inquiry of his own, "what kind of father would I have proven to be? What message would my absence have sent? And perhaps, just perhaps, another of you might have been taken from us to further entice me to return. I wanted to alert you in person and give you time to ask such questions."

Tim, Patty's and Stan's twenty year old son asked, "Uncle Eli, what did your family say? Are they scared, too?"

Eli looked at Tim and told him about Ed and Rita's profound disbelief. Of course, like Erin, Rita knew ahead of time that his job was dangerous. But his stepson, he told them, absorbed the initial shock and eventually proved to be understanding.

"That's easy for him. He's in Montana!" By this time Erin's father was standing above Eli. He was posturing; his displeasure could not be masked.

Eli never did get up from his section of the couch. From training he knew it would appear confrontational. Actually he had anticipated just such a reaction from somebody, so he waited for voices to quiet for a third time. They awaited his reaction. "That might have been true until I surfaced here. Now my return home could very well lead the assassin right back to them."

Patty hoped she could help cooler heads prevail. She finally spoke from across the other side of the room as she leaned against the archway into the dining room. "Dad, Eli discussed this with me before he returned here. He offered me choices. I could have prevented his visit. I could have prohibited him from even making this very announcement, but I agreed it was best if we were all here and totally informed." Then she looked at Eli. "Eli, tell them the rest."

Through the remainder of the evening, Eli spoke of President Rittenhouse's personal involvement. He reassured them that they would be extended every courtesy for their safety. He told them of his partners and how they were affected by all of it. He was asked about government protection. The issue of cost came about. "Will our kids be safe in school?" Through the evening, Eli patiently continued to field more questions, and he promised that he also would be available to all of them as needed, no matter where he called home. He did not leave the room until he felt everyone had exhausted their individual concerns for the moment.

By night's end, Erin's and Patty's family seemed to have calmed down. As awkward as it was for them, Eli's brothers did not desert him, but stood quietly by as they observed. Everyone simply needed time to process the information he had shared with them. Eli purposely avoided mentioning that the White House specifically suspected a Korean female. He did not want them living in fear of each Asian woman who crossed their respective paths. He did advise each of them to be more aware of their surroundings.

Compared to his whirlwind cross country flight, the next seven days would seem like a marathon. So much raw emotion would wear on all of them. By the end of Eli's week-long stay, Patty's side of the family would be drained. Forty-eight hours earlier Erin was still alive, and the son he now held in his arms still had a mom.

All in all, by the time Eli had gone to bed in one of Patty's guest rooms, he felt things had gone about as well as could be expected. In the dark, he sat on the edge of his bed and looked through the window. Off in the distance a street light made a pair of federal vehicles clearly visible. He felt helpless. No matter how well his public speaking engagement went over earlier that night, he knew that any of them could be dead by morning. Now it was just a matter of making himself available to all of them while he was still in Pennsylvania. Deep inside part of him was hoping his wife's killer would follow him home, thereby insuring the safety of everyone here on the east coast. He felt he would have more control. Yet another part of Eli did not want his ex-wife's killer anywhere near Montana, for it meant a heightened level of danger for Rita and Ed.

CHAPTER 26

No different than anyone in Falls Port, Alan was fascinated not only by Falls Port Airport's military visitors, but also by the lively gossip the event had spawned and the speed at which it traveled. He had no reason to believe that Eli and his work were important to national security. However it was clear to Alan Wing that Eli Parks would never again be considered just another face around the city of Falls Port. In a way, too, whatever happened to Eli took some of the spotlight off of Alan when it came to local gossip.

To test that theory, Alan stepped into the Driftwood Café on that chilly Friday morning. He had not been in there in quite some time. He stopped partly to fill his belly and partly to see how he would be received by the locals, one of the braver things he had ever done. He casually walked inside for his breakfast and selected a stool at the counter located in the inconspicuous corner by the entrance to the rest rooms. His father's old friend never said a word to him, and some more of his worries were allayed when the young waitress who approached him had no idea who he was. She held two pots of fresh coffee in her hands. One was regular and the other, with the orange handle, was decaf.

"Coffee and a menu, Sir?" she asked in a friendly tone. Her blue eyes had not given him more than a passing glance. Her reddish-brown hair was tied behind her head with a purple and gold elastic. Her snug Café t-shirt also sported the local school's colors.

"I'd like some regular coffee," he announced quietly as he leaned back and watched her pour, "and I'd like one of your Belgian waffles with a side order of sausages well done, please." His ex-wife would have been impressed with his manners.

"Some orange juice?"

"Thanks. Yes. I'll have a large glass please."

With that, she was gone as quickly and casually as she had approached him. Up to that point, none of the regulars acknowledged his presence either. Customers were enjoying each other as well as the great breakfasts that had become the Driftwood Café's local claim to fame.

Quickly Alan became even more certain Eli was responsible for much of the conversation. He had made Alan practically invisible. As conversation goes, Eli Parks was as hot as Alan's sausages sizzling on the Driftwood's grill. He evidently had entered the café at a good time amid much lively conversation.

From his everyday spot in his favorite booth, Gene Hopkins loudly professed what he believed took place yesterday at the airport. "Our Mr. Parks ain't native to Falls Port, folks, and he had to have picked our quiet little city for a place to hide."

Without even turning around at her grill, Brenda shot back almost indignantly with, "Hide? From what? And he married one of the more popular people in our area. That's not exactly hiding, Hoppy."

Alan continued the role of observer. He had never before perceived the Driftwood Café as a source of entertainment. Not in a disrespectful way, on this day he found its patrons fascinating. Actually he just was not mature enough to appreciate them prior to Friday morning. For the first time that he could remember, he had no reason to feel defensive among them. Around the community, his behavior of late had been that of a responsible adult.

As he sat off to the far side of the counter, upon a stool that had been host to thousands before him, Alan enjoyed the banter and the constant clatter of background noises. There were dishes being stacked, and anyone could detect the distant hum of the café's industrial strength dishwasher if they bothered to take notice. Conversation echoed and flowed while the jingling of bells above the entrance door brought new players to the stage every few minutes. Occasionally others who unknowingly had acted out their parts found it time to leave the stage, making room for new participants. Stories came in, and stories went out. The Driftwood Café was a busy place, and there was something comforting about all of its nuances. All the while, Alan enjoyed being in the audience.

"Brenda! You've got to admit that it didn't look right when three choppers were needed to ... apprehend one man!" The entire time Gene Hopkins spoke loudly across the counter from his seat in the booth, he managed to continue eating his scrambled eggs, salty hash browns and sausages. And his eyes rarely missed the face of anyone who entered the café. Hoppy loved having a feel for his audience, so Alan wondered how he was missed when he walked inside.

"Apprehended? Now you're claiming he was a fugitive!" Brenda finally had turned around to look right at Gene, pancake batter dripping from the metal pitcher containing the café's most popular recipe. It was then that she knew she had once again taken his bait. He was grinning from ear to ear as his shoulders bounced up and down due to laughter he could no longer stifle. "Watch it, Gene! You're lucky I don't leave eggs shells in your breakfast."

Gene tipped back his faded, red baseball cap. "I know what it's probably all about, Brenda. He's an alien, and I don't mean one of those illegal aliens neither. He's been dropped here in the mountains, and the government is just now realizing it!" He took a sip of coffee, his third or fourth cup, and finished with, "I *just knew* those lights in the northern sky were up to something!" With that Brenda just shook her head and turned around to continue what she did better than anyone else in Montana.

For others, the topic of Eli's departure was not passed over so lightly. All of them wondered what it was they had witnessed. They just processed it in their own ways, mentally digesting Thursday's excitement in quieter discussions or by themselves. And none of them ever knew about Eli's close relationship with their President. It was not something Eli shared in social circles. There was so very much they just did not know.

When Alan had finished his breakfast, he glanced at the morning paper's front page headline. Jim Kaufman left it next to his gratuity when he departed. Alan sipped his second mug of coffee as he scanned the article which was almost an echo of the morning's speculation he had overheard as he sat quietly eating. It seemed the reportage was unable to provide any hard facts by the time the tri-weekly went to press. There was not even a photograph. In an age of digital photography, evidently no one took the time to collect any pictures that were of satisfactory quality.

As he read the article, he was startled by the ring tone from his own cellular telephone. When he answered the phone, he felt sheepish and thought he might just be discovered after all. Hoo Lin claimed she was calling from Chicago to let him know she would be arriving at the Missoula International Airport in a few days. She was still uncertain as to when. She had more people to meet. As he said goodbye, he wondered to himself whether or not she was aware of all that had taken place in Falls Port yesterday. If the citizens of Falls Port did not know what they saw, how could she?

CHAPTER 27

After Hoo Lin called him earlier that day Alan realized this was his first opportunity to snoop around a bit without having to worry that she would return at an inopportune moment and catch him violating her privacy. He had returned from the Driftwood with a full stomach and a curiosity; an itch that he wanted scratched.

Carefully he searched Hoo's bedroom and then what she called her workroom. He was not searching for personal items, but anything that would hint at what she was writing. All in all the search uncovered rather mundane items: magazines and catalogs of a technical nature and a few notepads upon which she recorded her observations concerning places he had shown her. One thing he did note was that several of her entries referred to "vantage points". It was apparent she had even evaluated them. Alan assumed that she was planning camera angles for possible movie scenes. To him, that made perfect sense. "Maybe she really has been writing," he quipped.

There was only one other place of interest that he could imagine: the barn. It was not a large barn. It was red like so many others, and it had been recently renovated to a degree. The structure could easily have been used as a garage, but since it was located 100 yards or more behind the house and located slightly above it, neither of them put their vehicles inside. Far above the property ran highway 93 North towards Kalispell and south toward Falls Port. Vehicles passing by were rarely noticed. The distance from the highway to the house made them barely audible.

When he climbed over her bin's wooden frame into her side of their mutual storage area he was careful. He was glad he had taken the time to create a sturdy framework that would hold his weight. Once inside Alan thought about his approach to the few belongings Hoo was storing there. He could not resist the urge to explore, but initially he studied all of her property so that he would remember to put it back seemingly untouched. Her belongings were scant, and she kept them neatly stacked upon shelving Alan had installed for both of them weeks ago. His bin was a mess compared to hers. He could not imagine Hoo being curious about his collection and realized that he would never have known even if she had perused his things.

Temporarily he concerned himself with whether or not things were kept in any kind of order. It was clear that she had been in the barn to check or maintain her property because, unlike his boxes, there was little or no dust upon her things. So intent was he on studying the location of each and every item that he nearly jumped out of his skin when a breeze off the lake below the property swung the creaky barn door partially shut. He gasped, paled, and turned while readying for confrontation. He had violated any trust he had earned, and he was startled to the point where he began perspiring.

"What am I doing?" he asked himself in a soft voice. His feelings of guilt nearly began to outweigh his curiosity. A few ideas began to creep into his mind. "What if she notices my boot prints in the dirt? What if I don't remove all of them?" Quickly he was chilled by yet another thought that flamed his paranoia. "What if Ms. Technology has installed a security camera?" He felt blanketed with goose bumps. Then he tried to rationalize his actions. "What if something happened to her? I should be better informed about what's in here."

There were no labels on the sturdy boxes and metallic cases she had placed in her bin. At first, despite his extreme curiosity Alan just could not bring himself to open a single item. Then he experienced an epiphany. Why had he not thought of it sooner? "Wait! I can blame anything I want on anybody else!" That was when he opened the first box belonging to Hoo Lin.

Having never seen Hoo strike a single key on a keyboard made him suspicious of her writing prowess on more than one occasion, but what he found in front of him was more than a mild surprise. Alan did not know if he should admire her or be deathly afraid of her. It was then when he uttered to himself, "What do we have here? Who *are* you, Ms. Lin?"

In front of him, in pristine condition was a Polish bolt-action rifle known as a Bor or an "Alex", so-named for its lead designer, Aleksander Lezucha. Alan had discovered a sniper rifle but did not realize it. He had hunted for elk and such when he was younger, but he had never seen a rifle like this. What made it doubly impressive was the fact that it was stored in four pieces between layers of charcoal gray, egg-crate packaging foam. "Some assembly required," he chuckled to himself.

It took ten or twenty minutes to figure out how to affix the various components including the Leupold scope that he found protected beneath one last layer of foam. Each click was a solid affirmation that he was assembling the weapon securely and correctly. As he held the final product in front of himself, he whistled softly. When he recognized the night vision icon engraved on the scope, he remembered that hunters do not hunt after dark, and he became a bit unnerved.

More than once Alan had marveled at the quality of Hoo Lin's laptop, camera, and even her cell phone. However this was by far and away the most impressive piece of technology he had witnessed yet. It was appropriately camouflaged; painted in flat olive-drab and brown colors from the tip of its barrel down the forty-one inches to its stock. As he held it, the weapon felt as if it weighed only about ten pounds. In combination with its sturdy, adjustable bi-pod under the barrel, the stock created a tripod for steady aiming and firing. As of yet he found no ammunition, but he felt it had to be in the vicinity.

By now Alan was speaking aloud to himself. "Why in the world would she have this?" Then in an even more surprised tone he asked, "And how did she ever get it here? There's no way airport security would have overlooked this bazooka." Then he recalled some late-night visitors with whom Hoo Lin had met, visitors Alan never mentioned. He was dumbfounded.

He was sure the weapon was worth thousands. He knew hunters who paid a thousand dollars or more for a rifle much less sophisticated.

Quite a bit of time passed as Alan sat on an old crate in the barn with the weapon placed reverently atop his thighs, and he tried to imagine the significance of what he had discovered. The only light in the barn at this point was afternoon daylight that angled in through the gap between the barn door and its frame. In the back of his mind he might have heard the occasional 18-wheeler passing by on the highway, gearing down while making its way uphill to Kalispell, but it was a flock of crows off in the distance that snapped him out of his reverie.

He stepped outside the barn into the chilly, late afternoon. He needed someplace upon which he could rest the rifle and take advantage of its bi-pods and look through the scope. "When in Rome..." he said to himself, and placed himself in a prone position upon the ground. Listening for the crows, he finally spotted one sitting atop a tamarack down by the lake. A few others sat perfectly still upon some telephone wires above the road that ran along the lake between the house and the shoreline.

The tree's golden needles and the lake's cobalt blue waters were the perfect backdrop for the shiny, black creature. He looked through the scope's two-inch opening, and Alan Wing suddenly fantasized his role as a Native American sharpshooter for the U.S. Army. The magnification provided by the scope, which was about twelve inches in length, was astounding. He could spot a single crow across the property and make it appear as if it was dangling on a branch at point blank range. Again he whistled his surprise softly; the kind of whistle one emits when he stumbles upon a treasure.

There were more boxes to investigate. Alan rose from the cold, hard ground, and he carried his treasure back into the barn. This time he hooked the door to prevent it from sliding with the wind. He did not need any more excitement of that nature. His heart was beating rapidly enough.

"Now what do I open next?" he asked himself aloud. He was almost afraid to proceed. This time he wanted to open a metal case but found that he could not. It required a combination. "If she kept this rifle in a box that I can open, *what in the world* would she have in here?" He moved on to the next box and subsequent others only to find more surprises.

CHAPTER 28

Pilots agree that turbulence at any altitude is little more than a nuisance. They are the potholes of the sky. It was turbulence that interrupted Eli's reverie as he was flown to D.C. At President Rittenhouse's insistence, no matter how insensitive it appeared, and since it was a matter of security, Eli agreed to arrive on Sunday night, one day before Erin's memorial and funeral services.

Funeral arrangements were handled by Erin's family Friday morning at a local establishment. Viewings were available Saturday and Sunday afternoons with a memorial service on Monday. Eli felt it best to pick his spots carefully, especially when decisions needed to be made. The only topic upon which he remained adamant was that he would cover any and all funeral expenses. Perhaps it was wishful thinking, but he hoped covering the costs would reduce tensions and decrease the level of resentment he felt was leveled at him. Erin's death was something her parents had not expected, of course, and after she married Eli they never conceived of a scenario in which they would have to bury their daughter. When the divorce was finalized Erin, her parents, and Patty had all overlooked life insurance. Fortunately after their divorce, Eli had kept life insurance policies covering his ex-wife and Jake. He had felt it was incumbent upon himself to do so.

On more than one occasion, there had been brief family conversations concerning logistics and what was to happen next. At the top of the list, of course, was Jake. Everyone knew it was a conversation that needed to take place, yet it was awkward. Eli felt it was best to take his son to a private part of the house and begin discussing it with him. At the same time, he did not want their dialogue to take on a formal tone, so he chose to discuss Jake's future with him at the picnic table on Patty's stone patio. Jake was a young adult and as such deserved to be treated as one. However, to think he would automatically work out his future all on his own would have been foolish. To Eli's relief, Jake appeared receptive. It was early Sunday afternoon.

The patio was made of blue stone, and it was sheltered on three sides by the u-shaped rancher's exterior walls. Summer's outdoor furniture had not been stored in their garage as of yet, so the table's telescoping umbrella blocked enough of the bright afternoon sun that provided ample warmth on that autumn day. Both were wearing sunglasses.

"Jake, before I go back to Montana there are some things I must do, and there are some decisions that must be considered." Eli leaned forward, elbows on the round glass table between them. "You are my first concern."

His son looked across the table at him with an expression of appreciation; a look of relief appeared on his young face. "Dad, I don't know what to do. Where should I live? If I don't live in our home anymore, who would want me?" The tone in this voice was worrisome.

"I don't think you should live alone, Jake."

"Because it wouldn't be safe?"

"I guess that's part of it," Eli replied quietly as he looked around them. "Although I don't think you are in any danger. If Mom's killer had wanted you...wanted to take your life...he or she would have."

"You don't think lightning will strike twice? That kind of thinking?" Jake's body language implied his inner turmoil. He wanted to be so grown up in front of all his relatives, but it was difficult for him to sit still. He rocked continuously in his blue and white lawn chair.

Eli remained calm. His career had not hardened him to emotion or enthusiasm, but he had learned to keep outward appearances in check. He hoped almost-casual behavior might help soothe his son, the victim of an unspeakable crime. "Actually I just don't think folks should live alone. That's an even bigger part of it. At first, independence and privacy are pretty heady stuff, but they grow old fast."

"So what should I do?" Jake bit at the edges of his nails.

"Well my first tip would be to assess your situation. Don't act too quickly, and don't overreact either." Eli leaned back from the table. It sent a message to Jake. It was time for Jake to react, time to hit the conversational tennis ball back to his dad.

"How do I do that?"

A gentle early autumn breeze rattled a set of wind chimes off to their side as they dangled from a decorative black, cast iron hook just under the eaves. As their attention temporarily turned to the mellow, musical notes, Eli searched for solid fatherly advice. "Start by being brutally honest with yourself as you weigh pros and cons. Write things down if it helps." Then Eli regrouped for a moment as Jake waited for more. "It's not necessary that you go public with your thoughts."

Jake examined his fingers as he spoke. "You don't want me to step on anyone's toes or hurt anyone's feelings."

"Exactly. Yet I truly believe this situation you're in can only be improved if you're honest with yourself. Be considerate of others, but be true to yourself, too. Actually that's advice you probably can apply to most of life's situations."

Eli let himself smile briefly. Jake picked up on it. "What? What's the smile about?"

"When you were little your mom used to send you off to school in what she called 'outfits'. It didn't take you long to come home one day and put a stop to that. You claimed kids were teasing you about your clothes. You were nice about it, but you stuck to your guns."

Jake smiled, too, as he recalled that part of his life. "She really was in to clothes. That's for sure."

As he looked back at his Aunt Patty's sliding glass door, Jake quietly asked for more input from his dad. "Off the top of your head, what do you consider my options to be?"

"Well you can continue to live at home, although I think that might creep you out. If you have buddies in an apartment, you might enjoy their company if they'd take you in with them." He looked at his son and continued. "Do you have friends like that?"

"Yeah, I do."

"Then there are doors number three and four. Number three has you living with relatives while lucky number four packs your things and moves you out west with me."

Jake assumed an overwhelmed facial expression. To Eli, it was evident that his son was suppressing a lot of emotions. His father could only guess. Certainly there was a tremendous sadness. Since Eli moved and married Rita, Jake's mom became the most important part of his life. Her input, of course, had shaped his decision making. Now she was gone forever, and that was sad. Nevertheless his sadness was rivaled by fear. If Erin was a target, would he be next? And some degree of anger was surely bottled up. Despite the passing hours, Eli still thought that deep inside Jake might be as angry with him as he was with his mother's killer. Eli suspected all of this and hoped he could get Jake headed back on track to feeling better no matter how long it took. Bringing him to Montana might have been best for Eli, but it might not have been best for Jake. His work, his friends, and the family he grew to know would all remain in Pennsylvania.

"I need time to think. Do I have time to think things over?"

"Of course, Jake. There's not a person in Aunt Patty's family or mine who wouldn't help you. They're good people who think family is important." Eli meant what he said. It was not just a random comment. He felt fortunate to have Patty's family as a safety net. "I think you can take your time thinking it through and making decisions. Even then, after you make some choices, they won't close their doors to you. Nor will I. If your first choice doesn't work out, we'll all try the next one."

As if it was rehearsed, Patty opened her sliding door and quietly announced to both that it was time to return to the funeral home. The next day would be the day Erin's funeral, and soon Jake's new life would be underway.

As they walked through the sliding door and into the back of Patty's kitchen, Eli's cell phone vibrated in his jacket's inside pocket. When he saw "P.O.T.U.S." upon the screen he excused himself to take the call in private.

At Patty's insistence, out of respect for her murdered sister, the weekend became a period of what she deemed proper mourning. She disallowed television, radio, and newspapers, while she even had telephones of any kind turned off. About these things she became fanatical; the only visible manner in which she had completely stepped out character throughout the ordeal. Only Eli was permitted to have his official cell phone operating, so to learn of the tragedy at West Point Sunday afternoon was an emotional after shock. Was anyone safe?

The turbulence brought Eli back to the present. Ordinarily skilled at controlling his emotions, he was upset that he had to leave Jake and Patty behind at such a terrible moment. He trusted his college roommate, so he departed without question. He had learned long ago that time was a commodity that often must be used wisely, and Eli now knew President Rittenhouse had good reasons to be concerned about timing.

It was Sunday evening, and Eli was nearly in D.C. President Rittenhouse had arranged for another military jet to transport Eli from McGuire Air Force Base to Andrews Air Force Base which led to his fifteen-minute ride back to the White House. Far away, afternoon events had unfolded, events that forced Eli to forgo his ex-wife's funeral.

CHAPTER 29

As if nothing she had done that afternoon was of great consequence, on the same day she had taken Erin's life, Hyun callously decided to travel north and learn what she could about Winters and Ripkin who lived in neighboring counties of New York state. It was if they were nothing more than names on a shopping list that was topped with the name of Erin Parks.

Her flights to and from upper New York state were short since Ripkin lived in Orange County's Newburgh, and its airport was easy to access on line. Winters lived only twenty miles north in Poughkeepsie located in Dutchess County. Upon her arrival, she discovered impressive measures had already been taken to heighten their respective security levels. Bad news traveled faster than her commuter jet.

As a result she simply returned to Lehigh County, planning to stay for a few days longer in Pennsylvania. She was certain Eli would arrive from Montana, and the opportunity to bring part of her mission to a close would be at hand. However, security surrounding Eli Parks and his family had become impenetrable. Around-the-clock armed government agents were a formidable foe. "The American President," she whispered to herself, "certainly values his retired friends' lives." For the time being, she was unable to assassinate any of her three targets, but she certainly had put security on a high alert.

After observing the precautions exhibited near the locations of each of her targets, Hyun resigned herself to the fact that she would have to contact Alan Wing, make transportation arrangements, and return to Montana. Once she was back there, she would initiate alternative plans by applying the technology her Seattle contacts had delivered to her late at night on separate occasions.

It was Friday when she called Alan. Fewer than forty-eight hours had passed since she ended her most recent victim's life. Early that morning Hyun awoke to a call from the Front Desk of her hotel. "Good morning, Ms. Lin! It's 6:00, the weather appears to be continuing its warming trend, and if we can make your stay with us more pleasant in any way, please let us know."

"Thank you," Hyun replied sleepily, and then she put down the beige-colored telephone at her bedside. Slowly she arose, and she sat on the edge of the queen-sized bed. Her soft, tan blanket was cast aside giving the bed the appearance of a wrinkled envelope. After she stood she stepped to the curtains and opened them slowly, giving her deep, brown eyes a chance to adjust to the light of day.

Casually her long legs carried her to the shower and Hyun lingered there. She enjoyed the hot water cascading over her slender yet muscular body. Satisfied, she toweled off with one of the many thick, lengthy, white bath towels which were neatly hanging like art work from chrome racks. "This is so typical of Americans," she thought to herself. "I am but one guest in a room for four, and so many towels at my disposal."

As she toweled off, a new idea came to her. A smile lit up her face, the kind of smile that appeared whenever she realized she had a worthy opponent worn out chasing her masterful volleys back and forth across the back line in a singles match. It was a matter of time now. She was so confident she attempted a 10:30 a.m. phone call to Alan to let him know she would be returning in a few days. He did not answer the phone. Her last phone call that day was to a local travel agent who booked her on a one-way flight back to Stewart International Airport just west of Newburgh, NY. For a second time she would be near the homes of Eli's partners. This time she had a plan.

Unlike Winters who traveled to Baltimore to attend Johns Hopkins University, Ripkin took a lot of kidding about his hometown and his alma mater, the United States Military Academy. Winters and Parks certainly admired him, but they were unmerciful about how he did not travel more than five miles from home to "go to college" as if West Point was of minimal notoriety. Parks would joke, "At least Gabe ran away from New York and home for a little while."

While they were testing one of their mutual acoustical inventions, during a moment when both should have been concentrating upon nothing but the project, Gabe once whispered to Jeff, "Your mother must be an incredible cook." Ripkin knew that he was intimating he was a mamma's boy, and immediately he began to laugh uncontrollably, thereby setting off the alarm in their lab. The premature activation of the alarm nearly made Jeff hearing-impaired for an hour while the clever Mr. Winters was wearing ear protection ahead of time. Such light moments reduced the pressure brought on by the nature of their work.

Parks sometimes teased Ripkin about his address. "You are so patriotic you not only attended West Point, but you grew up on Washington Street in Newburgh! Washington Street! Have you or your folks ever met ol' George while you were home?"

The young man took it all in stride. "Yep! And I lived right across from the "famous" Delano-Hitch Stadium, once home to the Newburgh Hummingbirds of '46. And did you know that two other well-known pro teams played baseball there? I actually attended Nighthawk and Black Diamond games!" He knew all three teams were known only to locals, but all the while he made sure he sounded boastful for having lived the experience. Early on he discovered it was the only way to silence his partners.

Jeff Ripkin made a name for himself at the military academy. He not only graduated with honors, but he became a well-known lacrosse player as well, from 1987 to 1989. He attained All American honors. Of course, that did not go unnoticed by either of his co-workers, and he was often dubbed "the All American Boy".

He served in the army before teaming up with Parks and Winters. The fact that both of them were not veterans was not lost upon Jeff, and he saved this information for special moments when it was his turn to tease the two of them. "The only uniform you two were permitted to wear was a Cub Scout uniform. The Boy Scouts wouldn't accept either of you!"

Long before the three of them chose to retire from the halls of Washington, D.C., and whenever he was back in Newburgh, Ripkin attended football games in Michie Stadium, the home of West Point's Black Knights. Located five miles southeast of Newburgh, the trip through locally famous Stoney Lonesome Gate and into the stadium was short, but scenic. Much of the academy and the stadium itself overlooked the lower portion of the Hudson River Valley. The area, steeped in centuries of American history, was always a good fit for him. This particular weekend was doubly special since rival VMI was pulling in to play the role of spoiler on Homecoming Day. Army was still undefeated as were the Keydets of Virginia Military Institute. However, it was a security nightmare for those assigned to watch over him. It became worse when Winters agreed to attend the affair as well.

CHAPTER 30

In a day and age when terrorist groups lay claim to their destructive activities quickly and with pride, U.S. citizens waited to learn the name of those who authored so hideous a plot as the one that killed civilians and cadets alike in the crowded parking lot outside of West Point's Michie Stadium. The fatal explosion at the United States Military Academy rocked the beautiful Hudson River Valley from one end to the other. Everyone from Rip Van Winkle to the current mayor of New York City felt the area was a safe haven. The news of an explosion which transformed a celebratory mood on a gorgeous, autumnal Saturday afternoon into a scene of horror, yet another atrocity against all Americans, suggested yet another chink in the armor of American security. Just when the United States had finished emotionally digesting the thirteen killings by Major Nidal Malik Hasan at Fort Hood in Texas, after his long-overdue execution seemed to bring about an element of justice, the killings of innocent victims at West Point reopened old wounds all over again.

Sunday afternoon Hyun Lee sat among several guests in the lounge of a Chester County, PA inn. Guests were stunned and still listening to news reports from the scene of the tragic event inside the U.S. Military Academy. To the approval of everyone in the lounge, the bartender flipped from national news out of New York City to local news reports from little Emmit, Pennsylvania's satellite station. Everyone in the room wanted to know who would do such a horrible thing, so surfing the channels was perfectly acceptable.

No claim was forthcoming; not an honest one at least. North Korea would never touch this tragedy with a ten-foot kimchi cucumber. Instead the North Korean government issued a statement condemning the act of terrorism, expressing its sorrow for "...a crime against all humanity." Denouncing such behavior deflected any suspicion of its involvement.

In the spirit of the moment, Hyun Lee, alias Hoo Lin, appeared to reflect the feelings of those seated about her by openly lamenting the loss of anyone's life. "I pray to God no children were involved." No surprise to her, eventually a young man next to her bought her a drink and smiled a coy smile. Men like him disgusted her more than anything she had ever done to any of her victims. After all, she was a patriot, and this had been her job. What he was hoping had nothing to do with patriotism.

Later when alone in one of the inn's higher end accommodations, Hyun found herself in a reflective mood. Music played softly from the entertainment system perpendicular to her bed; she no longer wished to hear the evening reportage.

"One person and so many towels," she reminisced. "One sporting event and so many people." In her mind, the Secret Service never stood a chance. Hyun long prided herself in acquiring details regarding her targets. Ripkin's love for his alma mater, its tradition, and its athletic teams in particular had nearly slipped her mind. When she observed the arrival of Gabe Winters that sunny Saturday morning, she could hardly believe her own good fortune.

For a brief time, as she observed the Ripkin residence, she could only hope that Winters, too, was going to the football game. Time passed slowly as she sat in her vehicle and then did some walking on the streets that were lined with trees shedding some of the season's remaining orange and red maple leaves. She pretended to do some shopping in a small, local market. Finally both men exited the residence and entered the front vehicle together.

From the outset, the agents protecting both men were uncomfortable with the idea of attending the West Point / VMI game. Up until Saturday, each twelve-agent team had divided its day into eight-hour shifts.

In doing so, no squad would pull repetitive shifts, a plan meant to help keep observation skills and reaction times at their peak. By the time they were to depart for the Academy, they twice discussed how an unpredictable and overzealous throng of thousands might be a security nightmare. As a result of both sessions, both teams were insistent that Ripkin and Winters ride with them inside either of the black, nine-passenger, Special Edition Escalades transporting them. Altogether twelve agents were faced with staggering odds if something were to go wrong.

They were not agents lacking experience. The youngest on the squad, Alex Memphy, was thirty-two years old. The oldest, Jack Foster, was thirty-nine. Ripkin and Winters felt the agents took every precaution day after day almost to the point of being an annoyance, like little brothers who hang around older brothers and their dates. They periodically scanned both men's homes carefully as well as their respective private vehicles. Ripkin and Winters were followed everywhere as inconspicuously as possible. Agents observed the travels of both men from near and far, constantly staying in radio contact with other agents, often rotating vantage points to avoid tedium.

Once inside famous Stoney Lonesome Gate, a time portal for longtime Black Knight fans, federal credentials aided the Secret Service in procuring front row parking privileges outside one of the stadium's main gates. One Colonel in particular, a powerfully built man with the stereotypical close-cropped military haircut became indignant when told his long-time parking spot had been taken for the afternoon. It was where he had parked "...for every home game since the cadets had begun to play!" Fortunately for him, as it turned out, Presidential credentials trump a Colonel's hand every time. On this afternoon, having to park two rows further back saved his life although his brand new, burgundy Buick took a hit when one of the wheel covers from an Escalade sliced through his vehicle's windshield and removed its headrest. Also, parking Winters and Ripkin in the front row unknowingly put even more unsuspecting, exultant Black Knight supporters at risk. At game's end, decked out in Gold and Black, hundreds of fans were milling around what came to be known as the Bomb Site.

No one even noticed as the beautiful and athletic Korean assassin suddenly vanished under the shiny, black Escalade which had transported the extra agents who followed Ripkin and Winters to the game. She simply followed an older couple between some cars on their way to the stadium entrance. Hyun made a point of speaking familiarly to the couple on the off chance some security guards might think she did not belong. Neither of the older folks ever questioned her disappearance because they were excited about the afternoon's competition. Hyun learned their grandson was a participant.

To a man, each agent agreed it was incumbent upon all of them to accompany their charges into the stadium. Surely Security would be carefully watching the vehicles of their commanding officers. That assumption proved to be a fatal mistake for agents, Security, and spectators alike along with Winters and Ripkin.

It did not take Hyun very long at all to install and activate the explosive devices. The blast was to be extensive enough to thoroughly destroy several parked vehicles in the area of the blast. For her, the most difficult task was remaining undetected as she observed ankles and feet in a sacred procession until she could exit inconspicuously.

After that a waiting game ensued. Not wanting to be noticed as the only person walking in the stadium's massive parking lot, Hyun stayed in her rental vehicle and kept herself busy reading. She had to wait for the football game to run its course. Occasionally she would see a few folks leaving early, perhaps to beat the traffic jam that was sure to follow. She doubted Ripkin would ever be one of those. Michie Stadium was his cathedral, and he was not leaving the service early for any reason.

Throughout the afternoon she experienced crowd noise, cheering and applause that seemed to wash over the top of the stadium walls, much like waves in a bucket that had nearly tipped on its side. She thought about days when competition was a bigger part of her own life, and how her achievements brought her the attention of spectators and teammates alike. One big difference was most of her athletic involvement was relegated to an indoor setting. Hyun found the outdoorsy briskness of a sterling autumn day to be invigorating. She did not resent having to wait at all.

As band music faded and the exodus of fans began to increase, her mind cleared and she became 100 per cent focused. Young men, old men, and women of all ages seemed to depart almost reluctantly. Happy that their heroes on the field had maintained an undefeated season for yet another week, they were all of good cheer. Finally she saw Winters and Ripkin surrounded by the only twelve nonplussed people to leave the stadium. She waited until all the men were inside their rides, and then she detonated the explosives from a remote vantage point from where she witnessed the final seconds of her victims' lives.

The fury of the blast surprised even her. Briefly there was a fireball, but it was the sound of metal ripping apart and the scattering of glass which was followed almost immediately by wailing and screaming that was by far and away most powerful. Her sense of smell picked up on smoke and then fuel from some of the nearby vehicles. Simultaneously, she could see several dead victims strewn across the archway into the stadium as well as the injured writhing all about, unfortunate collateral damage in her mind. All of this was during the first minute after the blast. As planned, she awaited the departure of some folks who felt they must escape as quickly as possible, and it was among their line of traffic that she exited the Academy.

Back in her room on Sunday evening, she scarcely thought about that event anymore. Instead Hyun again attempted to contact Alan. "Where can he be?" she mumbled angrily to herself. She walked to her sliding glass door and opened it. Taking a seat upon her balcony, she continued trying to reach him for nearly an hour. She felt there was no point in leaving any more messages especially since in his male mind he would perceive her as being needy. That was the last thing she wanted him to think. When the street lights began to glimmer along Old York Road, she decided she had made her last call to Montana and Alan Wing. She considered making arrangements to fly west and her return to the beautifully scenic area around Falls Port, ridding herself of an unreliable employee who just became yet another person on her list of targets.

CHAPTER 31

Eli was upset, and he disliked being kept partially informed. He did not appreciate being told, "We will bring you up to speed once you are here", even when it came straight from his friend, the President. Certainly his college roommate and all of his underlings had gathered a great deal of information regarding the Saturday afternoon deaths of Gabe Winters and Jeff Ripkin. Twenty hours had passed. When he first took the call from the White House while still at Patty's house earlier in the day, he had asked for more details, but was told to pack his bags, to be patient, and to meet his flight to D.C. at McGuire Air Force Base as soon as possible.

During the flight he was extended every courtesy including a call to his wife. Rita's voice belied her attempt to sound confident and calm. "Honey, there are more agents in Falls Port now. I've met several. We're safe." She paused and added, "Don't worry about us." After a bit more about the horror of what had happened on Saturday, Rita attempted to change the subject of their chat in order to sound relaxed and to help Eli worry about his family less. "Know what I'm doing? Right now I'm overlooking the lake through the windows in our living room. More signs of late fall are here. There's a hint of yellow and orange in the remaining foliage on the trees." He heard her slide back her chair when she paused, and then she quickly added, "The birds feed constantly on the mountain ash berries in the yard, and earlier a mule deer stood calmly in the garden munching the few yucky tomatoes we didn't pick! All of the animals are preparing for winter."

He could have feigned similar confidence, and let his wife continue on this new topic, but Eli instantly opted for honesty. "Rita," he replied matter-of-factly, "be prepared to grab Ed and travel to D.C. at a moment's notice. Start packing now just in case. If it has to be done, I'll call you with specifics."

"Okay," she whispered over the shiny black cell phone she pressed to her ear. "Whatever it takes, Eli. But promise me you will be extra careful, too. No hero crap."

"Yes, Dear." His humor surprised even himself when it slipped out; that one button he pushed when he wanted to lighten a moment.

"Eli!"

"Sorry. I couldn't help myself. I love you, Rita." Then to show he was listening earlier he added, "Don't forget to have Edward pick up a few fifty pound bags of bird seed. Like you said, winter is coming."

She could feel his warmth across the miles. Then he surprised her.

"May I talk with Ed now for a moment? I'll remind him, too." Then he added, "See you soon. Love you."

Occasionally the smaller jet would rumble or bounce due to turbulence. Wisps of clouds raced by on the tips of its wings. The Atlantic offered a cold, cobalt blue appearance. He overheard Rita speaking to Edward, the conversation muffled, before Ed's voice came over the phone clearly. "Yeah, Dad. Oh...I'm so sorry about your friends. I still can't believe it."

Dad? Had he ever called Eli "Dad" before? It felt good, but in micro seconds Eli was all business again.

"Thanks, Ed. Now I'm gonna be straight with you. The three of us might be neck-deep in something dangerous. I need your help."

Quickly Edward sipped in a breath of adulthood and said, "Talk to me."

Eli pictured him sitting down at the kitchen table back in Falls Port. "I just told Mom the two of you might be called to D.C. for security reasons. It might happen. It might not." Eli felt the jet begin its descent ever so slightly. As the right wing dipped he saw more and more of D.C. "I don't have much time, so I'll come right to the point."

"Go on." Somehow Edward appeared to have taken on an older, more mature tone. He was, in fact, seated in the kitchen just as Eli had envisioned.

"Do not let her out of your sight."

"Okay. I can do that." Then he asked, "Anything else?"

"Edward, without you she doesn't even go to the –"

"Dad, I get it. Is there anything else?"

Eli reiterated that it was important that they plan on coming to D.C. "Both of you should begin packing for a quick departure. Time might be of the essence." And then he thought of something else. "Ed, don't be surprised if the agents seem impatient. They'll be professionally courteous, but they'll worry about timing. Okay?"

"Gotcha. Consider it done. And, Dad, be careful. We love ya."

"Love you, too, Ed." All Eli heard for a few minutes after that was the whining of the jet as its descent continued. Eli leaned back hoping he had said all he wanted to say.

Then as if he materialized from thin air, a steward approached. "Mr. Parks, we'll be on the ground shortly. Please make sure you've fastened your seatbelt. You'll be greeted by four government agents once the cabin door is opened."

Minutes later he was touching down at Andrews Air Force Base where he was ushered into what the Secret Service affectionately dubbed the "beast". President Rittenhouse had sent a Presidential limo to transport Eli to the White House. He was accompanied by all four agents and escorted by two other limos. In turn, they were preceded and followed by District of Columbia police.

"I wondered what this was like," he uttered to no one in particular in a friendly, relaxed manner.

The agent next to Eli on his right responded in a professional yet friendly tone. "Each of these vehicles is a tank."

"What do you mean?" Eli asked curiously. He welcomed the diversion from his never ending thoughts regarding Saturday.

The agents looked at one another and smiled. Again the young man to his right spoke to him. "Would you like the virtual tour?"

"Sure! I've long been curious about this."

The agent's name was Mike McLain. He went on to explain to Eli many of the limo's safety features. "To begin with, in the trunk right behind you are both an oxygen supply and fire fighting system. It's sealed perfectly in the event of a bio/chemical attack." McLain also explained that the fuel tank was foam-sealed. "It shouldn't explode even if it takes a direct hit."

"That's comforting."

McLain paused, and Eli was amused when another agent, Bill McElroy, seemed eager to fill in the gap. "The body is made of steel, aluminum, titanium, and ceramic. And thanks to eight-inch thick armor plating, each door is the same weight as a 757's cabin door."

"What about the glass?" Eli inquired. He was enjoying the company, so he attempted to continue the discussion.

"It's called 'transparent armor'. The glass is layered so that upon impact a bullet's energy is spread laterally, layer after layer. The final layer is a poly carbonate which literally catches bullets." Then the agent ran his hand over the glass as if to make a point. "Despite fragments and cracks on the outside, the inside of the window will remain as smooth as a baby's bottom."

Then there was a lull. Outside street lights flew by quickly. The vehicle moved along almost silently. Then a third agent added sheepishly, "And under you is a nylon explosive-resistant cloth installed from front to back to baffle explosions from underneath. However, what should make you feel most safe is that the vehicles in front of you and behind you are staffed with sharpshooters whose weaponry is state-of-the-art."

As they slowed to pass through the White House gates minutes later, Eli thanked each of the men for the information and said, "I'm glad we haven't had to test any of the equipment tonight."

The limo came to a stop. "Wait here, Mr. Parks," was all that was said once the doors were opened. Next he heard, "Okay, Sir, follow us." To an outsider, it might have seemed that each agent's demeanor had immediately become almost dark, bordering upon cold. But Eli took no offense. He knew they had to be on top of their respective jobs every moment they guarded their assignment. In that last instant before he was taken inside the White House, he fervently hoped that his family would be given the same top notch protection.

CHAPTER 32

From her bedroom, Rita heard car tires slowly stirring up some of the gravel on their driveway. It was twilight on Sunday. Looking out one of their bedroom windows, she saw Cary getting out of her truck, a red, sporty pickup. With sunglasses atop her head and a thick, soft, red elastic band holding back her hair, Rita was sure her friend turned a few heads along her way. For a moment, Rita marveled that some folks like Cary found the time and energy to keep their vehicles so clean. Rita headed for the kitchen when she heard Cary enter from the deck.

"Hello!" The sliding door glided open and shut.

"I'm coming, Cary! I'll be there in a minute."

Cary stood over the sink and looked out the kitchen window at the woods surrounding Rita's house. She could see a man down by the water securing both the footlocker on the dock and the ten-foot-long, flat-bottomed, aluminum rowboat lined up adjacent to it. It was not anyone she knew. She looked at the sky to see a few early evening stars twinkling. By all appearances, it looked like a lovely, cloudless night was in store. She heard Rita's footsteps coming up the hallway. "Hi."

"Your truck looks great!"

"Yes, I washed it...selling it to my cousin."

"That's a surprise. You have always enjoyed your truck." Rita gave her friend a hug. "What else is new?"

"Funny you should ask. I'd like to discuss something with you."

"Thought you might." Rita was somehow able to put on a smile. "Let me guess. It's about our fan club that's growing at the bottom of the drive." As she talked, she poured each of them a glass of red wine.

"Yeah...and down by the water and even in town." She tipped her glass in Rita's direction and gently sniffed the burgundy, enjoying its fragrance. "Nice wine glasses, by the way!" Cary walked to the sliding screen door that opened to the deck and spoke over her shoulder. "So tell me what the heck is going on. The fine folks of Falls Port are abuzz with gossip. First the helicopter show and now the invasion of 'agent ants' as they're calling them in town. The Driftwood will be cranking out all sorts of tall tales by the end of the week."

Rita leaned back. "I just can't get over how these agents do so little to play down the stereotype concerning their appearance. They stick out like a sore thumb with their perfect clothing and their sunglasses." She sipped her wine. "You know what I miss? The fun we have whenever we get together and play cards. It just felt so right." Pointing out the window Rita added, "*This* doesn't."

"You're right. They do project a presence, but I'm guessing that's a good thing. If anyone needs them, they're easy to spot." After a pause and a sip, Cary asked, "So tell me. Why exactly do you need them?"

They both turned their heads as Edward came out of his room. "Hi, Cary." He dropped his duffle bag by the forest green couch. "I'm ready, Mom." He picked up a book and plopped on the couch parallel to their fieldstone fireplace.

"Ready?" Cary uttered in a soft voice. "Where's Ed going?"

Rita put up her hands. "Hold on. Let's handle one question at a time. But first, let's go out on the deck. It's not too chilly is it?"

Cary shook her head and began getting up.

"Edward, Cary and I will be on the porch."

His head popped up momentarily. "Okay, Mom. If you go anywhere else, let me know."

"Okay, Dad." She walked over to him and kissed him atop his head. Then she playfully tousled his thick head of dark hair.

Once they were outside, Cary sat at the picnic table across from Rita. She tilted her head in Edward's direction. "What's that all about?"

Rita smiled again. "How many questions did you bring in that truck of yours?" She took a big breath and decided it was time to bring her confidante into the loop.

"If you think I have a ton of questions, wait 'til you sit down with the ladies at our next poker game. Don't think for a minute that Pat's radar hasn't been doing its usual, thorough job. She's going to have a field day with you."

As an occasional evening breeze released a few autumn leaves to the ground, the woods around them grew dark and even quieter. The stars grew more plentiful and the night sky was a quilt work of sparkles. All the while Rita told Cary things she never told her before. Deep inside she felt she was so close to Cary that it was important that she be told everything. In the end, it might keep her safe. Rita told her about Eli's work, some of the places it took him, and even told him about Eli's history with President Rittenhouse. Then after some internal mental debate, she informed her of the murder of Eli's first wife, and how yesterday's tragic events near West Point took the lives of two of his best friends.

"Okay. Stop there for a minute. Holy crap!" Cary sounded a bit overwhelmed. She reached across the table and gently put her hand on Rita's wrist. "Submarines, the President, and an assassin? Girl, you've moved into the fast lane!"

"Cary, Eli's always felt that his job was not that big of a deal. He and his buddies keep subs running quietly. Somebody has to do it. As for Elijah, he met him in college, and they were roommates. That was just fate."

"Oh! Now it's 'Elijah' is it?" She feigned surprise.

In return, Rita reached across the picnic table and gently grasped her friend's hands. "Cary, they were college roommates. The guy has a name."

"Okay. Okay. I get that part. But the part about a murderer becoming part of your life, that part rattles me." As best as she could, she stared right into Rita's eyes through the growing darkness.

Rita spoke quietly but with a noticeable worrisome tone. "How do you think I feel? It could have been me who was murdered. I keep wondering why it wasn't."

Cary looked off into the distance. "So that explains the need for security around here. I admire that." Then she had an odd thought. "Hey. Why wasn't I stopped when I drove up here?"

"Promise you won't be mad?" Rita held back a smile despite the seriousness of the discussion.

"What? Why wasn't I stopped?"

"They know all about you."

Cary took time to think about that. For a brief moment, she could not decide if she should be offended by Rita's answer or be flattered. She settled for the latter. "You mean you've given them a list, so to speak, of folks who are not a threat."

"Exactly."

"Well that makes sense. I'm not driving a vehicle with a trunk either. I can't hide my weapons." They both giggled briefly about that idea. "But Pat? I bet she's carrying. You might want to warn her!" They both joked about the scene that might cause.

Edward came to the door. "You ladies want some more wine? You left the bottle in here." His silhouette was that of a young man. His voice was gentle, and his consideration of them was gentlemanly.

"No thank you, Ed. Are you going to bed?"

He just stood there for a bit before he said, "No. Not yet." Then he walked back to the couch. They heard the television come on.

"He's quite a young man, Rita. He'll be a great catch from some lucky gal."

Rita sighed. "Yes, but right now he's like living with my father. I don't know what Eli said to him, but everywhere I go he insists on tagging along. He's like my shadow."

As the pair sat quietly under the starry night sky, Rita was also thinking about their current danger. It felt like a blanket that enveloped them. For Edward and all of them, she hoped that soon they could come out from under that blanket and live lives free of worry about their safety. She hoped her son would live long enough to be "caught" by some lucky young lady someday. However she did not share those thoughts with Cary. Cary knew anyway. Cary was thinking the same thoughts.

"You could have worse problems, I guess, but tell me more." Then she yelled out, "Ed! I decided I wanted some more wine!" He was there in a heartbeat. "Thanks," she said softly and gave him a smile.

"You're welcome." Once again he turned to go back to the couch.

"Honey, if you like, you may sit with us." Rita had no secrets to keep from him. In fact, occasionally she wondered if he knew more about what was transpiring than she did.

"Really? Thanks. But I think I'll watch my movie. You girls are too old for me," he teased.

"Ouch!" Cary snapped at him as he left.

When it was quiet again, Rita continued to bring Cary up to speed. The more her best friend knew, the less she would have to guess. Therefore Cary would worry less, too.

During the course of their evening, occasionally they were approached by an agent. They just wanted her to know that they were on guard. They wanted her to feel safe. At these moments she would thank him or her and would not see another agent again for an hour.

"So you're basically on standby. Is your bag packed? I saw Edward put his by the couch."

"Yes. That's what I was doing when you arrived." They sat in silence and enjoyed solitude for a while. Then Rita spoke up quietly. "You know, Cary, I don't know what's going to happen, but if at any point you feel you'd be safer here, you're welcome to bunk with us at a moment's notice."

"May I have a ticket to D.C.? I've never been there."

Rita laughed, but she knew she had made her point. Cary was such a close friend, she might become caught up in all of this webbing that was being spun; spun by a spider whose face no one but Alan had seen.

PART THREE

Henry the IV
by William Shakespeare

Falstaff:

To die [to blame others or run] is to be a counterfeit, for he is but the counterfeit of
a man who hath not the life of a man; but to counterfeit dying,
when a man thereby liveth, is to be no counterfeit, but the true
and perfect image of life indeed. The better part of valor is
discretion, in the which better part I have sav'd my life

CHAPTER 33

Ordinarily the Winston farm went unnoticed by anyone traveling up and down route 93. It bordered a pretty smooth piece of wide, blacktopped highway that proffered a scenic view of Flathead Lake. The lake and the Mission Mountains beyond are what most often captured any traveler's eye. The old farm consisted of forty acres nestled between the highway and the lake, bordered on all sides by tall pines and tamaracks. During autumn its grass was waist-high and golden brown. It waved gracefully in the afternoon breezes all the way from the guardrails along the highway down to the small, red barn far below. That barn replaced the larger, original one that was built long ago below route 93 which ran from Kalispell to the south. Off to the left of the barn sat the brown and white two-story, gabled homestead where Hyun and Alan had been living. Behind the residence was a large root cellar dating back 100 years or more. It had been dug into the gradually sloped hillside that began up along the highway. The root cellar was so large it had been divided into three rooms, the walls of which were constructed of stacked fieldstone.

However, on this October Saturday afternoon the Winston property was impossible to overlook. The spectacle of flashing red, white, and blue lights atop the brown Montana Highway Patrol cruisers adjacent to the barn caught the eye of everyone who passed by. After more than a few beers on Friday night, and after he finished gawking at more weaponry inside Hyun's packages that she had stored inside the barn, Alan decided he was out of his league. "I figured nothing good could come from this," he told the Highway Patrol officer who initially responded and arrived at the barn. "I have no idea what else she might have hidden around this place." They were already inside the wire cage when a second and third cruiser pulled up alongside the first.

The initial officer stepped to the barn door and called quietly to his counterparts. "Up here in the barn, Troopers." Alan was a bit uncomfortable with their formality. All three of the troopers were perfectly attired in their brown uniforms, complete with hats that reminded him of cops he had seen in movies and on various TV shows over the years. Like himself, each of them was physically fit. He nodded at the two most recent arrivals nervously and finally he was introduced.

Alan tried to make a joke; an attempt to relieve his own misgivings. "Any time I've been pulled over by the police I was never nervous. Now for the first time I called the police for help, and I have to admit that I'm more than a little unsettled."

"Have you done anything illegal, Mr. Wing?"

"Absolutely not." Alan did not know if the trooper was trying to intimidate him or remind him there was nothing to worry about. Quickly he decided to stifle any further attempts at small talk. He would just answer their questions and do anything which was asked of him. He began feeling a bit better when he overheard their respective reactions to his discovery in the barn and what he wanted them to see.

"Mr. Wing, please tell these troopers what you've told me before their arrival. Take your time; leave no details out; and if you can think of more, then tell us all of that, too."

Alan was rattled. He was hoping he had done the right thing. He knew he was innocent, but he wanted to make sure the police knew it as well. To emphasize he was merely an employee of the Korean woman he had come to know as Hoo Lin, he told his story beginning with the night she had rescued him further north on 93, just south of Kalispell. He felt that if they wanted him to move his story along they would tell him to do so.

He found the troopers to be patient. That helped him to relax which, in turn, aided him in his recollection of more details. Occasionally he was asked specific questions regarding dates, times, and locations. They seemed genuinely interested in the various places he had shown her, places she wanted to observe. He did his best to recall details and to be consistent whenever questions required that he re-tell a portion of his tale. Alan felt helpful as he reported various locations he helped Hyun visit. He emphasized how important observation and vantage points were to her. "Back then I thought she was just considering camera angles and such." He recalled the powerful binoculars and camera lenses she possessed, how she always had them along whether they were traveling in her pickup or in a boat all around Lake County.

When that string of memories seemed to exhaust itself naturally, one of the troopers probed another area. "Just exactly what was it that motivated you to break into your employer's storage bin and then her property?" he was asked.

Alan anticipated this question and finally it had been asked. "It was a combination of things actually. The first was how little I saw her write." He hesitated for a moment and then continued. "I mean isn't that what writers are supposed to do? I guess you could say I've questioned whether or not she is really a writer."

"You said you had more than one reason to violate her privacy." The trooper had a way of sounding accusatory, so Alan decided it was time to play his best card.

"Late night visits. She didn't think I knew about them, but I've seen things delivered here, and it was always done late at night. It seemed secretive to me, and she never once brought them to my attention."

"Could you identify any of these visitors?"

"Again, to be honest, it would be impossible since they arrived and departed in darkness. I can't describe the physical appearance of someone I didn't see." Alan waited briefly before continuing. "However, I do think they were Asians as well."

"Why do you think that?" asked one trooper.

Another almost simultaneously interjected, "You said you didn't see them."

Alan was surprised the obvious had not jumped out at them. "They spoke to each other in a language that wasn't English. She once told me she's Korean. I could hear them from my room." The troopers' respective body languages and facial expressions, no matter how well trained they had been, belied their nonchalance. Alan was certain he had their interest.

"How about names? Did she ever question you about folks living in this region?"

Being able to provide any nugget of seemingly important information made Alan feel more comfortable among them. "Perhaps it truly was coincidence, but her interest seemed to pique when I mentioned the name of my ex's friend's husband."

Each of them focused upon Alan a bit more intensely, and again he recognized it. It was as if he had let them in on a secret.

"Who is he?" the initial trooper inquired patiently.

"His name is Eli Parks. He's married to Rita Parks, my ex-wife's amigo. When I think of it I guess that would be 'amiga'." He immediately felt stupid when he saw their reaction to his Spanish lesson.

"How well do you know Mr. and Mrs. Parks?" There it was again, that Highway Patrolman formality. He made one little joke, and they shifted right back into that mode that seemed too professional to him. It made him uncomfortable again.

"Not very well." He paused and tried to summon up what he truly hoped to be pertinent. "Rita's a native. He isn't. She teaches in our school system here on the rez." He hoped the information helped regain their acceptance as well as his credibility, yet he could not figure out why their acceptance was so important to him. "He's not from Montana. I've heard he's from back east. Had a government job back there if memory serves. He's retired I guess."

All this time they had been milling about the barn and on over to the root cellar behind the house. Despite seeming to be a natural spot for more storage, the root cellar was empty. Alan felt as if he was losing their respective interests. Each of the troopers was intent on inventorying what he had shown them. They were taking notes. Then he mentioned that once he thought he had been told that Eli Parks worked out of D.C.

"Politician?" asked a trooper as he looked up from his notes.

"No, I don't think so. At least I never heard of a title, a position, or any campaigning."

"Anything else?" Darkness was approaching. They had been present for quite some time and seemed to be finishing their inquiry, but Alan had detected it was the "D.C." part that made the patrolman want to move the conversation along. Perhaps he wanted to follow that lead.

After all, they were in the presence of some serious weaponry and technology. He had shown them a pair of Sigsauer p229 pistols. He heard a trooper tell how it was the gun of choice among Secret Service agents. What Alan thought was an Uzi was not. It was a FN P90 or "P90". The troopers told him it was much lighter than an Uzi and was more accurate. At first, all of them were stumped by what turned out to be a laser dazzler which emits a single-colored light in pulses, thereby blocking any assailant's vision even during daytime operations. But the real eye opener was buried in the bottom of the pile. They found and would not even touch any of the stinger missiles to which Alan had unknowingly led them. Alan thought it probably would be a feather in any of their caps if they could tip off Washington, D.C. to a terrorist cell. He wondered if that was what he had helped uncover. He also wondered momentarily if he would receive any credit.

After a thorough check of the homestead, not long before dark all three cruisers left the Winston homestead behind fully loaded with all the new gear they had confiscated. Alan had shared all he could and was feeling as if he had just done something important. It felt good.

As the quiet around him intensified, he could hear subtle noises that had temporarily escaped him while he had company. Walking back to the brown, two-story residence and its porch which faced the ten mile width of Flathead Lake, he first noticed the sound of gravel underfoot. Those loud, obnoxious crows were actually silent, and a chilly breeze off the lake drifted through the nearby tamarack trees. Nighttime brought on a stillness despite the movement of the air. And then it hit him. Where was he to stay? Eventually Hyun would be back even if he did not meet her at the airport. His act of citizenry might well have put him in danger, and Alan Wing had some new decisions to make.

CHAPTER 34

Much to Eli's surprise, after Andy O'Neill greeted the four Secret Service Agents and thanked them for a job well done, and after Eli thanked each of the agents, he was not escorted to the West Wing of the White House and into the Oval Office. Instead Andy led Eli up the Grand Staircase and straight to the President's private quarters.

Upon entering, there was little time to appreciate the beauty of the large Yellow Oval Room where guests and dignitaries often are greeted by the President of the United States. However despite the sense of urgency on this occasion, the view from this part of the residence was not completely lost on Eli. Over the President's shoulder were floor-to-ceiling windows covered with white sheer curtains. Atop of them but drawn back were curtains of a heavier gold-colored fabric which accented the light yellow paint on the walls, giving the entire room a regal appearance. Two parallel couches sat in the middle of the room, accompanied by several antique stuffed armchairs decorated in burgundy and blue. A creamy-white fireplace was along the wall perpendicular to the beautiful windows looking over the famous, curved Truman Balcony which offered a view of the Washington Monument when lighted at night. It was easy to believe that the White House and the grand views of Washington, D.C. were meant to intimidate visiting heads of state. As long as Eli had known him, Elijah Rittenhouse always sought a home court advantage.

Eli was greeted by the President and shook his hand. Quickly it became an embrace. Eli spoke first. "Mr. President, I arrived as quickly as I could."

"I'm so sorry on so many levels, Eli." He stepped back from his college crony and continued. "First we lost Erin, and now we have lost the lives of your friends and other good people young and old."

"I appreciate your condolences, Mr. President, but you shouldn't beat yourself up over all of this." Eli looked at Andy who stood respectfully off to the side of the exquisitely decorated room; creamy-white woodwork around the floor accenting the fireplace while shelving and crown molding along the ceiling of the same color created a comfortable yet classic setting in which anyone could be comfortable. "All of us knew that a perfect security plan was elusive."

"Eli, it has happened on my watch," said the President sadly.

A gracious host, President Rittenhouse offered both men refreshments after they agreed time was of the essence. Both men declined politely, but food and drink were left upon the mahogany table between the two couches. They were alone, and they sat comfortably as they prepared to discuss the weekend's events.

"Until Saturday afternoon, Andy and I had every intention of attending tomorrow's memorial service with you." The President tasted his coffee. Then he continued as he looked Eli straight in the eye. "We are certain it's her, and we have to bring all of this to a halt."

"Do you suspect I'm being followed? Was my journey here this evening meant to force her hand?"

"I'd be lying to you if I didn't admit I wanted her on our turf, but no." He sipped more coffee. "No, I just feel as if I can protect you better if you are in D.C. Not only that, but we simply have to formulate a better plan."

Eli realized the time had come to voice that which was uppermost on his mind. "Sir, I don't know what to do about Rita and Edward. Part of me feels as if they are vulnerable if I agree to let them to stay back home." Rittenhouse could tell Eli was quite concerned, and it was a high priority to him. "But if we fly them here, perhaps they will be an easy target if Hyun Lee is here, too. If they were to stay in Falls Port, we might be able to turn the table on her."

"Andy and I have discussed this very thing, Eli. We were wondering if she might just be easier to spot if she were to go west." More coffee. "In D.C. it would be much more easy for her to blend."

Eli stood up and strode across the room and took in the view of the district. With his back to his company he asked, "Do we even know who she is? What do we have on her? What does she look like? Anything?"

As if on cue, Andy grabbed a file from the table adjacent to the couch upon which he was seated. Getting up he extended the folder to Eli. He said not a word.

The huge, oval-shaped reception room was silent. Only the turning of pages, an occasional sigh, and the ticking of Lincoln's clock in the distance were audible. Finally Eli looked up from the brief. He returned the file to Andy and indicated his thanks with a polite nod.

"How in God's name did we get involved in such a mess?" Frustration permeated his words. "We're engineers. We're not a threat to Korea or anyone else. We're not spies." As quickly as an electric current could have passed around the room, a glance was exchanged between the President and the President's Chief of Staff. Eli detected it. "What? What was that?"

"Sit down, Eli. We have some new information to share." Now it was President Rittenhouse's turn to stand. He put down his mug, and inhaled deeply. "How do I tell you this without losing your confidence?"

"Just tell me, Elijah." As a rule, Eli was always careful to address his friend properly when they were in the company of someone else, even when it was Andy O'Neill who would overlook any familiarity that might be exchanged.

The President sat back down. "Do you remember the incident involving the U.S.S. Helena and Captain Witworth?"

Eli's head snapped up. "Remember it? I was the cause of it."

"No you weren't." Then Rittenhouse emphatically pointed at Eli. "I hope you haven't been carrying *that* around with you all this time."

"I had to have him call you. I felt like I couldn't fight my own fight. I had to call in my big brother."

"You did the right thing. His ego was way out of line."

"Fine. Now just tell me how that incident has anything to do with what has happened to us lately." With a gesture of open hands toward Andy O'Neill, the President deferred to his Chief.

"Eli, when we suspected all of you were in danger, the President demanded to know why and what we could do about it. As you know, you were involved in the latter."

"And a lot of good that did," Parks uttered to himself. Subsequent to his comment, a period of respectful silence ensued. O'Neill and President Rittenhouse understood Eli's anger was directed at no one but himself. "I'm sorry, Andy. Go ahead."

The Chief of Staff continued. "My job was to head an investigation as to why all three of you were targeted. Initially it appeared that there was no single event or offense that motivated any aspect of the Korean government to want you terminated. Political instability, individual attempts at advancement within their government, and your successes with technology that frustrated Korean scientists and naval officers seemed to be all it took.

"Then we discovered that Korean operatives successfully gained information regarding your team, information not found in publications or journals anyone could access. We know now that they bribed one of our officers."

"Intrigued by the concept, Eli was compelled to ask. "How did you reveal that?"

"We pooled the names of officers with whom you worked during top secret assignments. That was our starting point for our investigation since we figured mundane assignments would be of little or no interest to anyone."

"Go on."

Andy presented his findings. "Well our investigation quickly resulted in one man who possessed two important characteristics: he not only had new, unexplainable cash reserves in his accounts, but he also experienced a run in with your team that was documented."

"Witworth."

"The coincidence was just too visible to overlook. And upon even more investigation, it turns out that his wife was angry over their divorce. Her revenge tactic was to spend as much of his money as she could while she could."

At this point President Rittenhouse added, "In an attempt to offset her spending, he invested poorly. He took a financial bath. The man did not have a Midas touch. He was desperate. Somehow the Koreans knew it."

Eli leaned back, looked upwards then squeezed his eyes shut. He grasped his head and brown hair in his hands. It was clear he was upset.

Upon witnessing his friend's reaction, quickly the Commander and Chief recalled sporting events, parties, classes, camping trips, and scholastic achievements all of which revolved around the two of them. "Eli, talk to me. You can't bottle things up."

Eli blurted out what he was feeling. "Witworth's problem wasn't with Gabe or Jeff. I was the one who bothered him. And now they're gone, and I'm not." He sobbed softly for moments. The only other sound that was audible was the ticking of that 175 year old clock off in the corner.

Rittenhouse moved next to his friend. "Eli, that's crap. The three of you were a unit. The presence of the team bothered Witworth. But there's more...more that will make you realize your confrontation with Witworth was not the cause of any of these horrible murders."

More silence. Then Eli spoke. "What else have you discovered?"

"I'll take it from here, Andy. Give us a moment." At that, Chief of Staff Andy O'Neill left the room. As he did so, he simply said, "I'll be down the hall." The President nodded his thanks.

Once O'Neill was out of the reception room, and once Rittenhouse felt Eli had regained his composure he continued. "I wanted you to hear this part from me." From the duration of the pause, Eli knew what his friend was about to announce was not easy.

"Just tell me, Elijah. Just tell me."

"Long version or short?"

Eli tilted his head as if he was surprised that there could even be a "long version". "Let's start with the short version."

The President again waited a moment and then he just quietly told Eli, "It turns out that Jeff was a spy, or an agent collecting information."

"What?" was the loudest and most vehement word spoken the entire evening. Eli stood up and looked down at his President. "Did you know this?"

"Eli, if I tell you I did, you might walk out of here thinking I knowingly put all three of you in danger. And if I tell you I didn't, I'm not sure you'd believe me."

Eli was disappointed he heard what was just said. His tone reflected it. "How long have we known one another? Why would I not believe you?"

"Because the President of the United States is supposed to have his thumb on everything that goes on around here. Is that not what every American citizen expects?"

By now Eli was pacing. He had to think things over. Finally he broke yet another lengthy silence. "Elijah, you tell me what's true, and I'll take it to my grave. You're human. How can you possibly know all that's going on in this spider web we call our government."

A relieved President Rittenhouse simply countered with, "I didn't know it, Eli. He even was assigned a second identity: Mitchell Dirlam." Then he showed why he was such a successful politician and leader. "Eli, if we are going to honor the lives of those we've lost recently, Jeff, Gabe, and the agents who gave their lives guarding them the best they could, we've got to quickly bring all of this to an end. I need you at your best."

He was challenging a constituent to accept partial ownership of the problem and the solution. It was a gamble, for no one knows how emotions will influence decision making. He awaited Eli's decision. In the meantime, he found Andy and brought him back into the room.

Andy's job was to fill in the cracks. He went on to tell Eli things about Jeff that Eli had not known. They were not really secrets that one would store in a closet to hide, but more like assignments for which Jeff's background and schooling had prepared him. He was young, energetic, and patriotic to the bone. Things he had accomplished were done quickly while Gabe and Eli were vacationing or sent off on two-man assignments of their own. They had been told Jeff had earned some time off or he was back in the lab. Quite simply, Korea had been on his itinerary. Although Jeff had never once stepped on Korean soil, he managed to connect with several of its operatives. Unfortunately, somewhere along the line he had irritated someone and made them suspicious. That is where Witworth came in. He simply verified that Jeff and the man the Koreans were seeking were one and the same. Eli Parks and Gabe Winters were simply guilty by association. The President was kept out of the loop: plausible deniability was the reason.

For a few minutes each of them mindlessly took a drink and a snack from the table in the middle of the room. Finally Eli's demeanor became phoenix-like, and the President received the response for which he was hoping. Eli simply said, "You're right. We have to do something about this. Where do we go from here?"

CHAPTER 35

Eli's arrival Sunday night dramatically altered the agenda of the President despite the fact that he had been thoroughly scheduled Monday for events throughout the day and into the evening. Originally he was to meet with Congressional leaders regarding legislation concerning the Southwest's recent, escalating border woes. A junket had been scheduled to Camp David later in the day by White House Transportation Coordinator Kathryn Sonner for yet another meeting with Secretary of State John E. Dougherty. Before leaving for Camp David, he was to partake in a photo session on the South Lawn among the four-time World Champion Philadelphia Phillies. However, the Parks Situation became a front-burner concern for everyone involved with security, especially after the deaths of so many people including Erin, Gabe, and Jeff. Nevertheless Rittenhouse did stop to meet with the team since it tied up very little of his time. Not only that, he graciously passed along former M.V.P. Ryan Howard's jersey to Eli and said, "Please give this to Jake." Then he added with the tiniest of boyish smiles, "I kept his hat for myself."

Throughout that same day, Eli was easy to contact. He was the President's personal guest in the White House residence, and President Rittenhouse found accommodating Eli was an easy task. "I want you as close to me as my schedule and lifestyle will permit," he informed Eli on Sunday night. "For only a short time, I hope, you're my roommate again."

"My my how the accommodations have improved!" replied the White House's newest overnight guest.

Rittenhouse never married. He once told Eli there was no particular reason. "I just never met the right woman when I was younger. As I became more serious about a political career, I truly had doubts that I could promise a wife and children an appropriate commitment."

As it turned out, opponents tried to put a negative spin on his bachelor status every time he ran for an office. The biggest question was always the same: "How can a single man relate to the problems of the American family?"

It was a shallow argument which he waded through pretty easily. "I grew up in a family. I have siblings, and I have wonderful parents. All of them have helped make me who I am today." That usually quieted critics faster than anyone expected.

Having been there more than once, Eli knew how to find the Oval Office on his own Monday morning. He was by no means alone at any point along the way, but he had no trouble finding the West Wing.

Upon entering the Oval Office through the second door of the President's Personal Secretary's office, Eli found several men and women awaiting him. Andy and President Rittenhouse were huddled over his desk, the famous Resolute desk which had been used by a queue of his predecessors. A large, nineteenth-century partners' desk, it was a gift from Queen Victoria to President Rutherford B. Hayes in 1880 and was built from the timbers of the British Arctic Exploration ship *Resolute*. The desk's intricate detailing carved into the wood all across its front included the Presidential Seal in the center of the panel.

Others in the room were standing and talking among themselves. Not until the President sat down upon a burgundy and gold-striped, overstuffed, wingback chair in the middle of the office did anyone else take a seat. All of those assembled had met Eli before. Together again, they hoped to formulate a plan of action that would terminate any threat against Eli and his family.

After Eli entered the office, the door was closed behind him by the President's secretary, Tessy Murray. She was a vibrant, loyal worker who knew when her President wanted his door closed and kept shut. The door's gentle closing rendered a solid sound, and since it was identical in color to the walls of the Oval Office, a bone-white eggshell, and there was no molding on the office side of the door, it was difficult to differentiate between the door and the walls surrounding it. Like a jigsaw puzzle piece, it became the final part of the famous oval-shaped room, and the door's disappearance created an extraordinary sense of enhanced security and privacy.

The view on this day outside the Oval Office through the long, floor-to-ceiling windows was brilliant, crisp, and clear, an artist's depiction of a fall day on canvas or film. Eli hoped that just such a day might help to lift the spirits of his son and Erin's family who were attending Erin's memorial service without him. He had spoken to Jake earlier via a secure phone provided by White House staff. "You know I want to be there with you, Son, but what we're doing here right now will make life safer for everyone as soon as possible."

Jake was maturing by the day, or so it seemed to Eli when he heard his son ask, "Dad, they're not using you as bait. . . are they?"

Eli did his best to assure his son that any meeting with President Rittenhouse would not end by formulating such a plan. "However, Jake, no one knows whether or not I'm being followed. If I am, all of us are on safer ground as long as I am here." Jake appreciated his father's honesty and told him so.

The remainder of the day continued without any problems. The memorial service was well-attended by family and friends who knew Erin Parks very well. There were several emotional moments throughout the day including the time for final goodbyes, which flew from everyone's heart silently after the conclusion of graveyard ceremonies.

As is customary in many religious communities, a gathering of supporters assembled for a luncheon. Much-appreciated condolences were received in Stan's and Patty's home. It was catered again by a group consisting of members from their church. Stories were shared. Some were new to Jake's ears, and others had been tossed about on other occasions. All of them were complimentary of his mother.

Not long after two o'clock everyone had departed graciously. Throughout the entire day, never once did anyone suspect they might be in any danger, nor was the presence of the Secret Service ever noted. "That certainly is a compliment to them," remarked Stan to his son Tim who stood by him in their front window as they watched friends depart in sundry vehicles. "It speaks volumes about their sensitivity to our needs during such a time." His arms gently extended around both his exhausted wife of twenty-six years and his tall, handsome son, nearly the same height as his dad. "Let's find Jake," whispered Stan, and together they turned to the kitchen.

After lengthy discussions in the White House on Monday, it was decided that Eli's family might be best protected by having Rita and Ed stay in Montana. It was agreed that spotting an Asian in and about Falls Port would be more easily done than in D.C. "There's no doubt we have an ample supply of agents both in Falls Port proper and surrounding your home," explained Oliver Fox, Director of the United States Secret Service operations. "I'm told that the locals have dubbed our people the *ants*."

Knowing the residents of Falls Port, Eli stifled a chuckle. To himself he silently quipped, "I can only imagine the chatter in the Driftwood these days."

Another reason for keeping Eli's family in Montana was the prevailing theory that it was impossible for Hyun Lee to be in two places at once. If she was not working alone, the Secret Service felt it was prepared on both fronts.

It was not possible to be involved in every conversation and meeting concerning his situation. Since much of the research being done by the Secret Service and FBI was done outside the White House, it was important that they knew where they could contact him quickly. So Eli Parks simply roamed the White House much of Monday. Occasionally he was required to answer a few questions or voice an opinion, and he was contacted via his protection. Never alone for a minute, Eli made the most of his day inside by asking questions, much like a tourist would do if given the opportunity.

He questioned the two agents who escorted him throughout the building about their respective families and homes. He chatted with them about their schooling and training for their careers. Eli found himself answering a handful of questions as well, some of which were of a personal nature about his friendship with the President. Most questions, however, were about his travels to other parts of the world. The agents were intrigued when he spoke about the oceanic wonders he had visited and those he had experienced firsthand.

"The oceans are amazing, and you could say they are the last frontier on the planet." Then he astounded them with his favorite bit of oceanic trivia. "If Mount Everest, the highest mountain on Earth at 29,029 feet, were set in the deepest part of the Mariana Trench, there would be 6,811 feet of water left above it."

As they continued to walk about the White House, he told them of his days in Japan. "Just flying there from the United States is a monumental pain in the keister." Eli began to share details regarding his most recent trip to the Far East. "I boarded here in D.C. Then I flew to Detroit, and it was from there that I flew directly to Tokyo." As if to emphasize the enormity of such a trip, Eli rolled his eyes widely. "I was in the air nearly twenty hours, and that was followed by a ninety-minute ride to the base in Sasebo." The agents admitted they had yet to leave the continental United States on anything job-related. One of them had been to Hawaii on his own time.

When asked what he remembered most or found most striking about the Japanese culture, Eli taught them what impressed him most. "*Vertical* is an important concept in Japan since land is at a premium." He went on to explain that hotels had some parking, but public parking garages "... are like carousels in that you park your car on the ground level in a slot, get out, and the floor/elevator combination puts your car in an available location."

Eli enjoyed sharing much of what he had seen in Japan. "I climbed a portion of Mt. Aso, which is the largest active volcano in Japan located about two hours from Sasebo." Then his facial expression took on an excited look when he recalled Japanese castles, noting their respective architectural beauty and historical significance. "Japanese castles were fortresses composed primarily of wood and stone. They evolved from the wooden stockades of earlier centuries, and came into their best-known form in the 16th century. Like their European counterparts, the castles of Japan were built to guard important or strategic sites, such as ports, river crossings, or crossroads, and they almost always incorporated the landscape into their defense."

The agents enjoyed every minute they spent with their guest. They found Eli to be engaging and a great listener as well. They kept a leisurely pace, and the day seemed to pass quite nicely.

After the decision was made to keep Rita and Edward in Montana, Eli was desirous to rejoin his family. He could not let himself stay in D.C. much longer. He considered making arrangements for his return on Tuesday, but he knew it would take a little bit of convincing when it came to telling his old roommate. Twilight was setting in and stars were just beginning to dot the evening sky over the nation's capital. Due to time constraints and previous obligations, Eli did not see the President again until the following morning.

Tuesday morning was bathed in golden, early-morning sun, and at Eli's request, the two men temporarily left the President's Office in order for Eli to share his decision privately. He wanted his friend to know first, and he wanted to tell him to his face.

"You know I'd rather you stay right here, Eli."

"I know. I know, Elijah. But I can't live with myself if I do that. If Rita and Ed might be in danger, I belong there with them."

During the walk back to their next meeting with Security Advisors, the President assured Eli that he would have an aircraft available for him, and Eli would be back in Falls Port at his earliest convenience. All of that having been said, the two men departed the West Wing portico, and re-entered the Oval Office.

The President's office was abuzz. During the brief span in which the two men spoke privately, there arrived two reports from the J. Edgar Hoover FBI Headquarters blocks away. The first came from Pennsylvania while the latter arrived from Montana.

Presented with all the new information, Secret Service and F.B.I. agents from both states contacted their respective headquarters, emphasizing both agencies work closely together on this particular case. At light speed, what they had passed on to their Washington Field Offices found its way to the President's ear. It was with permission of the FBI that Secret Service Director Oliver Fox relayed this tale to the President and Eli. Andy O'Neill and everyone else present listened intently to the details of both reports and awaited their respective reactions.

The local police within miles of the Parks residence in Hillsdale had investigated yet another murder. This time the victim was a thirty-one year old male, and it was possible his murder could be linked to the death of Erin Parks. The victim's body was discovered by a housekeeper in a room he had rented while he was staying at the Crooked Billet Inn in Emmit, Pennsylvania. Hillsdale Township and Emmit collaborated on the case, so Chief Monroe was involved in the investigation.

Several pieces of information resulting from the Emmit-Hillsdale investigation were of particular interest. As in the case of Erin Parks, the victim appeared to have shown no signs of a struggle. His door was intact, and his room was orderly other than the blood that had been spilled. There were no signs of vandalism or robbery. And as in the case of Erin Parks, it appeared the gentleman had been shot with a .22 caliber pistol. Once again no shell casing or bullet was found.

It was a third piece of information that was of tremendous interest to Chief Monroe, Agents Bystrom and McGee, and the White House.

Emmit and Hillsdale detectives collaborated to assemble and interview all Crooked Billet employees quickly. It was fortuitous that Chief Monroe actually interviewed Sunday afternoon's lounge bartender. Monroe listened intently as the bartender reported having seen the victim with an Asian woman during Sunday afternoon's Happy Hour. "He bought her two drinks," recalled the young man. "I remember this because I found it amusing that an Asian would order Irish Coffee."

Detectives from both police departments were few in number, so they collaborated, especially since they knew the White House might benefit from their findings. Any surveillance recordings the Inn could provide were collected and screened much more quickly as a result of their team effort. Eventually Chief Monroe was contacted. As he stood shoulder-to-shoulder with the Emmit Chief, what he found in front of him on a monitor was confirmation that at the very least, an Asian Woman had been inside the lobby of the Crooked Billet Inn several times between Saturday night when she checked in at 10 p.m. and Sunday afternoon as she casually passed to and from the lounge. They established a face, but lacked an identity.

Next the Front Desk was enlisted. It eventually provided records of their weekend guests. Those records confirmed Chief Monroe's suspicions. The Crooked Billet Inn had been host to a Ms. Hoo Lin in Suite Number Seven. He recognized her alias from a list provided earlier when he said goodbye to Agent Bystrom. He cringed when he read her supposed place of residence: Washington Street in Newburgh, NY, a small city located only minutes from Saturday's disaster at West Point. He was not sure if she was bold or stupid.

The Front Desk at the Crooked Billet Inn assisted in determining that Ms. Lin had made a phone call to Gulliver's Travel Agency in Emmit on Sunday. The call had been made from her suite. During the subsequent interview with the travel agent, a Mrs. Opal Hocker, detectives learned Ms. Lin had attempted to book her flight to Montana via the internet. "She told me about that. She was frustrated with the various airline websites because none offered her a seat on flights leaving soon enough to meet her needs." Mrs. Hocker went on to share how Ms. Lin emphasized her need to be in Montana on Monday. "She was polite, but she was assertive. At great expense to her and with a bit of luck, I was able to board her on a 9:30 a.m. flight out of Philly. The cost of the transaction didn't faze her in the least."

When detectives presented four photographs of four separate Asian women, Mrs. Hocker immediately identified her unforgettable client. The police had proof positive that the Crooked Billet Inn's weekend guest in Suite Seven and the travel agent's visitor were one and the same person. They had a name to put with her face.

After speaking with Chief Monroe, both Agent McGee and Agent Bystrom thanked him. They requested that both police departments remain vigilant for any other suspicious activity in their townships. "Keep an eye on the Parks boy and his family, too, Chief. We know the President will appreciate that."

It was the final report that convinced the President that Eli should be on his way back to Montana. Citing the intel, Mr. Fox reported how a Mr. Alan Wing of Falls Port, Montana had contacted the Montana Highway Patrol, and how he had shown the troopers a cache of advanced weaponry he had discovered upon a property where he had been employed by an Asian woman. "Her name, he claimed, is Hoo Lin," added the Director emphatically.

As President Rittenhouse listened to Fox, he looked at Eli and noticed his friend's startled expression. "Eli, do you know this Alan Wing?"

"Sir, everyone in our town knows Alan. It's a small place. He was once married to my wife's best friend." Then he recalled something else that bothered him. "Mr. President, my wife's friend has lived at our house on occasion because she was afraid of Alan Wing. Now you're telling me he worked in conjunction with the Montana Highway Patrol? He knows Hyun Lee by her alias and worked for her?" The excited tone in Eli's voice cut through the otherwise quiet room. "And D.C. is just *now* learning about this? Mr. President, I have to get back home."

CHAPTER 36

Due to an extended weather-related layover in Salt Lake City, Hyun landed in Missoula at 5 p.m. Otherwise, her last-minute journey across the United States was uneventful. She had no inkling she had left the east coast a full day earlier than Eli Parks, or that he was even on his way home. It was only a stroke of luck on her part that he was departing on Tuesday.

Flying on Monday was doubly fortuitous. Being of Asian ancestry went unnoticed, so airport security was not a problem. If she had flown on Tuesday, her presence would have triggered red flags and alarms, but Monday was just another day.

On this trip, she decided to travel northwest under her own name, for it was doubtful the rental service would rent to Hoo Lin a second time. Alan's disappearance made renting another vehicle a necessity.

Dressed in a business suit of charcoal gray, hair tied back behind her neck, and wearing conservative heels, Hyun's appearance portrayed a professional image. Her choice of a four-door Pacifica was not a surprise to the young lady making the arrangements. Hyun's only request was a GPS unit. "I've never been to Falls Port before," a lie she produced in a matter-of-fact tone.

"Then a GPS unit will be a big help to you!" replied the smiling rep from across the counter. Her voice was sweet, and it would not have surprised Hyun at all to learn it was the young lady's first week at her new job. Sally and her shiny nametag oozed enthusiasm.

Hyun smiled and gently took the keys from her hand. Soon she was walking by the airport's ten-foot tall grizzly enclosed in glass and into the ladies room just behind the gift shop near the center of the lobby. She strode into the lavatory looking every bit the cover girl for "Successful at Business Quarterly" and exited in casual jeans, hiking boots, and a hooded, burgundy University of Montana sweatshirt, standard issue for half the people living in the Big Sky state. Her jet black hair was flowing, and her travel bag was over her shoulder. Any of this would have been scrutinized twenty-four hours later, but not on an ordinary Monday.

Riding up 93 North out of Missoula gave her time to recall the first time she traveled alone in Montana. Those memories reminded her of her initial encounter with Alan. It irritated her to no end that he had proven to be unreliable. "Never bite the hand that feeds you," she said to her invisible passenger. "I rescued your tail, and this is how you reward me?" Men who crossed Hyun Lee always regretted having done so.

Fifteen years earlier Hyun was becoming a rising star in Korea, and her family was hitched to her success. More than anyone, her brother had become an annoyance. Spoiled by the advantages of being a celebrity's sibling, he often complained that items he wanted were not coming his way fast enough. "Don't blow this, little sister," he said one day as they shopped in a mall which catered to privileged citizens. "I don't want to live like we used to live ever again."

Week after week and month after month she heard criticism from her father and her brother when the family ate meals together. Rarely did they congratulate her upon her successes, and never did either of them thank her for having improved their social status. They took her for granted, and more than a few times she wanted to quit, but that never could happen. As much as she was a member of the Lee family, she gradually became the property of North Korea even more. Quitting was no longer an option for athletes who could bring glory to their nation.

During one such frustrating moment in particular, Hyun found herself with her ungrateful brother yet again. They had just finished eating in a food court, and he insisted she accompany him through a technology store. He spoke to her as if she were a second-class citizen. Others present looked over their shoulders at him, and then they would look at Hyun. He had continued yet another series of disparaging remarks when she decided he had crossed over an invisible line. "I am not a subordinate to you," she screamed at the top of her voice. Subsequently her reaction to his jibes was as quick as it was powerful. Inhaling deeply, she summoned all her energy to a point in her fist, and she turned on him so fast he never saw what was coming. A two-punch attack not only broke his nose, but also damaged his voice box as well.

His collapse to the floor was immediate and was followed by a collective gasp from everyone in their vicinity. The manager and an assistant rushed to her brother's side, wide-eyed in wonder that a girl of such diminutive stature could level a muscular, young man of more than 175 pounds. Her brother gasped for air as he writhed on the cold tile floor, scared that he might not take another breath ever again. The reprimand she was later forced to endure from her father and her coach was harsh, but it was well worth it. Her brother never bothered her again. That day was a turning point in Hyun Lee's life. Never again would men intimidate her, possess her, or make her feel less important.

It was dark as she drove through Ronan just 25 minutes from the Winston place. "If he's there, I'll kill him. If he's not there, I'll find him and kill him." The further she drove the more irritated she became. Unfortunately she let her anger distract her, and Hyun lost track of her speed. When flashing lights appeared in her mirror, she glanced down to see a digital readout announcing she had the Pacifica cruising at more than 100 miles per hour. Somehow in a land where speed limits were famously unlimited, she had caught the eye of a Highway Patrolman. She slowed and eventually pulled over to the side of the highway just three miles south of Falls Port. It was only a little past 7 p.m., but it was dark. Only two cars drove by as the officer approached her from the rear of her rental.

She was seething. In the back of her mind, she had no time for Alan let alone a Montana Highway Patrolman. Time was of the essence. She felt that time was wasting. She believed that Eli Parks and his friend, the President of the United States, would be in her rearview mirror all too soon. Hyun's next decision was a snap decision.

The officer gestured that Hyun lower her driver's side window. He leaned down just enough to enable Hyun to see the fear in his eyes in that instant he realized his life was nearly over. It took only a muffled single shot to bring the patrolman down. The quick, intense pop from her silencer was followed by the heavy collapse of dead weight upon pavement. Air that rushed out of the officer might have been mistaken for a grunt. Emotion never came into play; not even for a moment. Hyun was on a mission, and she wanted to bring it to a conclusion. Nothing was going to stand between her and a successful completion, especially a man; even if he was a man with a badge and gun.

She saw a brief window of opportunity. No one was in sight up and down the flat stretch of dark two lane highway. As quickly as she could, she dragged the officer back to his cruiser. She turned on the ignition but killed the lights, and then she set him in his seat behind the wheel. For two hours occasional travelers passing by simply thought the patrolman was watching for drunken drivers.

"Here I come, Alan," was all that Hyun said as she pulled back onto the highway. No one was going to stop her now.

Thirty-five minutes later Hyun pulled off the highway onto the Winston property. The trip had seemed as if it was endless. She saw no lights at all inside of the house, and her rental pickup was nowhere to be seen. She wondered momentarily if Alan had passed her on his way to Missoula to pick her up at the airport after all. Then she also wondered if he might have stupidly traveled to Kalispell and the wrong airport altogether.

Hyun gathered her carry bag and opened her door. As she stood and then approached the house she saw headlights splash over the driveway, and she heard the tires turning slowly upon the gravel. Then for the second time in an hour, she saw the panel of red, white, and blue lights begin flashing atop another Highway Patrol cruiser. "This can't be happening," she uttered to herself angrily.

Not knowing they were assigned to simply watch the property, she watched them slow to a stop. Hyun Lee was not scared. She was infuriated. She was not intimidated by police presence. She felt as if she was being inconvenienced. "I can't deal with them now," she muttered.

Much to the surprise of the two officers assigned to watch the Winston homestead for her return, Hyun walked right up to their car. They never had a chance. She leveled her pistol and took out both patrolmen with two shots. Glass shattered and the screams of two young patrolmen died out as quickly as they were emitted. Like a nerveless automaton, she stood by the cruiser momentarily. Not even the sight of gold bands on their respective left hands bothered her one bit.

After she quickly ended their lives, Hyun wondered why the patrolmen were even on the property. Too, she wondered if they had been in contact with other officers. She had to work quickly under the assumption that they had.

Reaching in through the open window, her right arm grazed the chest of her first victim. She flipped off the panel of flashing lights, turned off the headlights, and turned off the cruiser's engine. Her own headlights faced the house, but they provided enough light for the beautiful, cold-blooded killer to gain access to the cruiser's radio unit. She turned up the volume a little, adjusted the squelch, and listened. In a few minutes, it was clear to her that no communication had been shared before she had taken the lives of two more officers. However she was smart enough to understand that they were on the property for a reason. She decided to gather her supplies in the barn and get away as quickly as possible.

Approaching the front steps to the old homestead that had become her base of operations, Hyun suddenly was aware of an incredible solitude. She felt the building's loneliness. It was a tangible presence that surrounded her. Prior to this Monday night, rarely was she alone on the property, so she never fully realized the disparity between her earlier city environs and Montana's rural nights. Even when Hyun was finally inside and had turned on a table lamp near the front door, she was not at ease. Much of what she accomplished in the recent past was done alone, but on this night loneliness never felt so omnipresent.

Entering the house she was looking for any kind of message from Alan that explained his disappearance. She found none. Needing light to simplify her walk to the barn, Hyun flipped the second light switch by the door. The gravel drive leading up to the barn was bathed in light. From the window, tall, brown grass could be seen bordering a path to the barn next to the driveway. She noted the barn's door was partially open, and to her that was a breach of security.

Her walk from the house took only minutes. Nevertheless, having rested little for days, Hyun was exhausted. Climbing the stony incline had become a chore she had not noticed other days. At her side, she carried with her a large flashlight in her right hand, and it seemed heavy. "If I could only get some sleep," she complained to herself in a whisper. Still she forced herself to continue; needing to gather the tools of her trade.

Opening the large, rustic door with her left hand, she raised the lamp in her right and activated it with her thumb. Suddenly a pair of white, heart-shaped faces and dark eyes of two barn owls silently swooshed their brown wings across the flashlight's beam, passing right over Hyun's head as she ducked. Despite weighing little more than a pound each, their forty-inch wingspans unnerved her. She dropped the yellow, plastic portable lamp to the ground. Unexpected harsh screams from the raptors were as piercing as her own scream of fear that echoed across the night. Hyun's heart pounded forcefully in her chest as if it were about to explode.

Many moments passed before she regained her composure. Bent forward at the waist and with her hands on her knees, she took deep breaths to calm herself. Eventually the dropped flashlight was noticed upon the ground in front of her. It was in two pieces, and its four batteries had scattered. Thanks to the splay of light from the peak of the house she was able to reassemble what first she thought was broken. Hyun turned the flashlight on again as she attempted entering the barn a second time.

From a light that pre-dated three-pronged electrical outlets and even WW II, she knew a pull-cord hung inside the barn door. Hyun groped for it with her outstretched left hand. At last, upon a wooden crate she clumsily dragged inside the barn door, she was able to secure the cord and turn on the light fixture high above.

Had there been a distant bystander, he might have mistaken her silhouette for that of a suicide victim, for Hyun stood perfectly still, atop the box, head down in disbelief for several moments as if she was suspended by the pull cord above. Her equipment, all of it, had been removed from her bin. She felt as if her intrinsic right to privacy had been violated despite the fact that she was a criminal, and assassin, who deprived seven children of their fathers' returns that night. Hyun Lee was the epitome of a cold-blooded killer.

When she finally stepped down from her vantage point, she tore into what was once Alan's storage bin twenty feet from her own. It, too, was empty. She formed an accurate scenario in her mind. She envisioned Alan discovering her equipment, calling the authorities, and leaving the property to avoid her wrath. Perhaps the police kept him locked up because of suspicion, but that was unlikely if he initiated the contact with them. They might have instructed him to contact them if she contacted him. She was on thin ice.

"He definitely called them," she thought aloud. "That's why the police were present immediately following my arrival."

The clock was ticking. She needed to act quickly and desired to know what he had told them; wanted to know how many wheels he had set into motion. She wanted to find him and make him suffer as she interrogated him. Then she would dispose of him.

"If I'm Alan," she quizzed as she massaged her forehead, "where would I go?" Hyun stood, deciding upon a best answer to her own inquiry. Finally she decided he would approach family and the few friends he might still have.

She did not even bother to turn off the light inside the old barn, and hustled back to the house as best as her weary legs would carry her. Although beset with complications, she required sleep, yet could not sleep in the house. Surely the police would grow curious about the disappearance of their co-workers assigned to the Winston estate. Hyun chose to gather her things and take time to rest elsewhere and soon.

Back inside the house a few essentials were gathered. She moved economically about what had been her room. No seconds were wasted despite how sluggish she felt. Training and experiences taught her the difference between necessary and frivolous items. Guerilla tactics required hiking boots not dress shoes or sneakers. She grabbed layers of clothing that would provide warmth without making her bulky and clumsy. A hood always served better than a hat. A butane lighter was a valuable tool, and it was easy to carry. Her nylon, camouflaged-colored shoulder satchel freed up her hands. After all of these items and others had been collected and deemed important to her success, she quickly searched for her set of keys for the pickup truck. "He might have it, and I want it."

To the casual observer she might soon encounter, she looked no different than any other exhausted outdoor enthusiast, a breed not uncommon in northern Montana. But before she went too far, she had to get some sleep.

CHAPTER 37

It was dark, and the night air along the lake's edge had cooled to the point where it was a little uncomfortable. Hyun knew she could not leave the Pacifica she had rented in Missoula at the Winston house, but she could not waste valuable time hiding it either. She rolled the proverbial dice by driving along the winding, macadam road that paralleled the lake's shoreline until she soon discovered a subtle, off road location, probably worn by high school kids who also wanted a place to hide for different reasons.

From there she walked back to the fiberglass boat which Alan had kept docked below the house since the weekend they had arrived together. Branches occasionally tangled in her hair, and on two occasions, scratched the left side of her face enough to sting. She was overtired, growing impatient, and swore under her breath when these things happened. "Sheikkeh!"

The boat belonged to Alan's parents, but it was he who used it most and cared for it as well. An avid outdoorsman, he loved to fish as well as hunt. And thanks to his careful maintenance, Hyun was able to insert the key she brought from the house and start the Mercury 90 hp outboard engine with no trouble at all. She then trolled as quietly as she could the short distance back to her car's location among the trees, dropped the small anchor she knew was at the stern of the boat under a seat, and slept under several beach towels while using a life jacket for her pillow. It was not in the least comfortable, but it had to suffice.

Hyun woke up to pronounced slaps of water against the hull of the red and white Chaparral as it rocked gently. Alan had preached to her about the dangers of sudden movements upon a boat. He had taught her other important things as well; things important to her success on this day. She had learned not only the whereabouts of his ex-wife's home along the lake, but also the location of his parents' house across the lake a few miles from Cary.

She had slept upon the boat for several hours. Before sunrise, the vibration of her cell phone and the beeping of her wrist watch were both a necessary annoyance. The night had been cool, but she was grateful for the rest. She felt energized compared to how she had felt only a few hours earlier.

From the twenty-five foot fiberglass boat's glove box, she retrieved the binoculars she knew would be there. "Alan didn't find these in the bin," she said quietly to herself. Unlocking and uncovering the refreshment cooler/console also revealed that he had not discovered all her weapons as well. "Never put all your eggs in one basket, Alan." The sky had only begun to lighten in the east above the mountains, a paler shade of sky blue, so she had time to make her plans.

Using what little darkness was left, Hyun lifted the fifteen pound anchor only to drop it on the side of her foot when the wet line slipped through her grasp. "Owwww, Shiekkeh!" she yelled and then she realized she might have just given away her position if anyone was in the area and looking for her. Quickly she turned the boat key in its ignition, grateful for the immediate desired result. For a while, she moved the boat quietly, for she did not want to produce any sound if she could help it. Alan might have taught her a few things about safe boating, but she was smart enough to stay within her ability level as she gradually accelerated across the smooth water of Flathead Lake.

In fifteen minutes, she slowly approached the eastern shore and moved towards the water's edge not far from the Wing residence, a lake-side cabin-like structure which sat thirty or forty feet above the level of the water. A rocky and tree-filled property bordered the wooden steps that extended from the back of the cabin to where the dock was anchored during the summer. For winter, the dock had been removed from the lake and drug upon the shore. In fact, most docks had been removed from the lake. Alan's makeshift dock at the Winston place was only one of a limited few still on the water.

As she had hoped, there sat the pickup she had first rented in Kalispell. "Alan is so predictable and foolish," she thought. "He probably left the keys in the ignition." Compared to snuffing out the lives of the three young patrolmen, stealing her own rental was nothing more than a blip on the screen. "I just wish I had the time to find that *jaji* and end his life as well." Luckily for Alan and his parents, she feared such an action might stir up more attention than it was worth.

She disembarked from the boat in ugly, green knee-high rubber boots that protected her from the shallow, chilly lake water under the boat. She pulled the boat ashore and did not care that the lake's rocky bottom might damage the hull of the craft. In fact, she thought it was sweet revenge for what he had taken from her. "Chasing this boat or dredging it up off the bottom should keep him busy for a time," she whispered to herself. She was going to push it out further, but then realized that if for some reason the truck did not start she might need the boat, so she just let the bow sit upon the rocky beach with the stern in shallow water.

Hyun removed the clumsy boots, and with much stealth she nimbly moved over the rocks and between the evergreens to where she finally was able to get inside the truck. "If there's no gas in this, I will kill him."

As she had predicted, a matching set of keys dangled from the ignition. Not wasting a second, she started the vehicle, cringed at its explosive engine noise, and accelerated carefully away from the Wing residence. Relieved to see there was plenty of gas, Hyun eventually began picking up speed as she approached their road's end where it joined East Shore Drive and headed south. Hyun accelerated toward Falls Port at the southern end of the lake. Out her window, above the tree-covered mountains to her left, the sky continued to take on a shade of lighter blue and gray.

Out the passenger side, below the western horizon, darkness enveloped lake's lower shoreline where Cary lived alone.

On that chilly Tuesday morning at such an early hour, Falls Port was predictably quiet. Hyun continued along East Shore Drive in a southerly direction until it intersected 93 North. As much as she wanted to continue at a greater speed, she patiently awaited the traffic signal's change and made a right hand turn that took her through town. In the Falls Port business district, 93 was locally referred to as 2nd Ave West, and upon it Hyun passed various stores unnoticed before driving over the bridge leading out of town.

Only the Driftwood Café showed signs of life, opening like it had every other day at six o'clock in the morning. The trucks of a few regular early birds were aligned in the Café's lot, all of them facing 2nd Avenue as if they were to be reviewed and revered by passersby. Proximity to the eatery's front door signaled the morning's earliest arrival. More often than not, that honor befell Hoppy and his mud-encrusted Dodge Ram. He considered himself the Café's unofficial greeter. He was fond of chortling, "One of these days Brenda's gonna break down and get me one of them blue vests like the old geezers wear when they greet us over at Wal Mart!" Hoppy was never shy.

After crossing the bridge, locating Cary's home took more time than Hyun wanted to spend looking for it. She was certain Alan would notify the local police when he realized the Ford truck she had rented was missing from his parents' driveway. What she did not realize was that in tiny Falls Port the Police Department was comprised of retirees and part-timers, so they rarely began their police work before noon. Hiring one or two full-time officers had long been rejected by the Community Council since salaries and benefits would have cost more than they were willing to spend.

At first glance, the beautiful albeit exhausted assassin did not recognize Cary's place and drove by it. Seen from Alan's boat from the lake side her home was largely decorated with field stone as was its fireplace. However the road side of her house, which was considered the rear to locals who lived upon Flathead Lake, was accented with dark brown wooden shakes. They had not faded at all, so it was obvious she kept her home in repair. It was the fireplace that caught her eye during a return drive down the cul de sac, and she recognized her mistake. Observing the house from the road and the many himu or ponderosa pines that populated the property, Hyun was surprised at the steep incline that began aside the building and stopped at the lake's edge. From the water, the grade had gone unnoticed.

After hiding her truck and having determined there were no agents on site after Cary's departure, entry into Cary's home was easy after Hyun located the alarm system's external wiring, disabled it, and shattered the kitchen door window. She was uncertain when Cary would return, but it did not matter. She would wait until late evening if necessary.

As she waited patiently, Hyun tossed around the idea of capturing Cary, Rita, and even Edward in order to lure her final target right into her trap. Temporarily she even considered taking them hostage right in Cary's home. However, despite its tempting creature comforts, the more she thought about holding them prisoners in Cary's house, the more she disliked that idea. "Too many obstacles, too many variables with the neighbors being right down the road, and almost no clear vantage point from any part of her house." She decided to adhere to her original plan.

CHAPTER 38

Eli flew back to Montana upon Executive One, or so it was named whenever President Rittenhouse was aboard. When he was absent, the lavishly appointed Gulfstream V was merely a C-37A, another United States Air Force transport of the 89th Airlift Wing out of Andrews that cruised just under Mach 1 when necessary. Eli once again found himself in the awkward position of being the jet's only passenger other than the two pilots, the flight engineer, the communications system operator, and one flight attendant. An empty navy blue couch and two mahogany desks as well as eight empty, cream-colored swiveling recliners were there to remind him the entire trip that he was their sole traveler. Ordinarily the plane was filled with government and Defense Department officials, but today it was all his once again.

As they raced across the sky above a thick, white blanket of cloud cover, he stared out his large, oval shaped portal at a brilliant, blue sky. Thoughts of all that had happened since earlier in the day, when the FBI reports arrived in the Oval Office, replayed in his mind. Eli flashed back to a moment when he was gathering his few belongings in the West Bedroom of the Presidential Residence. Eli walked across the Center Hall toward the Yellow Oval Room and his influential friend continued preparing him for his journey back home. The President assured his college roommate that every conceivable precaution had been made to keep his family safe from harm.

"Not only have we deluged Northern Montana with more agents and policemen, we have also placed more of our people at your home within obvious close proximity. And although it might be much too late, airport security is on alert.

"And, of course, we're keeping our eyes on your family in Pennsylvania as well." As if something had stuck in his throat, the President stopped talking.

Eli looked at his friend, and then he put a hand on his shoulder. "Elijah, I'm not going to say what you're thinking. No one ever expected Erin would be a target. I know everyone is doing their best."

After one more look at Washington, D.C. from the Truman Balcony, the pair left the Oval Room and strode down the Grand Staircase, resuming their private conversation. "Elijah, if Alan Wing's statement to the Highway Patrol is accurate, Hyun Lee has proven she will wait patiently. She was with him for weeks."

Above them hung a spectacular English cut crystal chandelier, complimented beautifully by the crimson carpet and its gold trim that flowed down the stairway under their feet. Pictures of twentieth century Presidents and their respective First Ladies adorned the walls.

Eli stopped and shook his President's hand. "He has unwittingly taught his employer the lay of the land. She certainly knows the location of our home by now, and she will wait for the most opportune moment."

Elijah Rittenhouse cringed noticeably, and Eli picked up on it. "Elijah, that's not to say I have little or no faith in the Secret Service or the FBI. It's just an observation or opinion on my part." Then Eli went on to say one more time, "Again, I am truly grateful for all that everyone is trying to do for us."

The President assured his long-time friend that he took no offense. "Eli, these are extenuating circumstances. I cannot fathom or pretend to understand the depth of your concern for your family's safety. I can only guess." The two men hugged briefly and Eli was on his way as he exited the Grand Foyer in front of the White House. Soon he was out the gate and passed famous Pennsylvania Avenue, perhaps for the last time.

As Eli was transported from the White House to Andrews, he placed a call to Jake and Patty. He passed along everything new that he could now share with them. He treated no information as Top Secret. After what happened to Erin, he felt they deserved access to everything there was to know.

During the course of their conversation, they shared that they had already seen an increased presence of security people. Agents were highly visible. A new protection policy seemed to be in place.

As he finished talking to his son, he made him a promise. "Jake, I'll be back in Pennsylvania as soon as we bring this to a close, and we ***will*** bring it to a close."

From his vantage point at 35,000 feet, it seemed to Eli he could see clearly to Montana if only the cloud cover would dissolve. Finding mental escape comforting, he continued his reverie.

After departing D.C. and lifting off the ground, the Communications Officer aboard provided him ample opportunity to call Rita over a secured line. "Take as long as you need, Mr. Parks. The pilots and I promise not to listen to your chat upon our extension." Eli laughed lightly, appreciating the officer's friendly demeanor during such a trying time. However, before he placed his call Eli thought carefully about how he could bring his wife and stepson up to speed without creating a panic.

It was late afternoon in Falls Port when Ed picked up the telephone. He was standing in their kitchen right by Rita's side. He had just brought her home from school ninety minutes earlier. Thanks to a gorgeous autumn afternoon, open windows afforded them a light breeze that abated the heat from their oven as Rita baked Eli's favorite pastry: her homemade sticky buns.

"Hi, Ed," Eli began.

"Hi!" he replied excitedly with a bit of a mumble. He had been sampling his mother's baked goods as the call came through. "How are ya?"

"I'm better now that I'm headed home." As he talked, Eli spotted a break in the clouds for the first time since take off. "However I have no idea where I am." Bright sunlight splashed through the left side of the jet's tubular cabin which was fifty feet long.

A bit of frustration leaked through Edward's earpiece, and he sensed his stepfather's desire to be home was measurably greater than ever before. "Where are you landing?"

"Missoula first, and then you and all of Falls Port will love the final leg of my journey."

"Dad, not again!" Edward replied almost in a chuckle. "Not the choppers!"

Eli had to smile in spite of their situation. He was even conscious of it and thought to himself, "How typically American. Someone put a price on my head, and we're both amused by a lighter side of all of this."

"I'm going to the Driftwood early tomorrow," added Ed. "You should come along with me!" At this point, the two of them were laughing nervous laughter. Rita wiped her hands and asked for the phone.

"Mom's here. She..."

Eli interrupted him. "Wait. Thanks for watching over her. How smoothly did that go for the two of you?"

Edward quieted a bit and told Eli that he thought his mother was tired of her shadow. In the background, Rita could be heard adding to her son's summary of their recent comradeship. Next Eli heard Ed relinquish the phone to his mom.

Rita pretended to be gruff with her husband. "Eli, what exactly did you tell this young man?"

"Oh hi, Honey!" Eli began with mock sarcasm. "So nice to hear your friendly twang."

"Stuff it, Parks. The kid hasn't let me out of his sight since you left." She motioned to Ed to disappear on the deck, and then she started to walk down the hallway to their bedroom. She closed the door. "Are you headed home?"

"Actually yes, but as I told Edward I have no feel for where I am right now. I've been told that we'll be in Missoula at 4 p.m., so we're moving right along." He leaned slightly to his left to see more blue sky above and some land below. "I'll call from Missoula, too. That way you'll have a better idea about my Falls Port ETA." Then he reclined and relaxed in his leather seat as he gazed down at the flatlands beneath him. "Has to be Nebraska down there."

"Why do you say that?"

"The ground below us looks like a quilt. I'm seeing perfectly shaped green circles inside of slightly larger squares created by local roads around the irrigated crops. I have heard that's a trademark of Nebraska."

Rita was sitting on the edge of their bed and looking out their window. Light blue sheers moved gently with the breeze. Not many mid-autumn days were warm, so she was enjoying the fresh air.

"How was school today? What have you been doing?" Eli asked. He was putting off the inevitable.

"Well, I made some of your favorite sticky buns this afternoon. You'll be okay if our boy doesn't devour all of them first." She was gazing out the window as she spoke. "Looks like the blackbirds are waiting for you, too. They're down there on the wire where they all love to hang out."

Eli could picture them. It was a daily occurrence for red winged blackbirds to gather above the water upon the wire that paralleled the tamarack tree line.

"Did I hear our son say you'd be arriving..."

"Can you believe it?" Eli chuckled. "Friends with benefits."

She smiled at his joke. "That President fella must be impressed with you."

"Yes, he thinks I'm a real dandy."

Rita stretched forward and made note of two agents at the edge of the trees. They were dressed in relaxed clothing, but stayed attentive to all things around them. "Tell me about this army we have here, Eli." Then she added, "Thank goodness I don't have to feed them."

He wondered how one tells his wife that she might be the target of an assassin's bullet. His pause did not go unnoticed.

"Eli? Are you there?"

"Yes, I'm here, and I'll be there as soon as I can be." He grasped for what to tell her next.

Her subsequent inquiry helped broach the subject, albeit an unpleasant one. "Are we in danger, Eli?"

"Rita, I won't lie to you about this. Nor will I sugarcoat it. That's why the agents are everywhere. We are reasonably sure that she has gained a twenty-four hour head start."

"Who gained a head start? Who?"

He just said it. "Erin's killer. We believe she's trying to flush me out by heading to Falls Port."

Now it was Rita's turn to pause. Eli listened but heard only the whisper of the Gulfstream's jet engines behind him in the distance. He noticed that once again the cloud coverage had completely hidden the earth below, and sunlight disappeared from the cabin like laughter had disappeared from their conversation. Very quietly Rita whispered, "Oh my God. When does all of this end?"

"Sparky, if she's in Montana we will find her. Just this morning we were presented with two very useful reports."

Rita was up and walking about their room. She tried to maintain a calm demeanor, but she was beginning to come a bit undone emotionally. As she continued to hold her cordless phone to her right ear, she cautiously pulled back a single sheer from their bedroom window. She wondered if she had the ability to recognize anything threatening or if anything was amiss. "Eli, what did you find out?"

Her husband could sense she was becoming more fragile as their conversation played out. Moments ago he was handling glass. Now delicate crystal was in his grasp, and he felt he had to be increasingly careful. "We've confirmed her identity, and we know what she looks like." Like his wife, Eli was now on his feet moving slowly about the jet's cabin.

"And?"

"Well despite that, she boarded a flight for Montana before we could stop her. We didn't obtain the best intel until this morning which was after we think she must have landed in Montana."

Again all he heard was silence until he heard the sliding of their deck door and Rita shouting, "Edward! Come in here right now!" Eli could envision the scene unfolding in their home.

"Rita, listen to me. Try the best you can to maintain your composure. We need you to do your best to be clearheaded now."

His wife was nervously moving about. She clenched her phone tightly. "Eli, I..."

"Rita. Listen." Somehow Eli was able to dial up a level of calm that might help his wife. "We know where she was when she was in Falls Port before." As soon as he had spoken those words, he wanted to hit the rewind button on his mouth.

"Before?" Paranoia was not far off on Rita's horizon.

"Yes, this morning we learned she had been staying at the old Winston place. To our knowledge, Alan was working for her there."

"Alan Wing? Cary's Alan?" The disbelief in her voice was palpable.

"Yes, but he wasn't intentionally helping her in a bad way. He was merely a hired hand, a guide, and a pawn. In all fairness, he actually did something very brave that will turn the tide against this woman." Eli was sitting down again. As he spoke he tried to envision where she was in their home. He heard her tell Edward to stay inside. He complied without question.

Rita then resumed her conversation with Eli. "So you're telling me Alan knows things that can help stop her?" Suddenly she had an epiphany of sorts. "Wait! I think I've got to warn Cary."

"That's probably a great idea."

"I'll bring her here. She would be safer here. Wouldn't she?"

Now Eli could sense Rita becoming more mentally tough. She was more in control of her emotions. He wanted to get her thinking more positive thoughts, wanted her to feel more in control. "Yes. Get her there. Good thinking. That's a very good idea." Then he wanted to speak to Ed once again and bring him up to speed. "Call her now on your cell, Honey. And while you do that, let me speak to Ed again."

"Okay, but please get here..."

"As fast as I can. I promise." There was another brief pause as he wondered if he would ever get another chance to say, "I love you, Sparky."

"I love you, Eli." She knew exactly what he was thinking. "Now get home and tell me to my face."

When Eli heard those words, he thought she was back on top of her game. He gambled and said, "Yes, Dear."

"Really funny, wise guy. Here's Ed."

The conversation between Eli and Edward was succinct. After thanking him once more for his assistance to date, Eli explained the need for increased security due to Hyun's apparent and recent travel plans. He also explained to Edward her probable intentions. Edward handled it well.

"Ed, if anything ... any little detail seems suspicious at any point you have to immediately contact any agent you can."

Ed assured Eli he would be on the alert and would continue to accompany his mother and Cary. Before ending their conversation, he asked Eli a straight forward question. "Dad, can you at least describe the people or person I cannot trust?"

"Geez, Ed. That's an excellent question. Everyone's been told but you folks. And you just now gave me an idea as well." Eli summarized Hyun Lee's appearance and then assured his stepson that he would do his best to prevent any agents of Asian ancestry from being on the case if he could. He did not guarantee that it would happen. "Until I know it's been done, I can't promise anything. But thanks for the idea. I can't believe we overlooked it."

Edward remained reasonably calm throughout, and Eli was impressed. Then before hanging up their phone he asked Eli what he promised would be his final question. "When this is all over, will you please tell me more about this job of yours?"

Eli promised he would.

Despite his anxieties, just flying west reminded Eli of the first time he arranged to fly to Montana. He and Rita were taking their relationship to a whole new level. After Washington, they exchanged a legion of letters, phone calls, and emails that led to the day Rita invited him to her area. He was about to meet her son as well. Although it played out several years before, he recalled the happy details as if it had happened quite recently.

It was June. The first of his three connections on that day left Philadelphia International Airport at six o'clock in the morning. Paranoid about missing his flight, he had been up since three o'clock and left the house wearing jeans and a casual shirt. However, on the outskirts of town he pulled over into his high school's parking lot, and at the risk of being observed, questioned, and embarrassed, he gave in to his more romantic side by donning his best suit and tie. How many times had she teased how she "...loved a man in a tie" ? He knew she would be pleasantly surprised and appreciate the gesture, for more than once he provided, "I love being myself in a pair of jeans and a comfortable shirt." It was an ongoing mock battle between two people falling in love. It was a second chance at love for both.

During each leg of his journey back then, Eli enjoyed the views from each of his window seats. He had flown quite a bit but still enjoyed seeing the snow atop the Rockies in June. After a burger and a Cinnabun in Salt Lake City's airport terminal, he enjoyed looking down at Missoula knowing Rita was below waiting for him.

They had previously made a pact. Because it was mutually agreed that seven was a favorite number, they thought it would be fun to purposely create, rehearse, and speak a seven-word sentence to each other upon their reunion. No one else would ever know, but to them it would be special. It would be romantic. Eli spent several minutes during his flights and layovers arranging and rearranging exactly what he would say until he finally was happy with his choice. Like a schoolboy, he was eager to hear what she would say.

Upon disembarking from that final Salt Lake City / Missoula flight, he looked across a sea of people trying to spot Rita's face. As he stood there watching travelers disappear, it became obvious she was not to be found. He smiled and enjoyed what he thought was one of her better pranks. What Eli did not know was that she had neglected to tell him security measures prevented her from being on the second floor to greet him when he got off the plane. He stood there alone in a gigantic, carpeted room surrounded on three sides by plate glass windows overlooking the runways. He fully expected her to page him as she watched him squirm. Then he saw the escalator. "I must have looked so lost," Eli thought to himself as he smiled remembering that June afternoon.

Sure enough, there she was at the base of the escalator wondering if he had ever boarded the plane back in Pennsylvania! He saw the look of concern on her face wash away. When he was nearly within reach, he heard a young male voice say, "Boy are we underdressed" which was followed by Rita's nervous little "Hi!" for which he teased her unmercifully later. Her eyes begged forgiveness and they kissed.

"You are even more beautiful in person," he told her. Seven words that made it sound to Edward as if they had never met before. He sensed it was important at that moment for her son to think there was never a clandestine moment between them. They would have plenty of time to explain later how they had accidentally met in Washington, D.C. Truth be told, Edward never noticed any of it. He was a teen asked to tag along with his mom to pick up some guy at the airport. Eli knew that, for they discussed it once years later. It always put a smile on Eli's face.

Eli's final recollection about that day was something Rita did moments later that more than made up for being nervous in front of her son. When they pulled away from the airport in her car, she turned on some soft music. Not accidentally the first song that played was one they both agreed to call "their song" months ago. She looked at him across the seat and smiled. Eli was hooked.

"That's really when our lives became one," Eli thought to himself. "And I'm not going to let Hyun Lee, or whoever she is, bring it to an end." As the jet began to descend into Missoula, its passenger quickly assumed a much more serious demeanor.

CHAPTER 39

If Alan had not been on the telephone making the first of several calls to Cary Tuesday morning, he might have realized much sooner that the 4 x 4 was missing. He had made the calls from the depths of his parents' basement so as not to awaken them. As he telephoned his ex to warn her, he sat watching the morning news on the television in the game room they remodeled for him years ago. Sadly Mr. and Mrs. Wing rarely ventured there after he left.

Alan was waking to a hot mug of his mother's brew. She was in the habit of preparing their morning coffee just prior to her bedtime each evening. As she had done so many times over the years, Mrs. Wing announced to anyone within earshot, "Just hit the green button and the machine will take care of the *kapi*." It was one of several Kootenai words still spoken in their home.

Preoccupied by his good intentions, Alan never heard Hyun confiscate her burgundy vehicle, nor did he see her drive away. It was an odd twist that the person he intended to frustrate had done it to him instead. He had remained true to his word, for he had settled into the room's soft, chocolate-brown recliner and watched the local news while awaiting Cary's return call. Even when he quietly trotted upstairs and back into the kitchen for a second mug of hot kapi, he did not bother to glance outside and notice the truck's disappearance.

Not until nine fifteen did his parents begin to stir. An alarm clock was no longer part of their daily regimen. "I don't even wear a watch anymore," Senior boasted of his retirement. "But Mother still does." So when his dad opened the door atop of the game room's stairway and called Alan to come quickly, his son was about to finally learn that much was amiss.

"Alan, said his dad curiously, "isn't that our boat floating out there just off the point?"

His son's eyes grew even larger when he glanced from the red and white craft three hundred or more yards out in the water to the empty space where had he parked the Ford 4x4 only twelve hours earlier. It was then that he realized what had taken place and how close all of them had come to being Hyun's next victims.

ᘐ

It was early when Cary received the first of several telephone calls from the home of Alan Wing Sr.'s residence. Caller ID tipped her off as to their origin, and she chose to not answer them. Right or wrong, she associated Alan's parents with her divorce. Anytime she encountered the diminutive, gray-haired couple, their faces wrinkled and leathered by decades of sun, wind, and worry, she was polite to them, but such moments were awkward at best. Cary was not proud of following the course she had mapped out to circumvent the Wings, but as time passed she found that keeping them at arm's length helped her make her ex-husband a distant memory. Therefore, despite her curiosity, she let her telephone ring until it rang no more. She even ignored the amber blinking light that indicated their messages awaited her.

Ordinarily she left her house at 7:00 a.m. and stepped into her bronze Volvo wagon. However the phone calls annoyed her a bit, so she left earlier than usual which at the moment was a serendipitous decision. She had no idea an intruder was on the way.

She left her driveway and rode over a few local back roads, weaving her way to 93 North and Kalispell. In her rear mirror she caught a glimpse of the agents departing her property as well. They would return at 6 p.m. as scheduled.

Things were happening too fast for his taste. Alan suspected all along that Hyun would come after him; she might even attempt to kill him. He had prepared in advance by loading a few of his own guns. He had to be careful, for if his mother knew about it, she would have been really upset to learn a single loaded weapon was in her home. He had loaded several and placed them about the house in inconspicuous places.

Before departing, out of respect for his mom, Alan felt he had to go and unload each one before he did anything else. It was clear to him that they had been spared, if only temporarily. There had to be a reason, and he figured that reason was that she had little time to spare. Therefore he, too, had little time to waste. Quickly Alan unloaded all of his personal weapons, and chose to depend on the weapons he had taken from Hyun's cache in the barn.

Another piece of planning on his part was actually quite clever. He had mounted her own transmitter to her Ford pickup! There was a slight problem however. He did not know how to use it as of yet. He thought he would have more time to learn. "How long will the battery let it transmit? How great is its range?" His biggest problem was figuring out how to understand the receiver's information. To his chagrin, Alan was clueless about this technology and time seemed to be running out. By the time he had emptied the guns in the house, fetched their boat from the lake, and began studying what he could about the receiver, most of it trial and error along with research from the internet, noon had come and gone.

Just before one o'clock, Alan's father walked in on his son as he was studying the computer's screen intently. "What's that on the screen? Is that a universal GPS locater?" his dad asked as he picked it up from the desk. "Why would you be researching that?" His question nearly had an accusatory tone to it.

Alan could not believe what he just heard. He spun in his chair to face Mr. Wing. "Yes, that's what it is, but how did you know?"

"Alan, I know you and I never were the best communicators over the course of our lives, but I did spend 38 years working communications for the army and then the phone company." Alan Wing, Sr. enjoyed the look of astonishment upon his son's face. "Oddly enough, communications was my life. I only wish I had done more of it around the house."

"Dad, slow down here." Alan ran his fingers through his hair more than once. "This might be the most important thing you ever told me, at least for now." Then he asked his father the million dollar question: "Do you know how to work this thing?"

"Sure I do, but you will need a laptop or one doozie of a cell phone to receive its signal outside of the house." Those were the only words it took for Alan to jump up out of his father's Rexine computer chair and hug his white-haired old man.

❧

The commute was always beautiful to her, but on this particular morning not much could be seen. Bluish gray sky leaked over the Mission Mountains to the east. All else was overcast. On occasion she wondered if other travelers she passed daily found their commutes to be as restful as she did. She once told her girlfriends during one of their poker nights, "I've done some of my most creative problem solving on that highway."

Another ritual to which she adhered faithfully was turning off her cell phone each night by 10 p.m. and not activating it again until she reached her Kalispell office the next day. Those ten hours of privacy boosted her enthusiasm for her occupation. An excellent counselor, an excellent consultant, and an even better confidante, Cary believed that allotting time to herself kept her that way.

"You can't help others if you won't help yourself," was advice she offered to colleagues when she spoke at conferences or workshops. "At first, it might sound selfish. You might have days when you will experience guilty feelings when you take time for yourself." Then she would emphasize, "Trust me. I want you to make privacy your drug of choice. It's legal. It's free, and you might never again say the words, ' I'm going to work now!' " Cary Wing never went to work. She felt she was traveling to her office " . . . to meet with some folks."

At her office when her cell indicated messages were awaiting her, she was not all that surprised. However hearing Alan's voice actually took her breath away momentarily. Three of her seven voice mails were from him. It was Alan who had been calling from his parents' home earlier. Having listened to his messages, she was equally surprised by his demeanor. He did not seem to be of the same disturbing mindset when last he contacted her months ago.

"Good morning, Cary," the call began quietly. "It's me. I'm staying with my folks for a while. It's been great to see them again."

Of course, she was suspicious. Alan's folks never took his side during the divorce proceedings, and that angered him. He let them know how it hurt him when they did not see things his way. He left them on bad terms having said some terribly mean and inconsiderate things to them. She wondered if it was possible that during his absence he finally matured and his parents might have forgiven him.

"I'm not stalking you, and I'm sorry to have been so persistent this morning as well. But to help the Parks family and anyone important to them, I think it would be prudent if we met as soon as possible. I just cannot discuss details over the phone."

After hearing what he said and recalling what Rita had shared with her recently, Cary felt more than a little unsettled. What could Alan possibly know or have to share? This thought and others crossed her mind in bits of seconds.

Although his final comment sounded as if he was more than a little anxious, he managed to say it calmly. "Cary, please don't think that by any means I am a threat to anyone, but just recently I have learned your friends' lives might be in danger. I want to help, and that is the reason I'm home. I promise you that my intentions are good." In case she had forgotten, he provided his parents' telephone number, assured her that he would stay where he was, and wait for her reply. Quietly he hung up the phone.

Cary's first inclination was to call Rita immediately. Then she realized her best friend was in school for the day. Even if some of what Alan told her was true, she felt certain Rita was safe there. "I'll call her when I get home." Sitting at her desk with both hands rubbing her temples, she mumbled to herself, "And she's going to think I'm crazy if I call him back."

Each morning a brief meeting was scheduled by Cary so that she could touch bases with her staff. She trusted them and valued their opinions and input. The feeling was mutual. Clients and possible solutions to their problems were discussed. No part of these inter-office meetings were ever recorded nor were permanent notes ever taken. They were brain storming sessions that Cary felt might occasionally make a significant contribution.

By nine o'clock, most of the counselors were meeting with clients in their respective offices. Cary always waited until ten o'clock before she saw anyone. Dollar-wise it was foolish. No money was earned during an empty time slot, but Cary felt it was more important to make sure the rest of the office was running smoothly. When she knew everything was in order, it was easier for her to focus on her own visitors.

However that Tuesday morning was different. Cary found it difficult to concentrate as she attempted to help her three morning clients. Repeatedly thoughts of Alan's message interrupted her professional thought process. By noon she admitted to herself that she had been ineffective all morning, so she did something she had never done before: Cary cancelled all of her afternoon sessions, apologizing for the short notice, and she headed back to her home in Falls Port.

As she drove south on 93, down mildly graded hills with Flathead Lake to her left, handling familiar, gradual curves she had negotiated so many times during her life, Cary grew increasingly frustrated. A call to Rita at the middle school was tempting, but she felt her friend would have insisted she turn 180 degrees and head back to the office. Too, she felt interrupting her was in poor taste as well, especially when considering the source of her consternation was none other than her own ex-husband. Instead Cary drove home. She planned to call Rita after school was out for the day. She decided she would invite her over for Rita's favorites: lite beer and pizza. "How can she resist?" she thought to herself. "She probably will welcome a change in scenery anyway, even if it means being followed by several of those ants."

CHAPTER 40

By returning home from her clinic much earlier than usual on Tuesday afternoon, Cary unknowingly caused a breach in her own security. She had never requested any agents on sight. Their presence was all her best friend's doing. And since the four-man team assigned to her property was not expecting Cary until her normal arrival time, it was conspicuously absent. Not considered a target risk or to be in any immediate danger, security was assigned to her residence only when she was present. After parking outside of her garage, she exited her station wagon. When she locked her vehicle using her electronic fob attached to her keys, there was a not-so-subtle click and beep combination. Like millions of other modern car owners, she never noticed either sound.

After opening her Tudor-style door, she immediately turned to the entrance wall on her right and entered her security code. And again, just like millions of other homeowners, Cary did not listen and notice the lack of an audible signal when the door opened. Nor did the signal's absence register with her when she entered each number of her four-digit code. Both the sound of her keyless remote and her home security system had become part of the fabric of her daily life, taken for granted like the Winchester Chimes on her grandfather clock.

Cary's low heels clicked casually upon the slate floor in the foyer until she reached a lengthy, navy, floral runner that paralleled the stairway on her left. The entrance hall, adorned with pictures of family and friends, led into her kitchen. During daylight hours, friends could enter her home, look down the hallway and across her kitchen, and be treated to an expansive, eastern view of Flathead Lake.

Adjacent to the stairway, she stopped at her cherry foyer table and tossed down her keys in a flowered dish next to her silver telephone trimmed in black. Its light was still blinking. Alan's messages had not magically disappeared. As she returned from Kalispell in her car that afternoon, Cary decided she would indeed further scrutinize Alan's messages.

Immediately fascinated by his demeanor, Cary listened closely while still marveling at how her ex-husband's character seemed to have changed since last she heard his voice. He sounded so sincere, and he begged her earnestly to believe him. Alan implored her to call him as soon as she could. Consistent with the messages she had heard upon her cell phone earlier, he promised to await her call at his parents' home across the lake. She found his calm, matter-of-fact tone to be compelling, for woven within the strands of his voice was a sense of urgency that did not go undetected. Cary replayed it two more times after she had listened to subsequent shorter messages which followed.

"Maybe you should have heeded his warnings," were the words that sucked away Cary's breath and weakened her knees. Afraid to turn and face whoever it was that had uttered the remark, Cary briefly became statuesque, both beautiful and inflexible in her innocence. "Turn around slowly," the soft-spoken voice continued. "I do not intend to cause you any harm."

Even though in her mind she absolutely knew the voice was that of a woman, in the instant she turned she still expected to see Alan standing before her. In microseconds, her mind conjured a scenario whereby Alan would at least be partnered with the voice. She would finally come eye-to-eye with her former husband, and all her doubts about his change in character would be justified. What she saw was an attractive woman of North Korean descent, seemingly dressed for a wilderness experience, aiming a gun in her direction. Cary was on the verge of crying yet managed to control her tears, but she could not control her trembling inside and out.

"I want you to try and relax. Breathe. I meant what I said. I have no intention of harming you." Hyun pointed to Cary's living room off the foyer. Despite the trees, early afternoon sun from the west lit the room more than adequately. "Just pick a spot and sit."

As she moved to her wingback chair, Cary kept her eyes wide open and said nothing. She focused upon each of Hyun's softly spoken sentences. There was such a shocking contrast between the tone of her voice and the threat of her gun. The sight of this slender, sensuous woman even holding a gun, let alone aiming it at her, was incongruous.

"A gun," Cary finally thought to herself when she looked to the silencer on the gun's barrel for the second or third time. "I have one of those."

"Don't even think about it, Cary. Your weapon is long gone."

"How did you..."

Hyun interrupted, "It's my job to know, but I'll tell you." She smiled a coy smile. "The third time you looked at my weapon you did exactly that: you observed it as tool or a piece of equipment. Right then I was reminded you are familiar with guns." As she spoke, she looked out the window toward Cary's car. "That's when I knew my gun was a reminder of your own."

Cary had an odd, private thought. "This woman has counseling skills." Then just as quickly as her composure had come, she lost it. Her fear began intensifying, and again she came close to tears.

"Nice car," Hyun interjected. "Good here in the winter?"

"Yes," Cary answered meekly as she wondered what was going on. "Why are you here? What does my car have to do with this?"

"Oh, Counselor, don't be stupid." Hyun's tone remained patient, but took on a bit more of an assertive quality. "I'm trying to help you relax. I don't want you to do something stupid that we'd both regret later." Hyun was lying. If she shot Cary at some point, it would be without regret. In fact, it might have to happen. Maybe not. "As to why I'm here? I want you to introduce me to someone." Hyun stood and walked to a beautifully framed photo on the mantle. It was taken one night when the ladies were playing poker. "I want to meet this person," she announced rather casually, and she pointed at Rita's face with the tips of her fingers. It was then Cary noticed Hyun's nails were perfect. It was yet another odd observation considering the circumstance in which she found herself. And, too, it was at that very same moment Cary realized the assassin seeking Eli Parks was now in her living room.

Alan was scrambling to understand all that his father could teach him in a brief period of time. Simultaneously his father was trying to understand why his son needed to be tracking anyone.

"Okay, I have to just say what's on my mind, Son." He looked Alan Junior in the eyes. "What are you involved in?" It was another question that sounded slightly accusatory.

Alan actually winced. Last month's edition of Alan Wing, Jr. might have snapped at such a suggestive inquiry, but the new edition admitted to himself that he deserved his father's miniscule interrogation. "Sit down, Dad. I only have time to present the abridged version, but I guess it will help in the long run if I fill you in." And with that introduction, Alan Wing, Jr. did the best he could to bring Alan Wing, Sr. up to speed. Senior proved to be an excellent listener, asking but a few questions throughout his son's explanation.

When it was all said and done, Senior's first reaction was almost comical although he meant every word of it. "Let's keep your mother out of this."

Side by side like birds on a wire, and perhaps for the first time in thirty years, the father enjoyed escorting the son down a path of things he needed to know. It felt good to be working together. In fact, Alan Sr. felt as if the layers of many unfriendly years between them were being peeled back, and his comfort level grew along with his son's attention and understanding.

Alan absorbed what he could and waited until Senior was through speaking. "So what you're saying is that by calling your former employer, Centurytel, this device can be activated in less than ... twenty minutes?" Alan's tone of disbelief was evident. He did not mean to sound as if he was questioning his father's veracity or his sanity, but that learning Hyun's whereabouts might be that easy. "Dad, that's incredible! Who do I call?"

"Let me do it, Alan," said his father proudly. "I'd be honored. And I have to say, now it makes sense why you went around the house loading all our guns." Briefly, for there was not a lot of time, he enjoyed the look of astonishment on his son's face. "We won't tell Mother about that either."

CHAPTER 41

Just prior to calling Cary, Rita's cell phone began to vibrate in her hand. In the background, Edward was finishing his conversation with Eli, so Rita placed the tip of her left index finger over her ear in order to hear better as she took the call. Her cell phone's CID indicated Cary was calling. Rita began with, "Hi, Cary! I can't believe you just called. At this very moment I was picking up my cell to give you a call." She moved to the deck since Edward was still speaking with Eli. "How are things at the clinic today?"

Cary anticipated just such a question, and still she could not prevent the tiniest of tangible pauses from taking place.

"Cary? Are..."

"Hi," came out of Cary's mouth feebly as she stood eyeball-to-eyeball with her captor, but she quickly followed with some banter. "I'm actually already at the house believe it or not."

"Oh. Are you okay?"

Cary lied as best she could considering her nervousness caused by her situation. She opted for a convincing partial truth to sound more credible. Calmly chatting was difficult when she was being observed so closely. "I received another of those phone calls from Alan today."

"Oh no. What did he say?" Rita believed her high school crony and now thought she understood why the call had begun as it had. A pause followed her subsequent inquiry, but Rita thought it was appropriate.

"I'd rather not discuss it over the phone, Rita." Cary changed her phone to her other ear nervously and nearly dropped it to the floor. Her reaction was to utter an audible gasp.

"Well I was about to call you and invite you to stay with us again." Rita nearly began explaining why the invitation was being extended but decided to withhold the information since Cary was obviously upset already. "Just pack..."

"Rita, would you please come over here first? We'll have your favorite drink while I tell you about this. How can you resist?" she said attempting to sound more upbeat despite what she felt was a horrible betrayal of friendship. Deep inside her, she wanted nothing more than to summon the courage to scream, "Call the Police!"

Hyun sat motionless as she critiqued each word for some encrypted message Cary might be attempting. Later she definitely would have Cary define Rita's "favorite drink." Cary continued. "At the risk of sounding rude, please leave Edward at your house. He need not be privy to all I want to tell you, if you understand."

During much of their telephone chat, Rita had been sitting upon her deck and simultaneously enjoying the view of the lake from her deck. Evidence of autumn was reflected upon its placid surface. The fall colors were magnificent and made Rita feel relaxed, something she needed considering what Eli had told her moments ago. So Cary's direct request that Rita leave Edward at home had the effect of a pin prick upon her reverie-filled balloon. Despite how it felt, Rita did not balk. "Sure, Cary. He'd rather witness Eli's return to the airport anyway. He wants to observe it firsthand. Trying to make the moment less awkward, she added, "How often does a young man get to eyewitness such an event?"

It had been Hyun's idea to eliminate the arrival of a third hostage. Too many hostages might slow her down and demand too much of her attention. She did not have a lot of time. Hyun began pointing at her wrist implying to Cary that time was of the essence. Cary acquiesced with a silent nod and asked, "Can you come soon?"

Once again Rita uttered an affirmative reply. "Sure. Let me clean up a little sticky bun mess I've created here, talk to Father Ed," she tried to joke, "and I'll be right over."

"Thanks so much. It means a lot," Cary replied, and both of them shut off their respective phones.

Hyun took Cary's cell phone from her gently. "You did that very well. Now let's just sit and wait for Mrs. Parks to arrive while you tell me all there is to know about her favorite drink."

"You simply have to contact the police, Alan. You can't take on this woman by yourself." Alan's father was truly concerned that his son, the twenty-first century version of the prodigal son, might be lost as quickly as he was rediscovered. He put his hands on his son's shoulders and looked up into his eyes. "You have to get help."

Alan knew deep inside that his father's wisdom was indisputable. Yet he hesitated. "Dad, how do I tell the police that not only have I stolen a truck, her truck, but that I've also withheld some evidence. This tracking device isn't mine. And we both know I'm not exactly on their good side. Palmer hates me. He wanted to marry Cary, and to this day holds a grudge. I know he does."

Alan was at a crossroads. Authorities might thank him for his input, but they also might tell him that he needed to turn himself in. "They don't know Hyun and what she does. For all I know, she has called them and reported that I've taken her truck." The more he verbalized his dilemma, the faster he spoke. "It's my word against hers."

The smaller man thought for a long moment. Alan stared at him and studied the thick, pure white hair atop his father's head and all the wrinkles that he had accrued over the years. Then Senior held up the index finger on his right hand as if to indicate he might have an idea. "I'll call them. They don't have to know anything about you. It's not important that they know where the information comes from. We just want them to know she's in the area."

His son stood in awe. It was that simple. It was as if his dad was reducing fractions effortlessly. It seemed that, given the necessary time, he had a knack for breaking down the complex into the simple. "When did you get so smart, Dad?"

"About an hour ago, I guess." And then for a second he smiled at his son. "But we won't tell your mother."

Alan Senior called the Falls Port Police Department. As predicted, Jack Palmer took the call. "Mr. Wing, how are you today?"

"Jack, I'm fine. Listen I just became privy to some news that might be of interest to you."

"Really?" Palmer replied in a supercilious tone. "What's the nature of your information?" He doubted Mr. Wing had anything helpful for him.

The old man began to take a few liberties with the truth at this point. "An elderly fella I know who has some connections with the Highway Patrol was telling me about three of their men being murdered last night. He said something about the Patrol looking for an Asian gal."

Palmer sat a little straighter. "How did you get this information about last night already, Mr. Parks?" His arrogant voice changed quickly. "Very few folks know about this."

Senior had Palmer's attention for sure. Then he threw him a curve; he used a little misdirection technique. "So it's true?"

Palmer was miffed. It had not taken long for the old man to verify what until then might have been hearsay, and Palmer did not like admitting to himself that Alan Wing's father was on to something or had duped him. "Mr. Wing, what did you call to tell me?"

"Well, Jack, it might be of little consequence, but I did see an Asian gal in the area this morning. She was driving a pickup truck. Maybe she stole it, Jack. I don't know. Just seemed odd to see an Asian gal around here, and the fact that she was driving a truck made it more odd."

"Nobody's truck has been reported stolen Mr. Wing."

Bingo! Senior could not wait to tell his son that piece of information.

Palmer asked for some details. "What kind of truck was she driving? What color ? Where did you see her? What time?"

Alan's father had to be a little vague at this point. "It was early, Jack. I was out for a walk near the shore road over here by my house. It was a Ford for sure. Myself I don't like Fords much..."

"What color Mr. Wing? Did you notice the color?"

Now he was just messing with Jack. He knew how much the cop hated his son, so he stretched it out a little bit more. "That's how I knew it was a Ford. I don't like the way they look."

Exasperated with the old man, Officer Palmer inquired about the color one last time. "Mr. Wing, this is really, really important. What color was the truck?"

Alan Junior could not believe this was his father he was watching. He had never before appreciated this side of the old man. Speaker phone made it possible for him to witness the entire dialogue, and he could just picture in his mind the teeth-grinding that was taking place on the other end. Despite the serious nature of all that was going on, Alan nearly laughed aloud when he heard his father reply, "It was a Ford, Jack. I know it was... and it was burgundy." There was dead silence. "Was that helpful, Jack?"

Palmer begrudgingly thanked Wing Senior, and hung up his phone. Immediately he picked it up again and called the office where he knew the feds would be. He hated feds. In his mind, their very presence was insulting. Someone could have contacted him to handle any problem in his district. He did not understand why so many ants were attending his picnic.

Back at the Wing household, Alan asked his father for his Dodge. "I've got to get this tracker running and find out where she is."

"Will you let me know? I'd like to be kept informed. What if she turns around and heads back here?"

Funny one minute and dead serious the next was Mr. Wing. Alan knew his dad's level of concern was real, and his point was a valid one. By the minute, it felt as if his respect for his father was growing. There was a flash in time when the thought "Why didn't I listen to this man long ago?" ran through his head. He nodded and said, "Dad, you'll be the first to know. Keep your cell phone charged and on."

The two men hugged, and at that moment Alan thought his dad somehow appeared older and more frail. Senior handed Junior the keys, but not before he quipped, "You had better be really careful, Son. It's really your mother's truck."

CHAPTER 42

Alan was not gone five minutes when Senior received a call from FBI Agent Robert Simmons. It was clear that Jack Palmer had wasted little time contacting him. It was clear, too, that Agent Simmons was more than a little bit interested in what Alan's father had to say.

"Mr. Wing, I'm calling to verify that it was you who spoke with Officer Palmer a little earlier."

Senior had no reason to play with the Agent's patience. He had had some fun at Palmer's expense, but he understood what was at stake. "Yes, Sir. I did. May I help you?"

"Well if you could be more specific about the time of day, it would be of help to us. And if by any chance you noted the plate number on the Ford truck, that would be of enormous benefit to us as well."

"Can you give me five minutes, Agent Simmons? I can call you right back or can you hold?"

The agent sounded shocked when he uttered, "You have the plate number?"

"Believe it or not, I might have it right here someplace. It's a hobby of mine."

"Then I'll hold."

"Yes, Sir. Be right back." Wing Sr. stepped into the next room and flipped open his cell phone. Alan answered his call.

"Alan, I have an FBI agent on the house phone. What are the chances you know the Ford's plate number?"

His son thought long and hard. "Dad, all I know is that it's a Montana plate. It's a Lake County rental plate...and the first three characters are LIL. I don't know the last digits or letters."

Senior jotted the info down and told his son to be careful. Back on the land line house phone he passed along the information to Agent Simmons. "I hope that helps."

"You still haven't given me a more specific time, Mr. Wing. Can you do that?" The agent was polite and patient.

"Sure. I was outside by 5:30. I walk a lot." He thought a moment. He knew she had not stolen the truck before 5:30, because that was when he was up to go to the bathroom. He had noted the truck in the driveway. "I guess it was about ten minutes to six this morning."

Agent Simmons was happy to have the information. He thanked Mr. Wing, and their conversation was over. When Senior looked at the clock in their kitchen above his wife's head it was nearly four o'clock.

"Who was that, Dear?" she asked.

"Just a nice man from the police department, Mother. It seems a truck was stolen last night, and I might have seen it go by."

"Really? Oh my." Then as if she had let that thought pass by quickly she asked, "Where is Alan?"

As he looked at their fiberglass boat which Alan had secured earlier in the day he said, "Mother, I think our son is out there trying to help them find it." Then Mr. Wing picked up the phone to call one of his oldest and dearest friends. The phone rang but once before the reunion began.

Sensing Cary's request was of a delicate nature, with some sticky buns Rita negotiated with agents that only two of them need to follow her. Along the way, it worried her not when their front tire flattened slowly, causing them to fall far behind.

The door was unlocked. As friends often do, Rita walked in and called "Hello!" to Cary, and it was Cary's distraught visage she saw first. "Cary? What's wrong?"

Her friend's eyes were clearly rheumy, so Rita surmised Alan had gone a little too far. The concept angered her. And then she saw Hyun to her right as she finished walking into the living room from the long hallway behind her. Rita felt as if she had been punched. Despite never having seen her before, she knew that in front of her stood the very woman her husband feared might be tracking them down. Before her, under the arch that led from Cary's living room to her dining room stood Erin Parks's executioner. For what seemed like a much longer time than it was in reality, Rita did not breathe or take another step. She was sickened by nerves all at once. There was a distinct tingling throughout her body, and she too quickly became teary-eyed.

As if she heard her friend from a faraway distance, Rita could hear Cary apologizing for bringing her into this horrible circumstance. Clarity came to her only seconds after she first saw Hyun standing there with a gun pointed at Cary's torso. Rita heard Hyun say, "Stop your babbling. It will do no one any good." Even though Hyun Lee meant not one word, she then said, "I told you several times that neither of you will be harmed if you follow my instructions." Then she turned to Rita and ordered her to sit at the antique, golden oak table that was once a wedding gift for Cary's great grandparents during the early 1900's. Cary sat at her side.

"I don't have a lot of time, so I want you to do what I tell you the first time every time. Do you understand?" By her tone, Hyun was beginning to sound more threatening by the minute. Both women sensed that their Asian kidnapper was moving on to another phase in her scheme. "Lean forward. Fold your hands behind you at your lower back." One captive at a time, Hyun placed a plastic fastener about their wrists and pulled them uncomfortably tight as if to make the point that she was in charge. In essence, the women were handcuffed without handcuffs, a technique which had become more popular around the world among enforcement agencies.

Looks of fear and furtive glances were temporarily all the communicating Cary could share. Neither spoke for fear of their captor's reciprocation. It had just become clear that inflicting pain upon others was not a concern. The hard plastic around their wrists felt as if it would both cut off circulation and rip into their soft skins. Finally Cary lipped the words "I'm so sorry" to her friend for which she received a nod in return.

Since being forewarned less than an hour ago, Rita had the opportunity to subconsciously at least become angry with Hyun Lee. Now the anger was escalating within. Cary on the other hand was an emotional wreck from the moment she found Hyun in her home. Rita believed that somehow she had to help her life-long friend regain her mental toughness.

"Time to go, ladies," the assassin announced. "Cary, tell me where you put your keys." More and more Hyun sounded like a drill sergeant. It will be easier to move the two of you in your vehicle."

Timidly she responded with, "An extra set is in my purse." Her voice was shaky and soft, not at all indicative of her confident self; not even close.

Hyun had little trouble finding the keys inside the black leather bag. She noticed the small can of hornet spray in there, too, intended to fight off attackers. She held it up and said sarcastically, "I'm glad you didn't use this on me."

Meticulous about details, Hyun peered out the windows carefully and decided it was time to go right then. She even left a light on inside the house to make things look more ordinary once evening set in. Grabbing each of her captives by an arm, she led them to Cary's Volvo. To Rita's and Cary's surprise, she lifted the tailgate and had Cary, the smaller of the two, lie down on her side in the storage area behind the back seat. In turn, Rita was told to lie upon her side in front of the middle seat. Hyun backed out of Cary's driveway, and to those few she passed driving down the road, she appeared to be the sole passenger in the vehicle.

Not too many miles away, on the northern edge of Falls Port where the bridge leads traffic towards Kalispell, Alan pulled over along the road side for the fifth time since he left his parents' home. This time the results were different.

"Whoa! There she is!" His heart started to pound. He was within six miles of his target, but he did not like what he was seeing. He picked up his cell phone from the console between the two front seats. He fumbled with the keypad as he tried too quickly to dial his father's phone number. Finally he made the connection.

"Dad...you're not going to believe this." His father inquired as to what he had discovered. "I don't know why, but Hoo Lin has holed up inside Cary's house according to this tracker." Senior instructed him how to accurately double check his findings. "Dad, it says she's there. Why would she go there? You're going to have to call the police." His father assured him he would not be doing that again.

"Palmer would have a coronary."

"Who do we call?" Alan asked anxiously.

"I'll call that Simmons fella directly. He left me his number in case I heard any more details."

Excitedly Alan interrupted. "Dad, do you remember how to get there? Can you give them the directions? Emphasize that she might not only have a weapon but a hostage, too."

"I'll take care of it right away. I'll call you back." Then his father added, "Alan, do *not* try to do something heroic." His son knew exactly what he meant.

CHAPTER 43

Alan watched from a distance. He was still leery of Palmer. The man was so upset when Cary became engaged he invented reasons to harass Alan. His miniscule staff was directed to ticket Alan "...if he so much as crosses the street in the middle of the block." Cary had never once shown Jack Palmer the slightest bit of romantic interest, but he sure had his heart set on her.

Everyone in Falls Port knew it was true, especially his staff, so everyone saw the things he did to Alan. They knew he was envious and jealous. What surprised everyone was his adversary's tolerance. Alan never sought revenge, due largely to Cary's coaching. Her counseling skills had come in handy.

Alan Wing Jr. let his dad handle the communications end of things that afternoon. Even Palmer would not dare transgress the generation gap no matter what he was feeling. However the sting caused by their history fueled Alan's angst every time he saw the man. There was one memory that popped in his head most often which centered around Homecoming several years back.

Friday night football was big at Falls Port High. The Pirates were a pleasant diversion after a week of work. No different than most high schools, Falls Port High thoroughly enjoyed the atmosphere of Homecoming. For most people in town, it was a time for reunion.

Just before halftime of the football game, Alan noticed Palmer standing at the center of the gray, metal bleachers acting self-important and scanning the crowd. His stomach knotted in anticipation of what would happen next. Alan sensed a big stage and the biggest audience of the year would be just right for officer Palmer. And sure enough, when he saw Alan with Cary about three quarters up the bleachers at about the thirty yard line, Palmer made sure he caught everyone's eye.

"There's that creep!" he roared like a bull. Then methodically he made his way through the seats while calling out, "Alan Wing! You are under arrest. Don't try to get away!" Everyone's head turned up in their direction to the embarrassment of the young couple. Cary placed her left hand on Alan's knee to keep him calm and seated, but Jack had achieved the effect he sought. It did not matter one iota to Jack Palmer that the entire scene was nothing more than a charade, and an arrest was never made. Later Palmer simply claimed it was a case of mistaken identity on a witness's part.

Every time Alan recalled that night he hated Palmer more. His hatred grew like interest on a thirty-year loan. It was sizeable, yet he would not act upon it. At least Cary had taught him that much. "There's nothing to be gained by seeking revenge, Alan," she used to say. "What goes around comes around." And Alan remembered his parents agreeing.

So there he was watching the *ants* and Palmer's men carefully approach and circle Cary's home. He never saw so many sunglasses and Kevlar vests in one location in his life. Some wore their vests over white long-sleeved shirts. Others were dressed out in camouflage. They had parked well down the road on both sides of the house, and formed a circle about it. When the ring had tightened sufficiently to satisfy the agent in charge, he did what all those agents in charge do in the movies: spoke into a bull horn to inform Hyun Lee of their presence.

No response. Alan could feel the tension from as far away as his lakeside vantage point. The Agent spoke more, and his message oozed out from the trees and echoed across the lake in garbled tones.

"What could she be doing in there?" Alan thought to himself. "What in God's world is she thinking?"

To all involved it seemed like a standoff. It was dangerous and a matter of patience. Surely Hyun did not believe she could out maneuver so many men and women. He became unsettled about what Hyun might do to Cary.

Then he heard it. Confirmation of what he thought might happen all along: an initial attempt at negotiations. "Ms. Lee! We know you have both Mrs. Wing and Mrs. Parks with you! Just release them first, put down any weapons you might have, and come out. No one has to be harmed!"

"Rita Parks? When did *she* get sucked into all of this?" were the words that Alan whispered to himself. Then he took notice of her car. "How did I not see it?" he wondered. "Wait a minute. There's *Rita's* car. Where is Cary's Volvo?" He knew it was possible that she parked it in the garage, but if she had not, then it might mean the house was empty. They might have escaped in the Volvo. "Oh great. Now I have to let these people know I'm here. This could get ugly."

Very very carefully, Alan backed away from the scene. To just stand up and announce his presence might end in getting himself shot. This was going to require some thought. He decided to skirt the lake's edge and back away until he could safely walk his way up to where the official cars were left behind. He decided to approach someone on the fringe. "Somebody has to stay behind and watch the cars. If there's a crowd of curious onlookers I can mingle with them first. Then I can approach an agent and explain my hunch."

Alan had this little conversation with himself as he moved through the tamaracks, maples, and pines on the property and one neighboring house where the owners had been told to evacuate. He was right. There were a few folks standing about, curious as to what was going on down at Cary's house. He approached the first agent he saw.

"Somebody find me Chief Palmer," insisted the agent in charge. "He's the one who said old man Wing was credible in the first place." He waited. Finally Jack Palmer was seen hustling carefully to the foreground. It was right where he wanted to be all along."Agent Simmons," Jack smartly announced, "I'm Chief Palmer. We haven't officially met."

"Palmer," replied a testy Agent Simmons, "we spoke on the phone earlier. It was you who told me that your good friend Mr. Wing could be believed. It was you who gave me his phone number." Simmons was losing his patience. He was wondering how the likes of Jack Palmer ended up as a Chief of Police.

"That was over the phone..."

"Forget it, Palmer. Just listen." Simmons was leaning against a huge tamarack and rubbing his forehead. It felt as if all eyes were on the two. "How well do you know this Wing family? Are they credible or are they crackpots?"

"Family?" Jack replied defensively. He was not sure where this line of questioning was going, and because of his feelings about Alan, he was certainly not going to lie again and call Alan Wing, Jr. his friend.

"Palmer, there's a guy back at the tapes...back by the cars who says he's Mr. Wing's son." At that point Simmons pointed back over his left shoulder with his thumb and said, "He claims he was once married to the gal we thought might be a hostage in this house. Do you know this guy? Do you know the younger Mr. Wing very well? Is he "credible" like you said the older Mr. Wing was "credible"?

The Falls Port Chief of Police was squirming on the inside. Any favorable impression he might make on Agent Simmons and his crew might hinge on what Alan Wing, Jr. has to say. He treaded lightly. "I know the guy."

"You know the guy. Chief, I asked you if he was a crackpot or not. Is he?"

Silence. Birds could be heard chirping and fluttering all about their disturbed woods. A breeze off the lake rustled the few leaves that were still clinging to the trees that surrounded Cary's house. It whispered through the evergreens. Palmer finally spoke, hoping beyond hope that if he picked his words carefully he might salvage some dignity. "It's true. He is her ex-husband. I don't like the guy much, but he's not crazy. Why?"

"Well, Jack, seems Mr. Wing, Jr. has a theory." Then he paused. "Let me ask you a question, Jack. Would you recognize Mrs. Wing's vehicle if you saw it?"

"Sure. It's a bronze Volvo wagon. My father sold it to her. Gave her a great deal, too."

"Palmer!" Simmons exploded. Do you *see* a bronze Volvo in the driveway?"

"No."

The agent, suddenly a bigger-than-life figure whose chest had begun to heave, began walking around Jack in a tight circle ignoring the threat of Hyun being in the house. If Simmons were a betting man, he was pretty sure she wasn't. "What do you see in the driveway, Chief Palmer?"

Even Palmer recognized sarcasm, but he had to answer. "A red Ford Focus."

"Now Chief Palmer, let's do the math here. If there's no Volvo in Mrs. Wing's garage, it's a good bet that no one is inside."

Palmer stared at Simmons. He was quite uncomfortable.

"So what we have here, Chief, is an observation made by Mr. Wing about a half a mile back that might be right on the money. He can't see the cars, but he's the one who suggested this entire event might all be for naught." And then he said it. "I wish the Falls Port P.D. had thought of it."

Jack Palmer was steaming. He was tired of hearing "Mr. Wing" repeatedly, and Agent Simmons had just publicly berated him for his poor detective skills. In his own sick mind, Palmer found himself hoping Hyun Lee and Cary...Cary Wing...were inside the house. They were not. As it turned out, Alan Wing, Jr., too, had departed. He left in the hopes that he could figure out how to locate Hoo Lin a second time.

CHAPTER 44

Edward kept his first promise he made to his mother. He leaked not one word about Eli's pending arrival. Almost. To do otherwise would have created a near circus-like atmosphere, the likes of which tiny Falls Port Airport was ill-prepared to handle. The choppers' staccato-patterned approach bouncing off the Mission Mountains to the west would be alarm enough to bring attention to their arrival as they brought home Falls Port's newest celebrity.

Before leaving D.C., Eli made the President *promise* him that once in Falls Port, Eli would ride with his stepson. Not anticipating the agents, it had been Edward's plan to put Eli in a vehicle and transport him quickly from the airport inconspicuously. He even attempted to borrow a buddy's truck in order to enhance their chances of going unnoticed altogether. However there was a snag. His buddy Waff insisted on driving. "Man, you might have more chances at reliving this, but I won't." Waff's eyes were begging him to give in to his sole condition. Ed smiled a huge smile and acquiesced easily. Even though Waff was a muscular, independent sort, at that moment Ed imagined him as a puppy pleading for a bone.

"I can't think of a better guy to have along," Edward told his good friend. He knew Waff, also known around Falls Port as Carl Beilman, son of the best mason in town, was right.

So there they stood adjacent to four federal agents looking down the valley and listening. Night had not fallen, but shadows had darkened the Falls Port side of the mountains. The first time they ever heard the *pucka-pucka-pucka*, when Eli was swept away back east, was from a location across town more than two miles away. On that day, they had felt the vibration in the air from one mile away. On this night, both boys excitedly wondered about the intensity of the choppers' presence from close range. It was their hope that they would be able to witness their approach since darkness was growing.

Suddenly they noted a change. Until the end of time, Carl and Ed would argue about who first heard the three military aircrafts approaching and whether or not they initially *felt* them approaching or heard them. Carl later swore he noted the vibration bouncing off the mountainsides. He claimed it gave him gooseflesh. "You didn't feel them first, Man? How could you not feel them?"

Eli was surprised to see Edward and Waff shoulder to shoulder waving to him against the backdrop of early evening's twilight. Then he observed headlights and a line of vehicles in the distance already headed up Airport Road. The boys could not be heard above the rotors, but they were calling and motioning frantically. Eli ducked under the spinning forty-eight-foot-long blades, jogged a few yards, and turned. Feeling it was appropriate, he saluted the crews of all three Hueys. Each pilot respectfully returned the gesture, and they were off.

Jogging through thick, swirling dust Eli began to understand the two boys' comments and was tickled by their excited guffaws. He could not help but smile when he saw them jumping up and down while waving at the departing dark green and brown Hueys as they climbed quickly with all their lights flashing to hundreds of feet. At the rate of roughly 1,750 feet per minute, the crafts soon reached close to their maximum speed of 125 miles per hour, and all the noise was gone. Like long, slow-moving waves, their sounds came in upon the shore, and then went away just as uniformly. It was a moment the young men would share all of their lives.

Carl found it difficult to control his enthusiasm. "Mr. P', you ride in style!" he called out at the top of his voice. "For sure! You *do* ride in style, Man!"

Ed grabbed Eli's bags and then quickly tossed them into the bed of the truck. "Get in, Dad, unless you're holding a press conference."

Despite his excited state, Carl proved to be adept at giving the trio's departure an ordinary appearance. He drove slowly but not so slowly that his speed gave passersby a reason to gawk. It helped, too, that his windows were a tinted charcoal gray. Due to the slightly darkened glass on his truck and the growing darkness outside, nobody noticed there were three passengers in the front seat of his vehicle as they passed.

"Where's your mom?" Eli inquired of Ed over the clatter of Carl's truck as they turned off Airport Road towards home and privacy.

For a second, Edward felt a pang of guilt. This was the first time he had left her side during non-school hours. But Eli's question did not smack of accusation, and Edward answered comfortably after a brief hesitation.

"Cary's house. She asked Mom to visit. It was some sort of private matter." Then he added humorously, "I cut her some slack. This is her first time out without me. She calls *me* 'Dad'! Besides, there are always ants at Cary's whenever she goes." Then Edward told Eli that it was Rita who gave him the job of picking him up at the airport. "I think she needed to get away from me."

Eli smiled as he looked out his window. "Thanks. You've done more than you know when it comes to giving me peace of mind." Then he teased his stepson. "I bet you were a little happy to get away, too." They both smiled at one another briefly and then were interrupted when Edward's cell phone began to chime.

❧

Loudly and sharply, Eli ordered Carl to pull off to the shoulder of the road. Both boys were shocked by his apparent mood swing, but Carl did exactly as he was told. "Stay here! Do *not* leave the truck!" Having barked those commands, Eli hopped out of the vehicle, slammed the door, and walked quickly back down the road one hundred feet.

"Who was that call from, Man? Seems like it really shook him up," Carl shared with Ed.

"It was my Mom. She just asked to speak with him. Nothing she said seemed at all out of whack." Edward figured she was anxious since they had been apart, so he had passed the tiny black phone quickly. Nothing she said to him in that brief instant sounded like anything that might set Eli off. Edward had never seen Eli react in such a manner over anything. It was unsettling for him. Both young men turned and looked through the smudged rear window at Eli Parks standing in the distance, bathed in the red glow of Carl's tail lights and the headlights of their escort.

Simmons took the call immediately when he learned Eli was attempting to reach him. "Mr. Parks, this is Bob Simmons..."

"Agent," interrupted Eli, "just listen. I've just spoken with Hyun Lee." Eli sounded anxious and out of breath. He did not have a lot of time, so he summoned what inner strength he had. "Does that name mean anything to you?"

"Yes, Sir."

"She has two hostages right now. One of them is my wife."

"You spoke with her?" Simmons returned in a voice not hiding his surprise. "Are you sure it was her?" He was obviously embarrassed and incredulous. "Mr. Parks, earlier today a local man, a Mr. Alan Wing, Sr., put me wise to the fact that she might be close by." Then Simmons went on to explain to Eli what transpired hours ago at Cary's house. "We've been in a holding pattern ever since. Again...are you sure it's her?"

"Yes, I'm absolutely certain." Then he began anew with his instructions for the agent. "I've spoken with her, and she demanded to deal with me and me alone. You and I both know that's not going to work."

Simmons was quickly impressed. Ordinarily spouses insisted on going it alone, following a captor's instructions. Authorities are told to stay back or hostages will be killed. From previous experiences, both Parks and Simmons knew that chances of a successful hostage release depended on all rescue sources working together. Even then it was a crapshoot that depended upon a kidnapper's nerves and skills. Simmons continued to listen. "Go on, Mr. Parks. What are you thinking?"

"This woman is a pro. She's not stupid. She will most likely act on the assumption that you and I *will* work together. She's a fool if she doesn't." As he spoke, in the back of his mind Eli felt as if he had already used up too much time, but he knew it was necessary to coordinate with Simmons and his team effectively.

"I've been told her location, but I don't want you or your team within a mile of the place. As in most kidnapping scenarios, she gave me specific instructions. As always, any violation of those instructions ends in a hostage or hostages being killed."

"What were the instructions?" Simmons was not being idly curious. In order to increase their chances of success, both men had to be on the same page.

"I'm to approach the Drake property and house from the road below it. I imagine it gives her quite a vantage point. And I'm to call out to her and clearly indicate that I'm not armed." Eli paused. "Like she really thinks *that's* gonna happen. That is why she needs the advantage of a clear and lengthy site line."

"Okay, so what's the next step?"

I'll meet you where 93 North intersects with Lake Shore Drive in Rollins. Can your people find that?"

Simmons gripped the phone tightly. He did not like those parameters. "Yes, I know where that is . . . but a mile?"

"If she even sees a headlight my wife and her friend will be killed. I'll make the initial contact. I'll try to make the trade she wants. She wants me and not them. I must try to make that work. It's my top priority...

getting them out even if it means sacrificing my safety." Eli paused, and then he asked, "Simmons are you married?"

"Yes, I am."

"Good. Then you can relate." Next Eli insisted, "I want you to promise me, Simmons, that their release will be your top priority at any cost."

Simmons understood Eli's point, and he knew Eli's history. It helped that he was dealing with an intelligent, experienced, brave person, but still it was hard to agree upon such a condition. Yet in the end, it was all that Simmons could do. It was that or storm the place and hope for the best. "Okay, Mr. Parks, but where are you right now? And once we're there, how do you want my team situated?"

Quickly they talked logistics. Simmons was to strategically place his people as per Eli's instructions, just as quickly figure out a way to access the target if it became necessary, and agree upon a means of communication with Parks. When all of that was established, Eli hung up the phone only to make another call.

CHAPTER 45

Senior was expecting a telephone call back from his dear old friend, so finding Eli Parks on the other end of the call surprised him. "Are you the fella who rides in the helicopters?" he asked after simple introductions were through.

"Just one chopper, Mr. Wing."

"Well that must have been really something to see. I didn't get the chance..." Senior was telling Eli.

As politely yet as firmly as he could, Eli interrupted the older man. "Mr. Wing, I'm sorry to be quick, but I really need to speak with your son. May I please?" Then before Eli could rewind it he said, "Cary's life and my wife's life depend on it." He hoped he had not offended the gentleman or upset him.

Alan's father handled it well. "I'd put him on, but he's not here."

Eli stomach became unsettled. He felt his chest tighten two sizes. "Is there any way..."

Now it was Senior's turn to interrupt. "I can give you his cell number. I've been talking to him off and on. He's attempting to track down the Asian gal he thinks is after Cary and your wife. I told him not to attempt anything heroic by himself. Can you get him the help you both need?"

The roller coaster inside of Eli was on its way back up. There was hope. "I can, Sir. Just give me Alan's number. Please." After Eli recorded Alan's cell number, he thanked the elder Wing and then thought to ask about the whereabouts of his son.

"The last I knew, he was on the other side of the lake by Cary's. For a while he thought his tracking device had led him to her.

"Tracking device?" The concept of such a device being in play surprised him. Too, he didn't expect Mr. Wing to know all he did about his situation.

As briefly as he could, Alan's father explained what had transpired that day. Eli listened carefully, for he had learned long ago that pertinent information was invaluable in crisis situations. He gained some respect for Alan after learning what Junior had attempted to do.

"But I don't know where he is at the moment. I wish I did."

Eli promised he would call Alan and have him call home the first chance he could. Then he thanked him one more time and ended the call.

Alan took the call despite not knowing its source. His phone's CID could not decipher Eli's calling signal. He pulled his mother's vehicle to the side of the road. "Hello?"

"Alan, this is Eli Parks." He was matter-of-fact in tone, sounding as if he had known Alan all his life. In truth, they never met.

Alan's voice indicated a degree of gratitude and hope. "Eli? You're back in Falls Port?"

"Yes, I just spoke with your father. He told me of your suspicions, your attempt to locate this dangerous woman, and how you attempted to warn the girls."

Again Eli wished he had more time to compare notes with Alan, but he knew time was of the essence. He continued to speak and got right to the point. "Alan, if I understood the agents in D.C. correctly, you might know Hyun Lee better than anyone."

"She goes by Hoo Lin. She was Hoo Lin when I worked for her, yes." Then Alan proceeded to summarize the entire Winston property experience as succinctly as he could, answering questions when Eli interjected them. He, too, realized they might be on borrowed time.

"Okay. All of that might be helpful someplace down the road. Now tell me what you know about the place where she's holding the women." Eli thought Alan was aware of their location.

Alan balked. He was confused. Then he asked, "Eli, do *you* know where they are?"

"Yes! The old Drake property. The deserted ranch house a few miles from the Winston's." As soon as he said it, Eli wondered if it was a mistake. Perhaps Alan had not known, and Eli remembered Wing Sr.'s warning to his son about attempting something heroic. "Stay away from there, Alan. I've been in contact with the FBI. A plan's been formulated."

"That's tremendous news. Thanks." However Alan's mind was already scheming even as he continued talking to Eli.

"Now tell me what you recall about the property there. It would be a great help to all of us." Eli looked at his watch impatiently, but he knew he needed to pick Alan's brain.

Alan visualized the property as he spoke. He had hunted the region many times, so it was not difficult to recall. "Like the Winston property, 93 North forms its border across the top. Nothing but mountain and trees across the highway north of the houses, and the land slopes to the lake more than most people realize. In a way, the acreage is terraced in that it undulates gradually all the way to the road below the homes. For the most part, each shelf is broad...at least fifty yards from back to front. There's a lot of rock ledge under the soil, so the footing is firm. The property between the highway and the road along the lake has very few large trees. In fact, both homes can be seen from 93. Tall grass is the only cover. She's going to have quite a view in all directions, plus the driveways and the land down to the lake road are steep. It's not an easy approach from any direction."

Eli analyzed Alan's input. "What can you tell me about the house itself?"

Almost apologetically, Alan told Eli he did not know much about the building. "There are large windows to the lake side and the south side just off the driveway. It offers quite a view of the lake in the Falls Port direction. That's about it." He paused briefly and added, "Wait! There's an out building on the upper side."

"Okay...thanks. Call your folks. I promised I'd have you call them. It would probably be best if you went back to your father's. We'll let you know as soon as Cary and Rita are safe."

"Eli, where are you right now?"

"All of us are about thirty miles out right now, but we'll be in position soon. By the way you've described it, we'll need to be careful." Eli thanked Alan for his help, and with that their conversation came to an end.

At that moment, thirty miles seemed like a million to Alan, and he was very close to Drake's, less than a mile. When he had left Cary's earlier, his hunch had been that Hyun might go to ground that was familiar to her, and he was not far from wrong.

Before Alan started out on foot for the Drake property in the dark, he checked his equipment. Then he called his father's cell phone one last time.

During their conversation, once again his father advised that Alan at least wait for help to arrive. "Don't be foolish, Son. Help has to arrive soon. Mr. Parks assured me of this."

"But what if it's not soon enough?" countered Junior. "I couldn't live with myself if I ever learned we were a little too late."

The old man said nothing. The lake's cool damp air passed over his face unnoticed. Light slaps of wavelets sounded against Senior's fiberglass boat which Alan had docked earlier.

For a moment, no one spoke, and Alan thought of all the times his rebellion must have hurt his father. "Dad, I just need you to..."

"Tell me that later. Right now tell me your plan such as it is."

Alan appreciated his father's bravado and interest. "I've got to try and draw her away from the women. That will buy us some time. And if I can expose her, I can stop her myself."

"If you get her attention," the old man advised, "if you get her on the line, keep her on the hook until the others arrive. You understand? You don't have to be the one who nets her."

"Yes, Sir. Thanks," and they ended their conversation.

CHAPTER 46

Rita and Cary were tied, gagged, and locked in the dark, damp basement of a forty year old rancher that was abandoned many years earlier when the owner's investments went down the toilet. Dan Drake had put all his assets into acres of cherries, and when a late, disastrous frost and snowstorm wiped out all the fruit, he was unable to make ends meet. Disgusted and disheartened he went back east.

Each was sweating profusely, for Hyun had not only transported them roughly, but she had hidden them in dark, musty, tight quarters as well. They perspired even more due to the duress they were experiencing as their nerves had been badly abused. Both wondered if they would ever see daylight again.

Upstairs on the main floor of the brick ranch house, Hyun continued planning the final stages of her assignment. She had chosen this building for two reasons. First it was located near her last rental car, the white Pacifica she had parked not far down the road. She also liked the lay of the land, the vantage point it provided.

Yet for the first time, she was experiencing doubts, and her weariness was eating at her. The scratches on her face from the branches had become sore to her touch as well. Hyun wondered if she had made a mistake taking the hostages. Of course, they were a valuable lure, but if she killed them she lost whatever leverage she had achieved. While in her custody, she felt she had the upper hand, but in a sense, killing them was suicidal. She had to hope that Eli Parks had not given that part of her plan a thought, and that his desire to save Rita and Cary was so great that he would not be thoroughly rational.

She paced the house's empty living room. In its day, the structure had been someone's pride and joy. Abandoned as it was, it had become depressing. The only images upon the walls were lighter, rectangular patches of beige paint where framed pictures had once hung. Her steps upon the dusty hardwood floor echoed lightly. Only the empty swivel-stools anchored to the floor offered any place to sit as she planned and waited. And now that she had revealed her location to Eli, she did not feel comfortable sitting on either of the stools at the bar since they restricted her movement, largely forcing her to sit with her back to the large, plate glass windows at the front of the house. When she tired of pacing she sat atop the bar. The imposition irritated her. She did not like the way it felt to be uncomfortable, to be inconvenienced. "I've done this before, so why am I feeling like this?" she wondered to herself. Then she heard his voice.

Across the darkness, across the rolling acreage that surrounded the house in which Hyun kept two panicking hostages, Alan called her name. He was well hidden, but his voice floated eerily across the distance because only the night separated the two of them.

"Hoo Lin! Or are you Hyun Lee tonight!" After he yelled, he deftly moved to his left about forty feet, following a ridge that was slightly higher in elevation and gave him a better line of sight. "Can you hear me?" he screamed. He was making no secret of his presence. Again he adjusted his location. To remain in one spot would have been more dangerous. At the moment he had discovered her cache of weapons, he suspected he had also discovered a worthy adversary as well. He believed that possession of such tools implied familiarity and skill with the same.

Hyun recognized Alan's voice immediately. She was already incensed since he had been disloyal to her and because he had stolen equipment from her, or so she thought. But now he had somehow discovered her location. And then it hit her: he had attached the missing tracking device to her truck. He must have followed her to Cary's house, and from there she had unwittingly led Alan Wing right to her lair. The million dollar question was whether or not he had taken the time to alert the authorities as to her whereabouts. Had he enlisted any help? Or was he being a hero? Was he out there with Eli at this very moment? Would Parks be that stupid?

"I have to work on the theory that he has help on the way," she whispered to herself, "and that I am running out of time."

Having no clue as to Hyun's disdain for competitive and assertive men, Alan unknowingly set a hook in his quarry. "You're going to have to deal with me, Lady. You're not the boss anymore." His monologue across the darkness was quick and detached. He yelled. He moved left and right across the ridge, and he yelled some more. "You're dealing with a different animal than the one you were training. There's not a better hunter within 100 miles of this place!" He challenged her, and she never could turn down such a challenge from any man.

"This shouldn't take long," Hyun said aloud to no one. She turned off her flashlight and carefully stepped into the darkness from the back of the building. When he spoke briefly again, she fired off a round and the game was on. She heard nothing in return, and that was a bit discomfiting. There was no sound of gravel underfoot. There was no hint of movement of any kind. She was impressed by his stealth.

Alan wanted only to buy time. His plan was not so much to engage her directly, but to draw her away long enough that help could arrive in time to save everyone including himself. Surely Eli Parks had informed the authorities of her new location. Alan's bravado would only serve him for a while. He wanted her to leave the ranch house in order to lead her on a chase. Through the infra red binoculars he had hidden from the Highway Patrol along with a holstered, semi-automatic pistol and a rifle the Patrol never knew existed, he attempted to keep an eye on her location. Hyun was still near the darkened house as far as he could tell. Ever so slowly, he relocated upon the ridge once again.

"I never understood irony before, Lady, but I think I do now!" Somehow Alan was able to summon a confident sound to his booming voice as he attempted to taunt his opponent. Again he changed direction as he moved along the ridge in the dark. "Imagine how it's gonna feel when your boss reads you were brought down with the aid of your very own equipment!"

First there was the flash and a cracking sound, followed immediately by rocks splintering all about him. He knew he had her attention. Alan silently moved to higher ground upon the rocky ridge. He found a smoother boulder that protruded from the ledge. His hands bled from scrapes and scratches he collected as he scrambled across the ledges, but he carefully searched for any sign that would indicate she had taken his bait and had begun an advance toward his location.

A greater fear began to creep into Alan's psyche. All along he knew what he was doing was dangerous, but now he was realizing the hunt was on. He was the hunted. Until this moment, adrenaline afforded him a courage that enabled him to move on with his plan. Reality permitted doubts to creep in, doubts that led to second thoughts.

Then he saw her. He brought her into a better focus. Hyun had carefully exited the house below and scurried behind its garage for protection.

The sighting activated his adrenal gland once again. Alan thought his plan might just work. "Wouldn't Cary be impressed?" flashed through his mind, and then he fired off a single round in Hyun's direction to make his adversary more wary if nothing else.

Moving quickly and as quietly as he could to gain a new vantage point, Alan Junior scurried down the ridge and away from the one story structure. Temporarily he forfeited any ability he had to watch the building where he suspected his ex-wife and her friend were prisoners, but he had to move away and hope Hyun would follow. He knew the terrain while she did not, and that was to his advantage.

His heart was pounding, and his mouth was dry. Alan Wing was learning what it was to be the prey as opposed to being the hunter. Listening carefully, he moved to a location between two thick boulders where he could peer through the night vision glasses again. He scanned the side of the incline. Another flash and another crack. He heard clumps of dirt scatter. Because the impact of the bullet was far to his right, he felt that Hyun might have been startled by something causing her to shoot errantly. The flash gave away her position, and he focused on her as he momentarily stayed in place.

"I've got to draw her further away," he whispered. "Further away." Again he fired off a single shot. Ordinarily a marksmen, his nerves affected his accuracy, and he knew it. It reminded him of youthful cases of buck fever. Then there was the fact that he had never tried to kill anyone before. He suspected she had, and that was to *her* advantage. It was imperative that he scramble quickly to keep his distance and misdirect her. The slope he descended was gentle and brief. With a decent foothold, he scooted for higher ground once more. Alan knew that during this time of year the earth was pretty firm underfoot, so he moved aggressively through the dark.

Not new to hunting, Hyun realized she was in Alan's domain, and knew he owned a bit of an advantage since he was familiar with the topography. She was careful. Each of her strides was purposeful and economic. Like a Eurasian Lynx back home, her movements were stealthy, making detection more difficult for Alan.

To lead Hyun along, to draw her away from Cary and Rita being held captive in the dark, dank, and grimy cellar of that house, he had to remain close enough to give his assailant false hope, yet stay distant enough to improve his own chances of survival. Ideally he wanted to continue increasing the distance between Hyun and the ranch house. By successfully taunting her and leading her on, Alan hoped the cavalry would arrive in plenty of time. "Even more irony," the native American thought to himself.

Alan began to suspect that help might not show up in a timely fashion. He hoped to outsmart his adversary by circling behind her, subsequently aligning himself between the hostages and Hyun. In effect, he would become their last line of defense. He had to keep moving so she would not have time to recognize his plan.

"Just turn yourself over to me now! Things will go easier on you!" Alan called to Hyun. Deep within he would have loved nothing more, but he understood that the reality was that she was on her way to kill him. Given the opportunity she would snuff his life out like his mother snuffed out dinner candles each Sunday night; that is to say, without any thought. It was just something that needed to be done.

Under the cover of night, he had been sneaking to her left occasionally, but when he retreated to her right in a serpentine path across the ridge in darkness, he covered a greater distance. The entire time he managed to nimbly follow the rolling contour of the land, much like spring's melting snow from neighboring mountains fluidly traveled watersheds into nearby Flathead Lake. His plan had become a problem of topography, geometry, and simple arithmetic, and the answer was 180 degrees.

CHAPTER 47

Rita hated bees her entire life. As a child she had seen siblings stung, and she was unable to forget their tears and screams. As adults at a family reunion years later, someone recalled the common practice of playing barefooted and subsequent bee stings. It was then that they realized that Rita had never been victimized, even after several bees once began a hive in her mailbox which sat atop a post at the end of her driveway. "Nor do I want to be stung!" she responded. They had many a laugh at their sister's expense.

However it was spiders and mice that evoked an even greater level of anxiety, especially spiders. During a camping trip when she was thirteen, Rita was bitten on the back of her left calf by one of Montana's more common spiders: the aggressive house spider. It had been the family's first camping trip of the spring, a traditional family outing, and Rita was in her brother Buzzy's sleeping bag which was shelved all winter in the basement at home. She felt something slightly more painful than a pin prick and then soon noticed itching and swelling symptoms that were followed by a headache that aspirin just could not relieve.

Concerned, her father had raced her to the local Emergency Unit located in the park grounds a few miles away. Given the proper treatment and medicine, the symptoms passed within twenty-four hours, but the damage to Rita's love for camping in a tent had been done. It was not until years later when her brother purchased an RV that she had relented and joined them again.

While Rita and Cary were forced to deal with the pain and anguish caused by their captor's crude and forceful bondage tactics, Rita's memories of past camping days brought forth an additional worry of possible spiders in the basement. Eventually Rita felt what might have been a spider crawl across the skin of her ankle in the darkness. She immediately became alarmed and startled Cary who herself had barely been able to regain any composure. So violent was Rita's reaction that her friend feared for Rita's mental state.

Alan's ex-wife fully understood the danger of their situation, but could not fathom what caused Rita's sudden, wild movements as well as her muted growls that bordered on being primal. And as the initial seconds passed, the intensity of her stifled howling increased.

Fear multiplied by more fear motivated Rita Parks to pull and jerk against the wooden beam to which they had both been affixed. At that moment, Cary thought she noticed that the force of her friend's sudden and desperate movements had actually repositioned the beam ever so slightly! So sure was she of the beam's movement, Cary began to grunt vehemently in the hopes of distracting Rita and gaining her attention. Cary's confidence was beginning to resurface. Simultaneously Cary did her best to impact that same 10" x 10" stud rhythmically with as much force as she could muster. In only a few seconds the fruits of her labor were apparent when Rita apparently understood her intentions and began duplicating her powerful thrusts.

Convinced they were going to die anyway, the pair cared little if knocking out a support might drop the flooring above upon their heads. At least it was a chance at increased mobility and freedom. It mattered not whether Hyun Lee heard them as she waited in the room above, and little did they know their kidnapper was already engaged elsewhere outside of the building. They just wanted to be free of the post, remove the gags from their mouths, and speak of whatever might become Phase Two of their escape. They sensed hope for the first time since this ordeal had begun.

Eli was honest with Edward and Carl, and he was terse. "Your mom's in the exact danger I feared," he blurted. Then he looked directly at Carl and spoke to him as if they were all in the chase scene from "U.S. Marshalls" starring Tommy Lee Jones. "Get out now. I'm going to need your truck."

"Sure thing, Mr. P'!" Carl was high on the electricity in the air, and the excitement of the moment. Years later whenever he retold this story, he always accurately depicted the adrenalin rush he felt at that point in his life.

"Dad, what do you want *us* to do?" Ed asked excitedly as Eli returned his cell phone to him.

Eli paused as if he was considering just how this pair could be of help. He looked right at Edward when he spoke. "Get yourself home somehow. Stay by your phone." Then he spoke the words they never would forget. "Shoot any Korean woman who comes in your direction."

The two young men looked at him in disbelief but took what he said to heart. With their eyes wide open, and left incredulous at Eli's instruction, they stood by the roadside on 93 North and worried not at all about transportation. Carl's truck and its new driver, seemingly transformed into a warrior, were quickly swallowed by the darkness.

"Call Brandon and Christian, Man!" bellowed Carl as he nervously danced a circle around Ed when he pulled out his cell phone. "They'll love *this* action!"

Moments later Edward's sidekick nearly freaked when he heard his buddy calmly end the phone call with the words, "Make sure both of you bring a rifle and some ammo."

Waff looked at Edward. He was as antsy as Ed was composed. "Rifles man?" he asked.

"We gotta guard the fort, Waff." Edward began walking along the highway in the direction from which his friends would arrive. "We gotta guard the fort."

About ten miles from Rollins and the house where his wife was being held hostage, Eli saw several headlights in his rearview mirrors. His instincts told him it was Simmons. "Thank God," was all he said.

When they pulled over where Lakeshore Drive left 93 N to the right and down toward the lake, Eli hopped out of Carl's 4x4 and walked back to meet Agent Simmons.

"Bob?"

Simmons nodded. Headlights were shutting down behind him. "Hello, Eli. What's the plan from here?" If they did not know, outsiders to the scene would have thought both men had known each other for years.

Eli looked over the large agent's right shoulder and witnessed other agents prepping for an altercation. "I'm going to need one of your vests." In minutes, he was outfitted and given a pair of Slovak K100's.

As Eli prepared himself, Simmons informed him that he had contacted the Highway Patrol and local law enforcement as well. "Eli, there will not be a road around here in any direction that people can enter or she can travel without being confronted, even if it's an elk trail."

His counterpart looked east. "How about the lake?"

"We thought of that, too, but it's a wide expanse. They've moved as close as they dare and will do their best." Then the agent added, "Everyone's been told to radio first and pull their triggers second." Eli understood that a radio transmission was tantamount to a blip or sighting upon a radar screen.

"This is what I want, Bob." Eli extended his sleeved left arm and pointed up the highway. "If you have the numbers, closely position agents until they've silently reached the Winston place." He waited for Simmons reaction.

"Eli, you would not believe how many people your friend President Rittenhouse has assigned me. My people can practically hold hands from here to there."

"And the road along the lake?" Eli inquired hopefully.

"Same thing." Simmons waited for more instruction as the two stood there between their respective vehicles in the dark. By then, all headlights were off.

"I'm going in first, Bob. I have to try."

"I know."

Eli peered down the darkened road that paralleled the lake. "Have your people move out ten minutes after I'm gone." Then he re-checked his ammo. Looking up at Agent Simmons he gave one last order as he put his hand upon the agent's broad shoulder. "As long as it stays dark, stay back. But if your agents see this flare, have them come a runnin'." Simmons smiled at the country boy jargon although Eli could not see it.

CHAPTER 48

That night a gibbous moon broke through, and its light was enough to enhance details far and wide across the open, terraced landscape. The cloud coverage progressively became piecemeal as if a wind in the upper atmosphere had gently shredded its blanket of vapor. Edges of the remaining clouds were silver against the indigo night sky which was spangled by stars as the minutes passed.

Keeping low to the ground was more important than ever. Wing Jr. scurried to a new position behind one of a few large rocks which Mother Nature had rolled down the slope from a ridge above it. Little by little he had gained some ground as he continued to swing around closer to the ranch house below.

"This is almost too easy," he whispered to himself. At that location from atop the ledge, he nervously scanned the Drake property for his adversary's location. As minutes passed, not knowing her whereabouts gave birth to more misgivings regarding his involvement. "Maybe Pop was right," he thought. "When will I ever listen?"

An air-driven zipping sound passed by his right shoulder followed by the explosion of dirt clods all about the base of the rock. In micro seconds Alan realized that his location had been discovered by Hyun, that she was above and behind him. If he did not take flight immediately he would not be alive for long. In those seconds he understood that Hyun had employed his own tactics against him.

Then he felt his left hand explode. He knew he had been shot, and if time had permitted it he would have compared it to being stabbed by a large, rough-edged blade of immense proportions. He would have described the bones in his left hand as shards of ice causing sunbursts of pain in his flesh each time he attempted to move it, blood running cold out the hole through his palm. Acting upon instinct he immediately jumped over the rock that was meant to be his cover, and he tumbled awkwardly down the bank below it, gaining speed as he fell.

Alan heard two more explosions against the landscape behind him, but the only new pain he experienced came not from his shattered left hand but his arms and legs as he rolled violently across the hard ground and edgy terrain through the darkness. Thin, tiny rims of rock scraped his shins and forearms, but he had managed to escape without being shot a second time.

When he managed to retard his freefalling momentum upon the steeply sloped headland, he finally brought himself to a halt with his right hand by grabbing the branches of sturdier bushes he crushed on the way down the slope. Thick and gnarled, they too had taken a toll on his torso and clothing.

As swiftly as he could he took stock of his injuries. Alan attempted to survey his position since the spectacular tumble had slightly disoriented him. Simultaneously he checked for the protection of new cover. He knew he had lost his rifle, yet somehow he managed to not lose the semi-automatic pistol he had found days ago in Hyun's bin located back in the barn. He was anxious, but Alan surprisingly remained in control of his wits. In fact, he had become more irritated than scared, grateful her bullet had not hit any other part of his body.

Eli ran as fast as he could. Moonlight shimmered on his patinated suit pants while his white, long sleeves alternately flashed in sync with his strides. In that same blue-white moonlight, his shadow depicted a powerful figure which he had struggled to improve just for Rita. The image of a middle-aged man racing on foot at night down a country road while dressed in a nice suit was almost comical, but the circumstances on that particular night were not.

As he advanced quietly, Eli suddenly heard what he was sure were gunshots. It stood to reason that for Hyun to be shooting so many shots, a few things could be happening up ahead. First he worried that Simmons's agents had broken from their positions and attacked, thereby risking his wife's safety and the safety of her friend as well. Or perhaps the women had miraculously escaped, and Hyun was in pursuit. There could be no other reason for gunfire.

In one sense the appearance of moonlight was a curse. Hyun would be able to see much better, and there could be no doubt a professional assassin would be dressed appropriately for the situation at hand. She would be difficult to see. On the other hand, the moonlight was an aid. Eli could cover ground more quickly and spot the old ranch house with ease once he was close. He knew it would be positioned above him and on the left side of the shoreline road.

He ran faster. Then suddenly to his right he spotted a boat through an opening that he was sure was meant to be her escape vehicle, a large boat which had been pulled slightly ashore. If not for that very same moonlight, he would not have noticed it. He raced in its direction thinking her plan was to kill him, and then she would eventually attempt to go aboard. From the boat's location, Eli advanced cautiously. The shooting had stopped. He wanted to take Hyun by surprise when she came down from the house looking for him once he contacted her as per her instructions.

The wooden beam finally cracked, victim of the relentless tugging applied by both nearly-exhausted captives. Drained of energy and frustrated, knowing they were so close to achieving what they had set out to accomplish together, Cary and Rita began to sob. First one, and then the other. Their clothes were filthy and soaked with perspiration. Their wrists, shoulders, and backs were tender and scarred, searing with pain. They panted from their exhaustion, and once their minds were off their task, when they once again had time to consider their plight, Rita began to choke.

Her gagging was minimal at first, but it escalated quickly. Hearing her friend's distress, Cary's adrenaline pumped one more time to an entire new level. Gaining leverage as best she could by placing her feet beneath her, Cary produced a guttural cry through the cotton cloth over her mouth. She pushed forcefully and lifted in one final attempt to move the old, wooden post to which they had been bound.

The result was the deep, dry grinding sound of metal inside of wood as the nails began to bend and escape their positions. Due to its new angle, a six-inch gap formed at the base of the old support post, and Cary finally was able to lower her wrists to the cool dirt floor and slide them free even though they were still bound behind her back. She was free but not untied. Briefly she looked up into the darkness and listened. To her surprise the floor above did not release and crash down upon them immediately. Then she realized Rita was no longer gagging.

Cary pushed with her feet and scrambled desperately in her friend's direction. She could not see that Rita's head was down, her chin into her chest. Because Rita had become silent and still, Cary scrambled to help her and anxiously prayed her life-long friend was not dead.

With her back against Rita, Cary straightened her legs and clumsily worked her way up Rita's torso by gripping her sweater with her fingertips. Finally she was able to locate Rita's face and the gag upon Rita's mouth. It was soaked with saliva and vomit, but Cary was able to pull it from her face on her first attempt. She felt Rita's body slump to her right. Her friend's grateful intake of air was not a great whoosh, but loud enough that Cary knew she would survive.

Next Cary lowered herself and returned to their back-to-back position. From there she worked Rita's hands free from the post. She needed only to keep her own composure, breathe the best she could despite still being prisoner to the cottony gag still wrapped over her mouth, and wait for Rita to return the favor. Cary sat still, listened to Rita's breathing become more patterned, and for the first time became aware of the cooling effect caused by her sweat-soaked clothing against her skin.

The shooting had stopped. Alan knew Hyun would be upon him quickly. The noise of his fall had been loud and easy to follow. During that moment of re-evaluation, Alan thought he heard the primal cry of a wild person in the rancher not far below him. It was momentary, but he recognized it as a cry of anger and defiance. Of that, he was sure. Then it ended, and in stark contrast, he heard nothing but the wind off the lake whispering through the ponderosa pine branches that grew along the shore. The milky moonlight and the breeze belied the danger that threatened his life.

Through that silence moments later, there were footsteps below upon some gravel. He drew his weapon and tried to summon the kind of courage that would enable him to shoot a person. He remained motionless despite his discomfort and the fact that he had yet to find new cover.

He wanted badly to move and relocate. He could not remain where he was, for Hyun would discover him and eliminate him. Then Cary would be dead. He had obviously annoyed this woman he was sure, so he figured if he were to die, Cary would be expendable. That would be Hyun's form of revenge.

Cary. Before Alan tried to move his aching body to a new sight, he wondered why some of his last actions and thoughts would suddenly be about her. Why did he value her more now than he had when they were married? He once again heard his dad's voice in his head, the voice that attempted to reason with Alan as he went through their divorce. "Son, it's been true forever. You don't know what you'll miss or appreciate until it's gone. It's true of people, too." Right then and there Alan also fully realized that if he died he would miss opportunities with his dad and family. It was one of those Native American mountaintop visions without the mountain.

He struggled to his knees. The pain in his hand was sharp and there was intense burning. His body ached, but it seemed no bones were broken. After that sudden leap and landing, he was more sore than he had ever been at any point of his life. Then he had an epiphany. He was between Hyun and the house! That thought alone spurred him to a new level of energy. More adrenaline.

Carefully he looked about himself. He felt he could even reach the house before she did if he climbed down from the rise where he finally had come to rest after his jump. "Only 100 yards," he thought. "It can't be much more than that." In the moonlight he saw the structure's rectangular outline as well as the outbuilding near it. He sought a way down the slope.

He heard the footsteps yet again. It was obvious someone was approaching cautiously, but this time the steps were more pronounced. A loud whisper came from the direction of the lake.

"Rita? Cary?" is what Alan heard. A man's voice quietly calling to the women and hoping not to attract Hyun's attention as he did so. Unbeknownst to the stranger, it was a near-impossible task. This brave soul was treading on territory so explosive that if he had known it he might have turned around. Alan looked up the slope for Hyun and then down the slope towards the voice. He took a chance.

"Be careful!" Alan called forcefully in his softest voice. "I don't know who you are, but there's a woman with a gun not far above us trying to kill me." Again he heard the wind through the trees. Whoever was approaching him had stopped. Alan figured he had to be thinking over his next move.

"Can you hear me down there?"

Then there was recognition. "Alan? Is that you?"

Face down as flat as he could be, Alan Wing, Junior slid to the edge of the ridge just above the voice. "Who's down there?" he whispered again. "How did you know..." and then it dawned on him. It was Eli Parks. "Eli? Is that you?"

Alan could hear Eli advancing. He could envision Eli's fingers clinging to whatever growth was available for him to grasp, wedging the toes of his footgear against hardened rock. In the moonlight, he first saw one pale hand grasp a rock tightly embedded in the top of the ridge and then another. Soon both were lying prone and signaling to each other their next move without making a sound. Out in the open atop the grassy crest they were easy prey. Side by side they began to rise to a stooped position.

"Stay...right...there." Her voice chilled them. It was a soft, but commanding voice. Alan felt nauseated, for Hyun now had the upper hand, of course, but Eli's mind was working. Three people and each of them was armed. However only one had her gun drawn, locked, and loaded.

"Just shoot us and end it." Alan spat out his words as if he was disgusted. "I don't want to hear anymore of your philosophical crap."

"You had no business stealing from me. I treated you well."

Alan and Eli looked up at her silhouette in the moonlight against the background of night sky. They could make out a few details, mostly the skin on her hands and her face.

It was Eli's turn. "Hyun, is that how you justify what you are about to do? Because you have weapons, it's okay to use them on anyone you wish?" He began to move in her direction. "Let Alan go. He was just protecting innocent people."

"You can't be serious!" she bellowed, "Nothing about you, Mr. Parks, is innocent!" Moving closer to them across the rock-strewn soil, walking down near the edge of the final ridge upon which both of them stood, she raised her gun towards Alan's torso. "But I'm not wasting my time explaining..."

Through the wall of quiet darkness each of them heard it in the distance. Only Alan knew what it was. One last time he dropped to the ground and pulled Eli along with him. The next thing they heard was the unmistakable sound of flesh being pierced by an arrow as it expanded upon contact with its victim. In fact, Alan was sure he heard two! Those distinct sounds were immediately followed by a short gasp for air and then the dead weight of Hyun's body hitting the ground, collapsing first to her knees and then to her left side. The cavalry had arrived.

CHAPTER 49

From the base of the slope, Senior's worried voice rolled up to Alan's ears. "Alan! Are you okay?" He and his friend had traveled across the lake in his boat through the dark, forgoing the use of any running lights. His lifelong friend's knowledge of Flathead Lake proved to be invaluable. Quietly they had pulled Senior's fiberglass craft to the shoreline as best as two elderly men could do.

With difficulty they had climbed to the road that bordered the Drake property and followed what they thought was a prudent course: stay down wind and do not shoot until she makes the first move. "An experienced bow hunter," he had taught his son, "never shoots his prey until it lifts one of its feet off the ground. With one hoof up, deer and elk can't jump very well after they have heard the release of an arrow. That's when they are most vulnerable - when they have a foot in the air."

Injured and dazed, Alan raised to a knee. One moment they were at Death's door, seconds from extermination. The next they were struggling to stand, free of any danger other than gravity. Alan was happy to feel the soreness all throughout his body, for it meant he was still alive. Meanwhile Eli carefully studied the body of Hyun Lee sprawled at their feet. He could see the whites of her eyes which accented the look of shock upon her face. Death had met her with a surprise.

"Yeah, Dad, but how did you know where to find me?" He was incredulous. Somehow his own father had managed to show up and save the day.

No longer worried about noise, his dad replied proudly by calling out, "I told you I've known about these tracking devices. I put one on your mother's truck years ago in case she got lost someplace." Alan felt pride as he enjoyed learning even more about this father of his. What he heard next put a smile on his face. "But we won't tell Mother about that."

"Well don't try to come up here. You might fall and break your neck."

Then he heard another voice, a deeper one. It was unmistakable as it boomed up the slope in the dark.

"Come up there my ass," the voice grumbled as if talking to no one and everyone. Again Alan smiled and nearly laughed when he heard it. "Don't you worry, Sonny. We ain't doing that. It's bad enough I had to drive him across the lake in the dark and then drag this ol' geezer's rear end from the boat all the way up here." It was Hoppy, and now he certainly had a story for Brenda.

Like a lightning bolt, Alan's emotional high quickly crashed to a low. In a panic he called out, "Dad! Please head for the house and look for Cary and Rita! I'll be down in a second!" After all that had happened, even though Hyun Lee's corpse was right at his feet, he had momentarily forgotten the women. "Please hurry!"

"I'm going with them," Eli said to Alan. He looked at his hand. Then he wrapped it as tightly as he could with a piece of cloth he tore from his shirt. "Stay here. More help is coming. You might be more badly injured than you think."

"Ok. But hurry." Then Alan watched Eli pull out his cell phone and listened.

"Bob...it's Eli. It's done. Call off your people, but get some medical help down here immediately. You'll see us. Some lights will be on." And down the final escarpment he went, hoping to find his wife alive and well.

He scampered down the lengthy embankment with little thought for his own safety. Recklessly he passed Wing Sr. and Hoppy, and twice he had to regain his balance by spreading his arms and leaning backwards. Upon reaching the porch and front door of the single story dwelling, he found the door to be locked. With no hesitation, Eli lifted his foot and thrust it upon the doorknob violently. The old lock provided little resistance. Immediately he began calling their names.

"Rita! Cary!" The larger challenge was finding a light switch and or a lamp. Only when his companions came through the door with their emergency lamps were they able to provide some light.

"Rita! Cary!" He did not know that both were directly beneath him, one unconscious and the other gagged. Worry for their survival increased. As the two older men searched each of the rooms on the main floor, Eli first found a utility closet and finally the door leading to the basement stairs. "Rita! Cary! It's Eli!"

What he found in the basement was a sight that sent panic through his entire being. Cary's eyes were huge, and he saw she was gagged by a strip from a filthy, cotton tee shirt. In a brave gesture, she repeatedly tilted her head toward Rita as if to tell Eli, "Take care of her first!" In seconds he removed the gag, and then she implored him to check upon her best friend. "Don't worry about me, Eli !" she exploded. "I'm fine. Please look after Rita."

As he called up the stairway to Alan Sr. and Gene, he dropped to the earthen floor. He tenderly took Rita into his arms, checked her mouth, and began gently massaging her face while softly calling to her. He listened to her breathing and was satisfied there were no obstructions to her airway.

From his seated position and with Rita now elevated upon his lap and against his chest, Eli once again called to the two men upstairs. He saw their shadows atop the steps. "See if the water is on! And bring down a wet cloth...anything!"

After only a bit of discussion, Eli heard footsteps working their way to the basement. Gene had agreed to fetch water and a towel while Senior descended the wooden stairway to see if he could help in any way. Cary was amazed to see Mr. Wing and continued to stare at him as he released her from her bonds.

"How is she, Mr. Parks?" he asked. "Is she hurt badly? Just tell me we're not too late."

Eli continued to comfort his wife and hold her against himself upon his lap. With a moistened towel which Hoppy had provided as quickly as possible, he cleaned some of the mess from her face and hoped it would revive her more quickly.

With the expression of a frightened little girl, Cary continued to first stare at Mr. Wing, wondering how he had become involved in their rescue, and then to the top of the stairs. Her former father-in-law finally understood and gently comforted her as he said, "She's gone, Cary. She will never hurt anybody again." Only then did Cary relax and collapse into the older gent's arms and begin to cry.

Gene Hopkins had gone back upstairs. In a subdued tone, he kindly directed the EMT's to the basement. "Right down there, folks. Be careful. Those steps ain't the best."

The sound of their boots upon the old, wooden stairs brought welcome relief. Eli gently exchanged places with the first of the three young people who arrived and with concern whispered, "She has yet to respond."

No sooner were the words out of his mouth when a barely audible moan grabbed everyone's attention. "Speak to her gently, Sir. She seems to be coming around."

"Rita," he said lovingly. "Honey...can you hear me? I'm right here. You're gonna be all right."

A surprise to no one, the first words from her mouth were, "Is Cary okay?" A tender kiss was her reward.

He smiled. "She fine, Sparky. She's right here with you."

While the EMT ran an I.V. of fluids into Rita's arm and prepped her for removal from the basement, Cary moved to Rita's side. "I'm here, Rita. We made it. We're going to be fine."

In a few minutes, everyone was out of the building, but the emergency lights were left on for the investigators who arrived next. Elongated sirens echoed and flashing lights moved closer. Almost intimidated by the attention and with the support of Senior's arm, Cary stood on the small porch not far from the shattered door. She watched as they moved her friend to an ambulance.

She called to Eli. Excusing himself from the ambulance for a moment, he walked back to her and they embraced. "Eli, before you go I want to say thank you for all that you've done tonight." Then he put his arms on her shoulders.

"Cary, you're thanking the wrong guy. There were many of us on the way for this rescue," and he looked up the embankment to where it was dark on the top. "However the person most responsible for saving your lives will be coming down from the top of that rise."

For a time, Alan sat alone in the dark. He was hesitant as he watched Eli crash through the front door and heard their calls as they searched for Cary and Rita, brilliant flashlight beams careening across the interior of the darkened house. Time seemed to slow down as he waited. He found relief when he saw more lights go on and more people arrive. Finally it was safe. He sought no attention, but rather he just watched the rescue play out below him, as if he were atop a natural amphitheater. At long last Alan Wing, Jr. became ecstatic when he saw Cary being escorted through the door by his father as she spoke with Eli. Atop the ridge he stayed on the hard, hard ground and sobbed deep, guttural sobs in the moonlight. Temporarily, his injuries relented.

EPILOGUE

Falls Port returned to normal more quickly than some expected it would. By mid November, all the *ants* were gone, and as a result, Falls Port seemed a little more spacious. There were residents who went to their graves years later never having noticed the invasion, while others took it upon themselves to become the font of many entertaining tales. Some of their stories were true and others were only partially accurate. A third category was comprised of myths complete with local heroes. No matter what the story, all were passed along for many years and seemed to go best with coffee and breakfast. Along with these tales and the return to a status quo came a few surprises.

To the surprise of Eli and his family, Gene Hopkins said little about what he saw and what part he played that night on the Drake property. Hoppy did take Brenda aside one day and, in a private setting, shared the details of his involvement. It was not at all a boastful presentation but more of a confession which helped him cope with what he had done that night. Some say Gene Hopkins was quieter after that...but not much. He still filled the role of official greeter down at the Driftwood, and Brenda never did put shells in his eggs.

The Wing family enjoyed the surprise re-birth of Alan, Jr. Father and son were seen together more often over the years, always enjoying each other's companionship. Mother continued the tradition of Sunday night dinners, and for quite some time four extra places were seen at her table. She never did learn about loaded guns in her house, her missing truck, or a woman from North Korea named Hyun Lee. Father and son agreed that, "We won't tell Mother about that."

Cary and Rita surprised their girlfriends when they quickly resumed their poker games. Eventually they spoke of their horrifying experience and, to the credit of their friends, none of it was ever repeated. Privacy was a thread which held their alliance together more securely than ever. Kathy eventually took all of them on a train.

President Rittenhouse raised a few eyebrows that autumn when he announced he was headed to Seattle, not only for an economic summit with Japanese diplomats, but also to see firsthand a Sunday afternoon game between his undefeated Washington Redskins and the NFC West's division-leading Seattle Seahawks. To the nation it was a pleasant surprise that the bachelor President paid his own way. Not one penny of the tax-payer's dollar paid for the outing.

Yet somehow Elijah Rittenhouse, friend of Eli Parks, neglected to mention he was stopping in Falls Port along the way. Imagine the tower's surprise when Marine I requested permission to land at the Falls Port Airport! Eli along with Rita, Cary, Alan, Edward, and Waff were on location to witness the historic moment. After lunch with the President inside the airport's tiny cafeteria, they watched him lift off for Kalispell where he once again boarded Executive One. As only he could, Carl summed up the experience as they walked to their vehicles. "Mr. P', you run in some serious circles, Man. You run in some *really serious* circles."

Thought next to impossible years earlier, there was a gradual reconciliation between Cary and Alan. They never re-married, but remained friends. He was asked by a buddy about marrying Cary a second time. He surprised his friend with his answer. "I love the relationship which we have right now...what she deserved to have all along," he said wistfully. "I just don't want to risk endangering it ever again." Eventually Cary got word of what he said, and one day she spoke to Alan about it. She thanked him and complimented him on his change. She never married anyone else, nor did he.

Rita had lived most of her life in the Falls Port area. As children, she and her many siblings left California with their parents to settle in Montana long ago. Falls Port seemed to be the last stop for Rita while her only brother and four sisters scattered like dry leaves on the wind. So when she took an unpaid leave from school and Edward pulled up anchor, their decision to let Eli show them the east coast raised a few eyebrows. A horrible experience drew them closer together, but they still felt something was missing. Perhaps they were shaken and needed a break from reminders of what had happened to them. Off they went to sample city life, in love more than ever.

The following spring brought forth a surprisingly late snowfall and eventually long-overdue, beautiful weather. Spring also was host to the greatest surprise of all. Having resumed his line of work again, Eli supervised three assignments which sent him around the globe. He worked with new teammates on important "boat doctor" style missions. After his third lengthy absence, Eli decided it was time for his second retirement. Although opportunities were enjoyed while experiencing the east coast, everyone felt something was missing. Jake found he loved being part of a family once again, and he was eager to live in Montana with his dad, Rita, and Edward for good. A return to Falls Port was their hearts' desire, and the future for old Pete looked bleak.

From: Eli Parks <eliparks@usg
To: Rita Parks < sparky7@usg
Sent: 6:30 p.m. mst
Subject: We're home...

Though a raindrop's course alters on a whim,
Develops as others are met,
And its identity seems lost,
Its beauty is constant.

Trickling from hillsides and oozing from underground,
Sundry rivulets of diverse origin
Unite and become one,
Picking up speed as they continue their journey.

A flow twists through grassy meadows and forests,
Finding the way of its ancestors
Of decades and centuries ago,
Over pebbles and rocks that decorate the way.

We are but raindrops, you and I, having begun apart.
Now united, we will follow the course of life and discover its secrets.
Together we will deluge the stones along a serpentine path,
Spawning changes all our own along the way.

Meander along with me...

From: Rita Parks < sparky7@usg
To: Eli Parks <eliparks@usg
Sent: 7:03 p.m. mst
Subject: Re: We're Home...

Yes, Dear ... (finally gotcha!)

Made in the USA
Middletown, DE
27 September 2016